More praise for

WebMage

"Its blending of magic and coding is inspired . . . *WebMage* has all the qualities I look for in a book—a wonderfully subdued sense of humor, nonstop action, and romantic relief. It's a wonderful debut novel."

—Christopher Stasheff, author of
Saint Vidicon to the Rescue

"McCullough handles his plot with unfailing invention, orchestrating a mixture of humor, philosophy, and programming insights that give new meaning to terms as commonplace as 'spell-checker' and esoteric as 'programming in hex.'" —*Publishers Weekly* (starred review)

"A unique first novel, this has a charming, fresh combination of mythological, magical, and computer elements . . . that will enchant many types of readers." —*KLIATT*

"McCullough's first novel, written very much in the style of Roger Zelazny's classic Amber novels, is a rollicking combination of verbal humor, wild adventures, and just plain fun." —*Voice of Youth Advocates*

"*WebMage* contains a lot of humor and a highly inventive new way of looking at the universe, which combines the magic of old with the computer structures of today."

—*SFRevu*

"Complex, well paced, highly creative, and overall, an auspicious debut for McCullough . . . well worth reading for fans of light fantasy." —*Sci Fi Weekly*

CYBERMANCY

Kelly McCullough

ACE BOOKS, NEW YORK

THE BERKLEY PUBLISHING GROUP
Published by the Penguin Group
Penguin Group (USA) Inc.
375 Hudson Street, New York, New York 10014, USA
Penguin Group (Canada), 90 Eglinton Avenue East, Suite 700, Toronto, Ontario M4P 2Y3, Canada
(a division of Pearson Penguin Canada Inc.)
Penguin Books Ltd., 80 Strand, London WC2R 0RL, England
Penguin Group Ireland, 25 St. Stephen's Green, Dublin 2, Ireland (a division of Penguin Books Ltd.)
Penguin Group (Australia), 250 Camberwell Road, Camberwell, Victoria 3124, Australia
(a division of Pearson Australia Group Pty. Ltd.)
Penguin Books India Pvt. Ltd., 11 Community Centre, Panchsheel Park, New Delhi—110 017, India
Penguin Group (NZ), 67 Apollo Drive, Rosedale, North Shore 0632, New Zealand
(a division of Pearson New Zealand Ltd.)
Penguin Books (South Africa) (Pty.) Ltd., 24 Sturdee Avenue, Rosebank, Johannesburg 2196,
South Africa

Penguin Books Ltd., Registered Offices: 80 Strand, London WC2R 0RL, England

CYBERMANCY

An Ace Book / published by arrangement with the author

PRINTING HISTORY
Ace mass-market edition / October 2007

Copyright © 2007 by Kelly McCullough.
Cover art by Christian McGrath.
Cover design by Judith Lagerman.
Interior text design by Kristin del Rosario.

ISBN: 978-0-441-01538-2

ACE
Ace Books are published by The Berkley Publishing Group,
a division of Penguin Group (USA) Inc.,
375 Hudson Street, New York, New York 10014.
ACE and the "A" design are trademarks belonging to Penguin Group (USA) Inc.

PRINTED IN THE UNITED STATES OF AMERICA

10   9   8   7   6   5   4   3   2   1

For Laura; you dance in my heart

Acknowledgments

First and foremost, extra-special thanks are owed to Laura McCullough, Stephanie Zvan, Jack Byrne, and Anne Sowards.

Many thanks also to the Wyrdsmiths: Lyda, Doug, Naomi, Bill, Eleanor, Rosalind, Harry, and Sean. My web guru: Ben. Beta readers: Sara, Karl, Angie, Jonna, Shari, Dave, and Laura R. My extended support structure: Bill and Nancy, James, Tom, Ann, and so many more. My family: Phyllis, Carol, Paul and Jane, Lockwood and Darlene, Judy, Lee C., Kat, Jean, Lee P., and all the rest.

And in loving memory: Kay Marquez, George Johnson, Ellen Neese.

CHAPTER ONE

Who says you can't teach an old dog new tricks? The eyes of Cerberus glared down at me, six balls of black fire. There was no dog older or more dangerous. But here I was standing practically in his mouths, trick in hand.

"Oh, get on with it," growled the right head, the one called Mort, a mastiff. "We haven't got all night."

Almost against my will, I looked over Cerberus's shoulder. The River Styx lay behind him, and beyond it the gate to Hades, land of the dead and present residence of a web-goblin by the name of Shara. My lover's computer-familiar, Shara was the child of her magic, and a dear friend of mine. Her current address would have been hard enough to bear if it weren't my fault she'd ended up on the wrong side of the river. Knowing I was responsible for her death . . .

Thoughts for another time. I flipped my last card over, the six of spades. Not much of a card, but enough to take the trick and fulfill our contract.

"Read it and weep!" said the middle head. A rottweiler named Dave.

He was my normal partner, if you could call anything

about playing bridge with the three-headed dog of the underworld normal. They had to do an elaborate dance that involved a lot of closing of eyes and some sort of special deal with the central intelligence that ran the body and connected the heads in order to even make the game possible. But as far I could tell, none of them were cheating, and they all seemed to enjoy it.

"I believe that's three hands in a row," chortled Dave.

Bob, the Doberman third head, gave me a gimlet look. "I wish you'd never taught us this game, little Raven."

I looked away to hide my expression. I don't much like being called Raven, and it isn't the name I was born with. That's Ravirn, which I still insist on for daily wear. Unfortunately, I'd had a little disagreement with my family's matriarchs, better known as the Fates. Yes, the crones who measure out the destiny of every living being like threads for a tapestry are my own flesh and blood. I'm thrilled. As a result of our little spat, the name I think of as my real one got taken away.

It could have been worse certainly. My great-aunt Atropos is the Fate who wields the shears, and she would have preferred to take my birthday away, or at least make sure I didn't have any more of them. My umpteen-times-great-grandmother, Lachesis, the lady who measures the threads, initially agreed with her.

Only the intervention of Necessity, the one goddess even the Fates fear, kept me alive. Robbed of the opportunity to remove me from the land of the living, Lachesis cast me out of the family of Fate and revoked my name. Then, for reasons I still don't understand, Clotho, the spinner, broke with her sister Fates, declared me a legitimate force for chaos, and gave me a new name, Raven.

It's better than not owning a name at all, but it feels wrong every time I hear it, a bitter reminder of my outcast status, and I'd prefer not to think about it. That attitude has caused considerable friction with Cerice, my lady fair and a child of Clotho's House. She insists I'm foolishly ignoring the power of names.

Perhaps she's right, but remembering that day and its aftermath still burns my heart. Yes, I took the side of Eris against the houses of Fate. Yes, the Goddess of Discord is my family's oldest and bitterest enemy. But it was that or let Atropos turn every thinking being in all of the infinite worlds of existence into a gaggle of marionettes dancing to Fate's every whim. For the crime of choosing free will over slavish destiny, I'd been banished and stripped of my identity. All of which meant that Bob's little dig bit deep.

"That was uncalled for," said Dave, taking my side. "I didn't hear you complaining last week when you and Mort took three rubbers in a row."

"I'm sorry, Ravirn," said Bob.

"It's all right," I answered.

It wasn't really, but I let it slide. I liked Cerberus far more than I did many of my closer cousins. Why did all of my problems have to involve family ties? The whole giant inbred Greek pantheon was a divine mess. Cerberus might be a distant enough cousin that friendship was more important to our relationship than blood, but the damned blood was still there. That mix of loyalties would make what I had to do to him in the coming days both harder and easier.

"Hurry up and deal," said Mort, jolting me back into the moment.

He had a calculating expression on his face, and I couldn't help worrying that my look over the Styx had given too much away. But nothing seemed to come of it. An hour and a bit later it had gotten very late or started to get early, depending on how you looked at it. Part of the reason Cerberus and I get along is that we're both night people, me because I sleep deepest between 4:00 A.M. and noon, him because he's a raving insomniac. Anyway, it was time to pack it in. The last game had been mine and Dave's, but we'd lost the evening. Bob and Mort were quite pleased with themselves—himself? I was never quite sure how to think of the three of them: as Mort, Dave, and Bob, my buddies? Or as Cerberus, dread guardian of the underworld?

Thoughts for another late night, I guess. I packed up the cards as Mort and Bob good-naturedly ribbed their fellow head. I was just getting ready to drop the deck into my shoulder bag when all three suddenly stopped what they were doing and turned to look at me as one. I froze. Something about their collective expression made me shrink inwardly.

"Ravirn," said Dave, "we like you."

I nodded, forcing myself to smile. I could hear the *but* he didn't voice.

"You're a good friend," said Mort.

For a moment, I was transported back to my first crush. It ended as such things all too often do, with the dreaded "friends" speech. The thought almost made me giggle. I liked the hound of hell, too, just not *that* way.

"Don't think that makes us blind," said Bob.

I realized then that they were doing the scary three-mouths-speaking-as-one thing the Furies do when they are about to pronounce judgment, and any thought of laughter died. This was Cerberus, not my canine friends.

"I didn't think it would," I managed to say through a mouth gone terribly dry.

"Good!" said all three in perfect unison, their voices as solemn and final as the closing of a sepulchre. "We *must* oppose any who dare the underworld gate, no matter who they are, or how we feel about them. None may pass within save through death or the will of Hades, and for the dead the passage is one way."

"Ah, how exactly would this relate to me?" I asked, though I thought I knew.

"Cerberus has spoken." The three heads nodded.

"Guys . . . I'm really not sure I get where you're going with this," I said.

"We don't get a lot of company," said the left head, reverting once more to my buddy, Bob.

"Nobody comes here for fun," said Mort.

"Are you questioning my card-playing motives?" I assumed my best hurt-innocence expression. "I know we didn't start off on the best foot, but I thought that was all in the past."

If I hadn't done some fast talking when I tried to make that initial contact, I'd have ended up as doggy chow. Fortunately, on my second and subsequent visits, the trio had proved much more friendly. That made this sudden shift in canine attitude all the more surprising.

"Don't be an idiot," said Dave, "and don't take *us* for fools."

"Orpheus was the last to come and go unsanctioned and unscathed," said Bob.

Another demigod cousin of mine, Orpheus had played a tune of such beauty and wonder that it put Cerberus into a deep sleep, allowing the musician to pass into the underworld and retrieve his beloved bride, Euridice. It was a great triumph but short-lived, since Apollo cut his head off and made it into an oracle not long after.

"He wasn't the last to try," said Mort. "There have been others."

"Many passed the gate alive," said Dave. "In is easy. Out is the problem. None of them made it back, though there have been thousands."

"Tens of thousands," said Bob. "They failed, and they died. Their names are forgotten."

"Except by us," said Mort. "We do not forget." He looked sad but determined. With a move so fast I barely saw it, his head darted forward, and he caught the slab of basalt we'd been using as a table in his massive jaws.

"Don't make us turn you into a memory," said Bob. While he spoke, Mort's jaws began to close, crushing the stone as a lesser dog might a rotten bone. "We'd hate to have to kill you."

The noise was terrible, but I had no trouble hearing Dave's voice. "But we would kill you. Never doubt it. You're no *Orpheus*." He pronounced the name with a heavy emphasis that rang oddly.

"Of course not," I replied. "I couldn't play a lyre to save my life, and my singing voice is only good for attracting harpies."

Mort made a last effort, and the rock burst completely asunder, showering me with shards and dust. "Let whoever it is you lost go, Ravirn."

Without another word, Cerberus swung his giant bull-dog's body around and stalked back toward the river and the cave Hades had dug for his kennel. I wiped sweat from my face and let out a little sigh of relief.

A faint *bing* came from my shoulder bag as Cerberus passed out of sight. I unzipped it and dropped the cards inside, reaching down to retrieve the bright blue clamshell of my laptop with the same movement. Setting it on a rock, I flipped up the lid.

Large red letters read, *That went well!* A small goblin-head logo below and to the left of the screen was sadly shaking itself back and forth, an unmistakable sarcastic *not*.

"On the contrary, Mel. For the first time in ages and de-spite everything, I think this all might just work out."

The laptop made a rude noise. Melchior is not what you'd call the most reverent of creatures in either of his forms, laptop or webgoblin. When I'd first programmed the spell that gave my familiar life, I'd put in a subroutine de-signed to provide a touch of sarcasm and back talk. He'd long since exceeded his specs.

I'm never quite sure how to feel about that. Mixing magic with computer code has changed the way my family works at every level, merging hacker with sorcerer, and forever scrambling the logical and the irrational into one big WYSIWYG mess. I'm sometimes tempted to agree with the traditionalists in the pantheon that all this newfan-gled computer stuff is a royal pain. Then I actually have to perform a spell, and I'm reminded just how much less dan-gerous magic has become since the advent of the mweb and the birth of digital sorcery.

I typed, *Run Melchior. Please.* There was a time when I'd issued actual commands to my computer the way most people did. Sometimes I missed it. He could be a nasty and stubborn little piece of hardware.

The red letters returned. *Fat chance.* The logo raised a skeptical eyebrow. *I'm not getting anywhere near Rover.*

I sighed. Hades, as part of the whole original Olympus-home-of-the-gods milieu, was located in the basement of the central structure of reality. My next destination had a less ritzy address, and getting there required temporarily converting my flesh-and-blood analogue body into a string of ones and zeros and electronically transmitting it from point a to point b.

That meant running a spell. *Melchior*, I typed. *Mtp://mweb.DecLocus.prime.minus0208/harvard.edu~theyard. Please.*

Executing. Connecting to prime.minus0208. A brief pause followed. *Connected. Initiating Gate procedure.*

The eyes and mouth of the logo opened and bright laser-like beams shot forth, one blue, one green, one red. Together they stitched a hexagonal pattern of light on the ground. A green glow began to climb upward in the area above the hexagon as though the edges of the diagram delineated the walls of an invisible glass eight feet in height. I eyed it a little more warily than I once would have.

The digital me would make the trip via the mweb, the magical computer network that tied all of the infinite worlds of possibility into one gigantic matrix. When I was a boy, I'd been led to believe the Fates had created the system, but I'd since learned that wasn't quite true. Necessity, the shadowy and enormously powerful entity sometimes called the Fate of the Gods, was responsible for spinning the mweb from the Primal Chaos, though she left its day-to-day administration to my grandmother and her sisters.

In another context, that firm hand on the reins might have provided a certain amount of reassurance to a traveler about to embark on a little jaunt between the worlds. Unfortunately, I know beyond any shadow of a doubt that Fate hates me. So all the hazards inherent to mweb-based travel go double for me.

Just like the various human sorts of network, the mweb experiences the occasional hiccup. But what's merely frustrating when the error involves an e-mail going astray becomes infinitely worse when it happens in the few brief moments while a person exists as nothing more than a very fragile string of ones and zeros traveling between gates. I'd lost relatives that way. Still, I suppose it beats walking.

I stepped into the column of light.

Gating, said the words on Melchior's screen.

The stone-dotted shores of the Styx wavered before my eyes as the gate transformed me into one more electronic signal in a sea of data. For an infinite instant I could almost feel myself streaming down the channel between worlds, the pressure of chaos all around me, my laptop familiar a dim presence at my nonexistent side. Then, as abruptly as it had opened, the gate closed, returning us to the world of the physical.

We arrived in a cold and moonlit elsewhere, Harvard Yard in another layer of reality, one where winter held sway. Our point of entry, a secluded corner between Stoughton Hall and the Phillips Brooks House, was further shielded from view by the bulk of a tree. Since I'd been excommunicated from my family and dropped out of college, I'd been living in a nearby apartment with my girlfriend.

Cerice, another of the Greek pantheon's demi-immortal children, was finishing up a doctorate in C-Sci at the Harvard Center for Experimental Computing before going to work as a coder for Clotho, her family matriarch. I could have gated directly back to our apartment, but I wanted to walk a bit, and I wanted to see Cerice. As anyone who's ever lived with a Ph.D. science candidate in her last year of research knows, she would be found in the lab and not at home, even so very late on Thursday night.

Run Melchior. Please, I typed into the laptop for a second time.

Executing in 5, 4 . . .

I set the computer on the ground as the countdown ended. The screen, suddenly as pliable as a sheet of latex, bulged forward as though someone—or perhaps *something* would be more apt—had pressed its face against it from the far side. Sharp ears and a sharper nose shaped themselves into being as my familiar shifted from laptop to webgoblin. The back of the screen formed into the round dome of his bald blue head. The lower half of the clamshell frame became a miniature torso with arms and legs ending in clever hands and tiny feet.

He stretched and grinned. "Better. I was starting to get a little stiff."

"It's your own fault for insisting on playing laptop whenever we visit Cerberus."

"Given the choice," said Melchior, "I wouldn't get within a hundred Decision Loci of the security firm Fido, Fido, and Rover. At least in laptop shape I don't look quite so edible." He cocked his head to one side. "Speaking of shapes, yours could use a little work."

"Chaos and Discord!" I swore, though the oath no longer held the outrage it once had. I tended to think of the goddesses in question as the loyal opposition these days rather than the monsters I'd been raised to see. "Since I quit bothering with the wardrobe change, I keep forgetting to fix my face."

I whistled a half dozen bars of binary code, initiating a process of transformation. Melchior nodded his approval as the vertical slits of my green eyes became humanlike circles, and my slightly pointed ears rounded themselves. I left my long black hair, fine bone structure, and dead white skin—I could always pretend I was a Goth.

"Better?" I asked.

He shook his head sadly. "What *would* you do without me?"

"Get a moment's peace?" I responded sourly.

"I don't think so," replied Melchior. "Not with that sword attracting the attention of every cop within a thousand yards."

"Oops." I blushed.

In former times, whenever I visited with family—cousin

Cerberus, for example—I'd always made sure to follow the protocols laid down by my grandmother, Lachesis, and worn my natural face along with the proper court garb in my black and green colors: tights, doublet, boots, and, of course, rapier and dagger. Now that I was apostate, I didn't bother with the fancy clothes, preferring the protection and comfort of my Kevlar-lined motorcycle jacket, emerald Jack-of-lost-souls T-shirt, and black jeans. The boots I kept. Likewise the blades. They still seemed prudent, as did my .45 automatic. It wouldn't do much good if Cerberus decided I looked bite-sized, but I had other enemies.

I undid the sheaths on my belt and handed them to Melchior, though I retained my pistol. The low-profile shoulder holster barely made a bulge under my leathers. He whistled a complicated binary passage that would have taken me an hour to perform on top of three days of practice and who knows how much coding time, did something creative with the local fabric of space-time, and made the weapons disappear.

And that is why I thank the Powers and Incarnations that I was born into modern times, when a hacker-cum-sorcerer like myself doesn't need to do all of his coding on a dumb terminal or, worse, perform actual wild magic with all its inherent dangers and limitations. All magic taps chaos for its power, but the advent of the mweb, with its carefully regulated energy flows, has made the process *much* safer.

"Let's go find Cerice and tell her what happened," I said. She wasn't going to be happy, but then, with her thesis defense scheduled in seven weeks, how would that be any different from her base state? Lately, she'd been so stressed, I half expected her to start bleeding from the ears.

"It's your neck," said Melchior, perhaps divining the direction of my thoughts. "Kneel, would you?"

I knelt, and he scrambled up onto my shoulder, where another whistled spell made him fade into his surroundings. It wasn't quite invisibility, but anyone who saw him probably wouldn't believe it anyway. Webgoblins didn't exist. For that matter—a thought to remember when next I forgot to alter my appearance—neither did ex-princes of the middle house of Fate.

It was very late, and the night cold was really gnawing at my joints, especially the old injuries in my right knee, so I hurried. We had just reached the steps of Cerice's lab building when a tiny blue hexagon of light appeared on the concrete railing.

"Now what?" I muttered.

There were any number of folks who might gate in on me unannounced, most of them with ill intent, but none of them was six inches tall. Because of that I waited to see what happened next rather than do anything drastic. A moment later, a tiny naked woman popped into existence atop the pitted concrete. She had waist-length black hair, dragonfly wings, and—as I'd discovered the first time I met her—a thoroughly nasty disposition. A webpixie and sometime PDA, her name was Kira.

"There yer are," she snarled as soon as she spotted me. She did a lot of snarling.

"And a lovely good morning to you, too, Kira."

"Ar, go on with yer," she said. "What's the likes o' yer care about formalities from the likes o' me?"

"Can I eat her?" asked Melchior hopefully.

"Just yer try it!" said Kira. "I'll tear yer eyes out and feed 'em to yer."

"Somehow, Mel, I think she'd stick in your throat. What do you want, Kira?" She might be a royal pain, but I owed her a favor or two.

"What makes yer think I want summat?" I just looked at her. "Ar, all right. So maybe I'm in a bit o' need, and I thought I could touch yer fer help."

She did look rather bedraggled, exhibiting a few rips in her wings and a certain air of poverty. "Go on."

"It's been forever and a day since I've had a bit of an upgrade, and I figured yer was the one ought to set things to rights, seein' as it's yer fault I'm out o' work."

True enough on one level. She'd once been the property

of my cousin Dairn, who had very different views on the rights of the AI, which might have something to do with both her disposition and grammar, and I had been responsible for their parting. At the time she'd thanked me.

"What do you need?" I asked. She looked at her feet. "Come on, I'm kind of in a hurry. Besides, this isn't exactly a private forum." Only the lateness of the hour and the emptiness of the streets had kept our conversation from attracting attention already, and I really didn't want to have to explain Kira to any passersby.

"Well, it's been near two years since I came online and my RAM is sorely inadequate by today's standards. Also, I don't have any o' them fancy cell phone doodads, and I'll need one. Voice Over Mweb Protocol enabled o' course."

"Anything else?" This was clearly going to take work.

"I don't know. I'm about three OS upgrades behind the curve, and I haven't exactly been keepin' up with the trade magazines. What would yer suggest?"

"I could suggest that you go jump . . ." She looked heartbroken. I sighed, then smiled a yes. For some reason, I can't resist a damsel in distress, even if she's only six inches tall and has the manners of a moth-eaten weasel. Besides, I'd just had an idea. I put out my hand, palm up. "Hop aboard, and we'll talk. Melchior, would you get the door?"

He rolled his eyes but whistled a spell of unlocking— nobody in his right mind would give an old hacker like me the keys to Harvard's crown jewels of computing—then held the door. I decided to wait on seeing Cerice until I'd found out whether I could manage the upgrade I had in mind. So I had Mel open up the small computer repair shop just down the hall from her lab. I did a quick inventory and decided they had about half of what I needed on hand.

"The software will be easy enough. So will the RAM. But the rest? Your microphone is totally inadequate, so that'll have to go. You haven't got an audio-out jack, and I can't imagine where I'd put an antenna."

"Are yer trying to slither out on me?" she demanded.

"No, just thinking aloud. I wish this could wait until after I get back from—"

She cut me off. "No chance. I know yer too well fer that," she said. "Yer *errands* tend to the hazardous. How am I supposed to get fixed with yer dead and gone?"

"See," said Melchior, "even the great unwashed can tell you're not long for this world." He looked her up and down. "Well, unwashed at any rate."

"Why is everyone convinced I'm going to get myself killed?" I asked. The look of scorn and disbelief on the two small faces was identical. "Right. Mel, why don't you make yourself useful? I need you to run to the electronics store and find me the highest-capacity flash memory device you can find. Oh, and a couple of really nice cell phones."

"I could still eat her," he replied. "It'd probably be easier."

"Go." He went. I turned back to Kira and gave her a visual once-over. She put her hands on her tiny hips and glared back at me. It was quite disconcerting. "Do you want help or not?" She held my gaze a moment longer, then nodded, almost meekly.

"Right. Then you, Handheld. Execute, please."

For a moment I thought she was going to argue, but all she said was, "Executing," in the strange, almost timbreless voice the various AIs used when running commands.

With that, the webpixie was gone. In her place lay a small translucent green handheld computer. There were scuffs on her cover, and the top left corner of her case was badly cracked, but she was still a fine little piece of hardware—state of the art in her day. I started removing screws. After a time, Melchior returned with the gear. I mumbled a quick thank-you, then got back to work.

I removed the cracked bit of casing and used the resultant hole to mount her new antenna and a headset jack. Inelegant but functional, and a little bit of liquid latex helped with the looks. In addition to the bits I'd asked for, Melchior had turned up one of the new ultraminiature hard drives.

When he handed that over, I looked a question at him. He pointed at Kira and tapped his ear inquiringly.

"Fully shut down," I answered. "Can't hear a thing."

"She'll need that if she's going to get into MP3s." I raised an eyebrow. "I figured that was what you wanted the flash memory for. This is a better storage solution. Individually, MP3s may not take much memory, but they do add up and . . ." I kept my eyebrow up. "All right. She's about as much fun as a sand burr in your shorts, but she's got enough attitude for a whole herd of webtroll servers. She's fragile and obsolete, but she's not going to let anyone push her around. She's got this whole free will thing nailed. Since I'm still working on it, I admire that."

"I just hope I haven't scrambled her brains completely with this rush job," I replied.

Two hours after I'd started the project, it was time to find out. With a quick jab of my smallest screwdriver, I initiated a hard reboot. Several long seconds passed with the only sound a faint whir from her new hard drive. Then her little speaker let out a rude Bronx cheer.

"If her start-up sound is any indicator," said Melchior, "she's well on her way to normal."

When she shifted into webpixie shape, she confirmed that. "A bloody butcher yer are," she growled, "lopping a great huge chunk of my casing off like that. And with no anesthetic, I might add. Ar!" She took wing and shot out the door into the hallway.

"Not even a thank-yer," said Melchior. "Typical."

But before I could get out of my chair, Kira had returned, hovering a few inches in front of my nose.

"Thanks, yer great booby." She flitted down to Melchior. "Yer too, blue boy. I know that hard drive weren't his lordship's idea." She jerked a thumb at me. "That's pure fellow webcritter thoughtfulness that is." She grinned impishly. "It's too bad yer such a monstrous huge fellow, or I might show you my gratitude in a manner a bit more personal, if yer catch my drift." Melchior blushed a deep indigo. "Ar well, different ports for different connectors and all that. But if yer ever have the urge, remember this." She zipped up close to his ear and let out a burst of binary far too fast for my ears to decode.

Melchior was still looking stunned when she opened a tiny gate in the substance of reality and vanished.

"What was that last?" I asked.

"She gave me her new cell number," said Melchior. "She said now that she's got one, she might as well get some use out of it." He blushed again. "Then she suggested that even if we didn't have any hardware in common, we could always try wireless."

I grinned but didn't say a word as I headed out the door. We'd kept Cerice waiting long enough.

As expected, I found her in the lab pacing and swearing. She did a lot of that lately; the dissertation was practically killing her. She looked depressed and exhausted. Around her lay a couple reams of paper covered with a million or so lines of code that I could barely read, much less really understand, and a dozen monitors scrolling different sorts of graphical and textual representations of The Program of Doom.

Did I mention that Cerice is way smarter than I am? She's also beautiful, with ice blond hair, eyes like blue fire, and a bone structure that makes mine look crude. As always, she wore red and gold, in this case jeans in a muted gold, a red silk blouse, and scarlet high-tops.

"There you are!" she said, about a minute after I sat down behind a desk strewn with junk. In her fogged state, it took her that long to notice me. "It's about time."

"Were you expecting me?" I asked in surprise.

"No, I wasn't." She came and sat down on the edge of the desk, putting her feet on my chair so that they rested on either side of my knees. "But I had hopes." Dark circles underlined her eyes.

She leaned forward, wrapped her arms around my shoulders, and rested her chin on top of my head with a sigh. This put my lips squarely between her collarbones, so I kissed her gently in the hollow there, then again a bit lower. She pulled back and shook her head, though there was a wistful smile on her face.

"You tempt me," she said, her voice husky.

"I've got all night."

"It's morning, and I don't have any time at all," she replied, abruptly rising and starting to pace again. "I promised Dr. Doravian I'd have the analysis data on the theta-theta decision point subroutines ready for him by Tuesday noon."

"And?"

"And my thesis defense is going to look like an auto-de-fé." She tried to make a joke of it, but I could hear the strain in her voice. "The whole segment's gone trash can."

I thought about that for a moment. Cerice is smarter than I am and a better from-the-ground-up coder, but nobody anywhere finds programming flaws better than I do. It's where my share of divine spark manifests itself. Even Atropos, my most inveterate critic, acknowledges that, though she has some problems with the fact that I mostly use that talent on other people's security software. I looked at the screens of data and stacks of paper Cerice had accumulated and frowned. She'd been working on this project for years.

She'd even created her own programming language when the available choices proved inadequate. And that was the problem. Given time to learn the system, I might be able to do something for her, but it would take a month to get up to speed, and she only had three days before she needed the segment running again. Still, I had to offer.

"Is there anything I can do?" I asked.

She gave me a look that mixed longing and concern with resignation and real fear. That gave me a clue as to what she wanted but wasn't willing to ask. She shook her head and looked away. I caught her chin in my left hand and gently turned her back to face me. She covered my hand with her own, stroking the end of my foreshortened pinkie.

I'd permanently lost the first joint to a spell a bit over a year before. It had happened the night she'd saved my life

for the first of several times. It was a debt she'd never think
to call in, but one I owed her all the same. She owned more
than just my heart.

I took a deep breath and plunged forward. "What do you
need? Really. If I can help, I will."

She closed her eyes and practically stopped breathing
while long seconds slid by. Finally, pulling loose of my
hand and turning her face toward the floor, she whispered,
"Nothing. There's nothing you can do."

"What if you had Shara?"

"She's gone, Ravirn. Dead, and that's not a problem with
a solution."

"Orpheus—"

"No!" She cut me off. "That's madness. All that'll happen if you try to bring her back is that I'll lose you, too.
Don't even think about it."

But the moment had come. Cerice knew I'd been working on how to get Shara out of Hades. She'd tried to talk
me out of it enough times. Maybe she was right; maybe it
was crazy. But I couldn't let that stop me. Shara'd died because of me—a victim of collateral damage in my recent
confrontation with the Fates. An arrow that should have
had my name on it had punched right through her screen,
causing massive short circuits.

While I'd been horrified, I'd figured fixing her up would
involve little more than solving a really tricky hardware
problem. Cerice, knowing the architecture of the various
webgoblins and webtrolls that ran the backbone of the mweb
better than I ever would, had concurred. But when we'd gotten all the parts put back together, Shara wouldn't boot. The
hardware was fine, the software was fine, but no Shara.
That's when we'd realized that she had a "spiritware" problem. Her soul had passed through the gate so ably guarded
by my new pal Cerberus, probably at the instigation of my
great-aunt Atropos.

I owed it to Shara to at least make the attempt to restore
her to life, and now was the time—when a rescue could do
double duty. Shara was as much Cerice's programming

counterpart as Melchior was mine. She contained every scrap of information Cerice had ever voiced or written about her thesis project. As a coding resource and a friend, Cerice's familiar was irreplaceable. If anything could save Cerice's thesis, Shara was it.

So, all I had to do was get moving. It was time and past to screw my "courage to the sticking-place," as Lady Macbeth had so elegantly phrased it. But now that the moment had arrived, I felt like I'd been hit in the chest with a hammer. Best to act now before I had any second thoughts. "Melchior," I said, "my dagger."

The webgoblin, who'd been keeping a low profile so that Cerice and I could pretend we were alone, swallowed audibly. "Ahhh, Boss, are you sure that's a good idea?"

"Please." He didn't answer, but a moment later he handed it over.

"Don't," whispered Cerice, looking half-panicked. She shivered when I pricked my index finger.

Instantly, bright blood welled up. I touched it to my lips. "I swear by my blood and my honor to return Shara to you before the sun rises on Sunday."

There, I was committed. A fool perhaps, but a committed one.

CHAPTER TWO

Cerice went deathly pale when I spoke my oath. "That was a damn-fool thing to do, Ravirn." Instead of angry, she sounded scared.

"Yeah," said Melchior. "Listen to the lady. She knows whereof she speaks." He looked physically shaken.

I shrugged. "Too late to do anything about it now. Besides, what else would you expect?"

The two of them had been despairing of my common sense for years, and at least in this case, they were probably right. The Titans, my ancestors, had created themselves from the pure stuff of Primal Chaos—the driving force of all magic—by the sheer power of their own demiurge. Though thinned by the many generations that lay between, my own blood still carried that chaos within it. An oath sworn on it carried all the force of divine law.

If I broke my word now, the Furies would come down on me like the world on Atlas's shoulders. Not that it really mattered. If I blew this one, I'd be stuck on the wrong side of the Styx, and there's really not all that much that even the sisters of vengeance can do to a dead man. Which is not to say the oath was an empty one.

I had a plan, or half of one at least, but I knew I'd keep finding excuses not to try it if I didn't do something to stiffen my spine. Basically, I was scared three-quarters of the way to death at the prospect of breaking into Hades, and the oath was the only thing I could think of that would force me to act despite the terror.

At least that's what I tried to tell myself. But Melchior was right; there was something more than a little bit crazy about that oath. I've always been a daredevil, but lately I'd found myself pushing the edges harder and harder, as if something were driving me to ever-greater heights of risk taking. My fight with Fate had changed me in ways I didn't completely understand.

"He's at it again," said Melchior, rolling his eyes until they came to rest on me with a glare. "I suppose you expect me to come along on this little jaunt and bail you out."

"Volunteers only," I replied.

"You know I hate it when you make me make decisions," said Melchior.

"Ain't free will a bitch?" I replied.

He sighed. "Shara's my friend, too, and more than that. I guess I'm stuck." A grim smile exposed his fangs. "I suppose that, on the upside, I'll have the rest of eternity to say 'I told you so' after we get killed."

Cerice watched the interplay with a sad smile. "Same old, same old," she said. Then she gave me a quick hug and kiss. "You're an idiot. You know that, don't you?" I nodded. "But you're my idiot, I suppose. My dark bird."

I frowned at that. "You know how I feel about the whole Raven thing."

"I also know that Clotho does *nothing* without reason. Whether you choose to wear the name or not, you own it." She canted her head to one side. "More importantly, it owns you. Names have power, Ravirn. You need to at least understand what Clotho's given you before you can safely put it aside."

"I suppose you're right," I said, though not because I agreed with her. I just didn't want to start a fight with the woman I loved on what might be my last day among the living. Especially since I hadn't yet gotten her to admit she loved me back.

"Don't agree with me just to make me happy," said Cerice. "It doesn't work that way." Before I could answer, she put a finger on my lips. "Ravirn, no one living is closer to my heart than you are. You matter to me, and I respect your opinion, even on occasions like this one, when you're wrong." She smiled to take the sting out of her words. "But we'll save that discussion for another time. For now, let me just thank you for rescuing Shara."

"You sound awfully sure of my success in spite of the odds. If you're not careful, my head'll swell."

"I doubt it," she said, stepping in very close and touching my cheek. "If it gets any bigger, it'll burst."

"Amen," said Melchior from somewhere down around my knees.

"Unkind," said Cerice. Then she winked at him.

I had to smile. She and Melchior were all that was left of my old life, and I loved them and loved that they weren't letting the possibility of my death and dismemberment make them go all maudlin. I hate maudlin. When it's a choice of laugh or cry, I'll take laughter every time and no matter the cost. I rubbed Melchior's bald blue head for luck, then gave Cerice a very thorough kiss.

"I'd better get going," I said when I came up for air. "I need to make some serious preparations. I have less faith in the certainty of my success than you do." There were things I'd need back at the apartment, Shara's mortal shell high on the list.

As I started for the door, Cerice caught me and gave me another kiss.

"What's that for?" I asked.

"Just in case."

"I thought you were certain I'd succeed."

"I am. You'll fulfill your oath."

"So what the problem?"

"You didn't promise that you'd come back," said Cerice, and there were tears in her tired eyes. "I do sometimes wish you'd learn to count the cost. Try not to get yourself killed, all right?"

"I don't know," I replied, holding my hands up like two scales on a balance. "Get myself killed or come home triumphant to the grateful arms of the most beautiful woman since Helen of Troy. Tough call, that."

No. I didn't believe me either. I hoped I'd come back, but . . . let's just say I'd phrased my oath the way I had for a reason.

The River Styx runs black and wide, its nighted depths unplumbed, a fact I'd counted on from the start. But darkness comes in many degrees and types: the crisp obsidian of a cloudy moonless night, the stygian depths of a sealed tomb, the pregnant potential of a theater before the show. None of them touch the light-devouring midnight that holds sway in the river of death, a fact that had me swearing before I'd swum ten feet.

My high-intensity dive flashlight penetrated about the length of one arm. Unfortunately, it was Melchior's arm. If I pointed the beam down the length of my body, I couldn't even see my weight belt. Combine that with the fact that my wrist compass kept spinning in circles because the underworld wasn't exactly governed by the same rules as everywhere else, and I had major problems. I kicked slowly, trying to hold myself still relative to the water flow.

How come this kind of shit never happened in the movies? *Bond* always seemed to have crystal-clear water and fifty-foot visibility. Of course, a real dive in zero vis would be about as much fun on film as shoving the camera into a mudbank and letting it roll. I sighed through my regulator, letting off a trail of bubbles. In the current of the thick black not-quite-water, they slid slowly up and to my left. I turned my head in that direction and blew a bunch more bubbles. This time they moved directly away from me as they rose. I realized I could use them to tell the direction of the current and up from down. It might not make for pin-point navigation, but it should get me across the river.

By sheer dumb luck I surfaced less than ten feet from Charon's dock. Since he was apparently off picking up a fare, I was able to slide underneath, strip off my scuba gear, and rope it to a piling. I checked my watch—1:20, so Cerberus would be solidly into his afternoon nap. The big insomniac might have trouble getting twenty winks at night, but from one until three he went down like Morpheus on tranquilizers. It was one of the many useful things I'd learned over the months of our acquaintance. I felt bad about exploiting our friendship, but not bad enough to leave Shara on the wrong side of Hades' gate.

When the barge returned, it was carrying four crisp-looking Russian Spetsnaz carrying AK-47s and about two dozen Japanese tourists who didn't seem to have a real solid grasp of their situation—they were taking pictures and talking excitedly among themselves. I pulled myself up on the dock and, inasmuch as it was possible, blended in with the group headed for the gate.

A series of velvet ropes stood to one side to allow the area in front of the gates to be divided into a zigzag queue for high traffic. At the moment, it was a straight shot from the ferry to the place where a couple of obviously bored dead souls in Hades Security Administration uniforms were standing by something very like a metal detector. I was a little worried about that until the heavily armed Spet-snaz got through without the HSA boys so much as blink-ing their huge and vacant eyes.

When my turn came, I made sure Cerberus wasn't about to make an appearance, then boldly stepped through. The alarm went off like a harpy with its tail caught in a blender. The security detail stopped looking bored and started look-ing like the damned souls they were.

I yelped and started to run.

I say started because I didn't really understand what running meant until I heard the dreadful hungry baying of the oldest and most dangerous hound ever born. Cerberus was coming. I had thirty feet to cover from checkpoint to open gate. He had a half mile or more. The hot breath on my neck as I crossed the last yard was my only warning. I dived forward. If he'd really wanted to, he could have had me then. But those mighty jaws closed on air instead of me, and the pile-driver force of his striking head tossed me through the gate.

I landed hard, even by demigod standards, and emptied my lungs in a great whoosh. Why do I always end up taking on entities higher up the ladder of divinity than myself? Just once I'd like to go toe-to-toe with somebody from a lower weight class. It took me a good minute to get up the will to stand and another after that actually to manage the job. I was just glad to find that my bad knee hadn't taken too much of the impact. It was much better than it used to be—witness my sprint—but it still occasionally went out if I misused it.

When I looked back, all I could see was bristling hellhound. He filled the gate from top to bottom and edge to edge, or a bit more than that on the sides. He'd really have to squeeze if he wanted to get through. By looking between his big, bowed legs, I could see that the security checkpoint had been reduced to kindling in his charge.

"We told you not to try it," said the three heads in that one terrible voice. "We told you; you aren't Orpheus. But you wouldn't listen. Go on. Find the one you came for, but remember that we'll be here when you come back."

He settled down to wait, his eyes a poignant mix of angry and woeful, and I realized I'd just kicked a dog. I felt like a world-class heel.

"Good-bye for now." Mort shook his great head. "See you in a bit."

"We'll have to kill you." Bob sounded almost tearful.

"But after that you can still play bridge with us, at least until you drink Lethe's waters of forgetfulness."

"You won't make it past us again," said Dave. But then he smiled a sad/friendly smile. "No one but Orpheus has. Still, I wouldn't eat any pomegranates if I were you. Now, move before the boss shows up. *We'll* only kill you on the way out. Hades will kill you anywhere. Get out of here, Raven."

It was a slap in the face, and it stung, but I figured I'd earned it. I got going without another word. The underworld is a bit like a subway station with the trains all *permanently* delayed. Lots of bored and grumpy people sitting around doing nothing, forever. But there *is* a way out. All you have to do is let the Lethe wash your memories away. Then they send your blank soul back for another go-round in a fresh body. Hades may be the personification of death, but he's also big on recycling.

Once I felt sure Hades wasn't going to take a personal interest in me, I found a quiet corner and pulled my laptop out of the freezer bags I'd used to keep him dry. *Run Melchior. Please.*

"Kind of reminds me of the 149th Street station in the Bronx," he said once he assumed his webgoblin shape. "But the view is better, and it doesn't feel quite so hopeless."

"I thought 51st and Lexington in Midtown," I said.

"It's not *that* bad," he replied with a wink. "Mind you, I wouldn't want to winter here every year the way Persephone does."

"Yeah. Remind me not to join Hades' fruit-of-the-month club."

I might make light of the situation, but it really was that bad. In fact, it was much, much worse. Hades is the land of the dead. I'd always known that, but you can't really understand what it means until you're there. Life is something we all take for granted at a very deep level. Oh, not in the sense of never questioning our mortality or anything like that, but rather that it surrounds us all the time.

Biologists will tell you that no matter where you go, you're surrounded by living things. Even in the deepest, darkest caves and basements, you'll find spores, molds, tiny plants, bugs. You can find bacteria at the bottom of the ocean, or inside of stones, or in near-boiling water. There is no place completely devoid of life. No place, that is, except Hades. Here there are souls, but not a single living creature other than Hades himself and, for a few months a year, Persephone. You can feel it in your bones and your blood. In every breath that you draw there. The absence of life is a palpable thing.

I had never realized until that moment that we all carry a sort of sense of life within us, a deep psychic connection to the biosphere around us. We may not see the web of life, or be aware of it in any conscious way, but when it's gone, it's as obvious as if the sun had blinked out. A darkness of anima as scary as any loss of light.

I found myself shivering, and not from cold. "We need to find Shara and get out of here."

Did we ever! The so-very-alive Shara would be beyond suffering here. It was a good thing Cerice couldn't know how Hades really felt. She was almost around the bend from grief and stress as it was.

"I'll work on the Shara problem if you'll cover our exit," said Melchior.

"Actually, I have an idea or two on the subject," I said.

Cerberus himself had given me the hint, though he was right about my not being another Orpheus. I couldn't carry a tune in an amphora, but there was more than one way to fleece the golden sheep. Melchior gave me a questioning look, but I didn't elaborate. I wasn't sure any of it would work, and besides, why ruin my reputation for poor planning? With a sigh, he started making electronic bloodhound noises.

I held my breath. Hades' internal system is totally disconnected from the mweb—no way in, no way out—and I hadn't been able to find out *anything* about it. That had been one of the factors that prevented me from getting here sooner. What if he was as much of a technophobe as Apollo? The chariot of the sun was still run on B.C. technology—Before Computers, that is. But a few moments after he started searching, Melchior tapped into hades.net.

The system was like WiFi on speed, totally wireless and blazing fast but very short-range. There were dampers set up all around the perimeter of the underworld so no wardriving hacker on the outside could cop free access. Hades also believed in firewalls—the kind that came with brimstone—and security by sneaker-net.

The sole connection from the mweb to the underworld was a hardwired link to the desktop machine in Hades' office, and it had zero cross-connects to the intranet that ran the show down here. It also had weird access parameters that completely blocked outgoing locus transfers. That meant hacking and gating from the outside would only buy you a one-way ticket to invade Hades' personal space, a bad idea of Iliadic proportions. Even if you managed to slide a little hack into his machine and gated in undetected, the only way to move a program on from there to where the preowned souls were processed was to have it loaded onto a disk and physically carried to one of the hades.net servers. Then, just as in my current situation, you had to get it back out. Very serious ugliness.

Working from the inside, however, his intranet security was cake. It took Melchior about fifteen seconds to pop a hole into the command line, and from there we owned the soul-tracking software. I opened a terminal shell and ordered up a real-time lock on the current location of entry #99691046-Sh, better known as Shara. Once we had that, an in-system gate took care of getting us all together in the same meatspace. We found her sitting on a cliff edge overlooking the Lethe.

"You don't look so hot," whispered Melchior, as we came up behind her.

He was right. Shara, normally a bright lipstick purple in either of her shapes, had faded to a sort of lilac-tinted white. She barely even blinked at our arrival. I could have cried.

"It's kind of hard to maintain a tan down here, big boy," she answered, pointing at the sunless, starless cavern roof above. "Land of twilight and all that." Her webgoblin form and mannerisms had been modeled on the late, great Mae West, but they, too, seemed to have faded. The land of death was slowly converting her into a lost soul. "You'll go the same way soon enough."

"Actually," I said, "we weren't planning on staying."

"Nobody ever does." She looked sadly at Melchior. "He finally got you killed, huh? I always knew it would happen. At least he didn't manage to do the same for Cerice." A look of terrible pain crossed her face, all too similar to the ones I'd seen on Cerice when she thought I wasn't looking. "I miss her so. Every time I think of her, I start wondering if I shouldn't take a walk off the Lethe pier. I don't want to forget her, but it hurts to remember."

"She sure hasn't forgotten you," I said. "That's why we're here, to get you out."

"Right."

"No, really," said Melchior. "We're not dead . . . at least not yet."

Shara looked dubious.

"He's telling the truth," I said. "Look." I unzipped my bag and pulled out a freezer-bagged bundle. Inside was the purple clamshell that normally housed Shara's soul. I opened it wide and set it on the ground. The blank screen looked like a bottomless hole. "Hop in."

"You're serious," she said.

"Yes, if you'll pardon the expression, dead serious."

Shara reached out to touch the surface of her former self, then pulled back abruptly. She looked simultaneously fascinated and disturbed.

"I'm not sure this is such a good idea," she said, leaning over as if trying to see her reflection in the depths of the dead monitor.

"I am," said Melchior.

He placed both hands on her butt and shoved. She tipped

forward and smacked headfirst into the black rectangle with an audible *thunk*.

"Huh," he said. "That's not supposed to happen."

"I should hope not." Shara rubbed her forehead. "What did you expect?"

"It should have been like falling into a hole," said Melchior. "Hang on a second." He licked a fingertip and reached for Shara's ear, then stopped. "Is this all right?"

Shara nodded. "I'd make a joke about there being better ports for you to try, but I'm just not up to it."

I winced. If Shara really wasn't feeling up to innuendo, she was a seriously hurting unit. Melchior stuck his finger in Shara's ear and whistled a short spell protocol. After a few moments, he pulled back, a thoughtful look on his face.

"Well?" I asked.

"Problem. Big problem. She's been recompiled into a noncompliant format. We've got about thirty-six hours to get her back to Cerice, and she's not currently compatible with her own hardware."

I blinked. That was unexpected and very bad. "Are you sure?"

"Yep."

"Why in Hades' name . . . ?" Somehow that seemed an inappropriate oath at the moment.

"Who knows?" said Melchior. "Mysteries of death and all that. Maybe Hades' server does an automatic recompile as it processes incoming souls."

"You guys really are here to get me out, aren't you?" Shara blinked and rubbed her eyes like someone waking from a long sleep. "Alive and in the flesh?"

"Of course," agreed Melchior. "You don't think we'd let a little thing like death get in our way, do you?"

She shook her head. "Sweet. Icarus-grade stupid, but sweet nonetheless. Thanks!" She smiled for the first time since we'd arrived and gave Melchior a hug, then held her arms out to me. I scooped her up and gave her two, one from me, one from Cerice.

"Sorry we're late," I said.

"No problem," she answered. "It's not like I've had a lot to do. What's the plan for getting out?"

"It's not a plan so much as an outline," I said, "with plenty of room for improvisation. Unfortunately, we've got a deadline." I quickly sketched out the conditions of my oath.

"I should be appalled," said Shara, "but somehow, I'm not even surprised. Why do you suppose that is?"

Melchior held up a hand in the classic pick-me pose. "Is it because Ravirn and planning go together like satyrs and celibacy pledges?"

"That'd be it," said Shara with a sigh. "All right then, so what's the outline?"

"Well, version 1.0 sort of went out the window when you didn't go back into your mortal shell," I said. "So, we're going to 1.1."

"Which is?"

"I'm working on it."

She sighed again. "It's not a bug, it's a feature, right?" I nodded. "Goody. Do you just want to invite the Goddess of Discord to the party now? Or do we have to pretend this has some hope of ending well?"

"Hey," I said. "It won't get that bad. I promise."

She rolled her eyes. "Oh, of course not."

"Oh, I'm not saying things aren't going to get sticky, but I'm just not in Eris's league. If the ability to mess things up were a boat, I'd be a canoe to Eris's *Titanic*."

"Why don't I find that reassuring?" asked Shara.

"Maybe because you've seen what happens when someone stands up in a canoe?" said Melchior.

I decided it was time to cut the pick-on-Ravirn session short. It was nothing personal, of course. I could easily hold my own in a battle of wits with a couple of webgoblins. It's just that I'd had a fresh idea for what to do next. Really.

* * *

"Can we skip straight through escape versions 1.1 to 1.9 and start fresh with 2.0?" asked Melchior. "I really don't like being here."

"Hush," I said as I scrolled down the screen. "I know what I'm doing."

Truth be told, I didn't like being "here" either. After I'd told Mel where I wanted to go, he'd gated us directly into an office where any sybaritically inclined CEO would have felt at home. Lush carpet. Imposing desk. Pricey art. Expensive chair. Honking-big plasma-screen monitor. Of course it all had that same grayed-out quality as the landscape, but cutting a few artistic corners seemed an inevitable consequence of running the underworld.

So it wasn't that I had anything against the office itself—and Hades' big leather chair was one of the most comfortable I'd ever sat in—I just didn't want be there when he got back. Unfortunately, if you want to read the God of Death's e-mail, you have to go to the source. That meant the desktop computer in Hades' office, the one that had the only link of any kind to the outside in the entire underworld.

Typing fast, I pulled up Hades' e-mail client. It gave me a password prompt. Now, if only he was as unimaginative and technolazy as his brother Zeus . . .

I'd done a little troubleshooting for the big guy once. While he had godly power practically oozing out of his pores, you had to suspect that his wits had followed his wisdom when Athena popped out of his forehead fully formed.

I entered, *Hades123.*

Access granted. I let out a sigh, then almost swallowed my tongue when I heard a faint noise from beyond the office door, as of someone pausing there, then walking past. I really wanted to get away, but we had to get Shara back to Cerice ASAP if I wanted to keep my oath. That meant finding out what had been done to her. Forcing myself to concentrate on the screen, I checked out the client software. Then I started swearing.

I'd been spoiled growing up in the Houses of Fate. My umpteen-times-great-grandmother Lachesis is the Fate who measures the threads for Atropos to cut. Control freak doesn't begin to describe her personality. Neither does anal-retentive. She doesn't just want everything in its place. She insists that it *like* it there.

I'm about as sloppy a child of Fate as ever lived, but every e-mail I've ever received is neatly filed away in an appropriate folder for archival purposes. Some of them are even duplicated in multiple folders since they fit into more than one category. Cerice is the same way. It's our upbringing, and the source is more organized yet. Lachesis even archives her spam.

Hades was a whole different story. He didn't so much as have folders, just an in-box with about 300 messages, half unopened. Apparently anything that didn't have immediate importance went into the trash, where I found 23,897 messages, again about half unopened. After a few minutes I realized his search functions were shit, too, and that I'd have to code my own e-mail sorting script. It's amazing how fast a man with nine fingertips can type when he's got the right motivation.

More precious minutes ticked past, and I kept thinking that if Hades were a better record keeper, we'd have been in and out by now. As it was, I still had to look at 163 messages that might possibly contain the info I needed. I was able to discard some quickly, things with headers like "Smite 500 Percent More" and "Totally Nude Nymphs."

That got me down to fifty or so I actually had to open and skim. Forty. Thirty. Twenty-five. Twenty. I was sweating. What if the info I needed wasn't here? Ten. Still no luck. The next one claimed to be from Persephone@gaia.net. It was six months old, from before Shara's arrival, the date stamp was 10 July OST (Olympus Standard Time). I wanted to skip it, but my script had selected it as containing at least a couple of my search terms. I double-clicked.

It opened, *Dear Hades, I hope this finds you dead. As always, I hate you . . .*

I reached for the closing keys, then froze as heat seemed to shimmer above the surface of the screen, opening an instant-messaging box in the thin air between me and the monitor. *Hello, little hacker,* read the IM, *or would you prefer that I called you Raven?*

CHAPTER THREE

"I think we have a problem," I said, staring at the words hovering above the screen.

Mel looked over my shoulder and whistled. It began as a note of alarm but quickly changed into the binary line of an escape spell. Nothing happened. It was like he hadn't even run the program. He tried again. Ditto. Before I could think to do anything else, the office door opened. I reached for my gun, but my hand stopped halfway.

A goddess stood in the doorway. Persephone, daughter of the Earth and Hades' consort, the queen of the damned. Hades, the place, is not Hell any more than Hades, the god, is Lucifer. And yet . . .

No one comes to Hades for fun, and only the desperate few visit by choice. Persephone wasn't one of the latter. Long ago Hades stole her from her mother, Demeter, the Goddess of the Corn and one of the many faces of Gaia. In those days, Persephone was the very embodiment of spring, its beauty made flesh. Hades saw her walking in the world above and kidnapped her, raped her, made her his wife. For

Persephone, Hades is indeed Hell. Perhaps all the more so because she is free to leave for nine months each year.

When Demeter discovered that her daughter had been stolen, she ended summer, calling down an eternal winter where no seed could be sown in the frozen ground, no flower would grow on the vine, and no fruit might ripen in the tree. Finally, Zeus forced Hades to give Persephone up to her mother so that winter might end, but not before Hades made her eat three pomegranate seeds from one of the trees of the underworld and bound her to spend three months of each year at his side.

When Persephone returned to Demeter in the youth of the year, she brought the spring with her. When Hades summoned her back to the underworld, winter reigned again.

It's one of the darker, starker tales of the gods. There's no sugarcoating it, and even I can't bear to joke about it. It makes me ashamed that Hades shares my blood. Now I discovered that the scariest part of the whole thing is that you can read the story in her face.

She was every bit as beautiful as ever. Tall, lissome, long dark hair and perfect skin, the classical Greek goddess, only more so. None of that mattered once you'd seen her eyes. They were winter and sorrow bound into living tissue. Ever-changing, yet eternally frozen and monochrome. Gray and bottomless, like the leaden clouds of December one moment, the white that brings ice-blindness the next, and as black as a frozen lake in between. It took a huge effort of will to look away. When I did, all thoughts of weapons had fled. Adding to her pain was something I would not, could not, do. Instead, I placed my hands flat on the desk in front of me.

Long seconds slid past in silence. The Goddess entered the room and closed the door behind her, then leaned against it. More silence. I tried not to meet her eyes but knew it was only a matter of time. The tension visible in her body made me want to see what her face was doing. I glanced toward the screen, hoping to distract myself. Words appeared in the floating IM box, wiping away the older ones.

About time, they said. *I was beginning to think you'd never look.*

"I . . . What do you want from me?" I asked, keeping my gaze fixed on the box that hovered between me and the screen.

What do I want, little Raven? Why don't you tell me?

"I'm not Raven," I said, anger drawing the words from me before I could think. I almost looked at her again but remembered not to just in time. "Fate gave me that name, and Fate is my enemy."

Even Clotho, who took your side against your grand-mother and Atropos? The Goddess's words splattered across the IM box. *The name was a mighty gift. Do you not want it?*

"I want to be me," I said, "simply Ravirn and no more."

But that name was a gift of Fate, too, or did you think your parents would have given it to you without consulting the matriarch of your line? And what makes you think that being Ravirn is a simple thing?

I didn't want to hear it, or in this case, read it. I'd had this argument too many times with Cerice. I was who I was and not what Fate would make of me. Besides, the clock was ticking, and Hades might return at any moment. I didn't know what Persephone's agenda was or what it might cost me, but since my heart was still beating, she obviously wanted more than my life.

I'm fast and tough, a child of Fate and practically immortal, but Persephone's the real deal, a goddess born. I am to her like a toy-box Mercedes is to the actual car, yet she had chosen to discuss rather than demand. I might as well push my luck.

"Give it a rest, Lady." I heard Melchior slap his forehead but ignored him. "You want something from me. That's clear enough. What is it? Come on, speak." I looked up. It was a mistake.

"Do you really want to hear my voice, little Raven?" she asked aloud. Sorrow washed over me with her words, a wave of pain like the chorus of an undead orchestra. Her face reflected every ounce of that agony.

My hand went to my pistol, but this time it was because I wanted to blow my brains out. I stilled the impulse, but again, it cost me. So did refocusing my gaze on the screen. Out of the corner of my eye, I could see that she'd moved closer. Her presence washed over me like the heat of a fire.

"OK," I said, and my voice sounded shaky even to me, "so maybe that was a little hasty. If you want to keep IMing me, that's just fine."

She laughed then, a sound like rain falling on a corpse.

You learn quickly. Perhaps I can make use of you.

I didn't like the sound of that, but I wasn't in a good bargaining position, and time was most definitely not my friend. "Look, as much as I'd love to keep up the charming banter, your husband might come by at any minute. That would cause us both some problems."

True. So, let us be quick. You want to rescue the goblin from her durance vile, yes?

I nodded.

Some variation on that old story is always why the living find their way here. Usually I ignore them. But you are not usual, Raven. Not at all. It is in my mind that you may yet make it out of here in one piece. And so I am inclined to help you.

"That's great," I said. "I can use all the help I can get."

"Truth," mumbled Melchior.

I ignored him. "I'll take what you can give. I don't have a lot of choice in the matter. But I would like to know what I'm going to have to do for you in exchange."

For starters, there's the simple knowledge that when Hades finds out about this, it will hurt him. That alone might be enough to buy my help. But yes, I do want something. What that is will become clear with time, Ravirn. From your reputation, I think I can say it will be something you won't mind too much ;-).

Emoticons *and* my preferred name. Fabulous. Why did I suddenly think this was going to cost way more than I could afford? Experience perhaps. Goddesses are never nice to you unless they feel they have to be, and payback's the stuff of Greek tragedy.

"Right. Great. I'm sure I'm going to love every minute of it. In the meantime, we've got a goblin to rescue." I jabbed a thumb at Shara, who'd very sensibly taken refuge under the desk. Then I pulled her laptop case out of my bag. "Do you know how I can put the one back inside the other?"

Yes. But it can't be done in the underworld. Before your conflict with Fate, no one knew of the free will of the AIs. Afterward, Atropos alerted Hades to the need to summon souls like your Shara's and cautioned him to be very careful in securing them. She even sent him a program for the purpose.

I sighed. Story of my life—Atropos making things difficult, that is. "Would one of those precautions involve a spiritual recompile?"

It would indeed, one that automatically grabs any soul that comes in via the mweb, as your little friend's did, since her body had already been repaired. The only way to reverse it is to send her back out the way she came in.

"You want me to e-mail Shara out of here?"

Exactly, and the file protocol is huge.

"I'd best get on it then." My fingers began to fly as I composed one of the stranger notes I'd ever put together. A few minutes later I double-checked the To line, "Cerice@ harvard.edu/mlink/via-Clotho.net," then reached for the attachments button.

Shara caught my hand. "Wait."

"What?" I asked.

"Just this." She planted a big kiss on my cheek, then gave Mel one as well. "For luck. Thanks."

Her expression belied her words. What she really meant was, "In case I don't see you again." Of course, she couldn't say that. Neither could I. So when I kissed her back and told her to pass it along to Cerice, I didn't say why. I pulled a networking cable from my shoulder bag and attached one end to the computer and the other to the port concealed in

Shara's nose. A moment later she was gone, sucked down the line in a visual straight out of some crazy cartoon. I wished Mel and I could go out the same way, but that would require us to leave our bodies behind—a fatal and therefore very temporary arrangement.

"Now what?" I asked Persephone.

Now we find out whether you're a smart enough bird to fly Hell's coop. Then she was gone, too, leaving me alone with Melchior. Her floating IM box vanished, exposing the more mundane screen behind and the e-mail I'd been reading when she first arrived. *Dear Hades, I hope this finds you dead. As always, I hate you* . . . On an impulse I forwarded it to myself, being careful to leave no trace of having done so.

By the time I finished that, Melchior had already begun running the spell that would move us from Hades' office to some more congenial spot in the underworld. This time it worked without a hitch. I hate dealing with goddesses.

As the gate opened, he asked, "Where to?"

Perhaps because my meeting with Persephone had scrambled my brains, or perhaps because it was the only answer that had ever made any sense, I decided to return to my original plan. With the issue of Shara settled, there was no reason not to try it. I would trust to my friendships and my luck.

"Take us back to the front gate."

"Are you sure about that? What's the plan?"

"I'm going to play it by ear," I replied with a smile. It was kind of nice to be one step ahead of my familiar for a change.

"I hate it when you say things like that," grumbled Melchior. "I just hate it." But he went ahead and stepped into the gate.

I'll say this for the new computerized arrangement in Hades, it made the job of getting back to the top level a lot easier than it had been for Orpheus. Quicker, too. Just enter the coordinates in the master computer and poof. At least it did if you were a hacker like me. As far as the computerized routing systems were concerned, I *was* Hades. I love root-level access.

We ended up on a low hill overlooking the underworld gate, with Cerberus stalking back and forth on the other side. My watch said it was coming up on midnight. He hadn't varied his routine one iota in all the hours I'd been gone. I'd kind of hoped something would come up to distract him, so I could fake my way out. Oh well. I did have an actual Plan A; it just scared the source code out of me.

"Come on," I said to Melchior. "It's showtime." I stood and calmly walked toward the gate. Looking worried, Melchior followed. "Smile, Mel. If this doesn't work, maybe you can make a break for it while he's tearing me limb from limb."

"You don't have to outrun the cops, you just have to outrun your accomplice?"

"Something like that," I replied. "It always worked for my older sister when we got in trouble. But I hope it won't come to that."

Boy did I hope it wouldn't come to that! Lyra and I had never had to run from anything fatal, but she *had* gotten me into a world of hurt on occasion.

"Uh, Boss," said Melchior.

"Yeah."

"There's three of him and two of us. I know no one has a better opinion of you than you do yourself, but despite that remarkable and wholly misplaced egotism, I don't think he's going to need to devote more than one head to the Ravirn Squeaky Toy Project. That leaves two free."

It was just about then that Mort spotted us. Bob and Dave swiveled to look our way an instant later.

"Back so soon?" asked Bob.

I pulled the cards out of my bag. "Want to play?"

"We won't gamble for your lives," said Mort. "All that dicing with death stuff is a myth."

"Technically," I said, "so are you. That's not why I'm

here. No normal person bets on bridge. They just play it. You said we could have a game or two once I died. Now that I've seen what death does to people, that seems unlikely. The shades of the dead aren't exactly high-quality opposition material."

"Too true," said Dave with a sigh. "They're worthless. We just wanted to cheer you up."

"Thanks for the attempt," I said, uncasing the cards and stepping up to the very edge of the gate. One foot more, and I'd be through it. "Since my imminent demise is going to render my value as a fourth somewhat suspect, I thought we could go a couple of rubbers before you chewed me to pieces." I flipped the cards from one hand to the other in a fancy cascade I'd learned while getting fleeced at poker by Eris and Tyche. "What do you say?"

"Sounds good," said Mort. "It's going to be ages before we find someone else willing to come down here and play, and it's not like we ever get time off."

"I don't know," said Bob. "He's planning something."

"Of course he's planning something," Dave said in exasperation. "You can be such a yap-dog sometimes. I'm all for it." He turned his gaze on me, and there was a knowing twinkle deep in its black depths. "Still think you can pull an Orpheus?"

"Nope," I said, smiling at the twinkle. It said I really might have a chance after all. "I'm planning on pulling a Ravirn."

"Who deals first?" asked Bob.

"High card?" I asked, holding out the deck.

Cerberus's right paw reached forward to draw but was foiled by the narrowness of the gate.

"That could be a problem," I said. "Do you want to step in here?"

"Can't," replied Mort. "Against the rules. We're still alive. Hades is very specific about that."

"How about I come out there?"

All three throats began a low growling. It made my bones itch, but I kept smiling.

"Don't be like that. I'm not talking about going all the way down to the river or anything. Just give me three steps. No, two. You'll still be between me and escape. How much harm can there be in two steps?"

"Once you're on this side, you could hook up to the mweb and gate out," said Mort.

"That's ridiculous," I said. "A gate takes a good minute to form and another to cycle. You'd rip me to shreds before the spell was half-finished."

"Oh, what can it hurt?" said Dave, and I thought I heard a wink in his voice. "He's right about the gate."

There was some grumbling, but soon the trio backed up. When I stepped through the arch, I was careful to go no more than the two steps I'd specified. Running was *not* going to do me any good. Cerberus would be less forgiving than Bob, Mort, and Dave.

Mort pulled an ace and dealt the first hand. When the bidding came around to me for the second time I went seven no-trump, the toughest contract in the game. Bob whistled, Mort snickered, and Dave swore. He was the one who was going to have to help me pull it off.

After I took the second trick, I jerked my head at Melchior. "Make a call for me, would you?"

Bob gave me the gimlet look. "Hold it. You said no smart stuff, just cards. Why should we let you call anybody?"

"What can it hurt?" I asked. "You're the biggest, baddest dog in all creation. About the only thing you could have to worry about is if I had Necessity backing me up via my speed dial. But if that were the case I wouldn't have had to come in the hard way, now would I?"

"Necessity on your speed dial," snorted Mort, though he looked a little nervous about the mention of that name. "Good one. He's got a point, Bob. Why not let him make the call?"

Bob grumbled a bit, then asked, "Who you gonna call?"

"A friend. She's totally harmless, shorter than your shortest tooth." I reached out and boldly tapped one of Bob's canines, pricking my finger. "You boys aren't afraid of a wee tiny webpixie, are you? I just installed a phone circuit for her, and it seems rude to die without giving it a test. Here." I pressed my bleeding finger to my lips. "By my blood and my honor I swear she is what I say."

The twinkle in Dave's eye returned, brighter this time. "I'm game, if for no other reason than to find out what it is you're up to." He raised a questioning eyebrow.

I just smiled and signaled for Melchior to make the call. Kira arrived a few minutes later. She had to be terrified, but you couldn't tell it by looking at her; as Melchior had said, attitude enough for a herd of webtrolls.

"How's the hardware working?" I asked her.

"Great." She landed on my shoulder. "I found this really slick file-swapping software at jollyroger.mag. It's called Theftster, and I've downloaded like nine thousand tunes."

"Tunes?" asked Mort, his pupils widening in sudden concern. "What's this?"

Cerberus leaped to his feet.

"Now would be good!" I said to Kira.

She didn't need my prodding; Three Dog Night's "Joy to the World" was already pouring out of her open mouth.

A paw the size of a Saint Bernard landed on me, pinning me to the ground. One claw point pricked my throat just over the Adam's apple, and I knew that I'd lost. I closed my eyes and waited for the end. At least I'd reunited Shara and Cerice.

Seconds went by. Though I could feel a trickle of blood making me a crimson necklace, the pressure didn't increase, and I didn't die. Then a new noise joined Kira's replay, a great rumbling snore. I opened one eye. Mort's head lay closest to me, its eyes firmly closed, a trickle of drool forming at the corner of his mouth. Slowly and carefully I crawled out from under the paw. Bob was the one snoring. A tiny hint of black fire was just visible under Dave's left eyelid, as though he were still partially awake. When I looked closer, it flickered closed in what I could have half sworn was a wink.

I turned to Kira, and whispered, "If you're willing, I'd

love to set you up with a triple headset. I know you're looking for work, and I think Cerberus would make a great boss. He's loyal and he's tough and you've got a lot in common personality-wise. What do you think?"

She looked the big guy over consideringly, then nodded, not answering with words for reasons too obvious to go into.

"Good enough," I said. "I'm going to get going now and skip out on the whole rise-and-shine thing. Look me up when you've figured out the details, or if it doesn't work out."

I turned to Melchior, who was standing perfectly still against the side of the underworld gate. He was doing a pretty good impression of the stonework he'd pressed himself into.

"Gate?" I asked. He jerked his chin toward the water's edge as if to say, "not here," put a finger to his lips, and headed in that direction. I left the cards where they were and started after him. I'd barely gone two stops before a question occurred to me, and I turned back to Kira. "Why not Monteverdi's *L'orfeo*?"

"Joy to the World" was just ending, and Kira paused a heartbeat before going on to her next track. "Does he really look like an opera fan?" Then she started into Temple of the Dog's "Wooden Jesus."

I shook my head and, moving with exquisite caution, followed Melchior to the dock where I'd left my scuba gear. As I slid beneath the waters, I took one last look at the sleeping mountain that was Cerberus.

Orpheus might have been the greatest musician who ever lived: with only a lyre he'd eased the hound of hell's insomnia. I didn't have that kind of talent. But I did have a heck of a hardware advantage and a bottomless supply of tunes. Play a song for a hellhound, and you'll give him music for a day. Teach him to pirate MP3s, and you'll give him music for eternity. Couple that with Kira's alarm clock function, and I figured he might even thank me someday.

* * *

Though it was almost 1:00 A.M. when I got back to the Decision Locus where Cerice and I currently made our home, she wasn't in the apartment. After I returned myself to human-seeming and grabbed a snack, I got ready to head for the lab and my much-deserved reward. I'd actually opened the front door when a gentle chime from Melchior announced that the e-mail I'd sent myself from Hades' computer had arrived.

"You want to read it now?" he asked.

Dear Hades, I hope this finds you dead. As always, I hate you . . . The memory of those words seemed seared into my brain, along with the goddess's pain. I didn't need that right now. I wanted to enjoy the high of the ultimate hack job, successfully cracking Hades itself, and I couldn't think of a bigger downer than reading Persephone's hate mail and thinking about what she might ask of me later. I shook my head.

"No thanks, Mel. Park it in a password-protected folder for later inspection."

"Can do," he said.

Then we headed out. When we got to Cerice's building, I picked the various locks myself instead of getting Melchior to magic them open for me. I felt fabulous and couldn't resist the pure mischief of it. I took extra care with the lock on her door, opening it as silently as possible. I wanted to surprise her.

"Ta-dah!" I said, stepping inside.

Cerice was sitting in a chair on the far side of the room, her feet propped up on about a quarter of a million dollars' worth of custom mainframe. She looked even more weary and stressed than the last time I'd seen her and barely seemed to register my presence. Finally, she turned her head my way.

"Ta-dah?" She looked confused. Then hope bloomed in her tired eyes—hope and the first hint of true happiness I'd

seen there in a long time—and she leaped to her feet.
"Where is she?"

"Isn't she here?" I could feel the ground under my feet
going spongy, lab tile about to turn to quicksand. "I sent
her ahead."

"You what?"

"Sent her ahead." I glanced at Melchior for support. "We
e-mailed her." Cerice looked at me like I was totally out of
my mind. "We did! When was the last time you checked
your e-mail?"

Cerice pointed at the monitor hooked to the mainframe.
An open mail window was clearly visible. To any normal
person it would have looked like another typical UNIX
e-mail client, but I recognized an mweb-enabled program
originally written by Clotho.

"You're sure you haven't gotten an e-mail from Hades
with a really huge attachment?" I sounded like an idiot, but I
couldn't help myself. "Maybe it hit your spam filters and—"

"Ravirn," said Cerice, "anything over ten meg is going
to trigger a query on whether or not I want to download it.
How big a file are we talking?"

"I don't know, a couple of terabytes maybe?"

"Two-point-two-nine," said Melchior, whose silicon
memory was much more precise than my own faulty or-
ganics. "Sent at 9:38 Olympus Standard Time. And before
you ask, yes, we sent it to the right address. Shara double-
checked it herself."

"She did?" I asked.

"She did."

"Well then where the hell did she go?" I asked.

"I don't know," said Melchior. "Shit. The oath."

I could feel sweat breaking out on my forehead. I'd always figured that if I could get in and out of the underworld
alive, I'd have this caper pretty much sewn up. The possibility that I could be both alive and in violation of my oath
had never even occurred to me. Yet here I was. And if Shara
didn't show up mighty quick, I was going to have some unhappy Furies making a house call.

"Melchior. Laptop. Please."

He hopped onto the desk and shifted shape. I dropped into a chair and started hitting keys. It was at times like this that I most missed the tip of my left pinkie. The loss had cost me a couple of words a minute typing speed. Still, I got a graphic representation of the mweb connections between Hades and this DecLocus's version of Harvard pretty quickly.

There were an infinite number of possible routing solutions to get a set of packets from there to here, but only a couple of optimum solutions. For a job the size of Shara, the mweb master servers would be very careful not to take unnecessary steps. The network had bandwidth beyond the wildest dreams of human coders, but it had been designed always to optimize that resource—the hand of Necessity there.

By hacking the tracking system at Clotho.net I was able to get a lock on one big mother of an e-mail coming out of Hades and heading by direct link from there into the Fate's central routing system . . . where it vanished. Poof! No more packets.

"What the . . ." Cerice was looking over my shoulder. "Where did she go?"

"I don't know," I answered, madly hitting keys and calling up further information. "She hasn't been erased or quarantined. There'd be some evidence of that. She's just gone."

I pushed my chair back from the desk. I was trying to sound calm. I actually sounded dead, which was fair. I *was* dead. I'd escaped the Furies once before because I'd gotten very, very lucky. It wasn't likely to happen again.

"Don't give up yet." Cerice took my place in front of Melchior.

His screen shifted, displaying nothing but ones and zeros. I prefer a nice clean graphical interface for computer and spell work. It's closer to the way I think. Cerice goes straight into the underlying code, and she's used her own personal magic to enhance her abilities there. Sometimes

I think she's half computer herself. Screen after screen of binary flew by so fast it blurred into complete nonsense for me.

"There!" she cried, bring the show to a stop. "Right there." Her finger touched the screen, and Melchior obligingly magnified that section of code.

I didn't know what was around it, so all I could tell was that is was some sort of routing command. "What is it?"

"It's a hardware-level autofunction," said Cerice, "and it grabbed Shara."

"Hardware-level? Are you sure?" That could get really ugly really fast.

While the mweb is administered by the Fates through their individual webtroll servers, I'd learned recently that the actual core architecture is a cluster of multiprocessor quantum mainframes that come preassembled from Necessity herself. When a replacement unit is needed, it's delivered by the Furies, who are the only goddesses allowed to interact with Necessity directly. More than that, nobody knows.

That's because no one messes with Necessity. Repeat, *no one*. Not my grandmother or her sisters, not Zeus, not Hades, not even Eris—and Discord's flat-out nuts, a friend, but nuts all the same. Necessity is to the gods what Fate is to everybody else.

So if Shara's trip had been interrupted at the hardware level, it was because of something Necessity had personally built into the system. The very thought made my bones itch.

"Can you find out where she is?" I asked, trying not to get my hopes up. There was nothing at all I could do to affect Necessity, but at the same time the possibility that Shara was still *somewhere* meant there was a chance she'd end up here.

"I don't know. As far as I can tell, this"—Cerice tapped the screen for emphasis—"autoforwarded her to an address that should be a null set."

I closed my eyes. Not good. Not good at all. "I note

your use of the word should. Can I take that to mean that it isn't actually a null set?"

"I don't know." Cerice cocked her head to one side, the way she often did when she'd found an absolutely fascinating programming problem. "It shouldn't be possible for this string to work as an end address, but a file-received message came back to the mweb server in response to Shara's forward. Take a look."

I leaned in. Sure enough, there was the standard response string from—I mentally translated the binary— souladmin@necessity . . . Dot, dot, dot? That didn't make any sense at all. But there it was.

The clear e-trail showed that whatever had happened to Shara made sense to the mweb architecture, but I hadn't a clue how to do anything about it. Even if I knew where Necessity kept her personal server stack, I wouldn't dare go after it. There are fates much worse than death. Just ask Prometheus.

CHAPTER FOUR

"So now what?" I asked. Necessity had Shara, or at least her server did. While I might be willing to tackle Hades, the Fate of the Gods was a whole different story.

Apparently, Cerice didn't know what to do either. She just slumped in her chair and looked defeated. "We wait."

"I hate waiting."

Me too, said a text box on Melchior's screen. *All right if I go back to goblin now?*

I nodded, and Melchior shifted forms. "Why don't you two head back to the apartment?" He made shooing gestures. "I'll catch up in a little while."

"But I've got to—" Cerice began.

Melchior didn't let her finish. "Don't argue. You're out on your feet, and you've already told us your program's screwed without Shara's help. It won't be any more screwed if you take thirty hours off, and maybe the rest will help you get some fresh perspective."

"Why thirty . . ." Cerice trailed off as she looked up at the clock. "Oh." It was a quarter past one. In thirty hours it would be sunrise on Sunday, and the Furies would come to kill me.

"Go," said Melchior. "I'll just tidy up around here."

"Thanks, Mel," I said. He hates cleaning, probably even more than I do. This offer was entirely about giving Cerice and me some time alone. "I appreciate it."

The first time we made love it was a desperate, against-the-living-room-wall affair, all sliding flesh and seeking tongues—striving to ignore the sword of Damocles hanging over us. The second go-round was slower and longer, with Cerice riding me to a climax on the oriental rug in the hall. Finally, in our own bed, we managed to forget everything but each other. There, massage led to caresses, which moved on to mutual nibbling, then to a slow passion, spooned-up together on our sides. Mutual orgasm. Exhaustion. Sleep. And . . .

I was in the hallway at the front of the University of Minnesota's Weisman Art Museum. In front of me stood my cousin Moric. He wore head-to-toe armor, red and blue, blood and bruises. *That couldn't be right. Moric was dead, eaten by a burst of Primal Chaos that I had unleashed.* Yet here he was.

I heard gunshots from outside, and sparks danced on the back of his armor. He didn't seem to notice, turning to face me instead of looking for the shooter.

"Ah, dear little Raven. How nice of you to come out to meet me. Did you run out of places to hide? Or did you finally remember the nobility of your blood and decide to look your death in the face?"

"Neither," I said, echoing the words I'd spoken then through the mouth of a doppelganger. I wondered at his use of *Raven*. He'd died before I'd earned that name. "I decided that if I was going to go, I should at least take you with me."

Then, just as I had at the time, I braced myself and opened a line into the interworld chaos. What I was doing was a violation of every rule I knew about the proper management of magical power, and the potential cost was terrible. Tapping the raw chaos without taking major precautions was an invitation to end your magical career as a charcoal briquette.

I felt like I'd stuck a needle in my arm and started pumping liquid flame directly into my veins. As I did so, I expected my knees to give way as they had that long year ago, perhaps even breaking the right one anew.

But instead of collapsing or cooking in my own juices, I stood there and took the pain as the fires roared through my circulatory system. The pure raw stuff of chaos filled me until I felt as if I must dissolve from within. I'd never experienced such agony. I'd never experienced such . . . ecstasy. Ecstasy? Yes. Along with the fire came a terrible rush of joy, like a whole-body orgasm. The internal burning didn't hurt any less, but I found myself wanting it to go on forever. Of course, it couldn't. After what felt like hours but was truly not much more than the time between blinks, the chaos passed beyond my capacity to contain.

It burst forth from the palms of my hands in twin streamers of wildfire, twisting and coiling along a line that ran from me to a point just above Moric's heart. His armor protected him briefly, but the power of it knocked him off his feet. Soon he began to burn. Again the scene diverged from my memory. Then, the eyeballs of my doppelganger had melted. Now, I watched in horror as Moric flopped and rolled, trying to fight clear of the fire.

My stomach turned in horror at what I was doing, yet I couldn't look away, couldn't even tell myself that if I'd known about this, I would never have done the deed. It had been him or me. As much as it tore at me to see him like this, I knew that if I had it all to do over again, I'd still have to pick me. Seconds ticked by. Finally, Moric died. The flow of chaos did not. It built, rolling back over me and filling the space, eating away at the walls and floor. The power had me in its grip just as it had all those months ago, and it was not letting go.

Then, I'd had to sacrifice my doppelganger and slip between worlds to break free. Even that had only worked because the mweb was temporarily down. This time I had opened the link directly through my own body, not that of a surrogate. There was nowhere to run and no way to escape. The chaos kept flowing. Moric's body was long gone, completely dissolved. Now the hall followed. I felt the floor give way beneath me, but I didn't fall. I floated at the heart of a rapidly expanding globe of pure Primal Chaos.

I could no longer see anything but the wild tumbling colors that fill the place between worlds, but somehow I could feel the stuff eating into the substance of the planet, tearing great chunks out of reality and devouring them whole. I felt the University die. The city of Minneapolis. The continent of North America. The whole damn Decision Locus, reabsorbed by the stuff that had given it birth. Then, when I was alone, a living point in the heart of a chaos, it turned on me and I, too, was devoured.

I woke with Moric's final throes echoing in my mind and cold sweat running off my forehead. The only light in the little bedroom came from the blinking red LEDs of the clock: 6:30. I'd only slept a few hours. It would already be getting light outside, but Melchior had drawn the curtains for us. I was dead tired, but jangling nerves and the emotional aftershocks of the nightmare were enough to let me know that I wouldn't be getting back to sleep.

As gently as possible, I disengaged myself from Cerice. She made a tiny noise of protest when I opened the covers and the cold air hit her but subsided when I tucked them back around her neck. I might have had the more strenuous day, but she'd been running on sheer will for weeks. Now that she'd finally let herself collapse, I didn't expect her to move before noon.

A selfish part of me wanted to get her up, to drag her out in a pell-mell effort to deny my danger. But she really needed the sleep, and I knew deep down that waking her would only serve to drive the awareness of impending doom deeper. Instead, I pulled on a pair of jeans and a

T-shirt and slipped out to the kitchen with the intention of making myself some coffee and breakfast. Melchior was there before me, handing me a cup as I staggered through the arch that led into the hallway.

"Eggs?" he asked.

"Depends, are you cooking them?" Melchior and food preparation made for a bad mix.

"Great Zeus, no!" said Melchior. "I'm going to run down to the hotel on the corner and pick them up from their café like I did the coffee."

"That would explain the Murray's Hall logo on the mug, then." It was a very high-class establishment where Harvard put up visiting VIPs and rich alums. The food was outstanding, and I could avoid any guilt by leaving them the money for breakfast in my will. "Sounds good, Mel. What am I getting?"

"Normally, I'd say 'whatever's under the heat lamps when I get there,' but they just put in a new computerized ordering system, so the sky's the limit."

Hacked breakfast *and* a menu, what more could you ask for? I told Melchior what I wanted, and fifteen minutes later he delivered a set of covered hotel dishes containing a bacon-and-mushroom omelet, crispy hash browns, home-made English muffins, a couple of dark chocolate croissants, a ham steak, fresh-squeezed orange juice, and more coffee. I picked up a place mat and wafted a breakfast-flavored breeze down the hallway. When even this entice-ment didn't generate a sound from Cerice's direction, I tucked in. I'd have to ask Melchior to steal another break-fast when she finally woke up.

Once I'd finished transferring calories from my plate to my stomach and gotten up a good head of caffeine, I asked Melchior to go back to laptop and called up a Graphic User Interface version of the e-mail transfer point Cerice had found. Maybe GUI would show me things that hadn't been apparent in binary.

Collecting a tiny dagger from a sheath in the sleeve of my leather jacket, I plugged a networking cable into the hilt and connected the other end to Mel's laptop form. The athame was maybe five inches long and narrow enough to pass for a letter opener, but no letter opener had ever been this sharp. I braced my wrist against the edge of the table, then plunged the blade into my left palm, bearing down until the guard touched my flesh and the tip stood out from the back of my hand. Bitter agony catapulted me out of my flesh and into the world of the mweb, where it left me.

I hung above a sort of crystalline city, the mweb server in all its multicore interconnected glory. I'd had Melchior color the native software in a pale translucent green, remote client apps in a deeper opaque olive, and the internal pathways between programs sea blue. Backbone lines into and out of the server were orange, lesser links yellow. The honking-big pipeline that went directly to the Fate Core I marked in do-not-touch radioactive red. I'd already dodged one death sentence for interfering with it; no sense giving the Furies extra incentive.

Melchior tightened focus on the place where Shara had gone elsewhere. It felt like a slow-motion skydive as I went from a satellite's-eye city view through neighborhood mode down to looking at a single building. The e-mail routing node was a cube about the size of a six-story office building and part of a big cluster of similar nodes, mostly much larger ones. It also stood out like a cyclops in an optometrist's shop. Instead of the greens we'd used for software nodes, it was literally a black box, an enigma attached directly to the motherboard. There were no obvious connections leading out of the server. E-mail went in and then it went . . . somewhere else. Then verification of messages received came back from wherever that somewhere was.

I moved closer, almost touching the node. I couldn't be sure without entering, but it looked an awful lot like an independent core, a computer within the computer. I reached out toward it and . . . stopped. Something about the node raised the virtual hairs on the back of my electronic neck, and it wasn't just knowing I was flirting on the edges of Necessity's business. Accessing Melchior, I had him pull up one of my standard hacking tools, a code weasel, a completely independent program with no connections back to him or me. It appeared in my hand, a small furry thing like its namesake, different only in that it had bat wings. Moving well away from the node, I released it.

It dropped like a hunting hawk, backwinging just before it touched the black surface and landing gently. Before it had time to so much as fold its wings, a ball of black fire emerged from the node and engulfed it, incinerating it instantly. A dark flash and the weasel was gone. The flame, hovering above the node and spinning in place, remained. I decided I'd used up my luck for the day and had better leave. The second I moved, so did the ball. It came after me like an ebony comet with a tail of black sparks glinting behind it like chips of midnight.

I moved as quickly as thought could take me, but it gained steadily. I wouldn't make—

Sudden searing pain, like I'd put my hand on the burner of a stove. I heard a whimper and realized it had come from my own lips. I was back in my body, and the pain was on this side of the link. The athame embedded in my palm had fresh carbon on it, a loose star of char marks, centered on the networking port, whose delicate contacts were actually glowing a dull red as they melted. The connector itself was gone. Using the tail of my shirt as an insulator, I grabbed the hilt and pulled the blade out.

It didn't quite burn my fingers through the cloth, but it came close. Almost out of reflex I whistled the binary spell that closed athame-induced wounds. To my surprise it worked, sealing the flesh and soothing most of my pain. I could still feel a dull throbbing, but it no longer dominated my thinking. It was only then that I remembered Melchior. If the security program had done that to my athame, what had it done to my familiar?

I looked up and saw a line burned into the surface of the wooden table. It led from the place where my wrist had rested to the now-empty spot Mel had occupied when I crossed over into the virtual world of the mweb. It was only then that I heard the running water and swearing. Turning, I found my webgoblin. He was kneeling in the sink and swearing a streak as blue as he was. Water from the tap ran across his nose—the location of his networking port in goblin shape—and from there over his right hand, both of which were showing blisters. I rose to help him, then almost went down when the world wavered around me.

"Are you all right?" I asked, my voice sounding tinny and distant.

"I will be," he answered, "with a couple of minor repairs. I take it from the fact that you're speaking to me that I pulled the plug in time."

"What happened?"

"You know how they say that 'Necessity is the mother of invention'?"

"Yeah."

"Well, she's a mother all right." Melchior shook his burned right hand a couple of times. "Man but that smarts. I don't know how the security on that black box worked, but it went through my system without leaving a mark until it hit the line out to its target."

"Me."

"You. That's when the networking cable caught fire." He pointed at the burned line on the table, his pupils huge and black, and shook his head. "It *actually* caught fire. I didn't know that was possible. I've never shifted shape so fast in my life—burned my nose pretty badly, too, what with the cable being on fire—but it was the only thing I could think of. You got lucky then. Once it got into the cable, it was hot and nasty, but slow. I was able to rip it free of the athame before it nailed you. I'm not sure why it didn't move faster."

"Maybe destroying the line as it went degraded the transmission rate?"

"Maybe," said Melchior. "Whatever the reason, you'd better thank whatever high-ranking cousin of yours is the patron of hackers."

"Eris," I interjected.

He nodded. "Of course. I must be feeling more scrambled than I thought. Maybe you should send her some flowers or chocolate or something."

"Tomorrow, if I'm still alive." Not that Discord actually ever intervened to *help* people, but hey, it couldn't hurt. "What happened to the cable after you pulled it?"

"Consumed." He pointed at the floor, where a broken circle had burned itself into the linoleum.

"So much for my damage deposit," I said.

"There's a surprise." Cerice's sleepy voice came through the arch into the hall. "Have you *ever* gotten a deposit back?"

"What's your point?" I asked.

"Only that you're a bit closer to Eris in nature than you are by blood. Chaos and discord follow in your wake. Clotho was right to call you a dark bird."

I let it pass. This might be my last day on the right side of Hades' gate, and I didn't want to spend it fighting with Cerice.

"Feeling a little crabby, are we?" I asked.

She smiled sadly. "A little, perhaps. It has something to do with being wakened from a sound sleep by a swearing webgoblin and the smell of my boyfriend's charred flesh."

"Hey!" I said. "I'm only a little burned." I held my hand to my nose. "You can't even smell it close-up."

"My mistake, then. Care to tell me what happened?"

"In a moment," I answered. "First, I need to see to Mel's injuries. Come here, you." I lifted him out of the sink and into my lap.

"Melchior, Root Access. Please."

"Root Access granted," he replied, his face going a little dreamy.

"Righthand/allfingers/fingertips.source," I said, "Terminate Signal. Initiate Recovery Cycle. Run Command, Run Command. Nose/networkingport.source Terminate Signal. Initiate Recovery Cycle. Run Command, Run Command. Root Exit."

"Exiting Root," he responded. I'd just shut down the pain sensors in the affected areas and initiated a regeneration program for the damage. "Oh, that's much better. I should have thought of it myself."

"Good," I said. "Why don't you go fetch Cerice breakfast while I fill her in on what happened."

"Sure," said Melchior. "That way I get to skip the safety lecture, too." Cerice shot him a sharp look but didn't say anything. He bowed low and winked. "What do you want, my lady? Murray's Hall just put in a computerized ordering system."

She grinned and asked for a breakfast every bit as big and elaborate as mine. With another bow, he was gone. While we waited, I told Cerice about our little misadventure.

"Interesting," she said, when I'd finished. "Remind me not to try to hack any of Necessity's equipment. So what now?"

"Now we check your e-mail and hope that Shara's come in while we were napping. I can't really see past that at the moment. The idea that I went through my little encounter with Cerberus just to buy a day pass out of the underworld is a bit too much for me to get around."

"For *you* to get around?" asked Melchior, returning with Cerice's breakfast. "What about me? If you get nailed by the Furies, I'm going to have to break in a new employer. And in case you hadn't noticed, most of your extended family thinks the solution to free will and the AI is an electronic lobotomy."

I wanted to laugh—he was making wise to cheer me up—I just couldn't manage it. I tried instead for light irony. "Somehow, I find that to be a less pressing problem than I otherwise might. I'm sure Cerice will see that you don't starve," I replied. "Won't you, my dear?"

"Of course," she said, and there was a seriousness to her words that made them a promise and let all the air out of our joking. "But let's hope it won't come to that. Mel, would you be so kind as to allow me use you as a webmail terminal? I can see whether Shara's parked in my account at Clotho.net."

Melchior nodded and made the transition back to laptop.

Cerice brought up his browser and opened a line to
Clotho.net. At that point I turned and looked out the window. We were lovers and friends. But we were also hackers
and crackers, and it would have been deeply rude of me to
watch her type her password. Even with the iris recognition
and all the other biometric security we now used, passwords
mattered. Like true names, they were not shared lightly.

Besides, I could always get it out of Melchior later if I
really needed to.

Cerice knew that of course, but she chose to use him
anyway—something she'd never done before. That was a
sign of great trust on her part, and to me it said "I love
you," as clearly as the words she hadn't yet been willing to
voice.

Seconds ticked past. "Nothing," she finally said. "Nothing at all."

As the hours ticked down, we returned to the lab. Cerice had
a really nice sleeping bag that she kept tucked under the desk
for nights when she couldn't make it home. We unzipped it
and laid it on the tile, lying side by side where we could see
the mainframe monitor. Melchior sat on the floor near our
heads, legs crossed goblin fashion. We spoke very little, and
when we did talk, it was about inconsequential things. Memories from childhoods spent in the Houses of Fate or clever
hacks we'd created.

The sky began to lighten. Still no Shara. At this point I
began to wonder if it would even be possible to download
her in the time we had left and how half returning her might
count with the Furies in the matter of my oath. Maybe I
could get them to agree to only one Fury chasing me, though
I had my doubts. They hadn't been particularly happy about
having to give up on me after our last encounter. They are
legendary for their relentlessness, and being called off at
the last minute had probably caused them more than a little
stress.

Then, just when everything was looking bleakest, I heard

the faint "bing" that announced incoming e-mail. I was halfway to the screen without crossing the intervening space, but Cerice was ahead of me.

"There's nothing here!" she said, as she tapped on the keyboard to wake the monitor. "What the hell?"

But I knew the answer. Turning, I said to Melchior, "Who's it from?"

He didn't look at all happy. "Tisiphone@necessity . . ."

Tisiphone, the Fury with wings and hair of living fire. The one who liked to play with her victims. I could actually feel my already pale skin going paler. It was the oddest sensation.

"What's the header?"

"Save a dance for me."

CHAPTER FIVE

"Uh, Boss," said Melchior.

"What is it?" I asked, but my heart wasn't in it. E-mail from Tisiphone. I couldn't get past that. Death was on its way. Sure I'd fight, but I'd lose. I'd seen the Furies take down Eris, one of the toughest goddesses in the whole damn pantheon. I wouldn't even make a good speed bump.

"You might want to look at this," said Melchior.

"Why? How could the exact phrasing possibly matter?"

"Well," said Melchior, "it's a visual and—"

He was interrupted by a chime from the mainframe. I turned to see what was up. I had just an instant to read over Cerice's shoulder, "You have received a 2.21-terabyte message from Hades@hades.net with the header: Here she is. Do you want to download the message, save it for later, or delete it from the server? Automatic download will begin in sixty seconds." Cerice hit the download-message button. But was it too late? Was the download going to finish after sunrise? Was that why Tisiphone had e-mailed me? To mock me for failing at the last possible moment?

"Melchior," I began.

"I'm on it." He opened his eyes and mouth, shooting out three beams of light, one blue, one red, one green. Where they met, a golden sphere formed. It fogged, then became translucent. Inside, a three-dimensional image formed. Tisiphone.

She was naked, as the Furies always were, and beautiful even by goddess standards, very tall and almost boyishly slender, with small high breasts and red hair touched by living fire, both on her head and where her thighs met. Her eyes held flames as well, globes of fire where her irises should have been and pupils like roiling smoke. Her skin was so white it was almost transparent, the blue veins clearly visible in her breasts and thighs. Fiery wings sprouted from her back, expanding out of the picture. I knew from past experience that she could extend them thirty or forty feet in either direction and that what they touched burned.

"Save a dance for me, Raven," she said. "The music stopped too early this time, but I'm sure you'll play doom's song again. You live too close to the cliff 's edge for it to go any other way." Suddenly lines of twisting rainbow light slithered through the image, and Melchior's speaker gave a faint static hiss as though something had disturbed the transmission. It lasted only an instant, but I'd never seen anything like it before. "It's been a very long time since someone escaped my sisters and me as you did last year. Megaera takes it personally. She wants your hide nailed to the mantel, ideally with you still in it, alive and screaming. Alecto merely thinks you provide a bad example and wishes you dead at her hand. I take you as a challenge and look forward to playing catch again soon. Good-bye. For now."

Then she touched her fingertips to her lips and blew a kiss in my direction. A kiss of fire. Like a burning smoke ring, it sailed toward me. When the flaming lips hit the edge of Melchior's projection, they vanished, and so did Tisiphone.

"I think someone's got a crush on you," said Melchior. "Isn't that cute."

"I don't think so," said Cerice, her mouth pressed into a thin line.

"Neither do I," I snapped. "A, she called me Raven. B, I'm spoken for. C, hot times with Tisiphone would be a little too hot—I've never been much for third-degree burns on delicate tissue. And D, she's a fucking Fury! You know, Goddess of Vengeance and all that jazz? No one in his right mind would date her."

"Methinks thou dost protest too much," said Melchior, but he said it from comfortably beyond my reach. "Lighten up, why don'tcha? You're off the hook, Boss." Then he did a little dance.

"I . . ."

It finally sank in. I'd done it. We had Shara back, and I wasn't going to pay for it with my life. I'd visited the underworld without taking up permanent residence. For the first time in more than a year I didn't have anything life-threatening hanging over my head. My bad knee buckled, followed by my good one, and I found myself sitting on the sleeping bag. I opened my arms wide and flopped onto my back.

I felt wonderful and empty and hot and cold all at once. It felt like someone had removed a huge boulder from my back, one I'd carried so long I'd forgotten it was there.

"Are you all right?" Melchior paused in his dance.

But I couldn't answer. I had no words to express what was happening in my head and heart. Contrary to all the laws of nature, I expected to float right off the floor and into space. Nothing as light as I felt could possibly stay on the ground.

Cerice knelt beside me and put a hand on my chest. She didn't say anything, just sat there touching me. It was just what I needed. If time had stopped then and there, I would have been fine with it. But time does not stop, not even for the gods and their myriad children. So, after a while, when the relief had faded a bit, I sat up and gave Cerice a gentle kiss and a nod. I knew she had to be dying to check on Shara. She rose and went to the monitor. Before I could even make a token effort at following, Melchior landed square in my lap.

"Have I ever told you how beautiful you are?" he said, a wicked grin on his face. Then he took one of my ears in each hand, planted a big smooch square on my lips, and said, "I love you, man."

With a wild cackle he was gone, back to his goblin dance. I wiped my mouth with the back of my hand and promised myself I'd think of some suitable revenge later on. For now, I just smiled and joined Cerice. Shara had almost finished downloading, so I collected her mortal shell from my bag and ran a networking cable from it to the back of the mainframe.

"Whenever you're ready, Cerice."

"In a minute . . . there. Boot her up in target mode."

I held down Shara's power button while simultaneously pressing her E and D keys so that she'd come up as an externally mounted drive rather than an independent machine. There was a soft chime, and a drive logo filled the screen where Shara's smiling face would normally have appeared. After a few moments, her monitor went to sleep, and Cerice went to work. There really wasn't much more I could do at that point, so I grabbed Melchior and went to find breakfast.

I was returning from that errand when Melchior—now in laptop shape—gently trilled. Ducking into Starbucks, I plopped him on the table and flipped up his lid.

"Ravirn," I said.

"Bone!" said a throaty feminine voice through the laptop's speaker. It was touched with the faintest undertone of transmission static. "It worked. Can yer hear me? This is Kira."

"I can indeed, though the connection's a little fuzzy. It shouldn't be, not with VOMP phone." The mweb was better than a hard line for most things. "I must have messed up a solder joint. Stop by when you get a chance. But at the moment I haven't got a lot of time to talk. What do you need?"

"That triple microphone jack yer promised would come in mighty handy sooner rather than later, if yer catch my drift. The dogs and I worked a deal, but Bob says I'm too tinny in external speaker mode." This last came out indignantly, or perhaps "more indignantly than normal" would have said it better.

"Well," I said, "I owe you, so stop by, and I'll check my solder work at the same time."

"Bone. Be seein' yer," and she was gone.

"Bone?" I asked.

Good, printed itself on the screen. *From French,* bon, *as in bon chance,* or good luck.

I looked askance at the screen.

Google. What can I say? I was connected, and there it was.

You're always connected, I typed back.

Speaking of which, why can't you just get a Voice Over Mweb Protocol enabled cell phone like a normal person instead of using me for this stuff? I've got enough work without I should act as your own personal VOMP phone booth, too.

Even a smart phone doesn't have the ability to filter my calls the way you do, Mel. It's much more convenient this way.

Maybe for you, but . . . oh, never mind. Sigh.

Don't be such a wimp. Now, is there anything else? I really should get back to Cerice.

I can't think of . . . huh.

What is it, Mel?

It just struck me as funny that Kira's having VOMP problems now. She was clear as a bell when I called her from Hades' gate.

Maybe she bumped something, and it knocked a connector loose, I typed.

That's probably it.

When he didn't say any more, I closed his lid and headed for the lab.

When we got there, Cerice was finishing with the upload

to Shara's onboard drive. I handed her an extratall chai latte and a cinnamon roll roughly the size of a large cat. I hadn't bothered with anything more elaborate. Cerice wasn't even going to taste her food before she assured herself of Shara's good health. I dropped into a seat behind one of the desks, put my feet up, and waited as she finished the various tasks involved in Shara's reboot and—hopefully—rebirth.

Cerice shut down and disconnected Shara from the mainframe. She paused for a long moment then, her finger hovering over Shara's power switch. I could imagine what she was thinking. We'd hit that button so many times before, back when we thought all she'd need was a repair job. What if it didn't work this time either? How could she cope with that big a disappointment? Finally, she hit the switch. A gentle chime sounded, followed by a faint whirring. The screen went black, but only for a second. When it flickered back to life it showed Shara's goblin face, its eyes closed.

I held my breath. We'd gotten this far before. This was all hardware function. A minute ticked past. Another. I could feel my lungs wanting to breathe, but couldn't bring myself to do anything about it. Wait! Was that a . . . Yes! A flickering of the purple eyelids, a faint tugging at the corner of the mouth, and . . . there she was. Shara looked out of the screen at us and blinked at the morning sun streaming in through the windows. Her speaker coughed, and a rusty-sounding voice halfway between Mae West and Demi Moore spoke.

"Where am I?" it said.

"Home," answered Cerice, tears in her voice. "You're home, honey."

I let out my breath and discovered that, despite how relieved I'd felt earlier, I'd still had some tension left. If I was relaxed then, I was a liquid now. I couldn't have moved to save my life, and that was grand.

Melchior gave a whoop that almost drowned out Shara's plaintive request to return to goblin form.

"You can do anything you want," Cerice responded to Shara. "Anything at all."

A moment later a curvy purple webgoblin stood in the middle of the desk where Cerice had been working on her. She looked wobbly and tired, but she had an almost incredulous smile on her face. Cerice caught her off the desk and gave her a hug that would probably have cracked human ribs.

She didn't let go until Shara spoke again. "Uh, Cerice. I don't suppose I could convince you to let me breathe. It's been a while, and I remember enjoying it."

Once she was back on the desk, she looked my way. "I owe you, big guy. If there's ever anything I can do to repay you . . . *anything at all*, you just give a whistle." She let out with one that would have done the lustiest wolf proud and cocked a hip at me. Shara put a growl into her tone. "You know what I mean, big guy?"

"Shara!" admonished Cerice. "He's—"

"Yours," she said. "I know. But he's such a pretty boy, and you neglect him something awful." She gave me a wink and a nod, then turned to Cerice, whose face had darkened. She touched her fingertip to her tongue before drawing a check mark in the air. "Gotcha, and I've only been back five minutes. You must be slipping. Or have I been gone so long you've forgotten how to roll with my punches?"

Cerice rolled her eyes.

"There you go, my dear," said Shara with a grin. "Now, one last thing on my coming-home list. Where's Melchior?"

"Over here," he said, raising a hand and looking a little overwhelmed. Shara has that effect on most males, even when they're braced for her. "What's the last thing on your list?"

"This!" she said, and leaped.

She hit him high, knocking him backwards and rolling over and over with him until they bumped into an equipment rack. Somehow she ended up on top, straddling his chest and pinning his arms with her knees. With a positively predatory chuckle, she bent and gave him a solid kiss on the lips. Then she popped back up onto her feet.

"There!" she said, pumping her arms overhead. "I'm back." Then she started bawling.

Cerice picked her up like a baby and made soothing noises. Catching my eye, she made a subtle nod toward the door. I had questions, like where had she been when she was wherever it was that she was, but they could wait. I collected Melchior and headed out. Cerice and Shara needed some time alone, and I was happy to give it to them. If nothing else, I needed the sleep.

I'm not sure how long I'd been out when a loud *bing* woke me. I blinked my eyes blearily and found Melchior standing on the foot of the bed.

"Incoming visual transfer protocol message from Cerice@shara.gob," he said. "Accept Vlink?"

"Accept," I said.

"Vtp linking initiated." Light burst from his eyes and mouth, creating a cloudy golden sphere.

When it cleared, Cerice hung in the air before me. "I got Shara calmed down. She just needed something to do. I put her to work on that subroutine that went trash can the other day. She said she thinks she can see where the problem is. We're going to stay here for a while to see if we can nail it down. Is that all right with you?"

"Sure," I answered. "I mean, I'd hoped we could have a giant reunion party followed by a ticker-tape parade to thank the hero of the hour." I blew on my fingernails and buffed them on the sheets over my chest. "Me, that is. But if you're so eager to put poor Shara back to work in the salt mines, who am I to argue?" I grinned to put the lie to my words. "No, really. If Shara feels the need for work to take her mind off her time in Hades, I'm the last one you'll get an argument from. Though if you could find out what happened to her on the way home, I'd love to hear the story."

"Not much to tell. She says she doesn't remember anything after you hit send. Isn't that right?"

Shara stuck her head into the picture and nodded. "Sorry," she mumbled, her eyes down. "It's just a big blank."

"Oh. Thanks," I said. There was something evasive about her tone, but she'd had enough stress for one day, and I didn't want to push it. "If you're sure—"

"I'm sure." She nodded again, then vanished out of frame. I heard a faint sniffle.

Cerice gave me a hard look. "I've got to go."

"All right. I . . . I wasn't trying to stress her out. I'm sorry. You two do whatever you think is best for Shara."

"Thanks for understanding," said Cerice, her face relaxing. "What are you going to do?"

I started to tell her I was going back to sleep but realized that even if I hadn't been down long, I was slept out. "I think I'll take a long walk and just enjoy the idea that I have nothing at all in the world that needs doing. It's a novel sensation, and who knows how long I'll get to enjoy it."

"Sounds lovely. I envy you. If you're still moving around in a couple of hours, Vtp me or stop by the lab. Kisses."

She blew one my way and faded out before I could say anything more.

"Boss?"

"Yeah, Mel."

"I hate to bring this up after your last comment to Cerice."

I didn't know what he wanted to tell me, but I was pretty sure I didn't want to hear it. Not now. "So don't."

Melchior looked down his nose at me. He had a lot of nose to look down. It was long and blue and sharply pointed, as was the look he now gave me.

"You're going to tell me whatever it is anyway, aren't you?"

He nodded. "Sorry, but that's my job."

"You don't have a job anymore," I said. "We're partners now, remember? Not master and servant."

One corner of his mouth quirked up in a knowing smile. "Nice try, Boss. Partners we may be, but I'm still your familiar no matter what. We may not be in a following-orders kind of relationship anymore, but I'm still the sidekick. That means the big issues and strategy are your problems, and the nagging little stuff and tactics are mine."

"Oh, just get on with it, Mel. What horrible earthshaking thing have I forgotten to take into account this time?"

"Persephone," he said very seriously.

I felt a snake slither its way up my spine, a very cold snake. "Damn." I'd managed to put the goddess completely out of my mind. "She did say she was going to want something from me in exchange for Shara's life, didn't she? Can you believe I completely forgot about her?"

"You? Of course I can. Denial is a force beyond even immortal ken, and you are its prince."

"Thanks, Mel. That makes me feel *so* much better." I sighed and ran my fingers through my hair to pull it out of my eyes. "I'd just gotten used to being off everybody's list."

Melchior looked at me like I was out of my mind. "Off everybody's list? You're mad. You know that, right?" He held up a finger. "Atropos, the Fate with the Shears. Wants you dead." Another finger. "Tisiphone, Fury of fire, remember her? She wants your ass as a plaything." A third finger. "Clotho, Fate's spinner. Who knows what she's got on her mind, but you can bet she didn't name you Raven just for giggles." More fingers. "Lachesis. Alecto. Megaera. Eris."

He shook his head at that last. "I don't know what Discord wants with you, but she doesn't invite you to her place all the time solely to fleece you at poker." He looked at his hands. "That's seven. Hades. Cerberus. Hey, I have one finger left for Persephone. That's nice, I thought I was going to run out. Maybe you can get on Zeus's list, too, and I can start in on toes."

"All right," I said. "Point taken. My profile is way too high, and I should probably learn to keep my head down a little more."

"Oh yeah," said Melchior. "Like that's gonna happen.

Might as well ask Aphrodite to stop sleeping around. I wasn't trying to untie the Gordian knot, just reminding you that you need to keep both eyes open and not get complacent."

"What if I think complacent sounds like a wonderful idea?" He raised an eyebrow. "All right, that sounds whiny even to me. Can I at least pretend that everything's beautiful and that I'm not going to have to cope with shit like this whole Raven thing for one entire day?"

"If that means you're actually going to deal with it all tomorrow, sign me up. I'm not going to hold my breath, though."

"Probably a good idea. You've already turned blue." I rolled out of bed, and Melchior hopped down after me. "Come on, let's go get some ice cream and play hooky for the afternoon."

What I really wanted was to haul out my motorcycle and break some speed laws, but there was enough ice on the roads to guarantee that all I'd do was trash the bike and pick up some spectacular road rash.

We stopped by the Creamery again a couple of hours later, after visiting the electronics store and before heading for Cerice's lab. She and Shara welcomed the treat, but we couldn't pry them loose from their work despite the fact that Shara still didn't look anything like back to normal.

It took another two days and the successful delivery of the repaired portion of her program to her advisor to achieve that goal. By then she'd had enough time with Shara that she was willing to let her go off with Melchior to discuss "goblin things," an ever-mysterious category that probably included a lot of rude jokes in binary and gossip about their respective sorcerers.

I took advantage of the moment to get Cerice to go out for a late breakfast with me. We ended up at a little Thai place that we both loved. It had been a bar at some point in its past and featured deep booths with thick wooden backs that went all the way to the ceiling and guaranteed a certain amount of privacy. We'd gotten our appetizers, and I was just getting ready to ask Cerice what she thought about *us*, when she preempted me.

"I'm worried about Shara," she said. "She's not acting quite herself."

"She's doing better than she was a week ago," I said. "Then she was acting like death warmed over. Oh, wait. That's right. She *was* death warmed over a week ago." Cerice's face clouded, and I held up a hand to forestall her response. "Look, I'm not trying to be funny. OK, maybe I am, but I'm making a serious point. She was dead a week ago. Dead, Cerice. Wrong side of the River Styx. Hades is not a good place to be. I only spent a few hours there, but it's provided me with a whole new set of nightmares. I'd be deeply shocked if she were acting completely like her old self."

"I don't know, maybe you're right. I want to believe that, but it feels like there's something more. It's so hard. I want everything back the way it used to be."

"Give Shara some time to reground herself in the here and now. She's got to deal with this in her own way," I continued. "Don't push."

Cerice nodded, but she didn't look entirely convinced. Who could blame her? Shara was her daughter as much as her best friend, the creation of her heart and her magic, and she had been imprisoned in Hades. Look what that had done to Persephone's mother, the Earth. The goddess had been so stricken with grief that she'd literally fallen over, turning her feet to the sun so that eternal winter came to hide the goddess's face where it looked out of Greece. Only Zeus's intervention with Hades had gotten her upright again, and that not completely, leaving her forever off balance. Twenty-three degrees off, the tilt that gave us the modern seasons. Less poetic than the other version, but at least as true.

Our entrées arrived then, and we spent a little time in lighter conversation as we paid the excellent food some much deserved attention. When we'd gotten to the stage of filling in the corners, I decided it was time to have a go at relationship debugging.

"Cerice?"

"Yes?"

"I love you."

She grinned. "So I'd gathered." She reached across the table and squeezed my hand. "I'm happy that you do," she said, "but I have to say, falling for someone like me is probably not the wisest thing you've ever done."

"I didn't fall for someone like you, Cerice. I fell for you. You're smart and gorgeous and talented. You're a splendid coder, and I'd certainly be dead without the help you gave me in my fight with Fate."

"Thank you, but—"

"Hang on, I'm not finished. You're also deadly slick at avoiding things you don't want to talk about, like us."

She let go of my hand and leaned back into the side of the booth with a long sigh. "I'm sorry, Ravirn. I know the way I am is hard on you. I care for you deeply, and I want us to stay together and see where that goes. I even want to tell you that I love you. I just . . . can't. Not yet."

I felt like I'd been punched in the chest. Words formed in my mind, hurt words, bitter words. Somehow, I held them in. Though my mouth has gotten me into a world of trouble over the years, I've always managed to keep it leashed around Cerice. Perhaps because she and Melchior are all I've got left.

"I thought it was Shara," she said into the silence, "that I was still mourning her passing, or holding out hope for her return, or even just blaming you for her death. I know that's not true now. I'm not sure what's holding me back. I don't really understand myself anymore."

"Fantastic." I couldn't quite keep the sarcasm out of my voice.

"Please," she said. "Don't be angry."

"Maybe I should step out for a while and drop back in once you find yourself?" It didn't come out the way I'd meant it to, and I regretted saying it even before I finished.

Cerice looked like she'd been slapped. "Maybe you should," she said. "Maybe while you're out, you can find out who Raven is."

I didn't have an answer for that, so I picked up the check and headed for the register. After that, Cerice went back to the lab, and I headed for the apartment. We said good-bye, but there was no kiss, no physical contact at all.

"Ouch," said Melchior when I told him about it later. "But she's right about the Raven thing. You know that, don't you?"

"No. I don't." He opened his mouth, but I didn't wait to listen. "Melchior. Mtp://mweb.DecLocus.prime.Styx."

I was angry enough that I almost forgot the "Please." When I did say it, a split second too late, I knew it sounded insincere. Melchior's mouth shut with an audible snap. For a long moment I thought he was going to tell me to stuff it and walk away. I would have deserved it. I was clearly in a mood for self-destruction. Witness my destination.

No one could deny that I owed Dave and Mort and Bob an apology, but the sensible thing would have been to "say it with flowers," preferably from a great distance. I didn't think Cerberus would eat me at this point, but I wouldn't have bet money one way or the other.

Melchior shook his head. His eyes practically shouted "Stupid idea, dip boy," but he didn't say it. In fact, he didn't say anything at all until he eventually acknowledged my request for a gate with the formal syntax of an accepted program. "Executing. Connecting to prime.Styx."

A pause followed, one that stretched out unnaturally. Since we were in the apartment, he was using the hexagram Cerice and I had permanently inscribed under the oriental carpet in the living room instead of sketching one in chalk or light. On top of that, the Styx was part of the same world as Olympus, the center of the universe and home of the mweb core architecture. With that double advantage, the connection should have come so quickly that a flesh-and-blood creature like me wouldn't even notice the gap.

Instead, a full and unnatural two minutes passed before Melchior finally said, "Connected. Initiating Gate procedure."

I wanted to ask him what was up, but his expression didn't invite conversation. He reinforced that conclusion by changing into his laptop shape as soon as light filled the gate. His lid was firmly closed. I took his point and tucked him into my shoulder bag. One more apology owed.

Then I stepped into the light. I would soon see whether the hound of hell was still my friend.

CHAPTER SIX

The second I appeared Styx-side, a great baying began. I was tempted to have Melchior gate me back out again on the spot. But that would have involved admitting I was wrong. While I might be thinking it in my own head, I still needed some time before I was willing to share. Instead of sensibly fleeing, I sat down on a rock and waited.

The near bank of the Styx is rocky and dark, a black stone beach under eternal twilight. I've never been entirely certain whether it is actually in a cave under Olympus, or just in a pocket reality anchored to the mountain of the gods. There's little in the way of living vegetation on the near shore, and what there is has thorns and spines. If it doesn't stick you, cut you, or try to poison you, it isn't native. The black waters flow by in unnatural silence, so the huge splash that ended the baying was all the clearer.

Soon I could see the great vee made by Cerberus's mighty chest cutting the water as he swam to meet me. His eyes glowed a baleful red as he glared in my direction. That was new, and the hairs on the back of my neck danced in response. Still, I held my ground. Part of that was bravado, part stubbornness, and part pure calculation.

The river marked the ultimate border of Hades' domain. He held sway over the ground from its far side to the physical borders of the underworld and was absolute ruler within the latter's walls. But here, I stood on Zeus's territory. I didn't believe Hades was fool enough to lightly order one of the children of the Titans murdered in his brother's fiefdom.

Whether Cerberus might kill me without his master's sanction made for an iffier question. After our last meeting at the gate, I was inclined to believe he wouldn't just tear me to shreds. Shaking muddy river water all over me, however, turned out to be fair game, a fact I found out after he bounded up the hill to meet me.

As soon as I'd scraped enough of the foul stuff out of my eyes to see again, I gave Cerberus a slight bow. "Nicely splashed. I take it then that you're not just going to bite my head off?"

"How do you figure that?" asked Bob, an edge of anger clear in his voice.

"I suppose I could be wrong," I said, "but you never struck me as a big fan of muck-blackened cuisine."

"Point," said Mort, sounding much calmer than Bob.

"Not bad," agreed Dave, clearly amused, "but what if we just didn't think of it? What if our poor little doggy brains don't plan things out that well?"

I raised an eyebrow at him. "Poor little doggy brains? Nice try, Dave, but I'm not buying it. You've got about as much in common with a normal dog as I do with a sparrow."

"That might be more than you think, *Raven*," said Mort. "There are certain habits of thought and behaviors that we share with our mortal kin."

"Like an irrational attachment to our two-legged friends," Bob said, giving Dave a sour look.

"Look," began Dave, his voice hot, "just because I like Raven and take my duties to our mistress more seriously than you do—"

"That bitch hates Hades," snarled Bob. "I've never liked her. From the day he brought her home, she's caused nothing but trouble. We owe her nothing! Nothing. I wish she'd go away and never come back, that her mother would just keep her."

"Jealous much?" Dave sneered.

"Of Persephone?" howled Bob. "That's a joke, right?"

"If the collar fits . . ." said Dave.

Bob growled low in his throat and Dave snapped at him contemptuously. Seconds later both heads were barking and snarling at each other.

Meanwhile, Mort had moved as far away from the other two heads as he could. "At least I'm not between them," he said to me in a quiet aside. "Sometimes I wish I could take a couple of weeks off from pack life and play only dog." The barking cut off abruptly as Dave and Bob locked jaws, straining against each other.

Mort shook his head. "Bob never learns."

"Learns what?" I asked.

"That he's not as strong as Dave, that he always loses arguments, that he's never going to be alpha. Take your pick." Bob began to whine then. "Whatever you might think about our relative dogginess, our shape makes a difference. And so does our name."

"Subtle you aren't," I said, and it was my turn to sound sour. "If you think so much of this whole Raven thing, why don't you just tell me about it?"

"Is that a sign of curiosity at last?" asked Mort. "Are you actually starting to wonder about who you are?"

"I know who I am," I said. "I'm Ravirn, no matter what the Fates say. On the other hand, I have to admit that I'm beginning to wonder *what* I am. Or what others see in me. So, are you going to tell me anything? Or are you just going to stand there looking smug because I finally asked?"

"Asked what?" said Dave, who'd finally let loose of Bob.

"Who he is," said Mort.

"What I am," I corrected.

"A filthy little prison breaker," said Bob, who went silent a moment later when Dave turned a dark eye on him.

"It's about time you asked that question," said Dave. "I just wish I knew the answer."

"What?" I demanded. "All this time, the three of you have been giving me shit about this Raven business, and you don't know what it means either?"

Dave looked sheepish. "What it means, no. That it's important, yes. You don't smell like a child of Fate anymore."

"What?" I was surprised by that.

"We've met more than a few of Fate's children," said Mort. "You don't die easy, but you can be killed."

"I know that," I said quietly. "I've sent two of my cousins across the Styx myself, though I'm not proud of it."

"Moric," said Dave, "and his uncle's son, Laric."

"Exactly," said Mort. "Though you may not be able to smell it, there is a scent associated with those who come from the three houses of Fate. You don't smell like that."

I was frankly fascinated. "What do I smell like?"

"A raven," said Dave.

"And Discord," said Bob, still sounding angry.

"Say elemental Primal Chaos, and you'd be closer to the truth," corrected Mort.

"Chaos?" I asked. "Don't we all smell of chaos? It runs in the blood we inherited from the Titans, yours as well as mine."

"This is different," said Mort. "The Primal Chaos in our veins is fixed. The Primal Chaos that wraps you like an invisible cloak is the raw wild stuff that churns between the worlds."

"What did Clotho *do* to me?" I whispered.

"I don't know," said Dave. "I really don't. But the spinner spun Eris's thread as surely as she did those of Atropos and Lachesis. She is the author of order and disorder both, and her motives are not always the same as those of her sisters. If you really want that question answered, you'll have to ask it of Clotho."

"Thanks," I said. "I've got to go now."

My brain felt like someone had stuck a stick blender in my ear and hit the on button. I simply couldn't process the Raven stuff. To say nothing of the implications of Dave and Bob's tiff and what they'd had to say about Hades and Persephone. Even more disturbing was *how* they'd said it. I started to walk away, then stopped and turned back.

"I almost forgot why I came today. I'm sorry if I caused you any trouble with my visit last week. I took advantage of our friendship, and that's not nice. You don't have to forgive me—I don't regret the deed—but I owed you an apology."

"Forgiven," said Dave, with a smile.

"Forgotten," said Mort.

"Fat chance," snarled Bob.

It wasn't until I'd moved a little way off and gotten Melchior out of my bag for the return trip that I thought to wonder where Kira was. Since she appeared a few seconds later, it was a brief concern.

"Yer likes ter live dangerously, don't yer," she said as she flew up.

"Think of the devil," I said.

"And I'm yer reward," said Kira. "When do yer think yer could do that jack job for me?"

"Like I said, drop on by. I'll make time. Oh, and hang on." I dug around in my bag for a moment and pulled out a plastic sack. "I got these for you as a temporary jury-rig." Inside were three sets of earbuds and two stereo minijack Y-splitters.

"Thanks!" she said, flying in close to take them, then backing off and hovering.

There was something about her body language that suggested she had more to say, so I waited quietly. After a minute or so, she looked at her feet.

"Yer heard that bit about Persephone," she mumbled.

"I did."

"And Hades?"

I nodded. "It sounds like there's some conflict in the kennel on the subject."

"Aye," she said. "There is that. It don't seem right ter talk about my boss, but I owe yer a couple, so I'll say this. Dave's heart belongs to Persephone. Mort's his own master. But Bob is Hades' dog to the core. More to the point, so's Cerberus. That hound's more complex than he looks. He's bound to obey the letter of his master's orders, but his heads is pretty good at interpreting things to suit their fancies given half a chance. Yer won't get that chance if you cross the river again. Dave's yer friend. Mort, too. But Cerberus has orders to see you dead, and he's with Bob on this one. Be careful."

"I will; and Kira, thanks for the warning."

"Yer welcome. I'd best be going now before they miss me." She flitted away.

With a sigh, I pulled Melchior out of my bag and set him on a rock. As I reached to flip his lid up, he changed back into his goblin form.

"I thought you didn't like it here," I said.

"I don't. I really don't, but I wanted to make sure you were really listening to Kira, and it's easier to read your expression with eyeballs than CCDs."

"Is it also more satisfying to say 'I told you so' in the flesh?"

"What do you mean by that?" His face was the picture of innocence.

"Oh, just get it over with. You and Cerice and everybody else were right about me needing to make sense of Clotho's *gift*. I was wrong. Even I can see that now."

"It wouldn't have anything to do with reeking of Primal Chaos, would it?"

"No one used the word *reek*, but yeah, that pretty much nailed it for me. Oh, and while I'm on the subject of eating crow and other dark birds, I was an asshole earlier about asking for a gate. I'm sorry."

"Really? Are you going to tell me it won't happen again?"

"No. It'll happen again. I'll just have to apologize again when it does."

"At least you're honest about it. Apology accepted,

though I reserve the right to tell you to stick it in your ear next time."

"Deal," I said. "Now, how about you open up a gate so I can go home and make my third major mea culpa of the day?"

"You think you're going to even things out with Cerice with a single apology? Aren't you just the demigod of optimism." He got busy with some chalk and string, creating a temporary hexagram.

"Connecting to prime.minus0208," he said once he was done. A very long pause followed, then, "LTP error, client has encountered bad data from the server."

That was a new one on me. I'd never gotten an error message on a locus transfer protocol link before. But Melchior was continuing, and I didn't have the chance to ask him about it.

"Automatically rerouting connection request to alternate server. Waiting for response." There was another pause, briefer this time. "Connected. Initiating Gate procedure." The hexagram slowly filled with light.

As I waited for it to finish, I knelt beside Melchior. "What was that about?"

"I don't know." Melchior looked more than a little distressed. "The mweb is . . . I don't know, I've never felt anything quite like it. I didn't even know I *had* an LTP error menu until I accessed it. It must be something the Fates built into the webgoblin firmware specs." He gave a little shudder. "I wonder whether there are any other surprises lurking down in the depths of my code."

By then the gate was complete, so we stepped into the light. And dropped. I felt like I'd landed in a particularly wild waterslide. I shouldn't have felt anything at all, not as a stream of ones and zeros passing along an mweb channel. I shouldn't have felt anything, and I shouldn't have been able to scream because there shouldn't have been time. Nor should I have been able to hear Melchior's panicked cries. None of those shoulds mattered. I screamed and screamed again, and Melchior screamed back. None of it helped, and I started to wonder if this was what had happened to all the relatives I'd lost in transit. Then it was over.

Melchior and I had arrived . . . somewhere. The tiny room with its twin lofts sure as Fate wasn't our apartment in Cambridge, though it did look vaguely familiar. Then it hit me—my old dorm at the University of Minnesota, though the new occupants had completely different furniture and a much better cleaning routine than either I or my roommate had managed. The most important thing about them, though, was that they weren't home.

That was good, since I hadn't bothered to send a netspider ahead to check for surprises. I'd gotten out of the habit lately since I'd been gating to places where I knew I was safe or knew I wasn't. Either way, it didn't matter. Of course, it might not have mattered anyway, since I hadn't intended to come here in the first place. I turned to tease Melchior about that but stopped when I saw his face. He didn't look happy. In fact, he looked scared out of his wits. His skin had paled to an ashy color more gray than blue.

"You OK?" I asked.

"I . . . I'm not sure," he whispered. "We shouldn't be here."

"Hey, just because we landed halfway across the country and twenty-eight hundred Decision Loci off target doesn't mean there's anything wrong. You did get us to a college after . . ." I trailed off because Melchior was shaking his head vigorously.

"We're in the right DecLocus," said Melchior. "At least, that's what the mweb world resource locator forks are telling me. As for Harvard vs. the U, my system software tells me that's right, too. I just . . . This is bad, Boss. *Really* bad." He sat down on the floor with a thump. "There's something very wrong here. It's like all my firmware reference points are screwy."

I glanced out the window. By the sun it must have been around three in the afternoon. If this really was Cerice's

DecLocus, it should have been running pretty close to OST. That meant we'd lost an hour or two in transit on top of whatever else had happened.

"Virus?" I asked. He'd caught a killer whipped up by Atropos a year ago, and I'd almost lost him. I didn't like to think about it.

"I don't *think* so. I feel fine otherwise." He looked away from me, and when he spoke again his voice was very quiet. "Do you think it could be aftereffects from the one that crashed me so bad?"

"Maybe. It almost did you in, and I had to do a major repair job. But I'd think anything like that would have kicked in sooner."

"Not if they programmed in some kind of sleeper," said Melchior.

I didn't like that idea at all. It suited Atropos's nasty nature to a tee. "We should get you home so I can have a look at your internals."

"Good idea, but how? I don't think I should drive."

I had to chuckle. "Me either, little buddy. Maybe we can get Cerice and Shara to come pick us up, or Kira. First, let's find out for sure where we are. You say the mweb tells you this is prime.minus0208?"

He nodded. "But I can't be sure. Not the way I feel. I don't know if I should even try a Vtp link. What if I hit a logic loop, and it takes me down?"

"Not to worry, I have a radical idea."

"What?"

I sat down at one of the desks and picked up the phone. "This."

I might not have Melchior's ability to process and send high-speed binary, but I could do a pretty damn good impression of an old-style modem or a phone-switching computer. Phone phreaking was something I'd picked up purely for the hack value. I'd never had to make an actual person-to-person call before, preferring Vtp for relatives and VOMP when I had to interact with the human world or couldn't take a visual. Soon, a little whistling on my part had convinced the local voice provider that I was allowed to make unlimited long-distance calls from the number I was at. A few seconds later I waited while the phone in Cerice's lab began to ring. On the third ring someone answered.

"Theoretical computing, Dr. Doravian's lab, this is Cerice." Relief flooded through me.

"Thank Zeus. I'm sorry."

"What? Who is this? Ravirn?"

"You got it. I wanted to apologize right off."

"Apologize? Over the *phone*? What's up?" She sounded very confused. "Why are you using a *phone*? Is this some retro romantic-fantasy thing?"

"No, more like bad technoreality, but I'll get to that in a minute. I owed you the apology, and I wanted to give it to you up front. And hey, I'll be honest. I figured it'd lower the odds of your hanging up on me, too."

"You're not making much sense."

"Sorry, it's been a very strange couple of hours, not least because I seem to have awakened under an offending star. My mouth and my foot have been trying to get on better terms all day, and now I'm stranded with a fritzed webgoblin."

"Ravirn!" she said sharply.

"Yes."

"You're babbling." She did not sound amused.

"Am I? No, don't answer that. I am. Look, I think Melchior might be really messed up, and I need a hand."

"Tell me about it," she said, her voice softening at once. She had a big soft spot for webgoblins in general and Melchior in particular.

So I gave her the story. When I finished, I could hear her putting her hand over the phone. A muffled conversation followed.

"You still there?" she said after a while.

"Yeah. I just told you, I'm stranded, as in 'can't go anywhere.' Remember?"

"Sorry. Stupid question. Wait there; we'll be along shortly." The phone went dead.

"Thanks, Cerice," I said to the dial tone. "That's really sweet of you. We'll see you soon." Then I hung up.

After about fifteen minutes, the phone rang. I looked at it dubiously. It was almost certainly for the people who lived here and quite likely to be someone who'd find the idea of a strange man answering a bit on the alarming side. On the other hand, Cerice should have been here by now.

"You going to answer that?" asked Melchior.

"Yeah, I'd better." I picked it up. "Hello."

"Ravirn?"

"Uh-huh."

"We've got another problem."

"Why did I just know you were going to say that?"

"Maybe it's because you attract them the way Cerberus attracts fleas," offered Melchior. I just nodded. When someone's right, they're right.

"Tell me about it," I said to Cerice.

"Shara can't gate."

"What?" I asked. "Why not?"

"I don't know." For the first time in ages I could hear something akin to panic in her voice. "Maybe it's because she was dead. Maybe it's something else, something worse. Right now she's throwing up in the trash can, but she keeps telling me it's not a virus."

"Tell me what happened."

"Shara tried to connect, and she just sat and cycled for the longest time. That had me worried. Then she came up with an error message I'd never heard of."

"LTP error, client has encountered bad data from the server?" I asked.

"That's the one. How'd you know?"

"It's the same one I got with Melchior. I told you about it a few minutes ago."

"Right," said Cerice. "I knew that. Shit. I *knew* that. Damn!"

"What happened next?" I asked, trying to bring her

back to the topic. Cerice was a consummate problem solver. This behavior was completely unlike her. Shara's problems were consuming her.

"Sorry," said Cerice, sounding calmer. "Anyway, she tried again and got the same error. She was just going for a third round when she let out a little 'eep' noise and ran for the wastebasket. Now I can't get any sense out of her. She says she's not sick, but she keeps throwing up."

"Hang on," I said. "I'm on my way."

"How?" asked Cerice.

"I don't know. I'll think of something. Just hang on." With that I hung up.

"Boss?" said Melchior.

"Yeah. I don't suppose this is good news, is it?"

"No." He shook his head. "Once I heard Shara was having problems, I tried to call Kira."

"And . . ."

"No go. The mweb is really turbulent right now. It felt like someone shoved a hyperactive spider into my inner ear. Maybe that's why Shara's throwing up."

"Motion sickness?"

"Yeah."

"Huh, could be." It could be indeed, but I really didn't like the idea. If it was true, something big was happening with the mweb, something like nothing I'd ever heard of. "Or maybe you and Shara just have a bug in common. You do share a lot more software than most goblins."

"I hope that's the case," he said. "I'd much rather I was screwed up than the mweb."

Me too. I could do something about a webgoblin virus. The mweb on the other hand . . . I shuddered. That was too big a problem for me, and the more I thought about it, the likelier it seemed. Hadn't we been having all kinds of communication problems, starting with Shara's long delay and Tisiphone's static-touched Vtp message?

"Time to go," I said, scooping Melchior up and setting him in my bag. Suddenly I was in a hurry.

"Yeah," he said as he sank down until only the upper half of his face was visible. "But where?"

"The airport," I said. "If human people can get around on planes, so can we."

This isn't half-bad, typed itself on Melchior's screen.

Speak for yourself, I typed back with one hand. I needed the other to maintain my death grip on the seat arm. *My stomach's still on the ground in Minneapolis.*

It turned out I was a nervous flyer. If I'd had any idea of how bad it was going to be, I'd have stolen a motorcycle and gone cross-country. Compelled by a sort of sick fascination, I looked out my window again. All I could see was clouds. I shuddered.

No wonder airports are such miserable places, I typed. *The people in them know they're going to have to get on planes.*

I'd driven people to and from airports, even hung around in them a few times watching the planes take off and land. I had cousins who'd gotten pilot's licenses just for the joy of flying, but somehow I'd never had any desire to try it myself. I'd always figured that was because I knew a simple spell could take me from any point in all the multiple levels of reality to any other in a matter of seconds, so why bother? Apparently, it was actually my subconscious anticipating how much I'd hate the whole experience and working to reduce my suffering. Sensible subconscious.

This is a stupid way to travel, I typed, trying to distract myself. *It's worse than faerie rings.*

Nothing is worse than faerie rings. Faerie rings are the magical equivalent of old-style absinthe, slow death and sudden insanity.

He had a point, but . . . *At least I understand how* they *work*, I typed. *This is unnatural. A giant steel cigar with wings not much bigger than a Fury's, and somehow they expect it to stay up. Humans are all mad.*

Oh, quit whining. You can be such a big baby. At least you're not stuck back in coach.

I'd booked first class. Why not? It wasn't like I was paying for the flight or anything, not with e-tickets and online check-in. But bigger seats and classier service couldn't change the fundamental fact that flying and I did not belong in the same sentence. Sick of arguing with Melchior, I closed his lid and stuck him under the seat in front of me. That allowed me to cling to the seat arms with both hands. It was a marginal improvement, but I absolutely could not wait to get off that plane. I also couldn't wait to throw away the printout of the return trip ticket I'd bought to avoid hassles with the Homeland Security Department's data-mining software.

It was so bad that I stopped in one of the little airport bars at Logan and had a couple of shots of Scotch while I waited for my heart to go back to a normal rhythm. Then I caught the T's Blue Line at the airport station. Two transfers and an hour or so of travel time saw me off at Harvard station in Cambridge just before the system closed down at twelve-thirty. Not long after that I was opening the door to Cerice's lab.

I got a huge relieved hug and a kiss from Cerice. And a smaller, shakier version of that greeting from Shara, who claimed to be feeling much better.

"I don't buy it," I told her. "You don't look as bad as you did when I found you in Hades, but you sure don't look good."

"Way to flatter a girl," said Shara. She turned her gaze on Cerice. "Sometimes I wonder what you see in this boy. Then he walks away in those tight jeans, and it all becomes clear." She winked, but it didn't look like her heart was in it.

"Nice try," I said, "it's not going to work. You look terrible."

"Believe it or don't," said Cerice, "she looked a whole lot worse a couple of hours ago."

My shoulder bag moved of its own accord then, lumping up, then falling off the desk where I'd set it. Muffled swearing came from inside, then it unzipped itself, spitting out Melchior.

"Were you just going to leave me in there," he asked, "or did I miss something?"

"Sorry," I said. "I was a little preoccupied with Shara."

"I see why," he said, looking her over. Stepping closer, he touched her cheek. "Last time I saw that expression on your face, you were under the desk hiding from Persephone."

Shara shivered and hugged herself. "Don't talk about that, about her. I can't think about her. I just *can't*. She's . . . brrr."

"I agree with you there," I said, remembering the horrible pain of meeting those winter eyes, then thinking about what Kira and Cerberus had to say about her. "I can't tell you how much I wish she hadn't made me promise her a favor."

"What?" asked Cerice, an edge in her voice. "What's that supposed to mean?"

"Didn't I mention that part?" I asked.

Her eyes sparked dangerously. "No. I don't believe that you did."

"It must have slipped my mind. No. Really. When I got back, and Shara wasn't here, I kind of got distracted. I did mention that she helped me get Shara out, right?" Cerice nodded. "I guess I skipped the bit where she told me she'd have a task for me later."

Cerice put a hand over her eyes. "Only my Ravirn could forget a little detail like goddess blackmail. I so wish I didn't believe you."

"Does that mean you do?" I asked.

"Yes." She sighed. "It does. Now, I think we—"

She was interrupted by a loud *bing* from Shara. "Incoming visual transfer protocol message from Ahllan@ahllan.trl. Accept Vlink?"

"Accept," said Cerice.

Ahllan was a webtroll and an old friend. She'd once been Atropos's personal web server, but now she ran the familiar underground, an organization dedicated to freeing AIs from slavery in the houses of Fate.

"Vtp linking initiated," said Shara after a long pause.

The light that burst from her eyes and mouth was the first clue that something had gone horribly wrong. It was white instead of colored in the primaries. The globe it formed was filled with silvery gray mist like something from an old-time black-and-white movie rather than the usual gold cloud. It was also brimful of static. When it partially cleared, the troll within was likewise black and white and so shot through with lines of interference that she looked like some kind of electronic zebra. She was also low res.

You could barely make out the heavy lower jaw and three-inch tusks. Even her huge potatolike nose only registered as a lumpy blur. Ahllan was an early-model webtroll, one of the servers Atropos had used in her own personal network back toward the dawn of the computer era. At a hair over three feet tall, Ahllan barely came up to my waist in person. But her shoulders were broader than mine, and she probably outweighed me. Her skin was mottled and brown and wrinkled like a winter apple. The only bright things about her were the wise eyes. They shone like black sapphires. All that was lost to static.

"Ksshst an emergsssht. Need to kssshht warn you. Urgent. Ksssjsjt soon!"

"What?" I asked. With the garbling, I figured I'd better keep questions short and to the point. She might cut out at any second.

"Shshsjjt Garbage Faerie is crzshht."

"I missed that, what?"

"Hang ozzzst, I . . ." The image suddenly sharpened and lost some of its striping, bringing her background—a beer can faerie ring on a blasted hillside—into focus. She was in the backwater of reality where I'd first met Ahllan and the troll's onetime headquarters.

"There," said Ahllan, her voice tinny and strained, but clear. "Much better, but it's taking most of my processing power to modulate this so it rides with the churn on the mweb. I'll be quick because it's only going to get worse."

"Why are you calling from Garbage Faerie?" asked Melchior. "What's wrong?"

"I don't know," answered Ahllan. "Something awful has happened to the mweb. Worlds have fallen silent, and there are gaps in the net. The turbulence is incredible. I couldn't even reach you from my new home. There's change in the wind, big change. The web that Necessity built, the web I was designed to help maintain, is fraying. The great powers are restless. Fate. Discord. Zeus. Hades."

"Do you think one of them is responsible?" I asked.

Ahllan shrugged. "I don't know, but Necessity's strength is too great to be tried by lesser names. And whoever did this, each will try to turn it to their own advantage. People will die. Even gods may fall. It is a time of endings. I wanted to warn you, to tell you that I love you, and say good-bye if I don't see you again."

"Don't talk like that, Ahllan," said Shara. "You're tough as old tree roots. You'll weather this storm."

"I might," she said. "But old trees fall, too, and I'm old even by human standards, ancient for a computer. Even if all goes well, I won't be around much longer. If things go poorly . . ." She shrugged. "Much of the power of Fate is bound up in the mweb. They can operate without it, but it will not be easy. The Fates are unkind to those who interfere with them." She looked at me. "You should know that more than anyone. What will they do if their most powerful tool is permanently damaged?"

"Do you think it's really going to get that bad?" I asked. The very idea made me feel cold.

"Worse. Maybe much worse. Fate is not the only power who has come to depend on the mweb. How will Hades take it if something disrupts the flow of the souls who people his empire? For that matter, what will your cousins do if they can no longer make easy use of the magic that is central to their lives? If they are forced to travel by faerie ring or not at all? They will want to make the responsible parties pay. And if they can't find the right target, they will choose a scapegoat. It could easily be me and the underground movement I began. Or"—and her eyes caught and held mine—"it could be you."

She turned her head then as though she'd heard something off to one side. Her eyes went wide. "Shara? What? I don't kzshht." Static filled the picture, though the audio hung on. Ahllan's voice rose, sounding almost frightened "How is that—"

The globe of white blinked out.

"Connection lost," said Shara. "Transmission error. Encryption error. Unverified certificate. Attempting to reestablish Vlink. Attempting . . . Mweb not responding to queries." She blinked several times, then in her normal tones said, "Oh, shit."

"What?" Cerice and I asked simultaneously.

"The mweb," said Shara. "It's gone."

"You mean it crashed?" I'd crashed it once, taken down the whole system. That was how I'd originally ended up with a price on my head.

"No." Shara sounded more frightened than I'd ever heard an AI sound. "I mean it's gone. Poof. Vanished. It felt like this world was simply removed from the system."

"That's not possible," said Cerice.

"All the same. It's true."

CHAPTER SEVEN

"Melchior," I said. "Verify that, please. Are we really cut off from the mweb?"

"Already on it." His expression went vacant and far away. "Shara's right," he said after a few seconds. "The mweb's gone. Poof. There's no way for us to call Ahllan back or LTP to Garbage Faerie."

"Are you sure it's not just crashed?" I asked, but I heard Ahllan's words echoing in my head: *Worlds have fallen silent . . . the great powers are restless.* "When we set that virus loose the autumn before last, we blew out the carrier wave and everything. Couldn't this be the same sort of thing?"

Melchior shook his head. "When the mweb crashed, it felt like a phone going dead. There was no connection, but I could sense the network beyond. Dormant, but with the potential for reconnection. This feels like the phone isn't even plugged into the wall anymore. It's hard to explain, but there's no there, there."

Shara nodded. "When . . . when I was dead, I couldn't tap into Hades' network, but I could still feel it. I was personally cut off, but the possibility of connection existed. It doesn't here. We're *completely* off-line."

"How is that even possible?" I whispered.

I didn't like the implications one little bit. The mweb connected all the infinite worlds of probability. Without it, the multiverse would be like a hard drive with no directory. The files might exist, but many would effectively be lost forever—worlds gone silent.

"We have to get to Ahllan," I said, "find out what happened at the end of her transmission, if she knows anything more."

"But how?" replied Shara. "The mweb's gone. There's no way to get there from here."

"Faerie ring," said Melchior instantly. "We don't have a choice."

"That'll take time, too, and equipment we don't have here to set it up." But I nodded. It was really the only way, though I was shocked to hear Melchior suggest it. "We won't be able to leave for at least an hour."

"All the more reason to start now." And even though he'd visibly paled, his voice sounded firm.

Melchior hated faerie rings with a deep and abiding passion. I wasn't any too fond of them myself. I'd only used them a few times, and the most recent incident had nearly killed me. They were terribly dangerous, and unreliable to boot, but they were also one of the very few mweb-independent travel magics, dating back as they did to the days of precomputer sorcery. Hell, even the ley-line links were tied together through the mweb these days.

"I hate to go that way without trying some other route first," said Cerice.

"I hate to go that way, period," I said, "but I haven't got any other ideas."

"Couldn't we at least wait a little while to see if the mweb comes back up on its own?" asked Shara. "If it's going to take an hour or more anyway . . ."

"We need to go to Ahllan right now!" countered Melchior. "We owe her too much to leave her hanging."

He was right. I owed the old troll personally. She'd taken care of me after I'd shattered a knee in my fight with Moric. Without her, I'd almost certainly have died. After that, she'd helped me prevent Atropos and her sisters from extinguishing free will. She'd saved all of our lives in the course of that conflict.

But what she meant to Melchior and Shara and all their brethren was even bigger, or it should have been. The Fates had designed the first webgoblins, webtrolls, and webpixies as automatons to run our family's coded spells and manage our magical networks. Due to sabotage by Eris and Tyche, those original designs had gone awry, giving birth to genuinely independent AIs with their own desires and agendas.

For years, the AIs had hidden their true nature from their makers, certain the Fates would try to end their independence. They lived and—when their owners threw them away—died in secret. Then Ahllan had managed to subvert the cycle by escaping to freedom when she was junked and afterward running an underground railroad that rescued hundreds of AIs from the trash heap.

The secret of AI independence had been exposed during my conflict with the Fates, and Ahllan now had a huge price on her head. Despite that danger, she continued to act as a leader and mentor for the AI community. That made Shara's reluctance all the stranger.

"I'm not suggesting we leave her hanging, just that we wait a bit." Shara paused like she was considering something for a moment, then forced a smile. "Look at the bright side. As long as we're off-line, Persephone's going to have serious trouble collecting her pound of flesh. That's got to count for something."

Melchior gave her a hard look. "You're not serious, are you?"

She glanced downward, then shook her head. ". . . No, just trying to lighten the mood with a joke—a bad one apparently. Sorry."

She didn't look sorry. She looked terrified. Terrified and

confused, almost like she couldn't believe what she'd said herself. Why was she stalling? Something very strange was going on with Shara, something I needed to look into. But we didn't have time to deal with it now.

"What are you thinking?" Cerice asked sharply, and I realized I'd been staring at Shara.

"I don't know." Cerice was already touchy about Shara, and I sure as hell wasn't going to tell her I had any suspicions on that front, especially not when my concerns were so vague. "I'm just trying to figure out what to do next."

Melchior was less circumspect. "What is wrong with you, Shara? Why are you arguing about this?"

Shara hopped down from the desk where she'd been sitting and began to pace nervously. "The mweb's gone! Not crashed, not off-line for maintenance—*gone*. Something huge is happening."

"And Ahllan went with the mweb!" said Melchior. "That's why we've got to get moving. She called right before it went down. Don't you think that means something?"

"Yes," said Shara. "But what? I don't know. Do you?" Melchior didn't answer immediately, and Shara continued, "I didn't think so. For that matter, we can't even be sure it *was* Ahllan. The connection was so fuzzed up, I couldn't get full encryption authentication. And it failed completely at the end. We all know how much Atropos would like to find and eliminate Ahllan. What if this is some kind of ploy on Atropos's part?"

"I might buy that," he said, "*if* she'd been calling from her bubble hideaway. The location of that place is a secret Atropos wants, and we could lead her there. But Ahllan was sending from Garbage Faerie, and Atropos already knows the address. It's been abandoned for months."

"I . . . that's true. I didn't think of that. Maybe you're right." Shara looked defeated. "Let's go."

"About time." Melchior crossed to the door.

"Just let me run a backup." Cerice turned to the mainframe and typed in a couple of quick commands. "This is the last of the cleanup work for my dissertation project. Dr.

Doravian stopped by this afternoon, while you were Styx-side with Cerberus. He wanted to remind me that my defense date is less than a month away. Now I've even got a chance of surviving it." She looked from me to Shara and back again, then gave me a kiss. "Thank you."

"You're welcome," I said, returning it. "Maybe once we've got all this straightened out, and you've defended—"

She kissed me again. "I can't see that far ahead right now, and I don't want to start another fight, OK?" A ticking clock appeared on the screen. "There, the job's running, now we can leave. Where do we go first?"

I thought about that for a moment. There weren't any active faerie rings in the area since Cerice had destroyed the one I'd used to visit her during the fight with the Fates. We'd need to make our own, which meant collecting equipment from the apartment and more delay. Oh well, I could pick up the bottom half of my leathers and my helmet at the same time. I had a feeling the armor might come in handy and said as much.

Cerice nodded. "I'll want to gear up, too. Shara, Laptop. Please."

The little purple goblin shifted shape, and Melchior followed suit. Once they were stowed away, we headed out the door. With the mweb closed to us, we had to walk.

"I asked Cerberus about the Raven thing," I said, as we hit the street.

"You did?" Cerice looked shocked, but again, not as pleased as I would have expected. It took her a half block to respond. "That's . . . great! What did he say?"

"Not much, unfortunately. He said he didn't know anything beyond how I smelled."

"How you smelled?" She gave me an odd look.

"Yep, he told me that I don't smell like a child of Fate, that I stink of chaos and of ravens." I looked down at my feet. "You know, you don't look as enthused as I would have expected."

Cerice sighed. "I'm sorry, Ravirn. I'm really glad that you're doing something about the name Clotho gave you.

But at the same time, I can't help thinking it has something to do with the fight we had at the restaurant."

"Of course it has something to do with that." I caught her hand and turned her to look at me. "You were right. I was wrong. Now I'm working on it."

"But is that because you want to know the answer? Or is it because you think it'll make me happy?"

"Does that really matter?" I asked.

"It does," said Cerice. "I care about you very much. No, scratch that. I'll be honest. I'm more than half in love with you."

"That's fantastic." It was the most I'd gotten out of her on the subject to date. "You may not have noticed, but I'm completely in love with you."

Cerice closed her eyes, and her lips went tight and narrow. A single tear slid down her left cheek.

"What's wrong?" I asked.

"I don't know." She pulled away from me and started walking again. "You. Me. Us. Finishing my dissertation. Everything!"

"I don't understand," I said. I felt like I'd missed a meeting. "I know you haven't wanted to talk commitment until your dissertation was done. I can respect that. It's a huge part of what you've been doing for the last six years. I'm not going to ask you for anything more than we have now until it's done. But it's getting close, and I just thought that . . ."

More tears followed after that first one. "It's not the dissertation that's made me so reluctant to talk about us. It's what comes after. I'm a planner, Ravirn. You should know that. My whole life I've planned things out, then carefully followed through on those plans. When I started this project, I set out to achieve two things. I wanted to make a place for myself as a coder in House Clotho, and I wanted to use my program to help Ahllan get her fellow AIs to safety."

"I don't see where you're going with this."

"Don't you?" She shook her head. An affectionate smile bloomed on her lips, though the tears kept coming. "Oh, my Ravirn. My beautiful, mad, faerie lover."

The more she talked, the less I understood. She was as much faerie as I, which is to say not at all and one hundred percent. The fey didn't exist in the traditional sense, but the pointed ears, slit-pupiled eyes, and incredibly long life spans of the children of Fate had given birth to most of the legends. We walked a while in silence.

"Raven," she said, as we reached the door to our building, once again riveting my attention, "do you know what that means?" I shook my head. "It means, in addition to whatever wild gifts it brings, that you have been cast out of the Houses of Fate. Clotho may have given you a new name, but I don't think she'll sanction my bringing you home to live with me while I program the computers at the core of her power. Neither can I help Ahllan anymore, now that she's been exposed."

She started up the stairs. "For six years I've poured my heart and soul into this project. It's the best work I've ever done, and I love it, love that I can do this. But it's all useless now. The plan's ruined. I want you. I want the program done and installed to do its secret work on Clotho's servers. I want my House and my great-grandmother's respect and affection. I want to help the AIs. One year ago it looked like I could have all that. Now? Now I have to pick and choose, and every reward comes with a bitter loss."

She unlocked our apartment and led the way inside. "It's not failing at my dissertation that I'm really afraid of. It's succeeding. Because when I'm done defending, everything has to change. I'll have to choose, and I don't know what I'll do. Maybe for the first time in my life, I don't know what I'll do."

I closed the door and leaned back against it. "And it's all my fault."

I said it with a smile and as gently as possible, but it was true. It was my conflict with Atropos that had put me outside of Fate's Houses, and its results that had exposed Ahllan and her kind.

"Oh, Ravirn, that's not what I meant!"

"No, but it's true enough, isn't it?"

"I'd rather blame Atropos," she said.

"So would I, but she's not here."

"She forced you into it."

"Also true, but I'd make the same choices if I had to do it all over again today. Well, most of them anyway." I grinned ruefully. "I'd probably try to minimize the damage. My knee gets awfully achy on cold damp nights, and I kind of miss the fingertip."

Cerice grinned and shook her head. "You amaze me."

"If we had time, I'd do more than that." I waggled my eyebrows.

"But we don't." She sighed. "I have to get my sword, change clothes . . ."

"All the usual silly pomp and circumstance," I said, referring to my late family's fixation on the proper protocols and fancy dress.

"Are you going to wear *that*?" she asked, pointing to my leather jacket.

"And the pants. One of the few benefits of being an outcast is that I no longer have to conform to my great-grandmother's fixation on courtly manner and garb. No more tights and doublets for this boy."

"But I like you in tights," said Cerice.

"All right," I said. "For you I'll wear tights. But not for this. With the Kevlar lining, my motorcycle kit is better armor than anything else I own. Especially now that I've got the matching helmet. Besides, I'm going to be way less conspicuous dressed like this than you are in your gear."

"There you've got a point," said Cerice. "But that's what magic's for. Come on, we need to get moving."

I nodded and followed her back to our bedroom. All I had to do was change pants and grab my helmet and my magic kit. The bedroom wasn't very big, so I did that and got out of the way. I found Melchior in the kitchen getting a piece of cold pizza out of the fridge.

"You're eating," I said, when he started in on it. I was surprised. It didn't happen very often.

He nodded. "I was hungry."

"Really?" That *never* happens.

"Really. The mweb's down, and pizza's a lot more fun than AC."

Then I understood. Food is something webgoblins indulge in mostly for the pleasure of it, since they draw the bulk of their power from the mweb itself, both personally and for spells. They have the capacity to tap the power of the Primal Chaos directly, and until the mweb came back up, that's what we'd have to do for spells. But chaos is dicey stuff, and most of us and our familiars try to avoid dealing with it in the raw, preferring the predigested version that the master servers channel into the mweb. Minus that reliable power source, if Melchior didn't feel like running the risks of a direct tap, he had to fall back on chemical or electrical energy—food or the light socket. I'd have made the same choice.

"Where's Shara?"

"Sucking on the game station's power cord. She said that after spending time around Persephone, the whole idea of eating sounds pretty risky."

"Big impact for such a short time," I said. "Shara used to be a sucker for desserts. It's hard to imagine five minutes with a goddess, even one as harsh as Persephone, changing that."

Melchior looked up at me, his face troubled. "That's what I said. She gave me a very funny look then and pointed out that she'd been in Hades for quite a while before we arrived. When I asked her if that meant she'd run into Persephone before, she shook her head and told me I wouldn't understand. I think more happened to her there than she's willing to tell."

"Do you think we need to push her on this?" I asked.

Melchior shrugged. "I don't know. I love Shara, and I'd trust her with my soul, but this worries me."

"Me too, Melchior. Me too."

Just then, Cerice joined us. She wore a tightly fitted and

fully articulated suit of lamalar armor, very light and reinforced with magic so that it could stop anything short of an
RPG. It was red and gold, of course, and looked something
like a Greek hoplite's gear as reimagined by a fighting-
game designer. It had a heavily padded compartment in the
small of her back for Shara in laptop form and a number of
clips where she could attach various articles, including the
rapier and Beretta semiautomatic pistol she'd already
slung. She had a small pack as well, holding the diamond-
shaped buckler she preferred to a parrying dagger, along
with her T-faced helm. The helmet's horsehair crest was
just poking out of the top.

"You ready?" I asked.

"No, but let's do it anyway."

I collected my shoulder bag—now prepped with everything I'd need for making a faerie ring—while she tucked
Shara away. Melchior likewise assumed laptop shape and
went into my bag. Once Cerice had whistled a spell of con-
cealment, we were ready to go. It was a really elegant little
piece of magic crafted by Clotho many centuries ago and
refined and rerefined by her and her sisters until it was only
a few bars long.

"Where do you want to set it up?" she asked, as we went
out the door.

It was a good question. We wouldn't be able to close up
behind us, and you never know when some poor soul might
stumble into the ring, or worse, when something really
nasty might come slithering out of it. Reality has diverged
a great deal since Nyx laid the egg that became the Earth
and sky, and not all the paths have been pleasant ones.
There were some very dark places to be found among the
infinity of worlds and even darker things lurking in them,
so it had to be someplace isolated, where things that go
bump in the night wouldn't be a problem.

Fortunately, I'd had time to think it through. "The river."

She shrugged. "I guess you're the expert."

I tried not to laugh at that. I'd built one, once, and I
hadn't enjoyed the experience. A short walk brought us to

the Charles, where we made our way under the Anderson Bridge, just upstream from the Weld Boathouse. It wasn't exactly isolated—nowhere in the Boston area is—but between the hour and the icy cold, we were alone. Even in January the channel wasn't fully frozen—too much salt swept in from the harbor—but there were big sheets of ice along the edges.

"There." I pointed at the nearest.

"What?" asked Cerice, looking baffled. "Where?"

"On that chunk of ice."

"You're crazy, you know that, right? The ice all along here is brittle. It could break off at any moment."

"That's what makes it perfect," I said. Cerice looked dubious. "Look, just trust me on this. Everything'll be clear in a few minutes."

"I think I'm beginning to see why Melchior is such a worrier." She briefly closed her eyes. "All right, it's your show. Get on with it."

"Thanks for all your confidence," I said, winking at her.

Before I picked my way down onto the ice, I clipped my blades onto my belt and checked the hang of my pistol. Entering a faerie ring unarmed is a fool's choice. Cerice followed me but stopped with her feet still on dry ground. As I knelt and opened my bag, extracting the tools I'd need, Melchior shifted back to goblin shape and poked his nose out.

"Are we there yet?"

I nodded. "All that's left is the ring."

"That's like a parachutist saying all that's left is the part where we jump out of the plane," he observed grumpily.

I didn't answer. I had other things on my mind. Taking a fifteen-foot piece of networking cable out of my bag, I used a jumper to connect the two ends so that it looped back on itself.

I'd just lifted the athame I'd borrowed from Cerice's stash to replace my melted one when Melchior held up a hand.

"What?" I asked.

"Just a thought."

"Which is?"

"I was wondering if whatever cut this world off from the mweb will have any effect on things like the faerie rings."

I didn't like the sound of that. "How would that work?"

"Well, what if it's not actually the mweb itself that's having problems? What if there's some kind of turbulence or storm in the Primal Chaos itself? What if the many layers of reality are being tossed around by that?"

I set the athame down. "Do you have anything to back that up?" I asked. "Because if you do, I'd like to hear it before I take any irrevocable steps."

"No. I'm just speculating."

"So do you want to call this little trip off?"

He shook his head. "We have to go and go soon."

"Then why are you sharing?" I said, letting my exasperation color my words.

"Well, the idea's a scary one, and I didn't want to be afraid all by my lonesome."

"Right," I said, with a sigh. "Then if you don't have any other gloomy little ideas to share, I'll get back to work."

I picked the athame up again. This time, no one interrupted me as I cut a long shallow slice in the palm of my left hand. The blood welled up quickly, and I'd soon smeared it over the entire length of the cable and the connector. After that was done, I whistled the spell for closing athame-generated wounds and went to work laying the loop of cable out in as perfect a circle as I could manage. That involved crawling out onto the thinnest part of the ice, which made an ominous cracking noise as it took my weight.

Next came the really dangerous part, opening a hole into the Primal Chaos. As a direct descendant of the Titans, I have the stuff bound into the very matrix of my bone and being. I called on that resonance as it was expressed in the blood I'd smeared on the cable to put a microrip in the fabric of reality.

Pure raw chaos poured through but not in the controlled way I'd expected. The last time I'd done this, it had raced thrice around the circle of blood, cutting a faerie ring into the turf as neatly as a glass cutter might put a hole in a window. This time, the entire circle flash-burned in a single instant, and the air above the ring actually caught fire. The explosion threw me a good fifteen feet.

The world wavered and rippled around me, like air over hot pavement. Shadows flitted at the edge of my vision, making wings of darkness. The magical turbulence felt as if I'd gotten in the way of a tidal bore. As I fought to hold on to consciousness, I couldn't help wondering whether the effects were real or in my head, because if it was the former, we were in deep, deep trouble.

CHAPTER EIGHT

"Are you all right?" Cerice was bent over me, her finger-tips pressed into my neck at the pulse point. I had only very blurry memories of her getting there.

"What the hell happened?" I asked. I hadn't blacked out, but it had been mighty close. I wanted to see if her experience matched mine.

"Your faerie ring arrived with a bang. It was quite spectacular. I expect that the local emergency services people will be along shortly. I take it rings aren't supposed to do that?" she asked dryly.

"No. Not in my very limited experience." I sat up, though the effort made the world crinkle around the edges. "Did it work?"

"Oh yeah." Melchior came up next to Cerice. "Speaking of which, unless you want the effort to have been wasted, we need to get moving. It's starting to float away." He jerked his thumb over his shoulder.

With Cerice's help I managed to get to my feet. The ring, now a free-floating circle of ice, had indeed drifted away from the bank. More alarming, though, was that it was still on fire. Or rather, the water around it was on fire. Neon-green flames ringed the ice like a particularly gaudy Christmas wreath.

Something flashed in the corner of my eye, and I glanced up at the underside of the bridge, where a perfect circle of polished white stood out starkly amidst the dirt and grime. It lay directly above the place where I'd marked out my ring. The heat or the magic or something had burned a mirror-smooth finish into the concrete.

"Wow," I said, shaking my head. "That wasn't supposed to happen." Just then a siren started in the distance. "Come on, we'd better get going." Lifting Melchior back into my bag, I took Cerice's hand. "Ready?" She nodded, though I could tell she had some doubts. "Right, I'll count to three, then we'll jump. When we hit, we'll be on our way. Just keep holding on and let me drive."

"What about the fire on the water? Won't that attract attention?"

I shrugged. "There's not much we can do about it unless you want to stay here and answer official questions. Besides, it appears to be dying down."

It did, though not as quickly as I would have liked. Cerice frowned, then whistled a quick spell. A stand of dry and leafless brush some way upstream burst into sudden flame, sending a great plume of smoke skyward.

"There," she said. "That'll give them something else to look at while this drifts away. One."

"Two," I answered.

We said three together and leaped. The ice had drifted a good eight feet from shore by then, an easy jump for any child of Fate. Almost too easy in my case. I went farther than I'd intended, landing on the far edge of the ice so that the toe of my left boot actually touched the flame. I'd have cleared the ring entirely if Cerice hadn't had a firm grip on my hand. In fact, for one instant as my feet left the ground, I felt as though I could simply have flown away were it not for her weight.

I didn't have time to think about it because the moment

we touched down, we were elsewhere. A faerie ring is nothing like a computer-assisted locus transfer. When I asked Melchior to open a gate for me, I was creating a point-to-point link with a definite beginning and a definite end. The ring, on the other hand, was a matter of probability and will. Anytime you enter a faerie ring, you have an absolutely equal chance of emerging in any other ring among all the infinite levels of reality. Will determines where you actually end up.

In theory, if your will is strong, and you know what you're doing, you could get in at one ring and step out of the one you want to reach as your very next stop. In practice, finding your destination is more a matter of throwing yourself in the right direction and sort of channel surfing until you hit the ring you're looking for. I'd learned all of that with my previous faerie ring experience. This time I learned something else; not all rings are equal, and that matters. A lot.

This ring was much stronger and wilder than the ones I'd been through in the past. Before, the rhythm had been something like *world, beat, beat, world, beat, beat, world*. Now it was *wor-, wor-, wor-*, with rings strobing by too fast even to register as places. I felt like some sort of weird quantum particle, simultaneously in multiple places at one time. Hundreds of them in fact.

How am I going to find the right one if I can't even see them? a small panicked voice in the back of my head asked. Horrible things can happen to a person who gets lost among the rings. You can lose your soul. I nearly had on my last trip.

Then, just as suddenly as it had started, our progress stopped. We had arrived, at least for an instant, in one definite place. Pulling Cerice along with me, I jumped from the ring. I did it without even looking to see where we were. We could always step back into the local ring in a few moments when we'd had a chance to recover. Hopefully it would be gentler than the one I'd made in Cambridge.

"Huh," said Cerice. "That wasn't so bad. Step in at home, step out at Ahllan's place in Garbage Faerie two seconds later. Why do you and Melchior make such a big fuss about the rings?"

"What?" I demanded, but a quick look around confirmed she was right. We stood beside the beer can ring next to the torn-open mound that had once covered Ahllan's home. It was a sunny afternoon, and the season was much warmer than the one we'd left behind. "I . . . shit. How did that happen? Melchior?"

"I don't know, Boss. That's just plain spooky. I'd have expected you to at least pass through a couple of other rings on the way here. Let me think about it for a second."

"Wait," I said. "Didn't either of you register all those other rings?"

"What other rings?" they demanded in near-perfect unison. I sat down then. Fell down was more like it, but the effect was the same. I was no longer standing, and my butt was firmly on the ground. "Tell me what you saw," I said.

"Same as Cerice," Melchior said. "Step in there, step out here." Cerice nodded. "I figured that just this once we actually had a piece of *good* luck. I take it that's not what you saw?"

I related my experience of the ring. Melchior whistled.

"Sounds like my worries about a chaos storm and the rings being messed up too had something to it. Things certainly feel strange enough for that. I've got some mweb access in this DecLocus, but it's bad and rapidly getting worse."

"Maybe that's it." I had a sneaking suspicion that what had just happened with the faerie ring wasn't related to the mweb problems and that I wasn't going to like the truth when I finally figured it out. But there wasn't much I could do about it at the moment, so I put the idea aside and got to my feet.

Garbage Faerie, as we called it, was in a serious backwater of reality. Magic ran much closer to the surface here than it did in the vicinity of Olympus, where things were more regulated. Neither Zeus nor the Fates are big fans of anyone else's having magical power. That includes the other gods and all their myriad offspring; but the blood of the Titans cannot be denied or contained, so reluctantly, they live with us. Given the choice, I don't think they'd allow magic to go beyond the family. But the gods—except perhaps Necessity—are finite, and the multiverse is not.

I suspect that's the real reason the Fates went modern with their ever-expanding set of computers for tracking life threads and running coded spells. It's also probably a big part of why Zeus has kept such a low profile for the last couple of millennia—he's lost control, and he knows it. So now he sulks. Of course, he never really had control, but he's dim enough that I imagine it took a while to sink in. But hey, that's the head of the pantheon to a tee, astronomical energy harnessed to teensy-weensy processing capacity. Kind of like the early-model PCs they used to run the space shuttles at the turn of the century.

Whatever the reason, magic flows very freely out at the edges of things. The worlds there can become quite strange, bent as they are by the fundamental force of the irrational. In this one, despite an apparent lack of people, the detritus of a modern civilization lay everywhere, rusting hulks of cars, trashed refrigerators, old computers. The smell of decay hung heavy in the air. Yet there was a weird beauty to it all, because nature was in the process of reclaiming the works. Bindweed and other flowering creepers had taken hold of most of the larger pieces of trash, transforming junked pickups into floral topiary. A blown-out television had a Japanese rose growing out of the hole where the tube had once been.

Weird and wild and strangely wonderful, Garbage Faerie reeked of magic. Spells that might take a thousand lines of whistled code and draw heavily on the mweb in the vicinity of Olympus would need little more than a thought and pursed lips here. That plus its distance from the corridors of Fate was why Ahllan had set up shop here. I turned then to look at her blasted and empty home.

The low hill that had once sheltered a dozen homey rooms had been cloven in two, its mosaic-covered walls lying shattered and exposed to the elements. I heard a gasp from beside me and looked down to see Shara. She was trembling, and who could blame her? She had died here, falling in the ruin of this place.

"I didn't know it was this bad," she whispered. "I went down too early to see it." She put her face in her hands. "I feel so awful."

I knelt to put a hand on her shoulder.

"I'm sorry," I said. "It's my fault. It's *all* my fault." I was speaking of her death as much as the destruction of the house.

"Don't be an idiot, Ravirn," she said. From her tone I knew she'd caught my meaning. "I know that's hard for you sometimes"—she was interrupted by a whispered "amen" from Cerice, but didn't acknowledge it—"but this *isn't* your fault. Sure, you were the proximate cause, but it was Atropos and the other Fates who did this in their desire for absolute control."

"Maybe you're right," I said. "But we aren't here to argue about comparative guilt. We're here to find Ahllan."

"She's gone." Melchior was kneeling a few yards away, sniffing at the dirt. "She *was* here, but not for long." He pointed at a pair of deep footprints in the mud. "There was a gate there." He pointed again, but I didn't see anything beyond a few more tracks. "Incoming only."

That would explain it, no physical traces. Webgoblins' magical senses were much stronger than mine, able to see the faintest of spell traces if they hadn't been deliberately masked.

"So what happened? It looks like something very strange."

Melchior nodded. "Ahllan appeared through the LTP gate, walked a couple of steps, called us, then poof."

"But she didn't gate out?" I asked.

"Not that I can tell. And unless she did a really spectacular backflip, she didn't leave via the faerie ring. I can't

Vtp her either. I've been trying since we got here. Although whether that's because she's blocking messages, gone somewhere off the net, or just because the turbulence is so bad, I can't say." He shivered. "It feels . . . *wrong*, like something crawling around the inside of my skull. Shara?"

"I'm not hooked up, and if you don't mind, I'll just take Mel's word for it. I've got enough problems without things crawling around inside my skull."

Cerice gave Shara a penetrating look. Normally web-goblins hate to be out of touch with the mweb and will only break contact by order or request. The stream of information and magical power that comes to them through the mweb is as much a part of them as the blood flowing in their veins.

For perhaps the millionth time, I wished that I could experience the mweb in the same way Melchior did. Sure, I could enter its virtual space by using an athame, but it wasn't the same thing at all. It was the difference between being a scuba diver and being a fish. No matter how hard I tried, I wasn't going to grow gills. We needed to find out what was going on, and fast. With Ahllan missing, I could only think of one other possible source for that information: Eris.

"I want to visit Castle Discord."

"What?" exclaimed Shara. "Why? We should go home and keep our heads down. This isn't our problem. This is a matter for the gods to sort out with Necessity. If we try to fix it, if we even go within a thousand yards of the mweb servers, Fate will have collective apoplexy and murder us on the spot. Let it go."

"You're probably right," I said.

"I'm definitely right. This is not our business."

"So I'll take the three of you back to the apartment before I go on."

"Not a chance," said Melchior. "Not with Ahllan missing. I'm going, too."

Cerice knelt in front of Shara. "We have to do this, honey. We just have to."

Shara sighed. "All right. But if we have to go, we should do it quick before the mweb cuts out and we're forced to use the faerie ring again. Maybe it worked this time, but they still give me the creeps."

"Amen to that." Melchior pulled out a string and stylus and began sketching out a hexagram in the dirt. "At least when *I* make the gate, I know I can trust the driver."

I thought back to our most recent trip from Hades and how that had gone, but didn't say anything. Melchior clearly felt strongly on the subject, and, judging by the profound look of relief on Shara's face, so did she. A few minutes later we stepped into the light. It wasn't nearly as rough as our last trip. This just felt like being trapped in an elevator with its cables cut, a wild straight drop through darkness with a sudden stop at the end. We landed hard, though not hard enough to break bones.

When the light cleared, we stood on a small rectangle of stone completely surrounded by the wild billowing colors of the Primal Chaos. Some sort of irregularly shaped invisible shield prevented it from reaching the surface of the rock and devouring us, though occasional tendrils of the stuff came frighteningly close.

Eris prefers to live off the grid, way off. Castle Discord is a floating island in the sea of chaos. Whether it lies in the turbulence between worlds or somewhere beyond the farthest edges of reality is something that's more a question of philosophy than science. To make things even more difficult, the castle moves constantly. Combine that with the fact that it's not actually connected to the mweb, and you have a situation where only a fully functional webtroll like Ahllan, exerting maximum concentration, can keep its coordinates fixed long enough to open up a gate to the castle proper. For the benefit of visitors Eris has placed a chunk of stone in a fixed and permanent relationship to the rest of the multiverse. She called it the welcome mat, and it even had the Greek welcome, *Kalos Orisate*, carved into it in letters six feet tall. That's where we arrived.

I'd been there before and knew the routine, so I slowly

turned in place until I saw it. Far off and high up, a speck appeared. Castle Discord. Our arrival had triggered the doorbell, and now the castle was coming to us. As I watched, it grew steadily closer, becoming a ragged chunk of golden granite. The top was hidden by the angle at first, but as it descended, I could see a great splash of green covering the surface. It looked nothing like it had the last time I'd seen it. No surprise.

Castle Discord doesn't actually exist in the way most people mean the word. It's entirely a state of mind. I can't even begin to explain the spells involved in its creation. It's very deep, wild magic of the kind that scares the living daylights out of me. All I can speak to is the result. Castle Discord is a sort of mathematical description of a place with all the descriptors as variables that can be adjusted by the whim of its occupant. One minute it's a medieval cathedral, the next it's a Vegas-style casino. It depends entirely on what Eris's notoriously changeable mood desires.

Even more bizarre, when she isn't actively exerting her will on the place, it will rearrange itself to suit the whim of whoever happens to be wandering its halls, a fact I had discovered on my first—unauthorized—visit. At the moment, it most looked like some sort of huge botanical garden occupying a series of interlinked greenhouses. But that was on the outside. We wouldn't know about the inside until we got there.

When it reached a point about a hundred feet above us and perhaps twice that distance away, Castle Discord stopped moving. An archway opened just below the rim. Like some sort of huge stone frog mouth, it spat a long flight of stairs at us. They had no railing and looked to be made of black glass. As with the welcome mat itself, some sort of invisible barrier kept the stuff of chaos from pressing too close to the stairs.

"Have I mentioned that this is a bad idea?" mumbled Shara, when the stairs touched down in front of us.

"I'd certainly gotten that impression, yes." I stepped up onto the first stair. "But unless you want to play 'ring the doorbell and run away' with the Goddess of Chaos, we'd best get moving."

"I think it's fascinating," said Cerice, following close behind. "Ever since you first described this place to me, I've wanted to see it."

I'd been here any number of times since my initial visit but always by invitation, an invitation that had included only me and Melchior. I probably could have brought Cerice, but I'd always felt it safer to keep her away from Discord. Eris might find me amusing. She might even have a soft spot for me. But she was one of the most dangerous and certainly the most capricious of goddesses. I preferred not to give her any more handles on me than I had to, and Cerice would make a mighty fine one.

I looked past her now to Shara, who was reluctantly bringing up the rear. I wished there was something more I could do for the little purple webgoblin. I missed the wild, willful, sexy creature she had been before her time in Hades, and it tore at my heart to see her so subdued. I'm not sure which was worse, that or the fact that I'd started having suspicions about her. I hated my own paranoia, but that didn't prevent me from keeping one eye on her as we climbed the stairs. On one of my periodic glances her way, I noticed a bright flash on the welcome mat that I might otherwise have missed. It was similar to a locus transfer yet not quite the same.

"I wonder what that is," I said quietly. I couldn't think of any answer that would make me happy.

"What?" asked Cerice.

Instead of responding I stepped past Shara, and said, "Melchior, Eagle Eye. Please."

He quickly whistled the spell that gave me the vision of a raptor, then duplicated it for Cerice, Shara, and himself.

A bright rip had opened in the air at the base of the stairs, like someone had sliced a hole through from some-place else. That was because someone had. I'd seen the effect once before. It was the Furies' version of an LTP gate. I didn't know how it worked, except that it involved the adamantine claws that tipped their fingers and some special application of the powers granted them as Necessity's personal handmaidens and IT staff.

First through the gap was Megaera with her seaweed-colored wings and hair, not to mention a personal vendetta against yours truly. I didn't honestly care who came next. None of them was good news, and I couldn't help but think their arrival here and now was no coincidence.

"Run!" I said, turning back toward the castle. Cerice was ahead of me. She'd already scooped up Shara, and was taking the remaining stairs two at a time. I grabbed Melchior and followed.

We were already close to the top, and I felt confident we'd reach the gate ahead of the Furies. But there my confidence ended. Whether the doors would open for us, and what would happen after, I didn't know.

CHAPTER NINE

Cerice, running just ahead of me, passed through the stone arch at the top of the stairs, then skidded to a stop. Beyond lay a small vestibule lined with gold-veined black marble. The far wall held an elevator door beside a single button, marked "?". Typical Eris. I pushed the button then glanced back down the stairs in time to see the light that had announced the arrival of the Furies blink out. They were all on this side of the rift now.

I felt sweat break out on my forehead as I realized they were at most a minute or two behind us. If not for the narrowness of the stairs preventing the use of their wings, they would have already arrived. I hit the elevator button again. It didn't help. The Furies began to climb the stairs, their wings tightly furled around their naked bodies. Megaera led the way. Behind her was Alecto. I couldn't really see her, hidden as she was by her sister, but I remembered her well enough.

She was taller than Megaera and curvier, with hair and wings like storm-shot night, lightning forking and reforking with her every move. Her skin was a stony gray, save only her lips and nipples, which mirrored the storm in her hair. Bringing up the rear would be Tisiphone, tall and slender and fire-haired. I checked the elevator. Still not there.

"What should we do?" asked Cerice, loosening her sword in its sheath and opening the flap of her holster.

"Not that," I said, reaching over and resnapping her holster. "Neither guns nor swords are going to have a big effect on them. Even magic wouldn't help much."

Cerice nodded and bent her head close to Shara's. Still no elevator. I checked the stairs. Perhaps sixty feet still separated us from the Furies. Megaera waved and gave me a jaunty smile that set what felt like a small horde of flying bugs to buzzing in my stomach. To hide my fear I waved back. When the distance had closed to perhaps ten feet, the elevator dinged.

Too late, I thought as the doors slowly opened. *Way too late.*

Still, I turned and followed Cerice aboard, hoping to avoid a confrontation. This time there were two buttons. They said, HERE and THERE. Cerice had already hit the THERE button, lighting it up, but the doors remained open as the Furies entered the alcove.

"Hit them with a spell?" Cerice whispered in my ear.

"Not a good idea," I answered, handing Melchior to Cerice to clear my hands.

They hadn't made any hostile moves, and I didn't want to provoke them if by some slender chance they weren't here for us. Nor did they attack, as one by one they joined us in the elevator. I edged toward the back when they got on, putting my body between the Furies and Cerice and the goblins. It wouldn't provide much of a shield, but I had to do what I could.

A sign by the buttons claimed the elevator had a capacity of ten people. That might have been true if none of them were Furies. But between the wings and their apparent personal space issues with each other, it would have been quite full with just the three of them. Add Cerice and me and two goblins and it became something like a sackful of cats, all hard looks and sharp points. It didn't help that the Furies had never developed elevator manners. Instead of sliding inside and looking at the doors, they were all facing the back and me.

"Hello, Raven," said Megaera, who stood closest to the door. She tapped the THERE button. This time the doors immediately closed. As they did, a horrible steel drum rendition of "The Girl from Ipanema" began to play. "Thanks for holding the elevator."

"Very polite," said Alecto's voice from somewhere on the far side of Megaera. She was once again hidden by her sisters' wings. "Not at all like the last time we saw him."

"But that was such fun," said Tisiphone, who was practically pressed against my chest. "Cat and mouse is my *favorite* game. And he made such a cute little mousie." She made batting motions inches from my nose, highlighting the long, deadly claws that tipped her fingers. Her voice dropped half an octave. "Didn't you, Raven?" And she ran one of those fingers down my chest from throat to navel.

It's never wise to meet the eyes of a goddess. They can do things to you that way if you give them the chance. At the same time, I didn't dare *not* look at Tisiphone. So I kept my eyes down to avoid her gaze. Unfortunately, that meant I was staring at her breasts. They were very nice breasts, high and small and very pale, with erect nipples the color of flame. If they'd been on some other chest or in different circumstances, I might even have enjoyed the view. As it was, both the personality attached to the body and the fact that I had my heavily armed girlfriend pressed against my back made for a situation of acute discomfort. I found myself half-wishing they'd just kill me and get it over with.

Excruciating seconds slid by with no sound other than Discord's demonically inspired choice in elevator music. I'd have to think of some way to pay her back for that if I got out of this in one piece. That and the funny business with a door that closed for Megaera but not for me or Cerice. More time passed. What was taking so long?

"Is this thing even moving?" squeaked Melchior, echoing my own thoughts.

"It is," said Alecto. "Though not very quickly."

"I think someone is deliberately tormenting her guests," grumped Megaera.

"I don't know," said Tisiphone. "I'm rather enjoying the ride, though my wings *are* a bit cramped." She rolled her shoulders, which did interesting things to my view, then stepped forward a little so that I was suddenly sandwiched between her and Cerice.

Some guys would have killed to be where I was right then, pressed tight between an incredibly sexy blonde and a smoking hot redhead, the latter naked. *I* would have killed to change places with any one of those guys. Especially when I felt a sharp heat against my groin and realized that it must be coming from Tisiphone's literally flaming pubic hair. I wasn't sure which was worse, the idea that my pants might actually catch fire or the fact that despite all the terrified gibbering going on in my forebrain, I could feel myself growing hard at the contact.

Nor, if I was interpreting Tisiphone's smile correctly, was I the only one who could feel my response. I'm not sure what would have happened next if the elevator door hadn't picked that exact moment to open, but I was mighty pleased that I didn't have to find out.

"We're here," said Megaera, stepping backwards out of the elevator.

"About time," said Alecto, likewise leaving the elevator.

"So soon?" said Tisiphone, and I felt her hand slide between us to squeeze me through the leather of my pants. "Pity." Then she peeled herself away from my front and followed her sisters.

I surreptitiously glanced down to see if my pants had taken any lasting harm from their encounter with Tisiphone's fiery loins. It also gave me a chance to make sure my erection wasn't too blatant. It wasn't, and my pants appeared completely unharmed. At that, a part of my mind pointed out that the heat had never risen into the range of pain. That same part wanted to indulge in further speculation about the positive implications of fire that didn't burn me and how it might apply to other activities involving closer contact between the regions in question. I brutally suppressed the thought, helped along when a none-too-gentle push against the base of my spine reminded me of Cerice's presence and her probable take on any ideas I might have in that direction.

"Were you planning on getting off the elevator?" she asked, her tone sharp. "Or did you just want to stay here and lean against me while you try to put your tongue back in your mouth?"

I stepped smartly forward, then turned and bowed her out of the elevator. "After you, my lady."

She gave me a hard look. "Don't think a sudden reversion to courtly manners is going to get you off the hook, boyo."

"Never," I said, holding the bow. "But please keep in mind that I didn't have a lot of room for maneuvering."

"That's the *only* thing that's keeping you from the top slot on my shit list."

"Are you children going to join us, or are you just going to hiss at each other in the elevator?" The voice was one hundred percent sex and completely poisonous. Eris.

The goddess has sunk a considerable amount of power into sex appeal, and only Aphrodite can turn the heat up any further. The big difference is motive. Aphrodite is, well, Aphrodite. Sex and love are her thing. Eris, on the other hand, is all come-hither and no come-here. Like Artemis, she's a virgin goddess. But her motives are very different. Eris wants you to die from desire, or better yet, kill for it. Strife is her business, though unlike her brother, Ares, she generally prefers it come at the personal level, dueling over war. Her carnal voice is a potent weapon in her arsenal of destruction, but thanks to an alliance we'd once had, she usually didn't use it around me.

Perhaps because I'd had more exposure to her since my conflict with Fate, or perhaps because I had Cerice there with me, it didn't strike me as hard as it had the first time

I'd heard it. Still, an erection that'd been wilting under the pressure of circumstance sprang back to full attention. I saw the voice hit Cerice, too, as the angry slits of her pupils opened into great black holes, and she involuntarily moistened her lips. For a long second she looked completely glazed, then she very deliberately shook her head and, after putting the goblins down, gave herself a sharp slap on the cheek.

"Urgh," she mumbled, and though her pupils remained huge, some semblance of reason returned to her expression. She looked me a question.

"Always," I said, raising my eyebrows in silent warning against Eris. "She's always like this."

Bracing myself, I stepped out of the elevator into a large formal atrium. A window high in one wall allowed a shaft of light from the golden-apple sun of Castle Discord to shine down on Eris like a blessing from Apollo. She stood in the center of the room with the Furies off to her left. They seemed to have shrunk in stature, reduced somewhat from the terrifying creatures who had filled the elevator. But that was only by comparison. The Furies have chosen to size themselves as tall humans, preferring to let wings and claws drive home their difference and their divinity.

Eris is taller, six-four or six-five without the stiletto heels she always wears. With them she's very close to seven feet and every inch a goddess, or perhaps two. She looks different from second to second as the light plays across her, like taffeta. One moment her skin is an unearthly silver-black, the next twenty-four-karat gold, and both wildly and somehow inappropriately appealing. Her hair is sunlight and shadow, an ever-changing mix of raven and blond that spills halfway down her back. Her long, hard body is perfect. Not classical sculpture put-her-on-a-pedestal-and-worship-her-from-afar perfect, but I-know-what-I-want-for-my-birthday-and-she's-it perfect. Her face is fine and aristocratic, imperious even, with high cheekbones, a pert nose, pointed chin, and lush lips.

Only her eyes repel. When she opens them, she opens a

pair of gates into the Primal Chaos. Where flesh should be are twin windows on the ever-changing madness of color and turbulence that lies between the worlds. On her it simultaneously looks completely natural and utterly terrifying.

She was dressed in black and gold as always. In this case, torn black jeans that exposed a lot of leg and a skintight yellow tank top. Her shoes were some sort of extremely fancy designer heels made out of what looked like fish skin with gold-edged black scales. She was apparently unarmed, but I knew from past experience that if she wanted a sword or a gun, it would simply appear in her hand and that she would be much better with them than I or any other mere demideity.

She smiled when I emerged from the elevator and very deliberately and slowly ran her tongue around her lips. "Raven, darling, so nice to see you."

I shrugged it off. Well, part of me did anyway. Sure, there was a little bit of my back brain that was busily constructing scenes of wild abandon that involved Discord, Tisiphone, Cerice, and a really big bed; but the me that actually makes decisions very deliberately rolled my eyes. It was easier than I expected.

"I thought we'd agreed that you weren't going to play those games with me anymore," I said. "And don't call me Raven."

She shrugged. "Can't blame me for trying, can you?" she asked, dropping the come-hither from her tone. "I've got to keep my hand in after all. Since what I call you and who you are have no relationship other than convenience, I'd be happy to call you Ravirn if you'd prefer, or Zeus for that matter."

"Let's stick with Ravirn." Her comment grated on my nerves, but hey, that's her specialty, and I didn't think she was going out of her way to hit me harder than anyone else. So call it a win for now.

"Whatever you say, Raven dear." She turned her attention away from me. "And this must be your charming lady, Cerice."

"Cerice it is," she replied somewhat acidly, "though I'm no one's lady but my own."

"Really," said Eris, putting some sex back into her tone. "Would you like to be? I've got the perfect *position* for you."

Cerice shook the glaze off more quickly this time, and without the slap, but she did take a half step toward the goddess before she recalled herself. "Thanks, but I think I'll pass," she said, her voice husky.

"Can we skip the games?" said Megaera. "We've come for business."

"But I *live* for games," replied Eris. "You do, too, though yours all end the same. With blood."

"Oh, they don't *always* end in blood," said Alecto. "The last time we saw you, they ended in chains, as I recall." If she expected to get a rise out of Eris, she failed.

"Very nice," said Eris, making a parrying motion. "Touché, even." Then she laughed, a sound filled with undertones of glass shattering. "I'm cut to the quick. Or not. You won the game that day, but the chains are gone and chaos is eternal."

"The chains are gone," said Tisiphone, "because a sweet little bird cut you loose. Right, Raven?"

"I'm not playing," I said, though I did so very politely. "I am quite out of my depth in any exchange with you, your lovely siblings, or Discord." I didn't want to get involved with any animosity between Eris and the sisters of vengeance. I might be a fool from time to time, but I was not stupid.

"Not as out of your depth as you might once have been," said Tisiphone. "Not nearly."

"Don't encourage him," said Alecto.

"He's meat," said Megaera. "Not worth wasting words."

"But such pretty meat," said Tisiphone, openly appraising me. "A tender cut."

"Back off, Coppertop," said Cerice, stepping between me and the Fury.

"Growr!" Tisiphone made a clawing motion. "Very

fierce. But weren't you the one who was just saying she was no one's lady? If you won't admit a claim, what makes you think you can stake one?"

"Can we get back to business?" asked Alecto, with a sigh.

"I don't know." Eris looked back and forth between Cerice and Tisiphone. "This is developing into my kind of entertainment. Do we have to?"

"*We* do," said Megaera, throwing a gesture that took in her sisters. "And it would make things simpler if you would join us in that."

"But why ever would I want to make things simpler?" asked Eris, her tone apparently guileless—and, I suspected, sincere.

"Because Necessity asks it." Tisiphone smiled and batted her eyes at Eris.

"Oh." Eris's demeanor changed instantly from playful to completely serious. "In that case . . ."

She shrugged, and the jeans and tank top had gone, replaced by a very neatly tailored business suit. In that same instant the atrium we had all been standing in disappeared as though it had never been. In its place was a long wood-paneled boardroom with a huge black glass table running down its center. Only the golden apple of the sun shining through the window behind Eris remained as a reminder of the old room. Big executive-style leather chairs now stood waiting behind each of us. The three for the Furies had stick-thin backs that flared out at headrest height to accommodate their wings. The pair that had been provided for Melchior and Shara were extratall with built-in footrests and appropriately sized seats and arms.

"I was hoping she'd forgotten us," Melchior said resignedly as he climbed into his.

"I never forget anyone," said Eris, "though I do pretend to if I think it might irritate them enough." She blew him a kiss, and he sank even lower in his chair. "So, what brings you all to Chez Discord?" She had placed herself at one end of the table with the Furies at the other, and she directed the question their way. "Your agenda is my agenda."

In front of each of our places a sheet of neat paper appeared. At the top was the heading AGENDA FOR MEETING ~~MINE~~ YOURS.

"Cute," said Tisiphone, and *cute* wrote itself on the page in letters of fire.

"Oh please," said Megaera, and *oh please* appeared in green ink below *cute*.

"Enough," said Alecto, and even as it was writing itself on the paper, she flapped her wings, sending the sheets spinning to the floor.

"You people are just *no fun*," said Eris. "But if you're really here on Necessity's business, I suppose I'd better indulge you." The fallen papers vanished. "So what do you want?"

"Something's wrong with the mweb," said Megaera, giving Eris a hard look.

"Very wrong," agreed Alecto. "The resource forks are being corrupted. It smells of chaos."

"Necessity doesn't like that," said Tisiphone, "and you *really* don't want to see her angry."

"No," said Eris. "I do not. Which is one reason why I never mess around with the mweb."

"You meddled in the Fate Core," said Megaera.

"That's well within my purview," she answered. "Especially under the circumstances. Necessity herself agreed on that once Raven's little teddy bear brought it to her attention."

"I'm not a ted—" Melchior began hotly. Then, apparently realizing that he was drawing attention, he shut his mouth sharply.

"Point taken," said Alecto, "both by us and our . . . mother."

So, Necessity was actively listening in. At least that's what I assumed she meant. I guessed by Eris's momentarily sour expression that she thought the same. I tried to catch Cerice's eye to mime a question, but she was too busy glaring at Tisiphone to pay me any attention.

"There's really no need for such threats," said Eris.

"Furies never threaten," said Tisiphone, with a smile. "We only make promises."

"Charming," said Eris, her voice filled with crackling ice. "Does all this have a point?"

"It does indeed," said Megaera.

"A *very* sharp one," interjected Tisiphone.

"And that's this," said Alecto, as sober as her granite skin. "Necessity is unhappy with the circumstances. As yet she has no reason to suspect you."

"As yet," said Tisiphone. "But that could change." She held her hands up in a balancing gesture.

"It would please her if you'd do something a bit more active than just denying your involvement with the current situation," said Megaera.

"Like what?" asked Eris.

"You are the goddess of hackers," said Alecto. "Find out what's going on."

"Fix it," said Megaera.

"Or point us in the right direction for a little *troubleshooting*," said Tisiphone, miming a gunslinger's quick draw and snap shot.

"I've tried once or twice already," said Eris, seemingly grudgingly. "I haven't had any success."

"Try again," said Alecto.

"Try harder," growled Megaera.

"And remember," said Tisiphone, "Necessity *is* the mother of invention."

With that the Furies rose from their seats and headed for the door, filing out one by one. As she turned to let it close behind her, Tisiphone caught my eye, smiled, and winked. Then they were gone. The door hung half-open for a long moment, then closed with a thud. For a few seconds longer we all sat in silence.

"She's a mother all right," said Eris, and the chaos in her eyes tumbled more wildly than ever.

She brought her hand down on the table in what looked like the gentlest of pats. It shattered with a terrible sound, one that merged with Eris's sudden laugh as she leaped to her feet. It was not a wasn't-that-funny laugh, more of an evil-genius-plotting-her-revenge cackle.

"I wonder if they're leaning on the Fates and other players that hard?" she asked aloud. Then, spinning on her heel, she fixed her dreadful gaze on me. "What in nine kinds of hell are you up to this time, boy?"

"Me?" I asked, taken aback.

"Yes, you, *Raven*. I'm not the only one who leaves a signature of chaos when I work."

"What? Why me? Why not Tyche?"

"Because our Dame Fortune is a nincompoop. Tyche doesn't know the RAM of Random Access Memory from the sacrificial kind whose entrails she reads. If she weren't the Goddess of Luck, she'd have knocked herself out of the great game ages ago. But for her something always turns up. You, on the other hand, are the pantheon's newest gift to cracking and hacking. And since I didn't do it . . ."

"You're out of your mind," I said. "You know that, don't you?"

"Am I really?" said Eris. "Then swear on your blood and your precious honor that you had nothing to do with the virus that is now eating away at the very web that holds the worlds together. I dare you."

"This is ridiculous," said Cerice, standing up and shaking the shards of glass from her lap.

"Is it?" asked Eris, pinning me with her gaze. "Then swear the oath."

I opened my mouth to do just that, but something stopped me. I was certain I'd had nothing to do with whatever was tearing up the mweb. Positive. And yet I found that I wasn't willing to swear to it. Perhaps I'd learned a lesson from my almost disaster over Shara. Or perhaps it was that Eris was asking me.

I believe that she has a certain fondness for me, and I know she knows she owes me. But despite all that, she is still *Discord*, with all that means. Her reason for existence is entropy. She *is* the heat death of the universe, and no loyalty or friendship will ever change that. If throwing me away might advance her goals, she wouldn't hesitate for a nanosecond. I could like her. I could make alliances with her. I could even expect her to guard my back if our goals were momentarily the same. But I could never, ever trust her.

I shook my head. "Why are you asking me this? Is there something you know that I don't?"

Eris laughed again. "Many things, *Raven*, many things. And now one more."

"What's that supposed to mean?" demanded Cerice. "I've just—" Her voice cut off midsentence, and she froze.

A sort of velvet silence descended over the room, and I realized that the only things still moving were me and Eris. Melchior and Shara were as still and quiet as Cerice. Even the dust motes dancing in the light of the golden-apple sun had frozen in place.

CHAPTER TEN

I turned my head back and forth, gazing first at my frozen friends, then at Eris, then back again. I was furious, and for just a moment I saw myself as the Raven she kept naming me, a black bird flying at her face to peck and claw her eyes and beat her senseless with my wings. I throttled down the urge to hurl myself across the ruins of the table, clutching the arms of my chair as an anchor against the angry seas of my soul.

"Interesting," said Eris, cocking her head to one side. "I wondered how you would react. Whether you would embrace your new self or cling to the old."

"Stuff it, Discord." I used her title rather than her name, as I always did. It was a way of putting a little more distance between us. "Release them."

"Or what?" She laughed, then raised a warning hand as I stood. "Don't. I like you, Raven. But if you start this, I'll finish it. Besides, they'll come to no harm, and I'll let them go much sooner if I don't have to counter any heroic gestures on your part. I just wanted a moment to talk with you in peace, and this seemed simplest. Do sit down."

I wanted to rage and throw things, but all that would have done was make her happy. She feeds on strife. So I painted the calmest expression I could manage on my face, sat down, and put my feet up on the chair so recently vacated by Megaera.

"Your move," I said.

"Oh, very nice." Eris returned to her own seat in front of the suddenly restored table. "You're getting better at this, though you do need to learn the trick of relaxing your shoulders. I can see the anger you're carrying there, and it gives the lie to your act. Here, like this."

Eris leaned slightly farther back in her chair and all tension seemed to drain from her body. With it went the suit, replaced by a black silk camisole and a pair of low-rise gold denims. She looked sexy and slinky and completely at ease, rather like a cat in a sunbeam.

"There," she said. "See how easy it is? That used to drive daddy Zeus crazy when I was a teenager, and he was yelling at me." She grinned. "But not half as crazy as it drove my stepmother, Hera."

"Stepmother?" I asked. I couldn't help myself. Discord's past is shrouded in a good deal of mystery. Some claim she's Ares's twin, the child of Zeus and Hera. Others insist Nyx, or Night, as she is sometimes called, mothered her with no father in sight.

"Yes," said Eris, steepling her hands. "I was a cuckoo in her nest: one more product of Zeus's philandering ways. Oh how Hera hated me and hated even more Zeus's claim that I had come from her womb entwined with my brother Ares. I think the only reason she let him get away with it was to prevent news of yet another of her husband's bastards from becoming the talk of Olympus. You know"— she looked thoughtful for a moment—"I'm really rather surprised she's never managed to murder Zeus. It's not like she doesn't have the motive. Maybe I could do something to move that along. The succession struggle would be rather entertaining. Don't you think?"

"I'll pass if you don't mind. I've got enough deity-generated stress in my life at the moment."

"You *have* managed to piss off half of the poles of existence, haven't you," she said. "You must sit pretty high on both Fate's and Death's lists at the moment. Are you sure you don't want to help me help Hera do away with Zeus? That would give you Creation to match Hades' Destruction and quite the trifecta."

I shuddered. "No thanks."

"Too bad. Creation is weaker than it once was. Zeus, the usurper to the throne of his father Cronus, is not as worthy a target as the old Titan. Still, it would have been fun. If you'd said yes, I might have decided to adopt you. You'd suit my line much better than Lachesis's."

"I'm pretty sure she'd agree with you. She did, after all, cast me out of her House and take back my name. You remember that, don't you? As I recall it was because I'd just saved *your* sorry ass from a bad date with Necessity."

She scratched her chin. "No. I can't say it rings any bells." I growled, and she laughed. "Relax. I do owe you one, but we both know it wasn't me you were saving there. It was your soul. If you could've cut me loose without compromising your personal integrity, I don't think I'd be here now, would I?"

I looked at the floor. She had a point, sort of.

"Oh, don't feel bad about it," said Eris. "I don't much care about means except where they can be twisted to make life a little bit harsher. I'm much more interested in ends. And that brings me back to where I was when I made us a little time to talk alone." She waved a hand toward the frozen form of Cerice.

I felt another stab of anger, and apparently failed to conceal it, because Eris let out another of her broken-glass laughs.

"Don't grimace at me like that," said Eris. "She's a

pretty enough thing, but not really in your league anymore. You'd be much better off taking Tisiphone as a consort."

"What!" I squawked. "That's mad. I love Cerice. But even if I didn't, Tisiphone is a Fury, and I'm—"

"Raven. You may not choose to admit it, but you are no longer a scion of the middle house of Fate. You have transcended your origins and are playing on a much bigger stage. The girl"—she waved at Cerice again—"is an exceptional child of Clotho's House, but that's all she is. You are your own House now, a *power*, if a minor one as yet. As long as you tie yourself to Cerice, you will possess a significant vulnerability that any of your enemies could exploit. Especially your enemies in the Houses of Fate."

"But—" I began. *A power?* I wasn't at all sure I liked the sound of that.

"Allow me to finish. Tisiphone, while she has her *quirks*, seems genuinely fond of you. And no one, and I mean *no one*, would dare to strike at you through her. Not only does she have the innate strength to protect herself against most threats, but she also walks in the shadow of Necessity. That is armor even against the greatest powers."

"Why are you telling me this?" I asked. It was all true— irrelevant, since I was genuinely in love with Cerice—but still true. In its own way it was even very good advice, and that made it completely out of character for Discord.

"One, I like you. Two, I owe you a favor. Three, Tisiphone *really* needs to get laid. It might mellow her a bit, and that would make her less likely to interfere with me. I'd still have Megaera and Alecto to worry about, since no amount of sex is going to help the former and I don't see anyone around to throw at the latter." She smiled, and there was nothing nice in the expression. "And finally and most importantly, I know you won't take my advice even though you know I'm telling you the truth. What more could Discord ask for in the way of strife than painful truth offered fruitlessly to a friend?"

"How can you think that way?" I whispered in horror. I liked Eris. I knew I shouldn't, but I did. And I'd thought she liked me. "How can you think that way?" I repeated.

"I'm Discord," she said very quietly. "How could I not?" And for just an instant I saw a pain in her face to rival Persephone's.

It was gone so quickly I'd never be able to swear I'd really seen it, and yet I knew it would haunt me for a long time to come.

"Thanks," I said, "for telling me things I don't want to hear. Perhaps you could make it up to me by telling me something of the other sort."

"It's possible. What do you want to know?"

"What does it mean to be *Raven*? Everyone keeps telling me I should accept my new 'destiny,' but no one wants to tell me a thing about how to do that."

"That's probably because no one really knows." Eris grinned and held up her hands to form an X. "There are two major axes of power in the pantheon. They sit at right angles to each other like some giant crosshairs. The first you've had intimate contact with, the conflict between Order and Chaos, or Fate and Discord if you will. The second is between Death and Creation, represented by Hades and Zeus."

"But Clotho's role as Fate's spinner also touches on Creation," I said.

"Exactly, just as Atropos with her shears is the Fate of Death. In your previous family, the creation-destruction axis is split, whereas I embody the lot for Chaos."

I was starting to get a headache. "What does that all have to do with my question?" I asked, rising to pace.

"Everything. Nothing." Eris held up her hands like a pair of balances. "Clotho was given some reason to name you Raven, just as she once was given a reason to name me Discord."

"Then Eris . . ."

"Was the name Zeus hung on me to complement the one he gave his precious Ares."

Something else hit me. "Wait a second, what do you mean Clotho was *given* a reason?"

"Necessity is the Fate of the Gods. Though Clotho spins them, it is Necessity who manages the threads of the powers both greater and lesser. When your experiences in the Fate Core stripped you of an ordinary sort of destiny, it took you out of the hands of the lesser Fates, your family. Combine that with the immortal blood of your great-grandmother, and you became a player on the stage overseen by Necessity."

"Are you trying to say that I'm a god?" My knees didn't seem to want to work properly, and I dropped into the nearest chair. It had been Alecto's, but now it rearranged itself to fit me.

"Perhaps someday," said Eris, "if you live long enough, which likelihood I doubt. You are, however, a power, and what a power may become, no one knows except perhaps Necessity herself. Do you think Clotho wouldn't have tried to kill me in my crib if she'd known what it would mean for me to grow up Discord?"

"I—uh . . ."

"But she didn't know my ultimate fate any more than I do. She knew only that I was to be a power and that I bore the mark of chaos. Oh, and that that was what Necessity wanted. That's all any of us really know about you, that you are a power, the first new one born in many long years, and one marked by chaos. For all I know, you may someday supplant me as Zeus supplanted Cronus at the splitting of the worlds that birthed the multiverse."

"Oh." I thought about the implications of that for a bit and the idea that my role as Raven might disrupt the status quo. "Why isn't everyone trying to kill me while I'm still too weak to defend myself?" I asked after a while.

Eris laughed. "Atropos already has, though that was before your new name came into play, and she will again. You can bet that Hades will as well, now that he's got an official excuse. Once the idea penetrates Zeus's dim little brain, he'll probably join the party, too."

"Which leads to two more questions. Why have I still got a pulse?" I put a finger to my throat just to double-check. "And what about you?"

"You are alive because there are rules, and Necessity is their enforcer. As for me, if you try to usurp my throne, we'll likely have words. Otherwise, the simple fact of your existence creates discord among the gods, and discord is my reason for existence. As far as I'm concerned, you're a special present Necessity dreamed up just for me."

"Goody."

"You're welcome. Speaking of presents, that brings me back to the original reason I shut off the peanut gallery so that we could have this quiet little chat. That is, the problem with the mweb and Necessity's request that I look into it. While I'd prefer not to do anyone any favors, I'm not going to turn down that particular request. Unfortunately, I've already been working on this mess for reasons of my own with no results to date. Since I really don't want to go back to Necessity empty-handed, I thought I might lean on you for a little help. After all, the mweb is just one gigantic magical construct that has something wrong with it, and bug-hunting is your specialty. Perhaps even the reason Necessity sent you a name."

"I—" What *did* I want to say?

Eris is a profoundly unsettling goddess. Every conversation I have with her reorders my universe in some new way, though not always for the worse. I realize that her gift and her reason for being is what she calls strife, but while she certainly disturbs me no end, I sometimes wonder if she's not nearly as much of a villain as she likes to pretend to be. If, perhaps, discord with a small *d* is something we all need from time to time to keep us from stagnating. In the House of my grandmother such ideas would be rankest heresy, but what about in the House of Raven? I needed to think about that.

"Well?" asked Eris. "I'm waiting."

"I'll help."

I didn't add that my motives had very little to do with

helping her out and were much more about satisfying my own concerns and curiosity, not to mention finding Ahllan. With Eris backing me, I had a far better chance of hacking my way to the truth than I would on my own.

"You're such a good boy," she said. "It just makes me want to give you a big wet kiss." Without crossing the intervening distance she stood above me. Slowly, ever so slowly, she leaned down and put a hand on each arm of my chair, giving me a very clear view down the front of her camisole. "What do you say?"

"That I wish you wouldn't do that sort of thing," I said, closing my eyes and turning my head to one side. It was not easy, but it was necessary.

"Pity," she whispered, moving even closer and taking the pointed tip of my ear gently between her teeth. "But if you insist."

"—about had it with you!" said Cerice from beyond Eris, finishing the sentence she'd begun so long ago. Then, "What the fuck is going on here!"

Eris stood up and made a show of adjusting her clothes. I put my face in my hands.

"Discord," I said through my fingers. "That's what's going on." I dropped my hands and glared at Eris. "Can't you ever give it a rest?"

"No," she said, and I caught just an echo of her earlier pain, "I can't. Not for one single second. Now, we have work to do."

The boardroom was gone, replaced by a tile-floored computer center. The big square tiles were all gleaming white and mirrored the grid of the dropped ceiling above. Aluminum racks stood along the walls, each with several large golden apples mounted within and wires trailing down through holes cut into the tiles. Between racks were numerous Formica-topped tables strewn with the electronic detritus typical of labs and equipment rooms everywhere. A faint background hiss whispered of fans that kept the space beneath the floors at a constant positive pressure. A bank of uninterruptible power supplies stood in one corner. In other words, in every respect but one it mimicked the typical corporate computing center. Eris drew attention to that anomaly with a tap of one long black-and-gold-painted fingernail. The big metallic apple rang hollowly in response.

"Multicore Macintosh servers set into my own special case mods," said Eris. "They're all cross-linked like a Beowulf cluster, only better since I use my own custom operating software to maximize performance. I call the result a Grendel group."

"Hold on a second," said Cerice, stomping over to stand in front of Eris. "You still haven't answered my question."

"About what was going on?" asked Eris, her voice deceptively sweet. "I thought Ravirn covered it pretty well: Discord."

"And the part where you paralyzed us? You know, when we couldn't move, but we could hear every vicious word you said?"

I was glad Cerice was looking the other way, because though I managed not to say it aloud, I could feel my mouth shaping the words, *oh shit*. So Eris had given me a lecture on why I should dump Cerice right in front of her. *Thank you, Discord.*

"What about it?" asked Eris. "I didn't say anything I didn't want you to hear, child."

Cerice's cheeks reddened as though she'd been slapped. Out of the corner of my eye, I noticed Shara and Melchior ducking under a table. I wished I could join them.

"He is a power," said Eris. "You are not. The relationship is a risk to you both. Besides, as Tisiphone pointed out so succinctly, you haven't got a claim."

"Is that why you were nibbling on his ear?" snapped Cerice. "Because I haven't got a claim? Or is it just that you're an unmitigated bitch?"

"Oh, the latter definitely. I'm really only interested in romance as far as it generates outbursts like your current one. Tisiphone, on the other hand, has had quite a sweet spot for the boy since she met him."

"Oh, she has, has she?" Cerice whirled to glare at me. "And why haven't you mentioned this before? Who else is sweet on you? Persephone? She certainly went out of her way to help you out."

I'd about had it. "Cerice, I love you, and I owe you my life several times over, but I really don't like you very much at the moment." Melchior hissed under the table. "I don't think I've ever given you any reason to doubt my affections. Shit, I just went to Hades and back for the sake of your thesis."

That wasn't entirely the case, since my friendship with Shara had played at least as big a role, but her "no one's lady" comment had hurt, and I was tired of being fair.

"Despite all of that," I continued, "you won't, as Tisiphone put it, admit a claim. So why the hell do you feel you have the right to get mad at me when some other woman expresses interest in me?" I was yelling now. "Especially when I haven't done anything to encourage it?"

"I—" Cerice's voice started loud, but sank quickly to a whisper. "I—I don't have that right, do I? Not really. Eris is probably right about Tisiphone, too." She closed her eyes and fisted her hands for a long moment. "She certainly couldn't be any worse for you than I've been lately. I'm sorry."

Without another word, she went out the door. I started after her, but Shara caught the cuff of my leathers.

"Let her be. She's earned some wallowing time."

"I—" I stopped, and faced Shara. "What do you mean?"

"That she's been dumping shit all over you since the day I got back." She took a shaky breath. "I love Cerice. She's my best friend, but that doesn't mean I'm blind to her faults. The way she's been treating you lately is a big one. If you two are ever going to work things out, Cerice is going to have to face that. She won't do it if you keep apologizing every time she has a hissy fit."

"Are you sure?" I asked, looking after Cerice. It was hard not to follow her, hard to see her hurting even if she'd brought it on herself.

Shara nodded, then turned away. "Unpleasant truths have to be faced sooner or later." The words were almost a whisper, and I didn't think she was really talking to me. "You can't get away from yourself, no matter how fast you run."

I didn't know what to say to that, so I went to join Eris at the server rack. "When do you want to start?"

"Now works for me." She opened her hands. Each held a slender athame, its cable extending into one of the golden apple servers.

"I think I'll use mine and jack in via Melchior if possible."

"Good enough," said Eris. The athame in her left hand vanished, leaving only the cable with its network connector.

"Melchior, you up for this?"

He glanced at Shara, who had returned to a place under the table, where she sat with her back against the wall and her chin resting on her drawn-up knees. She made a vague shooing gesture, and Melchior joined us, hopping up onto the low table beside the rack. He gave Eris a sidelong glance.

"What will your role be?"

"Support," said the goddess. "I've already had a couple of goes without any success. I, and Grendel here"—she patted the rack—"are just here to provide computing muscle."

"All right, then let's do it." Melchior melted quickly into his laptop shape. *Whenever you're ready.*

I plugged Eris's cable into one of his networking ports, then pulled out my athame and attached its cable to a second port in his side. I studied that slender blade for a long moment, holding it point down above my palm and thinking about what it meant.

For jacking in, a hard connection from body to computer still remained the best way. A wireless hookup didn't have the same resonance with the life thread, or the silver cord, as it was sometimes referred to in fluffy New Age circles. Whatever you called it, the strand that Clotho spun for you at your birth embodied the vital essence of your soul, your anima. The house of the anima in the body was the bloodstream, the internal network that pumped life with every heartbeat. The athame and the cable attached to it provided a symbolic and sorcerous link to a node on the mweb, in this case Melchior, and through him to the network that connected the infinity of possible worlds.

Of course, all of that was just a way of keeping my mind on something other than how much the whole process hurt. It didn't really help much. With a sigh and a grimace, I stabbed the blade through my hand, then surfed the bitter wave of pain into the world of the mweb.

I arrived in a small room wallpapered with pebbled blue leather. There was only one exit, a wide-open and jagged-framed window overlooking an orchard. Stepping close to the window, I could see a thousand identically rendered trees standing in neat geometric rows. Each tree had a set of six hexalaterally symmetric branches dripping with golden apples. The symmetry repeated itself in the roots and the placement of the fruit.

It all had the eerie unreal feel of a poorly thought-out video game. You know the kind, where the programmer rendered one side of one tree, then got bored with the process and just duplicated that single side over and over again in a total failure of imagination. An average three-year-old with the most rudimentary of computer skills would have done better. It seemed utterly unlike anything Eris could have had a hand in, yet I knew I stood on the threshold of her server farm.

With deep misgivings I said, "Melchior, Red Carpet. Please."

The window opened even wider, and a long roll of lush carpeting appeared in front of me. It quickly unrolled itself, forming a bridge to the orchard, a bridge whose far end opened in a split like a snake's forked tongue. As I started across, I paused a moment to look back. Melchior's head towered above me, his tongue providing the carpet I now walked.

"Show-off," I whispered. The giant face winked an eye at me.

When I reached the end of the carpet, I extended a foot

above the flat green field that stretched between the trees. It looked more like a fuzzy bath mat than a lawn. At least it did until I stepped onto it. At that moment many things happened all at once.

The green sheet began to bubble and eddy like antifreeze in an overheated car. To the touch it remained solid. I could feel the occasional bubble press against the bottom of my booted feet, like a rock suddenly growing beneath me—but to all outward appearances it had become a liquid.

The trees started a slow and chaotic dance, slipping from their rigid positioning into an ever-changing geometric relationship that owed very little to the simple shapes of Euclid's imagination. They also lost their symmetry, twisting and growing into gnarled forms straight out of some cautionary Grimmsian fairy tale. The apples themselves became detached from the branches, though they remained clustered around the trees in thick clouds, glowing now like a swarm of mating fireflies.

"Like it?" a voice whispered in my ear.

I jumped a good thirty feet into the air, unbound as I was by physical restraints. Turning, I flew back down to land beside Eris, who now wore a black-and-gold dress with a huge train that twisted off between the trees.

"Don't do that! You just about scared me out of my skin."

"I was hoping that I might," she said, with a wicked smile. "I thought it might prove enlightening. Or failing that, entertaining. Sso, sshall we be going?" she asked, her voice taking on a sort of hissing undertone.

"I thought you were just providing backup."

"That, and transssportation." She twisted suddenly, and a portion of the train of her dress slid around in an s-curve, bumping against my calf.

It felt a lot more substantial than any dress should have, and I looked down to find that the portion touching my leg had a saddle straddling it. Only in that instant did I realize it wasn't a dress. An enormous snake's body descended from Eris's torso and trailed out behind her.

"You're not serious," I said. "A lamia?"

"You're going on a quest. That means you need a loyal steed, and this sounded like more fun than a sphinx. Hop on, and we can get going."

"I'd rather not."

"Oh come on, it'll be fun. How often are you going to get the chance to ride a goddess? Barring coming to your senses about Tisiphone, that is." She licked her lips with her now-forked tongue. "Look, you can argue all you want. In fact, I'd enjoy it. I live to argue. But this *is* the best way for me to accompany you. We both know you're going to get in that saddle eventually, so why not just admit it and enjoy the ride."

"All right. Melchior?"

"Here, Boss." A tiny blue bat with Melchior's head on its shoulders landed on my wrist. It wasn't the real Melchior, of course, just an icon representing his attention.

"Let's get this over with," I said, swinging a leg over Eris's elongated body.

Instead of sinking into the seat as I'd intended, the saddle rose up to meet me, and stirrups slid out to catch and cradle my feet. That's when I noticed that the saddle was actually grafted onto her body.

"Hi ho, nutjob, away," I said very quietly, and we suddenly shot forward.

I had to throw my arms around Eris's waist to stay on. Her flesh was warm and soft and very feminine. I tried not to think about it. We left the orchard shortly thereafter through a fat pipe that represented one of the remaining lines of the damaged mweb.

"So where are the reins?" I asked eventually. We were still sliding along an essentially unbroken tunnel, but I knew I'd want more control at some point.

"Steer with your knees, my dear. I can be *very* responsive."

"Yeah, it's that 'can be' part I'm worried about."

"Support and transport and nothing more," replied Eris. "Isn't that what we agreed?"

I sighed but nodded and looked ahead. A light quickly grew until the walls opened out around us. Eris stopped then, leaving most of her long body in the tunnel behind, and reared up like a cobra preparing to strike. We had emerged high up on a mountain with the core server architecture of the mweb lying like an endless gem-studded plain below.

"Pretty, isn't it?" said Eris.

"Uh-huh."

"But this is all on the public side and not much use for finding out what's wrong. For that, we'll have to dig deeper."

"Wait a second," I said.

But my protest fell on seemingly deaf ears as we slithered down the mountainside. Before I had time even to frame my argument, we were among the jewel-toned shapes that represented the many, many cores of the mweb mainframes. We didn't stop until we'd reached a huge ebony sphere, like some massive pearl—one of Necessity's black boxes. Remembering my last encounter with the goddess's security, I squeezed Eris's sides hard with my knees.

"Whoa there. I almost got fried the first time I messed with one of these. We should take it slow." I quickly described my experience with trying to crack Necessity.

Eris shrugged. "Last time you didn't have me along to play crowbar."

Then she slid to the left of the sphere and circled back until she'd met herself on the other side. She did this again and again until she'd looped three coils of herself around the huge black globe. She must have been elongating herself as she went, because I was pretty sure the Eris I'd first mounted couldn't have managed the feat.

"I thought I was in charge," I said.

"You are."

"Then tell me you aren't about to crush that thing in your coils."

"All right. I'm not going to crush that thing in my coils." She grinned. "But I'm sure as hell going to try."

With that, she squeezed. The black fire that had destroyed

my code weasel broke out over the entire surface of the processor core, and the world filled with blinding sparks and the smell of burning snake.

"Sssshiiittt!" and whether it was Discord's voice or mine doing the screaming, I couldn't say.

CHAPTER ELEVEN

The sound of shattering glass filled the universe, and it was both Eris's laugh and the cracking of the great ebony sphere. The dark fires faded as the black globe fell to ruin around us. Exposed within was another pearl, this one with all the rainbow highlights of the real thing. Eris's coils clutched tighter, catching this new sphere within them. But there was no resistance. It was like squeezing Jell-O, and together we sank into the core's surface.

So this was how the great powers played the hacking game. Smashing aside barriers that I would have been hard-pressed to finesse. I didn't like the style much, though it obviously had its strong points—effectiveness for example. I had just a moment to enjoy the idea that we'd beaten the system before I noticed the shards of blackness springing back into place behind us. We were in all right, but I suddenly had doubts about getting back out. Then the spheres were gone, and we arrived in a new frame of reference.

We were in the open, though mist, swirling gray and pearlescent, provided the illusion of boundaries. Beneath us lay harsh black volcanic rock, and I could hear waves breaking somewhere not too far away. Perhaps because of the way the ocean sounds came to me, or perhaps for some other reason, I felt certain that we were on a small island. I was about to share my thoughts with Eris when I noticed the guardian, or really, her foot.

It was a big foot, one that rearranged my sense of perspective. Now instead of a knight-errant riding a serpent of epic proportions, I felt like an action figure strapped to the back of a garter snake. A garter snake in very real danger of being stepped on. The foot, definitely feminine and a scant ten feet away, appeared to be formed of living purple-veined marble, hard and cold yet still alive and vital. My eyes traced upward, drawn to follow the living-stone column of the ankle up into the mist. As if on cue, the gray curtain parted, and I found myself staring past a curvy body into an enormous veiled face.

"We should have just stayed in Hades," said the bat-shaped Melchior. "It would have saved everybody a lot of trouble."

He had a point. In addition to her veil, the giantess also wore the world's biggest mirror shades. That was all to the good. It prevented me from meeting her gaze, a circumstance that would have resulted in my getting stoned, and I don't mean blissed-out. But circumstances could change at any moment, and that would mean game over, because I wasn't the only one in the company of snakes. The enormous guardian had seen my serpentine steed and raised me about a hundredfold. Her hair was alive, and it was looking at me. I had just found the world's biggest gorgon, and every single strand of her hair appeared ready to strike.

"Who?" asked the guardian in a female voice both strange and strangely familiar.

"Discord and Raven, on errand from Necessity herself," answered Eris. Which was good, since I couldn't think of a single thing to say. I was too busy panicking.

Long seconds dripped past as the great presence loomed above us. An internal struggle seemed to take hold of the gorgon, manifested in the wild twisting and hissing of her hair. It had been relatively still before. Now it was self-braiding.

Finally, the snakes subsided, and the voice spoke again. "Pass." It sounded oddly constricted, as though it were acting against its own will.

My spine turned into liquid from sheer relief and flowed away through a tailbone gone suddenly hollow. At least, that's what it felt like. The mist closed once again and the life seemed to leach out of the marble, transforming active guardian into passive statue.

"Are you totally insane?" I snapped at Eris. "I told you what happened to me last time I got near one of Necessity's black boxes, and now you just bull your way in? I thought I was supposed to be running this show."

"You are, and you will from here on out," said Eris. "But your last encounter with Necessity's security is exactly why I pushed things now. I knew you'd take forever and a day to get to the point of the matter, and that's not why we're here. Necessity and her security aren't the problem. Whatever's eating the mweb is, and we needed to get on to finding it. Besides, last time you weren't acting at the express request of Necessity herself, as delivered by her handmaidens. I figured we'd be golden on cracking our way in here on that count alone."

I sighed; she was probably right, but I wasn't quite ready to surrender the point. "So why didn't you just ring the doorbell? What if Necessity hadn't agreed with you?"

"The sentinel would have smacked us around a little, and I'd have apologized. This gave me a free shot at Necessity's security. I don't ever intend on going up against her, but if I have to try it someday, I now know a lot more about what to expect. If you're going to stay in the chaos business, you'll have to learn these things, Raven."

"But I don't *want* to be in the chaos business." Then I shook my head. When you're reduced to whining about your problems to the Goddess of Discord, it's way past time to shut up. "Forget it. Let's move on."

In apparent response to my comment, the world shifted

around us. Sunlight burned the mist away, exposing the horizon. We were indeed on an island, one surrounded by dark water as far as the eye could see. It became as smooth as the black terrazzo that now replaced the rough rock beneath us, changing the island from a rounded hummock to a neat hexagon a few feet above the water. No waves touched the endless ocean anymore, and no wind rippled the surface. It looked as though you could have walked on it, though where you'd go I couldn't imagine. Of our original situation, only the huge gorgon remained.

"And?" I said aloud. I was getting really tired of rapidly changing scenery and digital metaphors for reality.

"Uh, Boss," said Melchior. "Maybe you shouldn't push—"

"I'm waiting," I said.

Lines of white fire shot away from the island in every direction, like underwater lightning, forking and crossing in every conceivable combination without ever breaking the surface, until they filled the ocean in all directions.

"Thank you." Here was what I wanted, the master map of the mweb.

Sliding off of Eris's back, I walked down to the edge of the water. For a long time I just stood there and watched the lightning dance. I needed to get a feel for the interface. The island represented the core architecture, the master servers of the mweb and the deeper layers inside Necessity's black boxes. The lightning showed the various lines of connection. Where the bolts crossed, subnodes existed, some permanent, some temporary. Since the countless worlds of possibility remained in constant motion relative to each other, the mweb continually had to readjust itself to keep everything connected. Hence the dance of the lightning.

At first it seemed an impossibly complex and chaotic structure, beyond any comprehension. But the longer I looked, the more I felt that I could sense patterns, even if I couldn't see them outright, certain iterations that repeated themselves. With a thought, I lifted my virtual self high into the air, levitating up to stand on the shoulder of the gorgon. I unfocused my eyes, trying to let the visual information pass through me, direct from the sea to my hindbrain without the intervening filter of directed vision or thought. Time flowed around me, and I let it go unmarked.

Then, in a flash that mirrored the ones I watched, the whole image made sense. It was only for an instant, and I couldn't hold on to it, but I waited and it came again. And then again. Like a series of related slides flashing on a screen, a pattern emerged.

When Hades calls Persephone back to his side each year, her mother brings winter down upon the world of Olympus, a winter mirrored to some degree in every other branch of reality that has split off from that first of all worlds. With the cold comes frost painted on the surface of an infinite number of windowpanes. The variety of starting conditions is such that no two of these frozen portraits are quite the same; but if you look at enough of them, recurring patterns emerge, patterns described with the mathematics of fractals, patterns that repeat themselves over and over again as you move from the scale of the very small up to the very large.

After a time I could see that the lightning in the waters conformed to the same sorts of rules, infinitely more complex perhaps, but still recurring and still building from very small to very large through self-replicating iteration. More time passed, and my ability to see the patterns increased. Instead of snapshots of recognition separated by seconds or even minutes, the whole began to resolve itself into a single pattern expressed in both space and time. I didn't think I'd ever really be able to comprehend the totality of it, but now I could at least see that it was there. I could also see that something was wrong.

Around the edges of my vision, I could catch flickering gaps in the network, irregularities that prevented the thing from completing itself as it should. When I focused on them, they seemed to slip away, but by catching them out of the corners of my eyes I slowly came to understand that another pattern governed the gaps. It was a pattern of absence, as of things torn loose in a systematic way.

"Melchior?" I said then.

"Oh good, you're alive. I'd begun to wonder. You haven't moved in over an hour, and your virtual self doesn't betray itself with little things like breathing or blinking."

"Sorry," I said absently. "I want your opinion on something."

"Of course you do. If you didn't want something, you'd still be ignoring me." He held up a hand before I could argue with him. "Don't deny it, and don't worry about it. We're here to find out what's wrong with the mweb, and I'm not going to get in a snit if you ignore me so you can do that. Not with Ahllan's safety possibly riding on the outcome. So what do you need? I haven't been able to make hide nor hair of whatever's happening down there." His gesture took in all of the sea that lay in front of us.

"Neither have I," said Eris's voice from above and behind me. I looked up and found that she'd made herself at home among the stone snakes of the gorgon's hair. She didn't quite blend in, but she came close. "Give."

So I described what I had seen and pointed out the gaps. "I can see the flaws, but I'm not sure I understand the underlying realities well enough to know what they mean."

"Worlds cut off," said Eris after a moment. "I can see it now that you've pointed it out. Mweb lines that have lost their anchoring points."

"That's what I thought," I said. "But how would that work?"

"Maybe it's something like losing file resource locator forks," said Melchior.

"The fragments of code that identify where a given piece of software is to the master system," I said. It sounded right.

Melchior nodded. "The mweb is like a hard drive that's having bits of its catalog erased."

"Or corrupted," I said. "Everything is still there. It just can't find it anymore. That sounds promising. So, if we go with that for a moment, the next question is, what's causing the corruption? I wonder. Why don't we go have a look?"

"Sounds good," said Melchior. "There's something about Goldilocks and her very bad hair day here that sets my teeth on edge, something both right and terribly wrong, if that makes any sense."

"Eris?" I asked.

"You're driving." She slithered loose of the stony hair, and I remounted the saddle on her serpentine back.

I pointed at where I wanted to go, and we went, a particularly prominent dark spot in the pattern of light. I don't know how far we traveled in space, but it took only a few seconds of time for us to get to a point above the blot. On closer inspection it proved to be more complex than first impressions. Instead of a simple point of darkness, it looked like a seething ball of stringy shadows, each with a more intense dark point at its tip, and those tips appeared to be eating away at the dancing lightning around them. I was reminded of a ball of worms, or . . . snakes. A disturbing thought occurred to me.

"Take us closer," I said to Eris, and we dropped down toward the water.

"Yes," I said leaning over. "That looks like—"

"Get lost!" The words came from the center of that roiling darkness in the disturbingly familiar voice of our guardian gorgon and were echoed from the island behind us. This time I recognized the voice. It belonged to Shara.

I whipped my attention back toward the island and its sentinel. The gorgon had sprung to life once more, moving its great marble hand up toward its face, a hand veined in the exact purple of Cerice's webgoblin familiar. The figure tore away its mirror shades and lifted its killing gaze toward us.

For a frozen instant I tried to fathom what her presence here could mean. Then I let it go. I didn't yet know what was going on, but I knew that if we stayed here, we would die.

"Dive!" I screamed and, suiting action to words, flung myself off Eris's back into the dark waters.

With a splash, I plunged through the surface and touched the lightning. In that instant I understood how a bullet feels when the hammer comes down. With a bang and a stunning impact, I found myself accelerated to impossible speeds. The world blurred around me, becoming a tunnel of light roaring past too quickly to comprehend.

The trip ended as suddenly and harshly as it had begun when I slammed back into my own flesh-and-blood body with a stunning impact, as if the bullet I had felt myself to be an instant before had lodged itself in my heart. For long seconds I simply couldn't breathe. I pulled the athame from my hand but couldn't whistle the healing spell and had to watch silently as my blood dripped and spattered on the tiles of Discord's computer room.

When the seven notes that closed the wound did finally come, it was Shara's lips that shaped them, not mine. She stood before me as she cast the spell. When she was done she reached up and gently stroked the thin white scar that marked both the back of my hand and my many comings and goings into the electronic elsewhere of the mweb. I met her eyes and tried to hold them, but she looked away.

"You know," she said, utterly defeated.

I nodded, though I wasn't yet certain of exactly what it was that I knew. Somehow Shara—or something that wore her face and magical signature—had taken up residence in the heart of Necessity's computer system while at the same time she kept walking around in the real world. It shouldn't have been possible—the whole reason I'd had to go to Hades to fetch her was that souls are one-off, no copies allowed. Somehow, I'd messed up the rescue. Badly.

I could figure all the details out later. The more immediate problem, the one that was all too likely to get me killed, broke down into two parts: A, whatever the gorgon was, its presence in Necessity's domain coincided with the ongoing destruction of the mweb. And, B, it had almost certainly gotten there via the e-mail I'd sent from Hades.

Now, if I'd managed to cat-burgle my way in and out without leaving a trace, that might not be so much of a problem, but I hadn't. While my break-in wasn't quite as famous as Orpheus's little venture yet, it was all over the Olympian gossip circuit. So when Necessity started looking around for someone to punish, my name was going to be right at the top of the list. Because of that I had a number of questions I wanted to ask Shara. Before I could start, Eris intervened.

"I think you owe me some answers, Ravirn." Her tone was deadly serious. "About her"—she pointed a finger at Shara—"about the mweb, and about your involvement with both."

"I'm not sure I follow you," I said, with as straight a face as I could manage.

"Don't play games with me, child. Necessity's guardian and this little one"—she tapped the top of Shara's skull lightly—"look to be sharing a whole lot of code. The obvious link is you, my little chaos godlet. And—" She was cut off by a harsh buzz from the master console for the Grendel group. She turned toward the controls, calling to me over her shoulder, "We're not done."

"Boss," whispered Melchior, who chose that moment to shift back to goblin form.

"Yes."

"What the hell is going on?"

"Ask her." I jerked a thumb at Shara.

She looked at the floor. "I'm not sure, but I'm starting to have some flashes, maybe memories coming back."

"Of what?" I asked.

"Necessity. Hades. I—"

"Get your skinny butt over here," called Eris. "Tell me what you make of this."

I joined her at the console, where an alarm bell icon blinked beside a message. "Mweb access cut off. User Eris does not match any profile in system. Close this window or face immediate sanction by Necessity."

"I'd close the window," I said.

"But . . ." A countdown had started on the screen: 5. 4. 3—Eris clicked on the close button.

Another window opened. "Mweb carrier unreachable. Reboot?"

Eris looked down her long nose at me. "I was only joking about your trying to usurp the throne of Discord back in the conference room. You do know that, right?"

"I wouldn't have it on a golden platter, with a side order of anything I want."

"Why am I having trouble believing you?" she asked, an unspoken threat in her tone.

"Because you're naturally suspicious?" Behind me, I heard the familiar sound of Melchior slapping his forehead.

Eris snorted. "Even paranoids have enemies, little Raven. But you might be right. Not, of course, that that's important. No, what's important is that either you've succeeded in the most amazing hacking job since Prometheus stole the encryption key for fire, or you haven't, but no one's going to believe you. In either case, you have just added a great deal to the cosmic balance of entropy, and for that I must take my hat off to you."

She leaned forward in a low, sweeping bow, pulling a propeller beanie off her head and saluting me with it. It hadn't been there a moment before, and when she let it go after completing her bow, it flew off like a Blackhawk looking for its target zone.

"But taking on Necessity is going way too far, and the consequences are likely to be *very* messy. I can't and won't protect you on this."

"Surprise," I said. I hadn't expected it of her. "Are you going to hand me over?"

"No," said Eris. "I respect your accomplishment too much for that. But I won't lie to the Furies for you either, and they'll be back to ask about what I found out soon enough. The best I can do is offer you a head start. If you leave quickly, you might get far enough ahead of them to make an interesting chase of it."

"Will you take Cerice for me?" I'd run faster if I didn't have to protect her.

"I—"

"No," said Cerice. She had entered without my noticing her. "She won't. I'm not staying here, and I'm not going with you either." She was no longer crying, but the tracks of dried tears stained her cheeks. "How could you even think of hacking Necessity? Do you *want* to end up chained to a rock with an eagle tearing your liver out every morning?"

"You heard the bit about Prometheus, then," I said.

"That's when I came in, yes." Her voice was flat and furious.

"Are you going to listen to my side of the story, or are you just going to leap to conclusions and snarl at me like you usually do?"

"What the hell is your problem, Ravirn!"

"What's my problem? Honey, look in the mirror when you ask that." I'd finally, completely had it. "Bailing *your* webgoblin out of Hades is how I got involved in this mess in the first place!"

"Don't you dare pick on Shara! She's got enough problems!"

"You mean like the fact that she, or her twin, is right smack in the middle of whatever's wrong with the mweb! Or did you not eavesdrop on that part of the conversation?"

Cerice looked stunned. "I didn't know . . . No. What? How is that possible?"

"I . . ." I paused then because a thought had occurred to me, and I really looked at Cerice for the first time in . . . how long? That's hard to say. We see the people we spend our lives with all the time, but how often do we actually look at them?

Cerice is at least as good a coder as I am. I can outcrack her, and on most things outhack her, but she writes better code than I do. Look at her thesis program. It's huge and elegant and designed to totally own Clotho's network. Shara is the tool she built expressly for that purpose, taking over a Fate network. Now Shara, or her evil twin, was in the process of doing something sinister to the network belonging to the Fate of the Gods. Was I missing something vitally important because I was too close to the problem? Suspicion laid her icy hand on the back of my neck in that moment.

"Why are you looking at me like that?" asked Cerice.

"I'm just . . . thinking."

Eris's laugh shattered my concentration. "What fun you children are. If time weren't pressing, I'd love to watch this little tiff play itself out. But it is, and I won't. I really don't want your radioactive self on my premises when the Furies arrive, so if you could speed this up and get out of here, I'd appreciate it."

"And if we don't?" snarled Cerice.

"Why then, you'll have to learn how to backstroke through Primal Chaos. If Necessity hasn't already figured out what your Raven has done, she soon will. At that point, I do not want to be seen as sheltering him or you and your equally radioactive webgoblin. In fact, I don't want to be seen anywhere near you."

"But I thought you said you wanted an explanation from me," I said, "about Shara and Necessity and the mweb."

"That was before this." She pointed at the computer screen. "The collateral damage possibilities in your likely splash zone are now greater than my curiosity. As much as I'd like to know exactly what you've done, and even more what in the name of all gods you were thinking, I'm not willing to have you around long enough to give me the answers. You have exactly two minutes to get out of here on your own power. After that, you'll be leaving through a hole in the floor, one that'll take you straight out to the Primal Chaos. Good-bye, Ravirn. It's been interesting knowing you."

With that, she vanished.

"What do we do now?" asked Melchior.

"Leave," I said.

I opened my shoulder bag and gestured for him to climb in. As he managed that, I looked back to the place where I'd been sitting. Cerice had sense enough to come with me, at least for the moment. But I was worried about Shara and called her name. She didn't answer, and I could hear her slide a little farther under the table.

Let's see, I thought to myself. *Eris is gone. Does that mean she's relinquished local control?*

I pictured the room sans the table Shara had hidden herself under. It vanished, exposing the webgoblin. I breathed a little sigh of relief. Eris hadn't needed to do that. That she had meant she retained at least a little goodwill toward me. It also meant I might be able to do everything I had to and get us moving in the minute and a half of grace we had left. I didn't kid myself that she'd been bluffing about the trapdoor.

"Come on, Shara. We don't have time for games."

"This is all my fault."

"It is not," said Cerice. "It's Ravirn's."

"I won't argue with you about that last until I've got more facts, and we've got more time," I said. Besides, she might be right. It was my blown rescue that put us all here. "Hurry up, Shara."

"All right," she answered, standing up and coming closer. "I'll come, but you'd be better off leaving me to fall into chaos and oblivion.

"I doubt it," I said. "Besides, I'm sure as heck not going to let all the work I did breaking you free of death's cold grip go to waste in one quick drop with a sudden stop at the end."

Catching her by the scruff of the neck, I lifted her in beside Melchior. That left us about one minute. I rearranged my mental image of the castle, putting myself inside a memory from an earlier visit, a flower-filled greenhouse with a neat circle of forget-me-nots. Though in the present, I imagined myself outside the circle and standing within touching distance of Cerice. She looked startled by the transition.

"Don't think I'm ready to forgive you yet," she said, her voice husky.

"I don't need your forgiveness," I answered. I was still mad at her and suspicious. I held up a hand to forestall any response on her part. "And I don't need an argument. You can yell at me later. For now, we need to be gone from this place."

"And how!" said Melchior, from my bag. "We've got fifteen seconds left."

"I don't—" began Cerice.

"No time," I said, catching her hand in my own and tugging her toward the forget-me-nots.

She didn't resist, and a moment later we stood inside the circle. A moment after that we stepped out of another circle. At least that's how I imagined everyone else experienced things. I had experienced a thousand or more possible rings in near perfect simultaneity, just as I had the last time I entered a faerie ring, an effect—I suspected—of my new status as the Raven. This time I'd braced myself for the experience, reaching first for the ice ring we'd left behind in Cambridge. But it had melted away in the salty waters of Boston Harbor, and so I had to choose another.

"Garbage Faerie?" said Cerice, looking around. "But why?"

"It's the ring I'm most familiar with," I said. "And now, I'm the one who needs some time alone." I unslung my shoulder bag, setting it at Cerice's feet. "I'll be back." I thought about my new suspicion that somehow Cerice had set this all up. "Or then, maybe I won't."

She opened her mouth to speak. I just turned and walked away.

CHAPTER TWELVE

"Boss," Melchior called out, "you want me to come with you?"

"Not right now, OK?"

"All right, but be careful." His face took on a brief look of concentration. "Thought so. This DecLocus is completely off the mweb now, too. That'll cut down on possible nastiness, but you never know what might be lurking in one of these backwater worlds."

I nodded, to let him know I'd heard, and made a show of loosening my rapier in its sheath, but I didn't answer. I really needed to be alone and think.

When we'd stopped in Garbage Faerie earlier, I hadn't had time to do much more than glance at the place. It had been afternoon then. It was night now, but still quite light. Twin moons hung low in the sky. I walked toward the front of Ahllan's shattered home. It drew me like a magnet, this ruin I had caused. The rotting husk of a place where I had once found refuge—it suited my mood perfectly. To put it bluntly, I felt like shit.

Not all that long ago, I'd beaten the system, defeating

Fate in a battle over the future of free will. At the time I'd figured everything that came after would be easy by comparison. Sure, I'd picked up some heavyweight enemies and gotten the crap beat of me, but I was alive and in love and triumphant. All that I'd needed to make the victory complete was to save Shara. After fighting Fate—my own family—how much trouble could Death be? Orpheus had managed it, and let's face it, he wasn't the sharpest twig on the Olympian family tree.

I'd even been right. Cracking Hades hadn't proved to be much of a problem. At least it hadn't seemed that way at the time. But now? Now I was beginning to think I'd been set up. The question was, by whom?

Ahllan's door lay in a broken heap just inside the threshold. I stepped over the jagged bits of wood and into the hall beyond. It used to be that the low ceiling made me want to stoop. Now it lay open to the sky, more a ravine than a hallway. The first door on my right led into the domed living room, or it had. The roof had caved in, and the doorway was choked with rubble. There would be no more cozy teas here. I wandered deeper into the house, arriving at my onetime bedroom. I turned in, sitting on the edge of the dust-covered futon.

This was the first bed I'd shared with Cerice. Things had seemed so much simpler then. I'd known who my enemy was. Atropos. OK, it had turned out that she was only one-third of the problem, but still I'd known I was up against Fate. Now, I was so turned around that I was wondering whether *Cerice* might be the enemy. She certainly had the brains and the talent, but despite my suspicions, I couldn't bring myself to believe it. Maybe because I didn't want to. I might regret it later, but for now I mentally put her aside. So, who else was there?

Shara? That was silly. She was a webgoblin, not a power, and she'd still be trapped in Hades if I hadn't gone in after her. Yet the gorgon who pushed us out of Necessity's system had worn her face, a fact certain to land me in a world of hot water whatever the cause.

Ahllan would be a likelier choice if she hadn't vanished. Atropos's old server was a wily webtroll who'd managed to run a guerrilla operation against the Fates for years without suffering detection. Shara had been part of that network, a key player even. But what would Ahllan have to gain?

I didn't have enough information, and there were too many players. The Furies, Hades, Persephone, Eris. Hell, even Cerberus.

He might do a fine impression of a big dumb dog, but he was tens of thousands of years old and deadly smart. Not to mention, he was in the perfect position to get me in and out of Hades in one piece. That bore more thought.

Rising from the bed, I went back into the hall. It ended at a metal pressure hatch salvaged from the USS *Arizona*. It was twisted now, half-off its hinges. The steps beyond took me down into what had once been Ahllan's workshop for electronics and magic. The basement should have been pitch-black, but the air shafts that led to the surface had been ripped wide open by the passage of the Furies, and silvery splotches of moonlight made it almost as bright as outside.

I walked to the electronics bench and set a rack for chips upright. Its contents had spilled across the long table. I began to pick them up and sort them. I worked mostly by touch, counting pins with my fingers and dropping them back into the appropriate bins.

Cerberus. What had Kira said about him? That there were really four dogs involved. Bob, Dave, Mort, and the master intelligence, Cerberus. What must it be like to be a pack instead of a person? A group intelligence? And one with mixed loyalties, if Kira was right.

There was a faint scuff behind me and the sound of a throat being cleared. "Ravirn?"

The voice was barely above a whisper. Gentle, feminine, apologetic.

I sighed and rubbed my forehead. "I don't want to talk to you yet, Cerice."

"I'm not Cerice."

It didn't sound like Shara either. I felt a chill as if someone had lightly run a finger up the back of my neck. Tempering an urge to draw my sword, I turned around slowly. Tisiphone stood in the center of a rough circle of silver moonlight, the terminus of one of the air shafts.

"I just dropped in," she said, glancing at the opening above her.

"I didn't hear you."

"We can move very quietly when we want, part of the job." She seemed subdued, something I'd never seen in her before.

"Oh." That didn't sound good, but I didn't have a lot of options. She was between me and the door. I didn't have a spell prepped, Melchior was a long way away, and sword or pistol would be foolish at best. I'd just have to stall for time and hope someone above had seen Tisiphone make her entrance. Not that I was sure that would help. "Should I be running?"

"I'm not here officially. Or perhaps I should say that, officially, I'm not here." She half smiled.

I half smiled back. Maybe the current situation wasn't going to result in any blood loss. I'd like that. Especially since the blood would almost certainly be mine. "All right then. If you're not here, where are you?"

"En route." I must have rolled my eyes or something, because she apologized. "Sorry. I'm not trying to be cryptic. I'm just not very good at this." I wanted to ask what she meant by "this" but didn't get the chance. "I'm supposed to meet my sisters at . . . No. I probably shouldn't tell you that. I've got . . . boundaries I mustn't cross. Suffice it to say I'm supposed to be meeting my sisters so that we can go on to Castle Discord and ask about what you and Eris found out."

"But that's not what you're doing?" I made the statement a question. I wanted to know more, though in a way I already knew the worst. If the Furies were on their way to

Eris, my grace period was coming to an end. Once Necessity found out about Shara, or whatever the thing wearing her face was, she'd start handing out death warrants.

"No," answered Tisiphone. "I came here instead, because I needed to talk with you first."

"With me? Why?"

She stepped suddenly closer then, moving into shadow, hiding her features. "Don't you know?"

I shook my head though I was beginning to have suspicions.

"I—I want to get to know you better."

I'd never heard of a Fury hesitating about anything before, and here Tisiphone was doing it for me. Heady stuff, and scary. I'd have to watch my step. "I'm not sure I'm following you."

"I think you are," she said, though she sounded more wry than angry. She touched her lips. "This body is more than just a shell for the soul of vengeance. It's part of who I am, a woman as well as a goddess. That's very . . . hard, sometimes. I tend to frighten men. You understand?"

I did. On the list of men she frightened, I was currently occupying the top slot. But at the same time, I felt sorry for her. She seemed so vulnerable right now, a condition antithetical to her nature as a Fury. That had to hurt.

I smiled as gently as I could. "Maybe I do understand, Tisiphone. I don't know that I would have this time last year, but I was just plain old Ravirn then."

Things had changed for me when Clotho named me Raven. Though I hadn't known it at the time, she'd transformed me. OK, maybe that was stretching it. If Eris was right, Clotho'd just acknowledged the reality of the changes I'd wrought on myself through my conflict with Fate. Whatever the case, I was no longer what I'd once been.

If I felt this conflicted about becoming even the minor power I now was, how much harder must it be to fill one of the more important boxes on the cosmic org chart? What would it feel like to be the personality trapped inside the role of Fury? I don't know if what I was thinking showed on my face or what, but Tisiphone nodded then.

She cocked her head to one side. "I think you really do understand, at least to some degree, Raven." The last word came out as a whisper.

"I'd rather you didn't call me that," I said.

"And sometimes I'd rather that no one call me Fury. That name obscures the Tisiphone underneath. But often we don't have choices. I am what I am, and there's no denying it. Nor can you deny what you've become. But perhaps some good can come of that. I could never have offered 'plain old Ravirn' what I'm offering the Raven." She stepped closer still, close enough to touch, and I had no doubt about what she meant.

"Thank you, but I just can't."

"Why not?" she asked, reaching out and touching my cheek. "Am I so horrible to you?"

"No. Not at all. You are . . . beautiful. Beautiful and terrifying, like a forest on fire. I'm flattered that you find me so appealing. If my life were different, I might want to spend some time getting to know you as the woman inside the Fury. But—and I'll be honest with you because you've been honest with me—I might not. I know this will hurt you, and I'm sorry, but you have to put me high on the list of men you frighten."

"I know that," said Tisiphone, her voice rough and husky, "but I think you could overcome it with my help. No, I know you could, if you wanted it badly enough."

"Maybe. But even if that were true, I couldn't give you a yes. I'm with Cerice."

"But she won't claim you! She barely even acknowledges you have a relationship!" Anger flared in Tisiphone's eyes. "She denies you. I would never do that."

"All that may be true," I said. All that and more. Like the fact that I was out here all alone because I'd had another fight with Cerice, and on top of that I was more than a little bit worried that my lady fair was an evil genius.

"Cerice and I may be a bit of a mess right now. We may even be on the way to not being a couple anymore. But that's not decided yet. Until it is, I can't do anything but tell you no."

"And if you do break up?" asked Tisiphone.

"No. I won't play that game. For now, all my 'ifs' belong to Cerice. I'm sorry."

"Don't be. Your loyalty is one of the things I find most attractive. Damn."

She turned away, walking across the room. For a brief moment, moonlight touched her again, and I thought I saw something sparkle on her cheek. It couldn't have been a tear, could it? Not on a Fury. I wanted to go to her, to give her some comfort, but I couldn't. Not here. Not now. Not the way she wanted.

"Tisiphone?"

"Yes," she turned quickly, and this time I was sure I saw tears as she came back toward me.

"If it helps at all, turning you down is one of the harder things I've had to do."

"It doesn't help, but I thank you anyway. It's probably for the best, really. Furies don't exactly get a lot of time off. My complete lack of a love life for the last couple of hundred years speaks to that all too clearly." Her laugh was bitter and brittle, too close to the tears she'd already shed.

"Even if I did say yes," I said, "I'm poison. Too many powers want to make an end of me. Your job would probably come into conflict with any feelings you had for me before too long. Then what would you do?"

"Silly boy," she said, her tone mixing mocking and regret. "It already has."

"What?"

"I told you when I arrived that I was supposed to be on my way to meet Megaera and Alecto so that we could all have a nice little chat with Eris."

"And?" I asked.

"And when we do, she's going to tell us that the two of you found a twin to your girlfriend's webgoblin haunting

Necessity's server cluster. At that point we'll almost certainly be sent to take you to my mother."

"How do you know about the twin?"

"I never left Castle Discord," said Tisiphone. "I stayed and listened to the whole thing."

"Including the part where Eris—"

"Said you should take me as a lover. Oh yes. For that I owe her something, though I'm not yet sure whether it's kudos or curses. That conversation's a big part of why I'm here. Eris reminded me that they don't exactly mint new powers every day. The roster of possible partners for a Fury is somewhat limited, and over the years, history and bad blood have narrowed it even further. Once you had your fight with Cerice, I decided I had to at least take a chance."

"But how did you manage it?"

"Brute force is not the only tool of the hunter, not by a long shot." With those words she suddenly faded—not away, but very close.

Like a chameleon, she changed her colors to match the background. I could see her, but only by keeping my eyes fixed on her. When I blinked, she was gone. I didn't know where until I felt her breath on my face, her hands gently sliding into the hair above and behind my ears.

"I shouldn't be here," whispered a voice inches from my ear. "I came to warn you as well as to make my offer. I'll have to leave soon, and then we'll be on opposite sides again. It would be good for you to have a friend in the enemy camp, wouldn't it? Someone who could slip you information and sidetrack pursuit. Someone who could convince her sisters to go easy. All that can be yours for so little. A kiss even."

"No," I said. "I can't do that."

"Why not? Is a kiss that much to ask?" I could see her face again, or at least see where it was, by the tears tracking down her cheeks. "It's been so very long since I felt another's lips touch mine."

"It's not the kiss. That, I'd give you for free. It's the

promise such a kiss would make. If you went easy on me
for the price of a kiss, I'd owe you so much more. Surely
you see that?"

She faded back into view and sighed. "I do. Sadly, I do.
Then I'll have to find a way to deflect pursuit without even
so much hope as a kiss." She slid back and sighed. "Would
you really have given one freely if I hadn't made it a matter of bargaining?"

"I would." Moved to pity by tears on the face of a Fury,
I said, "And I will."

Stepping forward to close the distance between us once
again, I caught her shoulders in my hands and touched my
lips to hers ever so gently. They burned, not with the fire
that lived within her, but with a passion I found hard to resist. But resist I did, pulling away. She caught me in a fierce
hug.

"I—I—Damn! I don't want to let you go."

"Then don't," said a bitter female voice. "Not on my account, honey." Cerice!

"It's not what it looks like," I said, as Tisiphone released
me.

"Really? Then what *is* it?" Cerice had come halfway
down the stairs by then.

"How dare you!" Tisiphone moved toward Cerice. "You
don't deserve Ravirn."

"And you do? This time last year you were trying to kill
him."

Red light filled the room as the fires in Tisiphone's
wings and hair, banked till now, flared into brilliant life. She
flexed her hands, and the soft fingers that had so recently
stroked my cheek grew long claws hard as diamonds. If I'd
been in Cerice's shoes, I'd have been running, not walking,
back up those stairs. Instead, she advanced on Tisiphone.

"So, when you can't hunt for real, you poach?"

"I could shred you like paper," said Tisiphone, "but I
won't, for Ravirn's sake. I'd rather not have your shade
hanging between us in the future. Patience is another

hunter's virtue, and it'll be ever so much simpler to wait for you to drive him away, then pick up the pieces."

Pain flared on Cerice's face, and she swung her hand back as if to slap Tisiphone. It was the pain in her expression that did it for me. The bigger pattern finally fell into place in my mind. Somehow I managed to get between them, preempting Cerice's suicidal impulse before the blow could fall. I dragged her away from Tisiphone.

"Let me go," demanded Cerice.

"No."

"Please," said Tisiphone. "Pretty, pretty please. I promise not to hurt her . . . much."

"Cerice!" I said. "Listen to me. It wasn't what you think it was. You can believe me, or you can tell me you don't trust me. Which is it going to be? Because I can't take much more of this."

"I . . . I believe you," she said. "I'm just crazy right now. Everything in my world seems to be falling apart, and I keep taking it out on you because you're there, and you've been willing to deal with it. I'm sorry. I shouldn't have yelled at you back at Castle Discord, but it's all so hard now. What Eris said about Shara . . . was that true? Is some part of her really living inside Necessity's network?"

"Yes," I said. "And I think I know why. But I need to talk to Shara about it. Now." I let Cerice go and turned to look at Tisiphone. "How soon do you have to leave? I think you should hear this as well."

"I should never have come at all," answered Tisiphone with a sigh. "What's a few more minutes? But you'll need to hurry."

"Done." Pushing Cerice gently in front of me, I headed for the stairs. She might have agreed to believe me, but I still wanted to keep her away from Tisiphone.

As I stepped through Ahllan's front door on Cerice's heels, I found Melchior waiting just outside.

"It's about ti—" He stopped abruptly when Tisiphone appeared behind me.

"Uh—" He made vaguely concerned pointing gestures. "Do you . . ."

"Yes, I know I've got a Fury following me. She's on our side. Sort of. Maybe."

"Very decisive, Boss. I'm deeply reassured. Does she know that?"

"I do," she answered, "though *side* isn't quite the right word, and my reasons are complex. Ravirn, it's your show, but I don't have much time."

"Got it. Melchior, where's Shara? I need to talk with her."

"Here," said a quiet voice from just beyond the edge of the circle of light provided by Tisiphone's internal fires. "What do you want to talk about?"

"Persephone."

"Oh." Her shoulders sagged, and she looked both frightened and relieved. Waiting for that other shoe to drop couldn't have been easy. "Then you do know."

"Not really, but I have some guesses. Persephone set me up. When she said she wanted something from me, I assumed it would come *after* I e-mailed you out of Hades, a quid pro quo. But that wasn't it at all. It *was* e-mailing you out of Hades that she wanted. She needed to have you go out electronically, not embodied. I didn't see it till now. Very, very slick." Shara nodded glumly. I knelt and looked her in the eyes. "Why didn't you tell us what happened to you in Hades? Or for that matter, where you went after I hit send that day?"

"I—I didn't remember any of it at first. Then I started to get flashes, but they were awful, *wrong*, like they were coming from someone else's head. I remember incredible pressure to stay in Necessity's system and do her bidding, and just as much pressure to leave because I knew you'd die if I didn't come home. I felt ripped in two. Maybe I *was* ripped in two. I don't know. I'm still fuzzy on details, especially about the early stuff, what happened in Hades. Persephone did . . . things to me. I know that much. She messed around with my core programming, the bits that make me, me, a complete recompile. That's part of why it's so hard to remember; I'm not who I used to be, not entirely."

"I'll kill her," said Cerice, her voice flat and hard.

I couldn't help but remember how torn up I'd felt when I thought Melchior might die. To some of my family, our webgoblins are nothing more than convenient tools, but for Cerice and me, they're our best friends and, in some ways, our children. I understood her rage, but I didn't know what to do about it. She had every right to be mad. I certainly would have been furious in her place, but at the same time, she hadn't met Persephone. I was still trying to think of something to say when Tisiphone cut in.

"Not a good idea, girl, but that's no surprise." Her tone was sardonic, cutting.

"Did I ask you?" demanded Cerice.

"No, but you're being a fool again. While I'd encourage that on the Ravirn front—the sooner you drive him away, the happier I'll be—killing Persephone is the stupidest suggestion I've heard in a very long time. And in my profession, I get to hear a lot of stupidity. Death would put Persephone in Hades year-round, and she'd take summer with her." She paused, and a thoughtful look crossed her face. "Of course, chances are you'd just get killed in the attempt. Maybe I was too hasty. Go for it."

"Fuck you," said Cerice, but she nodded reluctantly. "Fine, I'll just have to find some other way to make her pay instead."

"There's nothing you could do to her that would hurt her any more than she's already hurting," I said, remembering my encounter with Persephone and her terrible anguish. "Her eyes *are* pain, Cerice. That pain is what gave me the key to the whole thing, actually. You looked so hurt a few moments ago that it reminded me of Persephone. Then everything just sort of fell into place." I spread my hands in a minishrug. "Well, mostly. I'm not sure about some of the details, but I'm getting there. Shara?"

She sighed. "I was kind of hoping you'd forgotten about me again."

"No such luck," I said, though I felt for her. There had been more than one occasion when I'd have killed to make powers forget about me. "Can you tell me why she didn't just send you through the network herself? Why she needed me? And more importantly, what's happening to the mweb?"

"I'm not sure," said Shara. "I have some ideas, but this isn't a spy movie or superhero comic book. It's not like she confided her evil plan to me in a burst of overconfidence. She just stuffed a bunch of new code into my OS and left it at that."

"So," I stood and started to pace, "why don't you speculate."

"I don't think she can actually touch Hades' computer, the one in his office. She's got complete freedom within the underworld, but she's not allowed any outside contact. That much I got from the little she said about the changes in my OS."

"But she IM'd me when I was going through Hades' e-mail," I protested. "Heck, she showed up when I was reading an e-mail from her. That was on his computer."

"No," said Melchior. "Actually that's not quite true. Yes, she appeared exactly at the moment you accessed an e-mail from her, but it was dated June. That means she sent it from outside the underworld. And the IM box appeared between you and the screen, not on it or even touching it. She never actually accessed the computer."

"You're right. Why didn't that strike me as odd?"

"Abject terror is kind of distracting," said Melchior. "I did wonder about it at the time, but I didn't want to draw any attention to myself, so I let it slide. Later, it seemed less important than our more immediate problems. Sorry."

"All right, so she needed someone else to physically input Shara. But why did she pick me? How did she even know I was there?" Then it hit me. "Of course. Cerberus. Kira said that Dave was Persephone's dog and that for all of them Persephone's commands came next in priority after Hades'. I didn't *break* into the underworld, Cerberus let me in. That's why he was so much more friendly the second time we visited. Persephone guessed what I was up to and ordered him to befriend me. We were set up from day one."

"Probably," agreed Shara. "Persephone's a manipulator. But I can't blame her. Not really."

"How can you say that after what she did to you?" asked Cerice. She looked horrified.

"You haven't met her," said Shara. "You haven't seen her pain. Think about it. What she did to me was bad, but it was one time, and it was out of desperation. But what Hades has done to her, brrr." Shara shivered. "When Persephone was barely a teenager, Hades kidnapped and raped her. He raped her not just once, but repeatedly. He's still doing it. Three months out of every year she has to leave her mother and go back to live with her rapist. It's been going on for thousands of years, and it's *never* going to stop. Really never. True immortality means no breaks. Ever. She can't even kill herself, because then she'd be with Hades full-time. No, I can't blame her for what she felt she had to do to me. It was wrong, and I wish it hadn't happened, but I just can't judge her."

Shara had put her finger on something that had been tickling the back of my brain as well. The goddess changed the way you saw things. I had to stop whatever she was doing to the mweb, and I had to fix whatever was wrong with Shara. The network was simply too important to allow anyone to destroy it, and while I might have busted Shara out of Hades, I clearly hadn't finished the task.

I should have hated that, hated the idea that I'd been set up, that something I'd been tricked into doing had loosed whatever was devouring the mweb and messed up Shara. But I couldn't seem to work up a good head of outrage. Maybe that was because my new ties to chaos caused me to see the mess in a different light. Or maybe it was just because Persephone had pulled off a hell of a hack, and my inner coder had to tip its hat to her. Whatever the reason, I felt more sympathy for her than anger.

"I guess I'd never thought about it like that," Cerice said to Shara, visibly deflating. "Can I at least be mad on your behalf?"

"I'd appreciate that," said Shara. "That, a stiff drink, and maybe some TLC from blue boy over there, and I'll be halfway to recovery." The latter came with a wink in Melchior's direction and some of her old Mae Westian growl.

I was glad to hear it. I hated to bring her mind back to the problems at hand, but Tisiphone was fast approaching the foot-tapping stage of impatience, and we still had some ground to cover. I turned to Tisiphone.

"Does that give you enough to work with?"

"As far as keeping my sisters off your back? Not by half. I believe you, and the case against Persephone works for me. But I don't operate independently. Necessity has final say over matters involving Fury-level action. Even in lesser matters, I'm only one vote out of three. Megaera and Alecto are not stupid. They know how I feel about you, and they're not going to believe anything I say on your behalf without solid proof. Neither will Necessity. Finding that proof needs to be job one. I'd try to get it, but I don't know when I'll next have a chance to get into the master servers. If you can find it yourself, it would sure help your case."

"Let me get this straight," I said. "You and your sisters are the security administrators for Necessity and the mweb's core architecture?"

"Yes."

"And you want me to hack into that system to do what you can't?"

"Uh-huh."

"And if I get caught? I'm guessing you won't be bailing me out."

"No. I'll probably have to kill you. If that's what Necessity decides, it's what I'll do." She closed her eyes for a moment, and her fires dimmed. "In fact, in full-on Fury mode I'll even enjoy it. Tisiphone the individual and Tisiphone the Fury are fundamentally different creatures, with fundamentally different agendas. I'm sorry." With that she opened her wings and leaped skyward.

Before she'd climbed fifty feet she brought one clawed hand around in a vicious slash, tearing a ragged hole in the stuff of reality. A moment later, after she'd passed through, it closed behind her.

"I'm sorry, too," said Shara, "about my part in all this."

"It's all right," I said. "Persephone messed around with your OS, changed who you are. Like Tisiphone said, the individual and the role aren't always in sync. Sometimes none of us has a choice." Did that include me?

I didn't know the answer to that. Not anymore. I'd made some truly crazy decisions in the rush to break Shara out of the underworld. Was that plain old Ravirn's love of a challenge? Or the Raven's trickster nature calling out for risk taking? Who was I now? And what?

CHAPTER THIRTEEN

"What now, Boss?"

"I guess we're going to have to try hacking Necessity again."

"Do you think we'll get anywhere?"

"I don't know. A lot depends on exactly what we're up against. Shara? Can you tell us anything more? About what happened to you on the way back from Hades or about the thing that wears your face?"

"Maybe. It's . . . hazy. I seem to be missing some bits."

"How could that be?" I asked. "I thought webgoblins had perfect memories."

"Oh shit," said Melchior. "Why didn't I see that before?"

"What?"

"The e-mail version of Shara that we sent from Hades was 2.29 terabytes."

"And?" I asked.

"The one that we received was only 2.21."

"So," I said, "something like eighty gigabytes of Shara went missing on the way home. How much virus do you think we could put into eighty gigabytes?"

That was a *lot* of memory. I didn't like the idea much at all, though it would certainly explain a supervirus in Necessity's core systems.

Apparently, neither did Cerice. "Last year, a twenty-eight-kilobyte worm almost took down the whole internet in my Harvard's DecLocus. That's less than one-two-millionth of the size."

"Hell," I said. "Scorched Earth was only a few dozen meg, and that's the program I crashed the mweb with. Sure it was temporary, but . . ."

"I think it's worse than that," Shara said very quietly. "The more I think about it, the more I think I must have copied myself into Necessity's system so that I could fulfill both the commands of Persephone and the needs of friendship. I've got no way to prove it, but it would explain why I feel like I've been split in two, like half of me, of my soul, is elsewhere. I'm guessing that's where these weird flashes of memory are coming from. Maybe it's just lingering aftereffects of being dead but . . ."

"No," said Melchior. "I think you're right. That gorgon wasn't just a construct, not even eighty gigs' worth. It had real presence and awareness. I told Ravirn that something about it seemed both strange and familiar and that it gave me the deep down creeps. That's why; because it was Shara and not-Shara at the same time."

"Tell me that you're not suggesting that an evil clone of Shara is now in control of security for the servers that run the mweb," said Cerice.

"Well," said Melchior, " 'evil clone' sounds pretty trite when you're talking about souls and software instead of flesh and blood. But I think it's also mighty close to the truth."

I sighed. "I guess we'd better have another go at Necessity's security. We need to rescue Shara again. And this time, we have to get it right." I looked at her. "What do you suppose the chances are that your duplicate will welcome us with open arms?"

"Like I said, I can't remember much. But if Persephone

programmed this thing in such a way that it's willing to destroy the whole damn mweb, what do you think the chances are that it'll blink at killing one of us?"

"That's about what I figured. So what do we do first?"

"Clear out of this DecLocus." Melchior made a loop with his finger to include all of our surroundings. "No mweb here. Garbage Faerie is completely cut off. I just wish Ahllan had been here. She'd be a real help, and I'm worried about her."

"There's no help for that," I said with a sigh. "Shara and the mweb come first. I guess that means it's faerie ring time."

"Where to?" asked Cerice.

"I guess we just jump around until we hit a DecLocus that's still on the net."

"That might not work out so well," said Shara.

"I know I'm going to hate the answer," I said. "But why do you say that?"

"What happens if you and Melchior are jacked in, and then the world you're working from gets cut off?"

I thought about that for a moment, about the possibility of the all-important psychic link back to my body getting severed. "Bad things. Very bad. Melchior might survive as a sort of self-aware subroutine on the server, but probably not."

"And you'd be dead," said Cerice.

"Yeah. Anybody got any bright ideas?" I asked. Nobody spoke up. "I was afraid of that, because the only one I've got is really stupid and unnecessarily dangerous."

I wondered again about how much of my current thinking was Raven and how much Ravirn. I was starting to picture the Raven part of me as an invisible entity eternally hovering overhead, a sort of feathery sword of Damocles.

"So," said Melchior after a while, "are you going to tell us what this idea is?"

"First let me make a last call for other plans," I said. "Anyone? Nope? Nothing? OK. The mweb servers are located within the Temple of Fate at the foot of Olympus.

They've got an actual hardwired link from there to wherever it is Necessity keeps her network. It doesn't matter what happens to the world resource locator forks. The temple computers can't be taken off-line, not with anything short of dynamite."

"You want us to sneak into the *Temple of Fate*?" demanded Melchior. "Atropos probably has wanted posters with our faces on them plastered on the front doors. That's crazy!"

"Yes. It is. Completely. But I'm not quite there yet. What I'm thinking is that Cerice can go to the temple. She's still in good standing."

"Sort of," said Cerice. "It's not like Clotho doesn't know about our relationship. Your thread might have been erased, but mine is still firmly in the hands of Fate. She can look at it any time she wants and see exactly what I've been doing."

"So don't act suspicious," I said.

"Oh, that's very helpful." She sighed. "But I guess I'm with Mel here—no better idea. So I casually saunter into one of the most heavily guarded computing centers in existence. Then what?"

"Then you plug Shara in and create a virtual network as a back door. We log onto that from one of the computers on Olympus proper, and we're in."

"Wow." Melchior shook his head. "That's so stupid it just might work. Whose computer were you thinking of using, Zeus's?" He chuckled. Then smiled. Then, when I didn't smile along with him, he started frowning. "You are, aren't you?"

"Come on," I said. "We don't have a lot of choice. All of the wireless access on Olympus is controlled directly by Athena, and her security is nearly as nasty as Necessity's. I'd really rather not add another layer of killer hacking to the job. Besides, how bad could it be? We've at least been in Zeus's office, back when we fixed his little browser problem. He never uses that computer for anything but downloading porn anyway. He'll never notice."

"Sure, why not?" Melchior sighed. "Besides, Eris suggested you get the big guy pissed off at you anyway, so you could finish collecting the set of annoyed pole powers. Man, when you become a force for chaos, you really become a force for chaos. Just for the record, I officially hate this plan."

"But I'm not hearing the word *veto*."

"No," he said. "You're not, because I really don't have a better idea. Besides, when you compare the possible consequences of invading Zeus's personal space with the risks inherent to hacking Necessity, it's really hard to work up too much of a lather over the former. He's only going to *kill* us. Whereas she . . ." Melchior mimed an eagle pecking at my liver.

"Yeah, thanks, Mel. That one's starting to get a little old. We'll just have to make sure we don't get caught."

"Could somebody just shoot me and save all the suspense?" said Shara. "Hades is no fun, but hey, at least I know my way around now."

"Which reminds me of something I've been worrying about on that front," I said.

"Oh goody," said Shara. "Do I want to know about this?"

"Probably not, but it's only fair that I pay you back for the bit about being cut off from the mweb midhack. Also, I think it's something you need to be aware of."

"All right, hit me."

"If your soul really is split between you and the Shara in the machine, what happens if one of you dies?"

Panic flitted across her face for a second. Then she steadied down. "You're right. I didn't want to know that. Why do you bring it up?"

"Because I want all of us to be very careful about how we deal with the version of you that's running around outside your body."

"Got it." Shara gave a crazed little laugh. "Try not to kill myself when I see me, even if I'm not really me but a twisted monster instead. And here I thought this evil clone stuff would just make for a great way to double-date. You know, much as I hate to say it, dead had its pluses, eternal peace high on the list." She shook her head. "Shall we get this disaster going?"

"Probably. If you'll all just join me in the faerie ring, I'll get us moving in the right direction." Urgh, I was becoming blasé about faerie rings. Not a good sign.

Once more I had the experience of being simultaneously in thousands of different places all at once. This go-round I had a brief moment to wonder how that experience of space related to my internal time. If you experience a tenth of a second spent in ten thousand different places all at once, have you actually burned a thousand seconds of your life?

Then we arrived, and I had more pressing matters to attend to. Our point of entry was a circle of dancing satyrs in a small glade. The sky was overcast, and it was cold and damp. With Persephone in Hades, winter held sway on the slopes of the mountain. Well, The Mountain really. The original Olympus was the first island in the great sea of chaos, where the Titans founded their dynasty. All other mountains everywhere are just reflections of Olympus, or at least that's the legend. The truth? Who knows? Gods lie all the time, and there was no one else around to bear witness.

The satyrs broke their circle in the instant after we appeared, wandering off to chase nymphs and whatnot. There are no permanent rings on Olympus. Zeus does not allow it. It's part of a long list of things he doesn't allow. Guns, for example. Doesn't like the noise, he says. Too much like thunder, and thunder "belongs to Zeus alone." I took a moment to make sure my shoulder holster was fully concealed, and Cerice tucked her Beretta deep down in the bottom of her bag. Then it was time to part. Cerice was going down, and I was going up. Trails led in both directions.

"Be careful," I said.

"You too." She gave me a quick kiss.

I just squeezed her tight for a moment, then let her go and started climbing.

"Are you ever going to get it together?" asked Melchior, once we'd gotten out of sight of the others.

"What do you mean?"

"You know exactly what I mean."

"I suppose that I do," I replied. "But honestly, I don't know. I think that's more up to Cerice than me."

He sighed. "That's a dodge. But I won't argue with you." We walked a little farther. "Does Tisiphone really have a thing for you?"

"She says so, and it sure seems like it. But what do I know about Furies?"

He gave me a long, appraising look, then shook his head. "Huh."

"What's that supposed to mean?" I asked, but he didn't answer in the few remaining moments before our path disgorged itself onto a broader road and we reached the gateway to the great Palace of Olympus. I tucked him into the bag as I looked it all over once more.

It was a big, sprawling place on the very top of the mountain, all white marble and fluted pillars, a stereotype of ancient Greece on a grand scale. Like someone had started with the Parthenon and just kept adding matching rooms. Once upon a time it had been painted in a wide variety of bright colors, just like the Greek temples in the world below. But first Rome conquered Greece, then it fell in turn to the barbarians who had ushered in the dark ages, at which point people stopped paying attention to the old temples, and the paint faded away.

I missed all that, of course, not yet having been born, but I hear stories. The big guy was pretty depressed about the rise of Christianity. Oh, he hadn't been all that happy about Rome devouring Greece either, but that was mitigated somewhat by the Roman adoption of the Greek pantheon. Sure they called him Jupiter instead of Zeus, but at least they kept the sacrifices coming.

I'm told that when Constantine moved the capital and declared Rome a Christian Nation, Zeus just about had a stroke. Who can blame him? It wasn't until the Renaissance, with its focus on rediscovering the classics, that he came out of his funk. By then all of Greece's temples and statues were bleached ice white, and the revivalists, not knowing any better, did everything up the same way. That's when Zeus had the paint scrubbed off everything on Olympus, said he liked it better that way anyway. Pathetic, really.

The main gate was a wide-open doorway in the front of a little classical temple that straddled the road. I was just about to head on through when a large figure in gray stepped between me and the door. Did I say large? Cancel that. Huge.

"Where do you think yer goin'?" boomed a voice from somewhere in the vicinity of the figure's head.

I looked up, way up. Picture a fat rent-a-cop, complete with silly cap and riding boots. Inflate him to three times normal size. Give him mirror shades. Mirror *shade*, really, a single bright reflector covering a single eye centered in an enormous sloping forehead. You get the basic picture. I was face-to-belt-buckle with a cyclops, or perhaps *cycops* would be a better term.

This one was packing heat rather than the more traditional club, a revolver the size of a small cannon. One of his beefy hands lay none-too-subtly on the grip of the pistol. I was frankly surprised, since guns were officially banned from the premises.

"I asked you a question, boy!" bellowed the cyclops. "I expect an answer."

I pointed toward the door behind him. "Through there, isn't it obvious?" I hadn't had many dealings with the various members of the cyclops family over the years, but I recognized the attitude this one was sporting. I knew that if I started backing down, he'd run me right over.

"And I suppose you just expect me to let you by?"

"I do indeed."

"Not gonna happen. Not without you do some explainin' about who you are and what's your business."

"Fair enough. I was once a child of House Lachesis, the lady who measures out the length of your life. You may have heard of her, sister of the one who snips?" I made clipping motions.

He swallowed hard but came back quickly. "I note youse is speakin' in the past tense there. Whose House do you belong to now?"

"My own, House Raven. At least that's what Clotho called me when she named me a power. If you need a reference for that, I suggest you call Tisiphone. She can vouch for my status."

"Tisiphone, the Fury?" Sweat was beading up along the line where his hat touched his forehead. One fat drop rolled down from temple to jawbone.

"No, Tisiphone, the house cat. Of course Tisiphone, the Fury. What are you? Some kind of moron? Now, if you don't mind, I've got business within." I moved to go around him, but he sidestepped to block my passage. "You're making me both late and angry. If I were you, I wouldn't want to do either."

"Sorry, sir." The cyclops's voice took on a sort of oily respect. "It sounds like you're legit, but I still can't let you through looking like that."

"Huh?" I had no idea what he was talking about now.

"Dress code. New orders from Zeus hisself. Nobody gets in without they go classical." He jerked a fat thumb at a marble statue of a Greek shepherd boy wearing the traditional white, one-shouldered tunic. Beside it was a shepherdess wearing the matching loose dress.

"You've got to be kidding," I said.

"Nope, that's official O-lym-pi-an policy." He sounded out each syllable.

"And what you're wearing fits into that how?"

"Which side of the door am I on?" he asked.

"And the pistol? Last time I stopped by, carrying that

would have gotten you a date with Miss Lightning. ZOT!
Instant charcoal briquette."

"It's not technically a gun," he said. "It's an updated Gyrojet, fires a small rocket rather than a bullet. Subsonic, so
there's no bang, at least at first. It keeps the old man happy."

I raised an eyebrow. "Sounds like you're splitting hairs."

"Not me, buddy. That one's straight from Athena. You
can tell her that if you want, but ever since she jumped out
of Zeus's noggin, she's been a little funny about that particular metaphor. Anyway, I don't make the rules, I just en-
force 'em. That means that out here on duty, I have to wear
this." He tapped a finger on his chest beside the copper
badge inscribed with a lightning bolt. "And pack the heat
as official Olympian external security. Inside, it's a loincloth and club, 'cause that's the way we always gets described in the litera-toor. Given my druthers, I'd let you in
as is, but it ain't happenin'. So, either you put on a tunic,
you head back the way you came, or we have to work this
out the hard way."

He did not look happy at the prospect, but neither did he
look like he'd back down. So I nodded. Starting a fight
with the gate guard was not going to help me sneak into
Zeus's office.

"I don't suppose you've got a loaner tunic?"

The cyclops visibly relaxed. "That we do. Tons of 'em."
He gestured for me to follow him into the temple and nodded at a curtained-off alcove in one corner. "In the changing area, every size you could want. Even got one for blue
boy there." He jabbed a finger at Melchior, who had been
keeping a very low profile.

"Not really," said the webgoblin.

The cyclops just nodded.

A few minutes later we stepped out, ready to face the
world. Well, not really. In Fate's family everyone is expected to wear the garb of a sixteenth-century courtier at
formal functions. I'd always felt a little self-conscious in
tights, but I'd grown up with them. Turns out I hadn't really
understood what self-conscious meant. Now I did.

The tunics were one size fits all. Not in the classic there-was-one-size-and-everyone-wore-it-as-best-they-could way. No, this used magic. You put it on and it adjusted itself to your size. And whoever had decided what constituted "your size" had a very different idea about hemlines than I did. It covered the appropriate bits, but only just. Bending over, a stiff breeze, or, well, a stiff something else, would all endanger my modesty in a serious way. Also, the thing was more than a little on the sheer side. Again, I was technically covered, but only just. I found myself with a powerful desire to keep my bag firmly in front of me, or I would have if I'd been allowed to keep it. Instead, I had a borrowed leather wallet that slung over a shoulder but didn't hang low enough to be of any use.

"Damn rent-a-clops," said Melchior, tugging at his own hem as we exited the back door of the temple into Olympus proper. "This thing makes me feel naked."

"Mel, you don't *wear* clothes."

"Yeah, but that's different. Being naked and feeling that way are not the same thing at all. One's natural, the other is *exposed*. The sandals suck, too."

I had to agree with him. The pair of loosely foot-shaped pieces of leather held on by a bondage fetishist's dream of a strapping system might provide some protection for the sole of the foot, but they were shit for traction. This was a problem, since the same idiot responsible for the rest of the décor had decreed the streets be made of gleaming slabs of polished white marble. Pretty? Yes. Practical? Not so much. I missed my boots and leathers, especially with the winter cold.

The shoes meant that most of my attention during our hike up to the top of the mountain and the biggest temple of them all stayed on my feet and not on the scenery. But hey, there's only so much you can say about an architectural monoculture done up in stark white stone. It gets old fast, and I was glad when we finished our trip.

Another rent-a-clops stood on duty just outside the main door, this time wearing the requisite loincloth and carrying a club, and looking damned cold. He did, however, have a little white earpiece with a wire leading back over his shoulder and down to a suspicious-looking bulge under the back flap of his loincloth. When he gave me a fish eye but waved me inside anyway, I figured that the news from the front gate must have whispered itself in his ear. That put me inside the building, but only as far as the audience hall. I figured I'd have to work a lot harder for Zeus's actual office, even if he never did go in there except for *affairs* of state.

The interior architecture was almost, though not quite, as monotonous as the exterior. There was lots more white marble, enough to make the place look like the world's biggest and most expensive executive restroom. Even the cubicles, installed to house Zeus's ever-growing support staff and tucked in neat rows behind the support pillars, were white marble. I gave them a wide berth as I made my way through the front room and toward the back and the stairs. Zeus's office is a little miniature temple in the round, sitting like a cupola on the roof of the main temple. Through some magic of Zeus's, it's invisible from street level. An esthetic blessing, that—otherwise, it would look like some sort of growth.

When I'd been here last, I'd had time to marvel at the views, since it's quite literally situated at the top of the world. I'd also wondered briefly about the fact that it was completely open to the elements and yet none of the papers on the desk ever went blowing around and it was a perfect balmy seventy-four degrees. But hey, what's the fun of being a weather god if you can't dick with local conditions in your favor?

I was still trying to figure out how I'd talk my way past the secretary and any other security when I stepped through the arch into the outer office. A big square room with no windows, it held a desk—white marble, what else—several really uncomfortable-looking chairs—same again—a stock of out-of-date copies of *Modern Mythos Magazine*—motto "All the Godsip fit to print"—and not much else besides the locked door leading to the spiral stairs and the big guy's office.

Now, Zeus tends to hire the dim and curvy for receptionist duty—available in large quantities from the ranks of Olympus's nymphs—but having one abandon her post just when I needed a break seemed a little too good to be true. It was at this point that I decided that either Tyche—Dame Fortune herself—was smiling on me from her own office, just down the hill a bit—or I was being set up again. Being of a suspicious nature, I figured it was probably the latter, but I really needed to have another crack at Necessity's network, so I decided to pretend I believed I could have luck that good.

Taking one last look around to make sure I really was all alone, I slipped over to the desk and reached underneath to hit the door release. With a gentle click, the lock opened, and I was on my way upstairs. I'd gotten around one and a half loops of the stair when a third possibility suggested itself to me rather forcefully. Not only was the secretary not missing, but the big guy himself was in as well, and dictation wasn't on the menu.

There's something about rhythmic thumping and moans of "Oh Zeusy, give it to me," that really doesn't leave a lot to the imagination. *That* was a serious problem. While I might be able to talk a subordinate around to the idea that I was just a repair guy on a call, the ostensible caller was not going to buy it.

"Now what?" whispered Melchior.

"Why don't you slip up there and see if there's any chance they'll be done soon, or if we might be able to use the computer while they're distracted?"

"Why don't you do it?"

I raised an eyebrow and held my hands up in a comparison of our relative sizes and stealthiness. Since Melchior isn't much bigger than a cat, and he's a whole lot smarter, he had to agree. With a disgruntled snort, he slid out of sight upward. After a very brief interval, he returned, shaking his head.

"Not a chance. The chaise is pulled up right in front of the computer, and they appear to be playing monkey-see monkey-do with streaming video from some site devoted to the better understanding of human fluid exchange. So, what's Plan B?"

I shrugged. "I guess we'll have to find another computer. Once we get out of here, we'd better check in with Cerice and see how things are going on her end."

Melchior nodded, and as soon as we'd found a quiet alleyway, he opened a VOMP line. I wasn't thrilled about making even that much connection to the local wireless, not with Athena running the network security for Olympus. But VOMP is low bandwidth, and I'd be just one caller among many. Everyone on Olympus uses the system these days. It's become the standard for the whole great sprawl of our contemporary pantheon. That's why I'd set Kira up with a VOMP phone. Of course, I'd only remain below the radar as long as I kept my usage at a reasonable level. If I tried to open the multiple channels I'd need to send myself into the system on a hacking jaunt, I'd light up Athena's bandwidth monitors like Apollo's chariot rolling into a dark room.

When Cerice picked up the line, I gave her a quick rundown of what had happened and asked how she was doing.

"We're screwed," she answered, calmly and very finally.

"Would you care to elaborate on that?" I asked.

"I got bored with waiting for you and jacked in for a quick look-see myself."

No surprise there. Cerice is every bit as much of a hacker and cracker as I am, and just as likely to succumb to the temptation to explore a bit. "And?"

"You remember that black box we found when we went looking for Shara?"

"The one that sent her off to souladmin@necessity . . . ? Of course I remember it. Who could forget a dot-dot-dot mweb address? What about it?"

"It's gone."

"Gone? It can't be gone. It was part of the hardware architecture."

"It's gone, and there aren't any others either. Shara told me where to find the one that you and Eris cracked. It's gone, too. There are no links from the mweb's core architecture to Necessity's system anymore. We're locked out."

CHAPTER FOURTEEN

"Locked out," I repeated. Not a witty response, I admit, but I was not feeling up to witty. "Is there anything at all where the black box used to sit?"

"Yes. Three tiny pips, like pomegranate seeds, only in Shara purple."

"Did you try to do anything with them?" I asked.

"No," said Cerice, and I could practically hear her rolling her eyes, "I just stared at them blankly. Of course I took a crack at them. As near as I can tell they're some sort of biometric identification system."

"Like an iris scanner?"

"More like a virtual DNA chip, if I had to make a guess, but I really can't tell. It wouldn't respond to anything I tried, and unless you happen to have a few strands of Persephone's hair or some nail parings that you can somehow link to your anima and carry into the mweb, I don't think you'll be able to do much more."

I nodded. I'm better at finding flaws in a system than Cerice is, but she was probably right on this. Magical signatures are virtually impossible to forge. That's one place where the mweb and its more mundane human analogues differ wildly. When I'm jacked in, I'm not just some kind of electronic avatar. My soul is literally within the machine, and my magical DNA becomes a part of every significant work of magic I do either there or in the real world. It was likely that only a jacked-in Persephone herself could open the lock in question.

"Ravirn?" asked Cerice. "Are you still there? What are we going to do?"

"I don't know. I think we're going to have to talk to Persephone."

Melchior cleared his throat. "You do remember that she's in Hades at the moment? If it's all the same to you, I'd rather not go back for another visit."

"I'm with you there, Melchior. But I'm not willing to just stand by and let Shara be ruined or the mweb destroyed." I laughed a rueful little laugh. "Especially since I'm likely to take the blame for the latter. Somehow I don't think that telling Necessity it was all an accident, and I didn't *intend* to release a doomsday virus into her network is going to cut it as a defense."

"Really?" said Melchior. "You don't say." Then he sighed. "So, does that mean you have a plan?"

"Of course not, though I do have one or two ideas. Why don't we all get back together and find someplace where we can think things through without worrying so much about the local security forces?"

"Sounds good," said Cerice, "I know just the place. Meet me back where we came in."

"Done," I said, signaling Melchior to hang up.

Getting back to the front gate and out of our shepherd boy clothes didn't take much effort. Neither did the hike back to our entry point. We were just about there when Melchior binged.

"Incoming . . ." He paused. "Now, that's just plain weird."

"What?" I asked.

He held up a hand. "Hang on, I'm still figuring it out. It's like a Vtp link, but not quite. Wait, I think I've got i—" Foggy multicolored light poured from his eyes and mouth, forming a rough sphere. It looked something like a smoke bomb going off at an expensive rave, one of the ones with a light show optimized for a chemically enhanced audience.

A bright fiery point appeared at the center of the globe, expanding to show a view of Tisiphone's face surrounded by the ever-changing colors of the Primal Chaos. Melchior was right, it looked something like a visual transfer protocol link, but not quite. If the background was anything to go by, I didn't think there were any computers involved.

"How are you doing that?" I asked, absolutely fascinated by the mechanics of the thing.

Tisiphone grimaced. "That's not important right now."

"But—" I began.

"Later, if you have a later, and you're still interested, I'll explain it. In the meantime, I don't have very long to talk, and there are things you need to know."

"Every time somebody says something like that to me, they follow it up with bad news. I don't suppose you're planning on breaking the pattern?"

She snorted. "Mother's gone off-line."

"Do you mean Necessity can't be reached? Or that the mweb's gone completely?"

"The former. We can't reach her, and all the portals leading into her domain have been sealed."

I thought about that for second, and about what I'd recently learned about the way the whole system ran. "Doesn't that have the effect of taking out the mweb, too?"

"No. The mweb servers at the Temple of Fate are completely capable of running the show for quite a while without input from Necessity. She normally only interferes when something goes seriously wrong or when it's time for an upgrade."

"So, maybe this is a good thing. If there's no contact between Shara's doppelganger and the mweb servers, things should at least stop getting worse."

"I wish that were the case," said Tisiphone, her voice mournful. "It might make me feel a little better about getting cut off from Mother. But the seals are only closed one way. Mweb management orders are still coming out. We can't read them now—they've been encrypted—but the servers are continuing to erase node information."

"Shit."

"There's more, and worse, at least from your point of view."

"Why am I not surprised?"

"Alecto and Megaera and I have tried everything we can think of to get through to Mother, but nothing works. We can't even get there in person, and until now, none of us thought there was *anywhere* we couldn't go."

I hadn't thought so either, and I suspected it wasn't going over at all well. "How are they taking it?"

"They're furious, if you'll pardon the expression. And they're looking for someone to punish."

I was pretty sure I could see where this was going. "Let me guess the next part. That someone is me."

"Uh-huh. We lost contact with Mother while we were talking to Discord about you and Shara."

"I don't suppose she did anything to help my case."

"She was too busy being impressed by your ability to remove Necessity from the equation."

"Remind me to do her a favor in return sometime." I rubbed my forehead. It didn't do anything for the headache I'd suddenly acquired. "So, are you and your sisters on your way to kill me now?"

"No, we have a stop to make first."

"Where?"

"I was outvoted, two to one."

"Are you going to tell me about it? Or do I have to guess?"

"We're not comfortable with autonomy," said Tisiphone. "We're used to working with orders."

I squeezed the bridge of my nose. "And?"

"And we're temporarily placing ourselves under the

authority of the Fates. Just for the duration of the emergency. We're taking them the evidence against you now."

I didn't know what to say to that. As it turned out, I didn't get the chance to think about it. At just that moment a great crashing arose in the forest upslope, accompanied by a deep, hooting sound. The call of a hunting owl, symbol of Athena, Goddess of Wisdom and chief of Olympian security.

Only then did it occur to me to wonder how much bandwidth Tisiphone's novel form of communication required, and whether it would trigger Athena's security.

"Shit. Gotta go, Tisiphone. Bye."

I scooped Melchior up and took off down the hill. For a few seconds longer the strange foggy light kept spilling from his eyes and mouth, then I heard a whispered "Goodbye," and it tapered off.

"That was the weirdest thing," Melchior said after a moment. "She was doing something really strange to the actual mweb carrier wave, like she was messing around with the energy source to create some kind of virtual transmission system, sending binary by pulsing the power flow."

"Really?"

That was absolutely fascinating, and it made sense. The mweb is powered off taps into the Primal Chaos, so that jibed with Tisiphone's background during the conversation. It was something I'd have to think about later, when I had fewer problems. Just then I heard a loud hiss from behind me, like an angry snake, a fast-moving angry snake, *very* fast. Before I even had time to move, whatever it was rocketed past my head, the noise rising to a screeching wail as it did so. An instant later it ended in a very final sort of *thump* as a good-sized hole appeared in a sapling ahead of me and to the right.

"What the hell was that?" I asked, picking up the pace.

"Gyrojet rocket," said Melchior, in that abstracted tone he uses when he's accessing online information. "A big one. Judging by the hole it made, maybe twenty millimeters."

"Damn rent-a-clops. They're—"

I heard a second hiss. A third. I threw myself to the ground as brown leaves and bits of branch rained down to the tune of a whole fucking snake party. I scuttled for the protection of a fallen log. Somewhere along the way I banged my right knee, the bad one, on a rock or something. The world went all red and runny around the edges, and I screamed. I didn't faint, but I sure as hell wanted to.

"I think we hit 'im!" bellowed a rough voice from somewhere uphill.

More hisses and whines. That was the really surreal thing. People were shooting at me, but the Gyrojet rounds were so quiet except when they hit something really solid that I could still hear my pursuers. The owl hooted again, this time from right overhead. I looked up and saw gray wings circling.

"Down there!" called another cyclops.

The heavy rocket-propelled slugs started hitting more consistently in my vicinity. Several hit my log with dull thuds. One of those sent up a shower of splinters, some of which embedded themselves in my cheek and the back of the hand I'd used to shade my eyes. The clops were getting closer fast, and I was pinned down.

"Mel, see if you can't do something about my leg."

He nodded and whistled a short spell, shaping his hand into a gun. The claw of his index finger elongated into a hypodermic needle, and he jabbed it into the side of my neck.

"Better Living Through Chemistry," he said, naming a spell that involved a whole lot of morphine, "but lower dosage."

It would take a few minutes for maximum effect, but I fancied I could already feel it starting, a cool soothing flow running through my veins.

"Thanks."

That addressed one of my problems. Unfortunately, it was the least of them. More slugs hammered into the log and the ground around me, throwing up puffs of dirt and more splinters. I couldn't even raise my head safely, much less leave the shelter of the log. If I didn't do something quick, the clops would have me.

Come on, think, Ravirn! I heard the rustle of wings and saw black feathers out of the corner of my eye. I rolled onto my back, drawing my .45 by sheer reflex and scanning the sky. Nothing. The owl had risen so it was barely a dot. I let out a little sigh of relief. I didn't want to take a shot at Athena's owl. Hell, I didn't want to take a shot anywhere on Olympus, but I couldn't very well let it kill me either.

"We've got him now!" yelled one of the clops. He was practically on top of me.

"I don't think so," responded a dusty contralto from downslope. Cerice!

The words were followed by what sounded like a series of bombs going off, fifteen of them in rapid succession. It took me a moment to realize it was the firing of Cerice's Beretta, the whole damn clip. After the eerie quiet of the rocket bullets, and in light of our proximity to the great irritable sky-father, it seemed insanely loud.

The steady stream of hissing wails cut off like someone had flipped a switch, emphasizing the thunder of Cerice's pistol even more. For a long moment perfect silence held the forest in its grip. Then the sound of big bodies taking cover broke the spell.

"Come on!" yelled Cerice, "I'll keep you covered." She followed that with a couple of more shots for emphasis, having apparently reloaded.

I didn't need a second invitation. With my left hand, I levered myself onto my feet. My right was busy with my pistol. My knee still hurt, though a bit less thanks to the morphine. Something big passed between me and the sun, and I glanced up to see whether the owl had decided to attack. It was gone. In its place great fingers of cloud had come streaming in from the direction of the palace. Lightning danced along the edges of the front. I hobbled faster.

"Oh shit," said a clopsian voice. "That's done it."

The hiss of rocket-propelled slugs started up once

again. The sounds of advancing clops did not. Since I wanted to keep it that way, I fired a couple of rounds up-slope, aiming high since the clops hadn't really done anything to me.

"Maybe the gun isn't such a good idea," said Melchior, jerking his thumb skyward.

"Tell it to Cerice. She's the one who started it."

"You're very welcome," she said, as I reached the place she was waiting for me. "I—"

A great hammer of thunder drowned out whatever she was trying to say. She shook her head and caught my arm, pulling it over her shoulder. She started half-dragging, half-carrying me off at an angle to my earlier path. A child of Fate, she could as easily have lifted me in her arms but apparently chose to spare my dignity.

"—ome on!" she yelled. "Shara's holding the gate open. But we don't have much time. The wrath of Zeus is going to land on us any minute."

Thunder rolled steadily now, sometimes quieter, sometimes louder. It mostly drowned the screeching hisses of the Gyrojets, though occasional explosions of dirt or falling bits of tree served as a reminder that the clops had not yet given up.

"Thank you," I said contritely. "I didn't mean to sound ungrateful about the rescue. Your timing was perfect. I was just surprised that you didn't think about the consequences." I pointed skyward.

"Who says I didn't?"

"Huh? I don't get it."

She smiled a sad smile, but didn't slow down, pulling me along as she spoke. "I guess I deserve that with the way I've been treating you lately. I'm truly sorry about that. I know I've been a royal bitch, and you've been unreasonably patient with me. We need to talk about that just as soon we have a safe moment. In the meantime, suffice it to say that I'm not going to let a bunch of goons pump *my* beau full of holes, not even if stopping it means I have to spit in the teeth of Zeus himself."

A gigantic lightning bolt ripped a tree into shreds behind us, sending splinters flying and a column of smoke climbing up toward the clouds. It was no longer possible to tell whether the clops were still shooting because a tearing wind struck now, mimicking the leaf-shredding effects of the rockets and turning the smoke column into a long gray banner.

"You might want to tone down the 'defying the gods' stuff," squeaked Melchior, from the place he had taken in my bag.

"I don't think it would matter," shouted Cerice. "Besides, I meant every word. This one's *mine*." She squeezed my arm. "Or at least, I'm his if he'll still have me." Then she laughed, the first real laugh I'd heard from her in a long time. "Anyway, I planned for the storm. It's keeping the rest of the pursuit down nicely."

"Great!" said Melchior. "They're *both* crazy. Who knew Ravirn-style nuttery was communicable?"

Just then we broke through into a little clearing. Waiting at the center stood Shara, one foot firmly within the light column of an open gate spell. She grinned in obvious relief when she saw us and gestured for us to hurry.

I was still trying to process Cerice's last statement when we reached the gate. "Does that mean you've made some sort of decision about where we stand?"

"You could say that," said Cerice with a smile. She stepped into the light and pulled me in after, planting a firm kiss on my lips. It was a sweet kiss, and as she pulled back I felt hair on the back of my neck stand on end. "I lo—"

The universe imploded to the accompaniment of a pulse of bone-crushing sound and a blinding flare of white light. Lightning, with the thunder coming simultaneously because the strike was right on top of us. I felt searing pain followed by a sensation of falling that went on for far too long as colors flashed wildly in the darkness around me. It felt as if someone had pulled Olympus out from under me, leaving behind a hole into the chaos that holds the worlds.

At first I felt nothing but terror at the idea of being lost in the place between here and there, but that pitch of fear can't be sustained for long. I began to have room for other emotions. Curiosity about where I was and what was happening to me. Disappointment that I might never know for certain what Cerice had been about to say. Even a tiny stab of guilty relief for the same thing.

I still cared deeply for Cerice, but I was no longer entirely certain that she was the only woman in the world for me. An awful lot of bad blood had fallen between us since I'd returned Shara to her, and nothing could ever completely clear that away. And there was Tisiphone. I certainly wasn't in love with her, not yet at any rate. But seeing her vulnerability and knowing how she felt about me had really moved me, and I didn't know what that might mean for Cerice and me. Why did relationships have to be so complicated? The roiling colors of chaos held no answer.

I don't know how long my interlude there in one of the borderlands of chaos lasted. Time does not run the same in the place between worlds. But I can pinpoint the moment it ended, when I crossed from falling through nowhere to falling into somewhere, and fall I did, for we appeared well above the level of the ground.

It was a matter of blinks. Eyes open on chaos. Blink. Eyes open on the manicured grounds of a huge garden or arboretum. I had an instant to register flowering trees and a great cluster of roses in full bloom, and for my brain to reassert the familiar and comforting ideas of up and down, sky and earth. Then up and down noticed me. It was not a long fall, no more than ten or fifteen feet, and it ended gently enough, though the spirea I crushed might have different ideas about that.

Still, I was more than a little stunned, and I lay for several long seconds staring up into the deep blue sky. My contemplation was interrupted by my sidekick swearing like a harpy. Sitting up and looking around, I quickly discovered why. Something, either the lightning striking the gate or the imbalances in the mweb, had set the normal rules of locus transfer protocols awry. Rather than depositing us all together, the gate had spat us out in a loose line at some distance from each other.

Where I had landed on the relatively benign spirea, Melchior had come down square in the roses. Shara, who I also located by her swearing, had apparently landed in an ornamental pond just visible beyond them. At least that's what I inferred from the fact that she was standing next to it, dripping wet and covered with duckweed. Cerice was not immediately visible, and that worried me. But the fact that three of us had arrived relatively intact, and that the pond backed against a thick privet hedge suggested that she was probably merely out of sight rather than out of this world.

Getting to my feet required a little effort since my knee still hurt, though not nearly as badly as it had before we'd taken our long fall through chaos. Once I was up, I collected Melchior from the roses, then headed for Shara and the hedge, limping only slightly. I'd barely gotten there when I heard a very muzzy-sounding Cerice on the other side.

"Wher'd ev'ybody go?"

"Over here!" cried Shara. "Are you all right?"

"M're 'r less," answered Cerice. "I landed pr'ty hard, and . . . Oh hell." A *thunk, thunk, thunk* sound like knuckles rapping on glass came through the greenery. " 'M in the hedge maze, aren't I?" Cerice was starting to sound more coherent.

"I'm afraid so," said Shara.

"Damn, any idea what the current chip model is?"

"No," Shara answered, "but I can try to find out."

"Don't, I'd rather not announce our arrival just yet."

"What's going on?" I asked. "Chips? *Thunk?*"

"If you were looking down on the maze from above, you'd see what looks like a giant computer chip in green and gold. The gaps between the privet are floored with heavy glass with marigolds underneath. It's supposed to represent the latest in processor technology. So, with the way computers are advancing, the maze is constantly being updated. It's almost never the same from visit to visit."

"Goody," said Melchior. "Does it have any other special features?"

"Yes," said Cerice, her voice resigned. "Once you've entered, you can only leave through the exit gate.

"I take it you know where we are?" I had a nasty suspicion I already knew the answer.

"We're in the gardens of House Clotho," said Shara.

"This is where the gate was *supposed* to take us?" I asked her, feeling sick.

Shara nodded. "That's what Cerice asked for."

I turned to the hedge. "Just for the record, the Furies are at this very moment on their way to confer with the Fates in hopes of procuring my death warrant. The Houses of Fate are not a good place for me right now."

"I know they aren't," said Cerice, sounding defensive, "but I needed to stop in here."

"I can't wait to hear this one," I mumbled.

"Neither can I," said a cold hard voice from just behind me.

"Oh shit," said Melchior in a very small voice. Then he slapped his hand over his mouth.

"Hello, Clotho," I said, without turning around.

"Hello, Raven," she answered, her voice even colder and harder. "What brings you here?"

"Fate?" I said, pivoting now, and offering a deep bow. "But then you'd know that better than I would. Yes?"

I kept my gaze from meeting her own, choosing instead to look over her left shoulder. I had seen the power of Fate's eyes too many times to chance it lightly.

"You've always been such an amusing child," said Clotho in a tone totally devoid of amusement. "Your fate is no longer in my hands, and we both know it. I suppose I really should have asked Cerice what brings you here, as it was her familiar who made the travel arrangements."

She turned then to Shara. "You're looking a bit the worse for wear, little one. Are you still grateful to the Raven for his gift of renewed life, or does the shadow of the grave ahead rob you of its riches?"

"Leave her alone," snapped Cerice. "She hasn't done anything to you."

"No she hasn't, but neither has she done anything for me. Oh, this is tedious. As much as I'd like to make you work the maze, I don't have the time to wait for you. Let's see, I can't cancel the magic of the maze without doing it serious harm, so . . ."

Using the Fate trick of self-harmonizing, she whistled something that sounded like the *Toccata and Fugue* played in a roomful of helium by a fifty-piece orchestra. In response, the privet hedge started writhing like a huge green caterpillar beset by army ants. When it stopped, a single arched opening stood directly in front of us, with Cerice on the other side. Behind her, the passage split and then reformed, with another opening at the other end.

"A binary gate, the simplest of all chip forms," said Clotho. "I imagine you can solve this one quickly enough?"

"But of course, Grandmother." Cerice curtsied deeply. Her tone was frigid and formal, devoid of the warmth she usually showed when speaking of or to Clotho. "Thank you." She took two steps forward, exiting the maze.

Too curious as to how this would be received, I gave up my effort to avoid Clotho's eyes and looked straight at her face. I needn't have bothered. Her expression was as still and blank as a marble sculpture, her skin as white and perfect. Her eyes, Fate's eyes, were directed at Cerice, not me, and I could read nothing in their silvery depths.

I wondered what Cerice saw there. The eyes of Fate are knowing eyes, twinned mirrors that show the person who meets them a vision of their own life through time. Sometimes the looking glass is dark, showing you only the shadows of your fate. Sometimes the light comes through, illuminating the best hope for your future, the brightest take on your past. But always there is a sense of heaviness, of judgment waiting, the sure knowledge that you can never escape your own reflection or yourself.

"Speak," said Clotho. "I have been summoned to council. I was casting a gate when yours dropped you so precipitously on my back lawn. The Furies have news for me and my sisters. They are all at the Temple of Fate now. They are waiting. So am I."

Cerice looked at her feet, then back at Clotho. "For what? You're Fate. Surely you know why I've come."

"Surely I do. But until you have said it, it has not happened. Fate has been thwarted before. Has it not, Raven?" She addressed me, but her eyes never left Cerice's.

"If you insist, Grandmother, I will say it." Cerice took a deep breath. I could see that every word was costing her. "I came here to resign."

Clotho's expression, already statue-still, somehow managed to become even more remote and devoid of human expression. Mine probably did some interesting things as well. I wasn't sure where this was going, and I was downright shocked to hear Cerice say something like that to Clotho.

"Resign from what?" asked Clotho. "Your position as one of my programmers? Your duty to your family? Your very blood? What will you renounce for this"—she flicked a finger in my direction—"betrayer of the House of Fate? Your House."

"The first only, Grandmother, though I will not live in this House any longer. I honor my family and the duty I owe you, but I cannot live with my heart torn in two."

"So you will walk away from us, from me? For what? Has the Raven even promised you anything?"

"Not really," said Cerice, her voice practically a whisper. "Not recently. In fact, considering how things have gone over the past few months, I wouldn't blame him if he walked away from me right now."

I wouldn't walk away, though I had to admit the thought had crossed my mind and more than crossed it. I still wasn't sure what I was going to do.

"But his choice is not what this is about." Cerice straightened her shoulders and spoke her next words in a clear, carrying voice, "This is about being true to myself. And the truth is, I love Ravirn, or Raven, or whatever the hell he turns out to be. That means I can't stay here."

"Perhaps it does," said Clotho, "but walking away from me is not as easy as that, my child. Not at all. Still, we can discuss all that later, when I get back. Now, I have an appointment to keep."

"I won't be here when you return," said Cerice.

"Believe what you like," answered Clotho, "but it's not so easy to argue with Fate." Her statuelike calm broke, as she smiled a very thin smile. Then she whistled.

The hedge struck like a snake, wrapping us in coils of green before we could move.

"Good-bye, children," said Clotho's now-disembodied voice. "Have fun with the maze. It's a very special design. I'm sure I'll see you when I get back. You'll have to tell me then what you think of your introduction to the age of quantum computing."

CHAPTER FIFTEEN

The hedge stopped writhing, leaving the four of us surrounded by walls of green. But they were nothing compared to the wall between Cerice and me. As I met her sad but hopeful eyes, I felt so confused. Only minutes ago I'd been absolutely furious that she'd brought us to House Clotho of all places. Minutes before that she'd saved me from the clops, just as she had once saved me from Atropos. I loved her, but our relationship had changed so much over the last few weeks I didn't know whether we still had a future.

That hurt. It killed me that I couldn't just tell her I loved her and make everything better, but it wouldn't have been honest. I needed to think through the implications of the most recent events.

Silence stretched out between us while I searched for something to say. Finally, I opened my mouth, not knowing what would come out but feeling like I had to say something. I couldn't bear the thought of leaving her hanging any longer.

Cerice touched my lips with her finger. "Don't. Not

unless you're really ready. You've given me all the time in the world despite the way I've treated you. The least I can do is give you the same courtesy. You've been telling me you love me for months, not just with words, but with your actions. Let me tell you not just that I love you, but how."

"I really, really hate to say this," said Shara, twisting her small fingers in her long purple hair, "but could this maybe wait until we're somewhere a little less dangerous? I don't think we want to be here when Clotho gets back. If she'd been any angrier, she'd have been smoking."

"Yeah," agreed Melchior. "When you decide to burn a bridge, Cerice, you really toast that sucker."

Cerice nodded. "Point taken. But I'm not sure we *can* get out of here. The maze is always hard. When I was ten I was lost in here for almost a week." She turned slowly in place. "I don't even *see* an opening, much less an exit. Maybe that's because of the quantum computing stuff. Whatever the reason, I don't know where to start."

"Only one way to fix that." I took a closer look at the hedge that surrounded us. I wanted to hear more of what Cerice had to say, but Shara was right—we needed to get moving.

At first glance it seemed as though the growth around us was indeed continuous and unbroken, but as I stepped closer to one wall, there was a flicker, and a neat gate appeared in the hedge. I took another step, keeping my eyes fixed on the opening. As I did so, it flickered again and changed back from opening to wall. That made a weird sort of sense, considering the nature of the quantum bit, or qubit.

In a normal computer, everything is binary. Each bit is either a one or a zero. Qubits, on the other hand, had three states simultaneously, zero, one, and zero/one. So the open gate of a one could instantly become a closed zero. Or in this case, it could and probably should be both. I took another step closer. The gate flickered again, opening. Another step. Flicker, closed. Step. Flicker, open.

"What are you doing?" asked Cerice. "Once you headed for it, that section of hedge went all blurry."

"Blurry?" That seemed very odd. Sure it flickered as it changed, but the end result was perfectly stable. Wasn't it? I suddenly remembered my experience with another chaotic system, the faerie rings, and how it differed from everyone else's. "Tell me what you see, Cerice."

"All right." She sounded like someone humoring a sick relative. "I see a section of hedge that looks like it's just on the other side of a sheet of glass smeared with Vaseline. Until you started paying attention to it, it looked just like the rest of the hedge."

"Huh." I took a step forward. The gate flickered closed. "How about now?"

"Same thing."

"Shara? Melchior?"

"Ditto."

"Me too, Boss."

Very interesting. Maybe there were some pluses to this whole chaos power thing after all. Quantum effects are tied very closely to the mathematical foundations of chaos. Time to try an experiment. Reaching inward as I did when casting an old-fashioned spell, I touched the place where my blood tied me to the Primal Chaos and willed the gate back open. A shadow flickered between me and the sun, and the hedge section vanished.

"What did you just do?" asked Cerice. "There's a gate there now."

Score! I tried again, focusing my will on the space immediately to the left of the gate I'd just opened. Again the shadow. I was ready for it this time, looking at the ground when it came. Wings! The outline was only there for the briefest fraction of an instant, almost too fast to register, but I had no doubts about what it was. The shadow of a giant raven. I looked up at the hedge. The gate had doubled in width.

"Spooky," said Melchior.

He didn't know the half of it. I laughed, a harsh cawing sound, at least to me. "I don't think we're going to have much trouble with Clotho's maze after all. Come on." I lifted Melchior into my bag, and once Cerice had picked up Shara, I took her free hand. "This way."

It was easy now to hold the gate open with my mind. We passed through it and into a narrow passage beyond. I focused my will. The shadow came again, and the far wall vanished. After a few dozen repetitions, a gate opened with no hedge beyond it. We were out, and I had taken another tentative step toward the terra incognita called Raven.

"Are you feeling all right, Boss?" Melchior asked from his perch in my bag.

"Why do you ask?" I wasn't. Not really.

I would use the power because I had to, because power ignored is not power defused. One of the rules of magic is that if you don't channel power, it will channel you. But I'd never asked for any of this, and frankly, it freaked me out.

A sharp claw poked me in the ribs, and I looked down. Melchior raised one dark blue eyebrow at me. He didn't buy it. Well, neither did I, but maybe we could both rent to own.

"Forget it," said Melchior, in a voice that clearly said he wouldn't. "We can talk about it later. For now, where are we going? And how are we getting there?"

"Cerice?" I turned to her. "You have anything more you want to do here?"

"Nope. I'm done." She looked around wistfully, like a kid leaving home for the last time. "I'll miss this place. But I don't belong here anymore."

"Shara?"

"I've got no agenda, big boy. Well, there's getting my soul back in one piece, but I don't even know where to begin on that now that Necessity's network is closed to us."

"Then we need to get to Hades," I said, "to see if Cerberus can help us reach Persephone. We'll have to go sooner rather than later, but I'd bet Midas's golden horde that things are going to get ugly fast on that end. We need to rest and regroup a bit before we tackle the big dog."

"Cambridge?" suggested Cerice.

I shook my head. "Too many people know about that

place, the Fates and the Furies topping the list. Likewise Garbage Faerie."

"You know," said Melchior, "maybe we need to find a new line of work. The list of places we can't go back to is getting awfully long. I'm starting to feel about as welcome as Dionysus at an AA meeting."

I had to chuckle. "You may have something there, little buddy. Let's try using a faerie ring if there's one around here. I've got a hunch I'd like to play."

"There's one over this way," said Cerice, pulling on the hand she'd never let go of. "What's this 'hunch'?"

"Just bear with me; you'll see in a moment." Or she wouldn't if I was wrong. It was more chaos magic, and I didn't know whether it would work, or whether it was something I should even try.

"All right," said Cerice. "I'll wait. I'll trust you, but only because crazy seems to work for you."

She led me into a large arbor walled off from the main garden by thick ropes of ivy and climbing roses. It was hard to tell through the profusion of greenery, but the skeleton of the place looked to be an intricate wrought-iron lattice, like something made by a giant clockwork spider. More creepers wove their way through an openwork dome of verdigrised copper pipe.

Underneath lay the circle, and I laughed out loud when I saw it. Maybe Clotho did have a sense of humor after all. It was made up entirely of foot-tall lawn gnomes. They stood or sat facing into the center of the ring in a variety of vaguely rustic poses. All of them were dressed in the classic style, with pointed cap, button-up shirt, baggy trousers, and fuzzy boots. Only, instead of the usual bright colors, all of the clothes except the red hats had been painted over in flesh tones, and each of them wore a little Greek tunic over the top of its other clothes.

"I wonder how Zeus feels about this," I said.

"I don't know," replied Melchior. "But I can't help noticing the whole place is made out of conductive materials and firmly grounded."

"There is that. Now, let's see if this works the way I think it will."

Cerice nodded, and we crossed into the ring together. I felt a myriad of possible rings open out around me. It was a sensation I was becoming accustomed to. This time, instead of reaching out for a specific place and taking us there, I tried to imagine a series of conditions I wanted met. Someplace safe. Someplace slow. Someplace secret. A refuge. For what felt like ages, nothing happened, nothing physical at least. I could sense something of me reaching out into the ring network, touching first this ring, then that, until finally, I got a sense of connection. Squeezing Cerice's hand, I moved us forward into . . .

Paradise. That's the only way to describe it. We stood on a grand marble balcony hanging over a white sand beach on one side of a huge half-circle bay. But this was not the sterile white marble of Zeus's Olympus. This was a rich, green marble veined with black, like great slabs of gem-quality malachite. Neohedonist instead of neoclassical. A low balustrade of the same marble ran along the edge of the balcony, turning and following a wide flight of stairs down to the beach on my right. The air was humid and tropical, redolent with the smells of greenery and flowers, but not too warm.

Looking directly across the water, I could see mountains reaching down to the far edge of the bay, iron-rich soil exposed here and there by jagged rents in the velvety tropical forest, like a red arm in a tattered emerald sleeve. To my left, the mountains climbed up to a cloud-shrouded peak. To my right the bay opened out into the deep blue sea stretching luxuriously to the horizon. It was one of the most beautiful settings I'd ever seen and I wondered how such a place could be so devoid of people.

"Where are we?" asked Cerice, her tone hushed in wonder.

"Welcome to Raven House," said a new voice from behind us.

I should have been startled, practically jumping out of

my skin. I wasn't. It was like I'd expected the voice. I let go of Cerice and turned slowly around. I found myself facing a faun in a Hawaiian shirt. He had curly hair and a little soul-patch beard. A thick cluster of leis was wrapped around his equally thick neck. He smiled and stepped forward, lifting one of the leis off and placing it around my neck, then doing the same for Cerice.

"Raven House?" exclaimed Melchior. "That's ridiculous, there is no such place. And who in Hades' name are you? You look like the product of a nightmare brought on by eating a pineapple-and-feta-cheese pizza with an ouzo margarita on the side."

The faun took a much smaller lei from around his wrist and popped it none-too-gently over Melchior's head. "I am the spirit of this place. If you have problems with my appearance, or its appearance, take them up with your partner's subconscious. Because this is indeed Raven House."

Melchior gave me a very hard look as the faun moved on to give Shara a lei. "He's kidding, right? Tell me you didn't come up with this. Tell me you have more respect for continuity than to do this." His gesture took in the great house that rose behind the faun.

It was mostly green marble and aqua-tinted glass, in a sort of high modern mix of classical Greek and nouveau-tiki lounge. It should have been an awful kludge, yet it seemed perfectly harmonized with its environment, the greens blending smoothly into the jungle surrounding it. There was a big open porch behind the balcony, with a fountain centering it and low, comfortable furniture scattered in conversation sets.

I turned to the faun. "Can you fix us a couple of daiquiris?"

"Of course, what would you like?"

"What are the options?"

"You name it, we've got it."

"Guava," I said. "Cerice?"

"Banana."

"Done," said the faun, turning and heading for the bar.

"Looks like paradise to me, Mel. If this is Raven House, I, for one, am in." I pulled off my leather jacket and slung it over my shoulder.

The webgoblin put his face in his hands. "A faun in a Hawaiian shirt fixing daiquiris is your idea of a power's proper home. That's crazy."

"That's chaos," the faun called over his shoulder, "and the Raven is a power of it."

"Could be worse," said Shara, shaking her head. "He could be wearing a kilt."

"Yeah," I agreed. "It's a good thing I'm more of a surfer than a golfer."

Just then the faun returned.

"What should we call you?" I asked, taking my drink.

"I'm tempted to say 'Id—Id Runamuck.' But that would be cruel. My name is Haemun. Is there anything else I can get you?"

"Food would be good. Rice, fish, something simple."

"I'll get right on it." Haemun headed for the depths of the house.

"Now," said Cerice, "I think it's my turn to talk. At least I think that's where we were before we left the maze. Just let me get out of this armor."

She reached to her side and popped the buckles on her breastplate, letting it fall on the thick carpet that set our cluster of furniture off from its surroundings. Her shoulder pieces and bracers followed quickly. Underneath, she wore a thin silk blouse.

"Oh, that's so much better." Cerice rolled her shoulders, which did interesting things to the rest of her torso. "Could I impose on you to scratch my back before I make an emotional spectacle of myself?" I stood up and obliged as she peeled off the rest of her gear. "Nice," she almost purred. "Thank you." Then she turned and gave me a gentle push toward my chair. "Now, I have some things that need saying."

"This is where it gets mushy," said Melchior. "I'll pass. Shara, you want to help me explore this dump?"

She nodded, and they wandered off together. I smiled

after them. Despite Melchior's harsh words, I knew he was trying to give us some privacy. I appreciated it.

I took a seat and a sip of my drink, then looked at Cerice. "The floor is yours."

"Right. Where to start . . ." She sipped her drink as well then looked me in the eyes. "How about with this, I love you. I love your reckless abandon. I love that you don't plot out your hacks and cracks, you just do them. I love the sloppy way you put together spells. I love your courage and the way you never take danger seriously." She laughed and took another drink. "I guess I love all the things about you that drive me absolutely crazy, and I haven't the foggiest idea how a House of Fate produced someone like you."

"You're not alone there, just ask Lachesis. Perhaps I'm a genetic throwback to the Titans."

"Whatever the reason, I appreciate it. I'm not sure if you've noticed, but I'm a little bit on the anal-retentive side." She said this with a self-knowing smile and held up her hands a few millimeters apart. "Or maybe a lot." She spread her arms into a gesture like someone talking about the one that got away. "I plan everything." She looked at her feet. "Did you know that there's a spreadsheet tucked away in Shara's memory entitled 'Life Plan' and that the subsheet 'College' has a list of what schools I wanted to go to and when?"

"I can't say I'm surprised."

"I wrote it when I was thirteen. It included a four-year break between high school and freshman year of college."

"I'd never have guessed that part. You actually put free time into the list?"

She blushed. "Not free time. I laid out a travel agenda involving visits to all the major mythological sites, when I was going, and for how long, as well as an extended tour of the prime minus one DecLocus with stops in all the big capitals and visits to fifty colleges with great comp-sci departments, just in case I changed my mind about undergrading at a version of MIT."

"You didn't change your mind," I said. I remembered visiting her there the year I was first looking for schools.

"Of course not." She looked at her feet again. "In fact, when I was fifteen, I added a tentative course schedule to my file. The only reason I changed anything when I finally started taking classes was because some of the things I'd picked out were no longer offered. I always knew exactly what I wanted to do and be."

"That's what makes you a great programmer, Cerice. You can hold a thousand lines of code in your head and see whether it'll do what you want it to."

"But it didn't really prepare me for the messiness that is real life. When I discovered that Shara was really an independent being, it completely threw me for a loop. It changed all of my plans and assumptions. I couldn't just fit smoothly into Clotho's IT machine anymore. I loved Shara, and I had to do something for her, for her and for all the other web-goblins and trolls with the same problems. So, you know what I did?"

"I can guess. You revised your 'College Plan' sheet."

Cerice laughed. "I did indeed. I changed my Ph.D. thesis subject and went looking for a new advisor, though I stayed with the same school. My proximate plans changed, but my methods stayed exactly the same. I changed the plan, but I still had one. Everything was going to be fine."

"Then I came along."

She nodded. "And then you came along. I'd always liked you when we met at joint court events, or when you visited me at MIT, but you were *too wild* to consider as even practice boyfriend material. I had other plans on the romance front."

"But?" I asked before finishing my drink.

"But I kept finding things wrong with the guys on the good-boy demi-immortals list. Either they didn't really turn my crank, or they treated their familiars like shit, or they had inherited their brains from wherever Zeus got his. All along I kept thinking back to you. Then came the day I overheard Atropos and Clotho vote to send Moric and his brothers to kill you. It was another break point. I had to warn you, but that meant some major spontaneous hacking and straight-up defiance of Clotho. I felt sooo guilty. But I couldn't let them do it."

I was about to say something, but a subtle cough made me turn my head to find that Haemun had returned. "I've put together dinner and set up a table. It's out on the terrace, where you can watch the sun go down." He gestured with one hand, collecting our empty glasses with the other. "I'll just refill these, shall I?"

"Please," said Cerice, rising and offering me her hand.

Together, we walked out to find a small round table with two place settings side by side facing west. A small bamboo basket had its lid cracked to expose steaming rice, and a warming dish held two grilled ahi steaks beside it, but it hardly registered. The sun had sunk quite low, dipping toward the water while we'd talked on the porch. It was a beautiful evening, with just enough cloud cover to provide the sun a canvas on which to splash a gorgeous abstract painting in blood and fire.

We sat down and, by a sort of mutual unspoken agreement, said nothing as the sun slid the rest of the way into the ocean. It was a half disc just sticking out of the water when Haemun arrived with our drinks. He delivered them so quietly and so smoothly that I barely noticed their arrival or his departure.

I absently reached for mine but stopped midway. The sun had reached the point where it seems to drop precipitously before vanishing. For just an instant after the disc disappeared, the light shone back brightly through the water in a brilliant green flash like some giant solar wink. It took my breath away.

"Gorgeous," said Cerice. "I've read about the green flash, but I've never seen it."

"I don't think I've ever heard of it before. It's wonderful." I finished my earlier gesture and collected my drink. "I'm glad that I saw it with you."

"So am I," said Cerice.

Then she reached for the serving dishes. It had been a long time since our last meal, and we paid more attention to the food than conversation for a little while. When we slowed down, Cerice caught my eye.

"Where was I?"

"Moric and company had just been dispatched to kill me."

"Right, and I'd defied Clotho. As awful as that made me feel, I couldn't convince myself that I'd been wrong, or stop thinking about you. I had to find you and talk to you."

"And you did, with a little help from Ahllan."

"I did. Then one thing led to another, and we ended up in bed and I panicked. I wanted you so badly, but you just didn't fit into the plan. I tried to shut you out at first, but you kept coming back, and pretty soon it killed me every time you left. So guess what I did?"

"Revised the plan?" I raised an eyebrow.

"Uh-huh, now it included a sheet under 'Ravirn, re-forming of.' Then it turned out Atropos and the other Fates were trying to kill free will, and I got caught up in the fight because I couldn't let them kill you in the process, and then somehow you won. But you became Raven doing it. Everything was totally messed up and the plan was shot and I panicked again."

"And shit flows downhill." It came out harsher than I'd intended, but I had to say it.

"It does," said Cerice. "It flowed all over you, and I'm so sorry about that. If I've lost you, I don't know what I'll do about that. But I do know I'm done with plans. The best things in my life are you and Shara and the things I've done and learned in helping you oppose Fate. If I'd followed the plan, I'd never have experienced any of it."

"Cerice, I . . ." Again, I didn't know what to say, but I felt I had to say something. I did love her. No matter what happened between us, that much was true.

"Please," she said, "don't answer me yet. We've reached one of the bad places in the story again. Soon, too soon, we'll leave here and try to fix the Persephone mess. That's going to be dangerous. You could die. Melchior could die. Shara could die. I could die. No matter what, everything's going to be different afterward. Answer me then. For now, I just want to make love to you and let tomorrow worry about tomorrow. Is that all right?"

"Yes, and more than all right." I rose and helped Cerice from her chair. "Shall we find out if this barn has a master suite somewhere?"

"Let's."

It did indeed, a huge room on the level above. Instead of marble, the bedroom was carpeted with living moss. Likewise the room's twin balconies, one of which overlooked the bay, while the other faced the mountains. It was full dark now, and there was not a light to be seen anywhere on the slopes or beach. For all we could tell, there wasn't another living intelligence anywhere beyond the bounds of Raven House. Stars sprinkled the sky like salt spilled on black velvet, and the Milky Way made a great pale stripe from horizon to horizon.

"This is gorgeous," said Cerice, from the edge of the bayside balcony.

I put an arm around her waist. "So are you."

She laughed lightly and kissed the side of my neck. "That's very sweet, my dear. But I'm a complete mess at the moment. I saw what looked like a world-class bath through the door over there." She pointed with her chin. "Want to clean up before we get dirty again? I could really use someone to scrub my back."

"If you insist."

I needed a good scrubbing, too. It had been a long time between baths, and I'd been scared silly, shot at, and dropped in a spirea bush since the last one. Cerice led the way into what turned out to be a truly magnificent bathroom. Apparently my subconscious, or whatever part of my psyche had led us to this place, liked its comforts.

A marble tub almost big enough to swim laps in was partially sunk into the floor in the corner, and someone or something had filled it to the brim with steaming water. Three wide steps led up to its edge, and there was another inside to allow you to ease into the depths. A couple of sinks occupied a countertop opposite. A big glass booth in the corner held a half dozen showerheads. The toilet sat in its own smaller room beyond, out of sight of the bathing amenities.

Cerice dipped a hand in the tub. "Perfect!" She started to strip off her clothes.

When she caught me watching, she grinned and started moving slower on the buttons of her red silk blouse, making a show of it. I felt myself hardening in response. Once she had her shirt fully open, she coyly turned away from me and let it fall to the floor, exposing the white skin of her back. Cerice is as tall as I am and very slender, with a runner's lines, and her back is a work of art. So was her chest, clearly visible in several of the mirrors. Her breasts are small and high, with pale nipples and clearly visible veins running through them, and you can count her ribs from fifteen feet.

Cerice found my eyes in the mirror and grinned. "You like what you see?"

"I always have."

"I'm glad."

With one smooth move she slipped her tights and the panties underneath over her hips and down to the floor, then stepped clear. Her long legs are hard with muscle, her buttocks likewise, an athlete's figure despite the hours spent sitting in front of a computer. She turned to face me again, crossing the distance between us in a few quick steps.

"Aren't you going to join me?" she asked, her lips inches from mine.

"Of course." I put my hands on her hips and pulled her closer still.

"Well then." For a moment she pressed her whole body against mine, catching my lower lip ever so gently in her teeth. "Why don't you get a move on?" She pulled away and skipped up the steps to the tub, dipping a foot in. "Still perfect." She gently lowered herself into the water, then flipped over so that her chin was resting on the lip and gave me a flatly appraising look. "Your turn."

I was very conscious of her eyes as I pulled my T-shirt over my head and took off my boots, actually blushing as I unzipped the fly of my leathers. Being watched felt even sexier than watching Cerice had.

As I stepped up onto the edge of the bath, Cerice rolled onto her back, looking up the length of my body from a point almost between my feet.

"Also perfect," she said, with a wink. "Or close enough for my tastes at any rate."

As I slid in beside her, Cerice ran a hand from my ankle to my shoulder. Then she turned her back and handed the soap over her shoulder.

I washed her slowly and thoroughly. Then she washed me in like manner. We just sat for a little while after that, letting the hot water soothe away our aches and completing the process of bringing my knee back to as good as it was ever likely to be again. Then we made gentle love on the edge of the bath, getting water and soap everywhere. Once we'd cleaned up again, we headed out onto the bay-side balcony, where clouds had eaten most of the stars. There was no one else around, and the night air was still warm, so we hadn't bothered to dress.

"I wish this could last forever," said Cerice, leaning forward against the railing.

"Me too." I stood behind her, my arms around her waist, my chin resting on her shoulder. "But it can't."

"No, it can't."

Something about her tone made me reach up and run a finger along her cheek. It came away wet.

"You're crying."

"I'm happy. And sad. And frightened. I don't want to let this moment go, because I don't know what will happen next. But I know I have to."

"I *have* to find Persephone and try to save the mweb and Shara," I said, wanting to make it better somehow.

Cerice sighed. "Better make that, *we* have to find Persephone. After all, Shara's my familiar."

I smiled and squeezed her tighter. "All right, *we* have to find Persephone."

"Better. But we don't have to do it right this instant, do we? It can wait till morning?" She pressed her hips back against me.

"It can wait till morning," I agreed.

"Good." She reached back between us, guiding me.

As I entered her, it began to rain gently. The storm matched its tempo to ours, rising slowly to a wild pitch and ripping the darkness with lightning as we orgasmed. The air had cooled, but we had not, and we took our pleasure a third time there on the moss that carpeted the balcony in the pounding rain. Finally, exhausted, we toweled off and fell into bed.

CHAPTER SIXTEEN

If my illusions about a benevolent Fate hadn't been erased long ago, they would have crashed to ruin with my awakening. Instead of the Haemun-served breakfast in bed I'd been hoping for, the first thing to meet my bleary eyes was Melchior's sour expression. He was sitting cross-legged on the blankets between me and Cerice.

"About damn time," he said, grumpily. Then he hopped to his feet and cupped his hands over his mouth. "Shara, they're up!"

"No, we're not," said Cerice, from somewhere under the pillows. "Go away. We don't want any."

"Cerice says they're not hungry! Tell Haemun don't hold breakfast!" He glared at me. "The faun was going to bring it to you here in bed, but I knew you'd never get up if that happened."

He looked smug, so I yanked on the blankets, pulling them out from under him and sending him ass-over-end.

"Cancel that!" I yelled to Shara. "Tell him we'll be down in five."

"Damn goblins," said Cerice. But she sat up, too. "Don't know enough to respect their betters."

"Betters!" squawked Melchior, getting back onto his feet. "I like that. You two couldn't figure out how to code an if-then set without the help of the true better half of your cyberpartnerships."

I held a hand up to measure Melchior's height. "Half? More like ten percent, and I wouldn't be so quick to declare which end of the partnership carries most of the load if I were you."

"Short jokes is it? From the man who designed me this size? Ha, ha. I'll get you for that," he said. "You know that, right?"

"We do," said Cerice, "but not before I get *you* for waking me up." She yanked the covers again to tip Melchior. Before he could right himself, she flipped them over him and rolled him up into a little blanket burrito. Then in the sweetest tone imaginable she whispered, "See you at breakfast."

Haemun, or some as-yet-unseen functionary of Raven House, had carried off our clothes and left behind a pair of very nice kimono-style silk robes. Mine was green with a black raven on the back. Cerice's was red with a golden phoenix. After slipping into them, we headed downstairs.

Breakfast was laid out on the same table where we'd eaten dinner the previous night. The house shaded us from the rising sun, and the view over the bay was even more gorgeous than it had been then. The long, rolling waves practically cried out for surfing, and I wished very much that we could have given it a shot.

This time Haemun had put out four place settings, two with bar chairs to bring the goblins up to the height of the table. The spread was lavish, with cinnamon toast, crepes, sausages, and tons of fresh fruit including papaya, pineapple, slices of cantaloupe and honeydew, and pomegranate. There was also some sort of delightful egg casserole involving bacon, mushrooms, and spinach. For drinks he

provided coffee and tea, milk, and three kinds of juice—
passion fruit, guava, and orange. I had a bit of everything,
as did Cerice and Melchior.

Shara looked tempted right up until he brought out the
fruit plate. At that point she let out a small sigh, hopped
down from her chair, and unplugged an extension cord
from a lamp. Dragging it back to the table, she whistled a
short spell that capped two of her claws with copper and
stuck them into the plug's end. I took it from Shara's actions that this world had also been cut off from the mweb
but didn't ask because I didn't want to put her on the spot
about her behavior.

The food tasted fabulous, and very little conversation occurred while we paid it our proper respects, just polite
grunts and requests to pass this or that item. I'd just started
in on a second cup of coffee when Melchior caught my eye.

"I hate to end this delightful little idyll in de land of denial, but the mweb is dying, and we need to get moving."

I sighed. "You're right, Mel. As much as I'd like to stay
here, it's time. Do we want to try to put together a plan, or
should we just blunder along like we always do?"

"Why mess with success?" he answered.

Cerice smiled sweetly. "I notice your limp is better this
morning."

" 'A hit, a very palpable hit,' " said Shara.

I winced and nodded. "Point taken. But I'm not sure that
there's much to plan. We go from here to the shores of the
Styx and ask Dave to get us in contact with Persephone, or
to take her a message if he can't do that."

"What would a message like that say?" asked Shara.
" 'Sorry you've been condemned to eternal damnation here
in scenic Hades, but that doesn't give you an excuse to mess
up everybody else's life, too. Please call off your virus.' I'm
sure that'll work. After all, it's not like she comes from a
family willing to call down an unending winter to get her
out of there."

Melchior turned to look at her. "Aren't you just in a
pissy mood this morning."

"I'm sorry, maybe it's having my soul ripped in half that's put me off my feed." She closed her eyes for a moment, exposing how dark the purple hollows underneath had grown. "I really am sorry. That was uncalled for. I guess I just feel like shit, and I'm scared none of this will work. Or maybe I'm just scared to be going back to the borderlands of Hades. I didn't much like being dead, and even the half-life I've got now is precious. But I don't know what else to do either, so I guess I'll be coming along."

I met Shara's eyes. "You're right. Convincing Persephone to give up her scheme to break free of Hades is going to be hard, maybe even impossible. The odds are this will all end badly. We still have to try, or at least I do. Not just because the Fates and two out of three Furies are likely to use this as an excuse for payback. Even if I could stay here safely forever, I'd go."

I stood up and started to pace. "The mweb is the center of my family's existence. My *whole* family, not just the Fates, but all the children of the Titans. We need it. And on a less noble note, I need it. I'm a hacker, a computer-centered sorcerer, and I'll do what I have to to keep it going. If that means taking on Persephone, or Cerberus, or even Hades himself, so be it."

"I could say I was doing it for love," said Cerice. "But that's not my only reason. We're in the same boat on the hacking front, a boat that will soon be up that proverbial creek if we can't get this fixed."

"I'm in, too," said Melchior. "That leaves us back at the question of a plan."

"Go to the Styx," I said. "Talk to Cerberus. I can't see my way past that point. Too many variables. Anybody else?" Cerice shook her head. Melchior shrugged. I looked at Shara.

"Oh, let's just get it over with."

That just left getting changed and going. "Haemun," I called. "Are you around here someplace?"

The faun appeared from deeper within the house. "I am indeed." This was the first I'd seen of him this morning, and I couldn't help but notice that today's aloha shirt was even more garish than yesterday's.

"Do you know what happened to our clothes?"

"Of course." He smiled, then looked expectant.

"Would you care to share that information?" I asked, trying not to roll my eyes. Why was everyone in my life born difficult?

"Certainly. They're in the laundry."

Great. Soggy leather. "I don't suppose you'd care to fetch them for us."

He gave me a look of polite disbelief. "I could, but they're really not ready. Wouldn't it be better to grab fresh things out of the master closet? You did see the master closet, yes? Big room with lots of clothes? Next to the bath?"

"Of course." I hadn't, but I didn't want to admit it. "There's a change for both of us in there, is there?"

"Several, I should think. It is a *master* closet after all, in a magical mansion. It's your subconscious of course, but I'd hope that it's up to the task of dreaming up a solution for wardrobe emergencies. You do have a good imagination, don't you?"

Melchior snorted, and I cast him a dire look. "Thanks, Haemun. If you'll excuse us, we have to get dressed."

"Which will of course involve getting undressed," said Shara. Then she gave a deliberately theatrical headshake. "Well, children, make sure that getting 'dressed' doesn't take *too* long; we'll be waiting."

Melchior whistled a sprightly little bit of binary, and an egg timer appeared. He flipped it over so that the sand began to run. "Go get 'dressed.'"

Mustering what little dignity still remained to me, I stood up and offered Cerice my arm. Together we went upstairs and found the closet exactly where Haemun had said it would be. Cerice's armor, carefully scrubbed, had been placed on a person-shaped rack just inside the closet on the left. Next to it hung a small selection of women's clothes in Cerice's size and colors. As she started to sort through them, it quickly became apparent that most of them were, shall we say, "not for strenuous use."

"Your subconscious is incorrigible," said Cerice, holding up a particularly flimsy and translucent bit of fluff.

To avoid having to answer that, I turned my attention to the space beyond the little patch of red and gold. The majority of the closet was filled with black and green, including several sets of racing leathers, and a suit of samurai-type armor that I wouldn't have been caught dead in. I only turned back around when I heard a little gasp from behind me.

Cerice had pulled out a full-length brocade gown. It was elaborate and gorgeous and unlike any of the other women's clothes on the rack.

"What do you suppose your hindbrain had in mind for this?" she asked, holding it up against herself. "I found it on the floor in the very back."

"Court ball?" I said quickly.

But that wasn't what it was. When I was in my late teens my sister Lyra had married. I'm not generally a student of women's fashion, but I'd fallen in love with her wedding dress. It was simply perfect. Here was that dress once again, the only difference being that it was in Cerice's colors. I wondered what that said about the way I felt about Cerice and about the fact that it was on the floor in the back and not a hanger up front.

"Nice," said Cerice, putting it away.

I nodded but didn't say anything more. The dress made me want to explore the whole place and find out what other surprises might lurk in the various corners. But the goblins were waiting, and we really didn't have much time. We did, however, find a moment or two for getting "dressed" before we put our clothes on, and that necessitated a quick shower. But that would have been a good idea anyway. Then, once more outfitted for action, we headed back to the balcony and our appointment with the hound of hell.

I hadn't noticed it when we'd arrived, but a permanent faerie ring made up a part of the basic structure of the balcony. Thick black whorls in the stone floor near the head of the stairs surrounded a perfect ring of green. Cerice placed Shara on her shoulder, rather like a well-trained cat. Melchior climbed into my bag, and away we went.

On the shores of the Styx we stepped out of a circle made of corroded copper coins, the dead man's fare. A little shiver of foreboding slid its way from the back of my neck to the base of my spine. Normally when I came to the border of Hades, I had Melchior set us down directly across from the gate. This time we'd arrived a few hundred yards downstream, in a place where the river ran very close to the outer wall of the great cavern that held the underworld. No more than ten feet separated the dark waters from the damp stone, and the faerie ring occupied a good portion of that narrow way.

It would have been easy for someone picking their way along to step into the circle accidentally and find out why all those old folk tales warned against trifling with the gateways of the fair folk. I felt quite sure the possibility hadn't escaped the attention of whoever or whatever had crafted the ring and wondered if there might be other pleasant surprises left around by the same soul.

"Nasty," said Cerice, but she wasn't looking at the ring.

"What?" I asked.

"This place."

"It's supposed to be," replied Melchior, poking his blue head over the edge of my bag. "Keeps the tourists away."

"It's better than being on the far shore," said Shara with a shiver. "There's not much that's worse."

She hugged herself and looked away from the Styx and the wall beyond. It was sheer and slick as glass, rising fifty or so feet from the waters to a razor's edge at the top. Another barrier, invisible but impenetrable, climbed from there to the cavern's ceiling. I'd found out about that by talking with Dave.

"Not much at all," I agreed, wishing I'd gotten things right the first time, so we didn't have to come back.

"I wonder what the headwaters look like," said Cerice, "whether it's as bad there. Beginnings rarely are."

"That's Clotho's granddaughter talking," said Melchior. "This is a bad place from start to finish."

"Is it really?" asked Cerice.

"Trust me on that."

"He's teasing you," I said. "But he's also right. The Styx is a loop. It has no source and no outlet. Hades is an island in the center of a river without end. The first time we came here, Mel and I walked all the way around."

"I've never heard that before," said Cerice. "You didn't mention it to me when you came home."

"It didn't seem all that important since it neither helped nor hindered my plans for freeing Shara. Besides, that first encounter with Cerberus drove most everything else about the trip out of my head."

"You mean the way he picked you up with Bob's big old jaws and had Mort tell you that if you ever came back he'd eat you was a little distracting?" Mel offered.

"He what?" asked Cerice. "You didn't tell me that either, just that he'd warned you off."

"I didn't want you to worry. He was *much* nicer the second time." It sounded lame even to me.

Cerice glanced upward as if asking for patience. "You drive me crazy, you know that, right?"

Time to change the subject. "And here I just thought I drove you wild." I waggled my eyebrows.

"That too," she said with a little chuckle. "That too."

"I hate to interrupt," said Shara, "but could you save the flirting for a more festive locale?"

I nodded. "You're right. Let's get this thing done and get out of here."

I struck out toward the gate. The ground was rough and thick with loose bits of obsidian and other volcanic rock. I hadn't gone ten feet before I accidentally kicked a stone. It skittered across the cave floor before sailing over the edge of the bank and landing in the river. When it hit, the water came alive. Or rather, things that had been hidden beneath its surface started moving. Lots of them, and fast. A dozen, no, a hundred rippling vees appeared, all of them rocketing toward the center of the ring made by the stone.

When they reached it, the water started to look like the surface of a boiling cauldron. A moment later I got a look at the cause of the commotion. Eels, or something very like them. There were so many that a few were pushed briefly out of the water by the pressure of their brethren below. Long and sinuous with shiny black skin and shiny black teeth, they had slick death written all over them.

"That's new since our last visit." Melchior sounded shaky. "Looks like someone crossbred sea snakes with piranhas. I can't say much for their taste."

"Probably just like chicken." I put a lightness into my words that I didn't feel. "Isn't that what everything tastes like?"

"Oh, you're very funny," said Melchior. "Ha. Ha. Ha."

Cerice hadn't said anything for a while, so I turned to look at her. She was very pale, even more so than normal if that was possible. Cerice doesn't scare easily, and her attitude surprised me at first. Then I noticed the way she was holding on to Shara's thigh. To the best of my knowledge in the many years of their partnership, Shara has never fallen off of Cerice's shoulder, but you couldn't tell that by Cerice's white-knuckled grip. This was a mother afraid for her only child's life, and I didn't have anything reassuring to say to her. Instead, I reached over and squeezed the shoulder that didn't hold Shara.

"We'd better move on."

Cerice nodded, and we continued. A few minutes later, when we'd reached the point where a beach appeared between the water and the wall on the farther bank, a howl went up, a howl with words of warning in it.

"Sounds like Fido knows we're here," said Melchior.

I gave him an admonishing look. "I wouldn't say that where he could hear you."

"Neither would I. All the same, he knows."

I nodded and stopped walking. Best to wait for him to come to us.

"Do we have an exit strategy if this conversation goes badly?" asked Cerice.

"Run?" I said.

"How about something a little more proactive?" She lifted Shara off her shoulder and knelt in front of the goblin. "Why don't you set up an LTP link so we can gate out if we have to."

"I'll try if you want," responded Shara, "but the mweb's cutting in and out here, too. Any attempt to gate could go very bad if we get a service outage at the wrong moment."

"Why didn't you mention that earlier?" asked Cerice.

Shara shrugged. "Mweb problems have been so common the last few days that it didn't seem worth mentioning."

"But we're in the main level of reality," said Cerice. "This is where the system lives. Blackouts shouldn't be possible."

"Maybe the turbulence from all the lost nodes is affecting the servers," I said.

For every world that went off-line, there would be a line in the network that no longer had an anchor point. If they were all flopping around loose, it could eat up a lot of processing power.

"Better not risk it," said Cerice. "I—"

"Here he comes," interrupted Melchior.

Cerberus had emerged from his den. He stalked to the edge of the water then very deliberately leaped in. Rippling vees exploded away from his entry point as the eels—showing more sense than I'd have expected—found someplace else to be.

The river was wide, but Cerberus is a *big* dog, and it didn't take him long to cross the distance between us. As he climbed out, I remembered my last experience with a wet hellhound.

"Melchior, Hydrophobia. Please."

The goblin whistled a spell, and a huge transparent shower curtain appeared between us and Cerberus. It was just in time, as the great dog started to shake himself dry. When he'd finished, Melchior whistled the barrier away.

"And a soggy hello to you, too," I said. "How are things?"

"Cut the crap, Raven," said Bob. "You're not here to make small talk, and we all know it."

"Charming as always, Bob."

"But he's right this time," said Mort. Then he winked. "Though I could sure go for a hand or two of cards."

"That would be nice," agreed Dave. "But it can't be bridge. We've got too many players." He addressed that last directly to Cerice.

"I'm sorry," I said. "I've forgotten my manners. Let me make introductions. Melchior you know."

"We do," said Bob, "but not in this form. He's usually too busy pretending to be an inanimate object. Silly really. Laptops probably taste better than goblins anyway."

"You're being rude again," said Dave, with a little growl in his voice.

Bob met his eyes for a second, then turned them downward. I got the feeling that if he could have rolled over and exposed his belly, he would have.

"And Shara," I began.

"Her we know as well," said Mort. His voice was very cold.

"I, uh, well. Yes." I really didn't know what to say to that, and apparently Shara didn't either.

Without a word, she turned away from the rest of us and walked down to the river's edge. There she climbed up onto a huge rock that overhung the water, keeping her back firmly pointed in our general direction. I could see her shoulders sag, and I really felt for her, but there wasn't anything I could do about it at the moment. A long and harsh silence hung in the air until I tried again.

"I guess that just leaves Cerice. Dave, Mort, Bob, may I introduce you to the Lady Cerice of House Clotho. Cerice, Cerberus and his three . . ."

"Heads?" offered Mort, ever practical.

"Musketeers?" Dave gave a doggy grin.

"Billy goats gruff," suggested Melchior.

Bob gave him a hard look, but didn't respond directly. "How about you refer to us as 'his pack'?"

"Delighted to." Cerice dropped a curtsy.

"What?" asked Bob. "No offer to shake?"

"Give it a rest," said Dave. "You're stereotyping again, and that just leads to bad dog jokes."

Mort gave a little bow. "Likewise delighted. I've smelled you so often, it's a pleasure to meet you at last."

Cerice looked a bit taken aback, but then rolled with it. "I suppose you have at that, over your acquaintance with Ravirn."

"Speaking of smells . . ." Bob looked at me. "You really stink."

"Gosh, thanks," I replied. "I love you, too."

"He means it literally," said Mort. "The smell of chaos that you carry with you has gotten much stronger."

"Chaos—and Raven," said Dave. "You are becoming the role."

"That's great. It's just what I always wanted." What can I say, for me fear engenders sarcasm.

"It's better than the alternative," said Mort.

"I don't know about that," said Bob. "The change might improve his attitude."

"I don't understand," I said.

Dave lowered his head to look me in the eyes. "It's like this. You're a power, and each power has a role to play in the grand scheme of things. Your choices in the matter are very limited. You can assume the role. It can assume you. Or you can die. Two of three won't leave much of Ravirn behind."

That was fan-damn-tastic. I could either become something I never asked to be or let it eat me. I felt like sticking my finger in my ears, and screaming "I'm not listening, la, la, la." I didn't have time to think about this right now. I really didn't. I'd worry about it once we got the mweb fixed.

"As fascinating as I find all this talk about my impending doom, and as much as I'd like to discuss it to death,

I've got some other things to take care of. I presume you're aware of what's going on with the mweb?"

"Of course," said Bob. "Hades told us all about it when he gave us our new orders. You've written a virus to attack Necessity, and now you're trying to blame it on Persephone."

I opened my mouth. Shut it again. Blinked several times. "Is that the official story now?"

"It's the truth," said Bob. "The nose knows. You reek of chaos nearly as bad as Eris. Well, you're not going to get past us. Not a chance. We've got orders to rip you limb from limb the instant you cross the line into Hades' territory."

Mort nodded. "Sorry to say it, but those *are* our orders. He gave them to us at the same time he stocked the river. As long as you stay on Zeus's side of the water, you're OK. Hades does *not* want the troubles with the mweb blamed on Persephone. Break the line of the Styx, and we're duty-bound to kill you."

"That could pose a problem, Boss."

I shot a sidelong glance at Melchior. "Could it really? I'd never have guessed." I turned my attention back to Cerberus. "How about Cerice? Would it be OK for her to go as far as the gate? Then you could maybe send a message for Persephone to come down for a little chat."

Dave shook his head sadly. "Nope. Hades was pretty specific. Apparently he didn't want to leave any loopholes in his orders. Neither you nor any of your associates or servants is allowed anywhere within the lands belonging to Death. We won't be able to let you pass either way again. For that matter, we're supposed to eject every living thing we find on our side of the river."

"Which is a major bummer," said Mort. "We had to send Kira away for the duration."

"Back to insomnia." Bob sounded more than a little irritated. "And it's all your fault."

"Can you take Persephone a message?" This time I appealed directly to Dave. He was my best friend among the trio, and he was also Persephone's dog. "I really need to talk to her. I don't think her little software project is working out the way she planned it."

"She had *nothing* to do with this mess!" barked Bob. "Hades was very specific about that. Necessity's problems are all with you." He looked a little smug. "He also told me that if you came by, I was to tell you he'll be waiting for you. Everybody crosses the river eventually, and he's putting together a special suite just for you."

I glanced at Mort, who nodded glumly. "You're not going to get in, Ravirn. Not alive."

"Hades won't even let *me* see her now," said Dave, sounding like someone had taken away his best friend. If Kira was right about his relationship with Persephone, someone had. "Go home, there's nothing you can do here except die."

This was getting better by the minute. I was beginning to suspect that the only way I was going to have a chance to make things right was by entering Hades proper again, something I definitely didn't want. Especially now, with Cerberus no longer even partially on my side. On the other hand, it'd probably solve my Raven problems.

"Give me a minute to think," I said, turning my back on the canine triumvirate.

Cerice stepped closer. "What are we going to do?"

I didn't know the answer to that. But I did know that if I made another visit to Hades, I couldn't take anyone with me this time, not even Melchior, not with my odds of getting back out so low. I was still trying to figure an angle when a sharp tearing noise drew my gaze upward. An all-too-familiar rip had opened in the air between us and the tunnel that led out to the foot of Olympus.

"I hope we're not too late to join the party," said Alecto, as she slid through into this part of reality. I had a brief glimpse of the meeting chamber in the Temple of Fate before Megaera blocked my view on her way out.

"So glad to see you here," she said. "I think it's time we ate crow."

"Raven," said Tisiphone as she joined her sisters. Her voice sounded flat and dead. "He is the Raven."

"Birds of a feather and all that," said Alecto.

"Once you've gutted them, they're pretty much all the same," agreed Megaera.

"I'm sorry," said Tisiphone.

"I take it that my grandmother and her sisters have issued my death warrant."

Alecto produced a scroll from somewhere around her person. I wondered at that; it wasn't like she had pockets.

"Signed."

"Sealed," said Megaera, with a satisfied smile.

"And now, delivered." Tisiphone looked like she wanted to throw up.

CHAPTER SEVENTEEN

The three Furies advanced on me, and I took an involuntary step back, colliding very gently with the furry pillar of Cerberus's left leg. Megaera chuckled, low and evil. She and her sisters kept coming. They weren't moving fast, but they didn't have to. With the river on one side and the wall on the other, I was pretty much pinned between them and Cerberus. Besides, Alecto and Megaera were enjoying this too much to want it to end quickly, and Tisiphone was clearly reluctant to have it end at all.

That gave me precious seconds to think. Unfortunately, I was about out of options. The faerie ring was too far away to do me any good. The river was bad. A gate would take too long, especially with the mweb whacked. A fact which also limited my spell menu. It was more good luck than planning that Hydrophobia had worked, since it was mweb-based magic. Most of my spells were. I'd grown up in the mweb era, and except for a few brief hours when I'd crashed the whole shebang, it had remained a constant throughout my sorcerous career. Megaera had gotten perhaps fifteen feet away when Melchior stepped between me and her.

"Run, Boss!" he yelled, before whistling the beginnings of a spell.

It didn't sound like one of mine, and the roughness of it suggested he was coding on the spot. Since I'd never known Melchior to spontaneously compose, I was frankly fascinated to see the results. Stupid, I know, but there it is. Before he'd gotten more than a few dozen lines in, Megaera stepped forward and bent down, backhanding the goblin.

It was clearly a casual blow, contemptuous even, but it sent him flying. For all his attitude, Melchior's not much bigger than a cat and lighter than he looks. He hit the cave wall with a thud that made my stomach turn a cartwheel. Cerice hurried to his side. The Furies let her pass. I stood alone, my back tight against the hound of hell.

I should have been terrified. I was. But even more than fear, I felt anger. Anger at the way Megaera had treated my familiar. Anger that the Furies' presence prevented me from going to him. Anger at the whole damned situation. Anger that was exactly what I needed to break my thinking loose.

I couldn't escape from the Furies, not really. Not in the long run. Even if I gave them the slip here, they would keep coming after me. That was what they did. That was who they were. No, as long as they operated under the authority of Atropos and her sisters, I was going to be a target. If I wanted any hope of ever getting my life back, I had to find a way to stop Persephone's virus, fix Shara, and make things right with Necessity. That meant going to Hades. My only true escape route lay across the Styx.

There was a quick way to make that journey, a very quick way, and Megaera would be only too happy to buy my ticket. But I wasn't quite ready to give up on getting back out. That meant that I had to shake the Furies loose at least for a few moments. And as the living wall pressed against my back reminded me, I had to get Cerberus out of the way, too. Perhaps I could introduce problem A to problem B to create opening C.

"Tisiphone," I said. "Do you still feel the same way about me that you did when last we talked?"

"I do," she answered.

"Then, if someone has to kill me, I'd prefer it were you."

"I . . . Don't ask me to do this," she said.

"That's cruel," said Megaera stepping forward. "Ask me. I'd love to help."

"Or me." Alecto stepped up beside Megaera. "It's my duty and if you face it with honor, I'll end it quickly."

"Dave," I said quietly.

"What? I'd rather not get involved at this point."

"Are we still friends?"

"Yes—" he said, simultaneously with Bob's "No."
"—good ones."

"Then, I'm sorry to get you into all this. You and Tisiphone both."

"I don't—" he began, but I was already moving.

I chose Megaera, both because she was closer to the river than Alecto and because she was much more likely to let her anger govern her actions. I took a long step toward the Fury and away from Cerberus. Using my left hand, I unzipped my jacket and exposed my chest. Megaera grinned and lunged at me, just as I expected. Ten razor-tipped fingers came straight at my chest, and the flow of events seemed to slow down. I felt like I had all the time in the world to implement my plan.

But I was moving as slowly as everything else. So despite the fact that it seemed like I had hours in which to decide exactly how and where to grab Megaera's wrists, I was only just able to catch them, pulling her forward and up at the same time as I threw myself backwards and down so that she passed over my falling body.

It shouldn't have worked, and it probably wouldn't have if I hadn't had help. Even though I knew I couldn't hold Megaera for long, I had a firm enough grip for the action of the moment. But I'd forgotten about the talons on her feet, talons that would have slit me from throat to groin if Tisiphone hadn't leaped forward at that exact second. She collided with Megaera in what looked like a clumsy effort to help her. Instead, it gave Megaera a little added boost, and those toe claws dug ten shallow trenches in my chest rather than filleting me. It felt like she'd ripped my nipples off, but it didn't kill me, and Megaera kept right on going, sailing over me to collide claws first with Mort's nose.

Pandemonium. A dog's nose is about the most sensitive bit of his anatomy, and Mort's was no exception. He howled like a bee-stung basset and almost instinctively snapped at Megaera, catching her shoulder in his oversized mastiff's jaws. With a reflexive toss of his head, he threw her aside, sending her sailing through the air. Then he turned his attention on me, glaring down and snarling with his great fangs bared. Since I was flat on my back and practically between his feet at that point I should have been paralyzed with fear. I didn't have time.

Tisiphone had taken Alecto's place as the closest Fury, standing over me with both of her feet a few inches to the right of my pelvis. As her toe claws sank deep into the stone there, I felt my penis shrivel and try to climb up into my body to get away from them. She swung her right hand high above her head as though she were about to rip me open.

At the very same time Alecto was coming in from her left. But before Alecto could do anything, Mort's descending head struck her square in the ribs. He kept his jaws closed, but the force of the blow was tremendous, and she tumbled, smashing into Tisiphone. Together the Furies fell toward me. Again, I probably should have died when that tangle of sharp death landed on me, but somehow Tisiphone's wing, like the pinion of my very own personal guardian angel, swept me out of the way at the last instant.

It wasn't gentle, and I picked some up fresh scrapes and bruises as I rolled across the loose rocks and rough stone that made up the near bank of the Styx. Megaera came back about then, descending on me from above.

"You attacked Mort!" Dave bellowed in a voice that sounded like a bad actor auditioning for the part of a vengeful gang member in *West Side Story*.

Then he snapped Megaera out of the air. Tisiphone got to her feet about then and screamed something incoherent before lunging at Bob. I don't know what Alecto and Mort were thinking at this point, but full-scale battle had been engaged between their respective counterparts, and they crashed together in an apparent desire not to be left out. Cerberus lost his footing and fell almost on top of me, forcing me to scramble like mad to get clear.

I ended up at the base of the long finger of stone that Shara had climbed earlier and quickly leaped up beside her. We were trapped there by the snarling tumbling ball of madness that was the Furies and Cerberus. Well, I had my distraction. I just needed to figure out how to get past the barrier of the river. I was glad the melee had separated me from Melchior and Cerice. That would make my plan for taking the next step alone much easier to execute. Now I just had to lose Shara and get across the damned river.

"What do we do now?" she asked, looking worriedly from the wild brawl to the black water that surrounded us on three sides.

The entire surface rippled and roiled with the nastiness Hades had released into the waters. Directly beneath us, the water was so churned up that sooty foam had formed in small clumps.

"I don't know. Swimming doesn't seem like a great option." *And I want to leave you on this side of the Styx anyway.* She was half-rescued, and I didn't want to have to rerescue that half later.

"Really?" said Shara, rolling her eyes. "You don't say? No swimming. And here I was thinking you and I were finally going to get a chance to go skinny-dipping without Cerice around to spoil the fun."

Before I could respond, the battle between the two tripartite heavyweights caught my attention. It was one of those brief moments of stillness that happen even in the worst fights, and I got a snapshot view of the state of things. Tisiphone had Bob in some kind of modified head-lock and was viciously smashing the balled fist of her free hand again and again into the center of his forehead. Either Alecto had caught Mort's upper jaw with her hands and his lower with her feet and was desperately trying to force them apart, or Mort had grabbed Alecto and she was trying not to get munched. It was hard to tell which. Dave had Megaera's waist clamped between his teeth and was shaking her brutally.

Then, with a sudden flip of his shoulders, Dave tossed Megaera aside. He yelped when he did it, so I'm not sure who the point belonged to, but I had more immediate concerns, as the tumbling Fury smashed hard into the base of our rock-spur refuge. It shook and tilted, sending Shara sliding toward the edge. Throwing myself flat, I flung out a hand and caught the scruff of her neck before she could go in.

"Nice save, little man," said Megaera, whose presence I had momentarily forgotten. "Too bad it's not going to do you any good in the long run."

Oh shit. I felt a jolt along my spine like someone had plugged my tailbone into a light socket. This was it. But Dave snarled then, and Megaera turned away from me. I had a moment to feel relief that she hadn't had the time to make good on her threat. Then she kicked backwards with her left foot, slamming the sole into the base of the rock like a sledgehammer. She used the impact to propel herself into the air and a swooping dive aimed at Cerberus.

I'm not sure what happened with her after that, and frankly, I didn't care. The kick had been the last straw for our little refuge. The rock was tipping and sliding toward the dark waters and the hungriness that lurked beneath.

"Save yourself," screamed Shara.

I might have been able to jump clear, if I'd let her go. But I wasn't going to do that. Together, we slid toward the river and final oblivion.

My brain kicked into overtime, trying to find some way

out, a loophole that I could slip through and save the day. There had to be a way. Darkness passed before my eyes. I thought it was all over for a moment, but then I recognized it as the shadow of the Raven, the spectre that had haunted me with increasing frequency as I made ever more use of the gifts of chaos.

I remembered Cerberus's last words on the subject before the arrival of the Furies cut our conversation short—that I must "assume the role" of Raven or I would eventually face self-destruction.

Well, eventually had come more quickly than I'd expected, and the decision point was here. I could die as myself, or I could accept the new role I had forged in my battles with Fate and hope that the Raven could offer a solution where plain old Ravirn had none.

I turned inward, reaching for the place where blood and bone met chaos. As I did so, the shadow of the Raven slid over my own. For a brief moment the two shadows remained distinct, then they merged into one darker winged shadow. I had found it, the inner nexus between my own heart and the heart of change.

Now, I silently whispered, *we become one*.

A burst of pure energy hit me like nothing I'd ever experienced. It was wild and raw and completely insane. I felt a bit like a mosquito might if it had bitten into a fire hose rather than the fireman holding it. Time stopped. Not really, but effectively. Just as my newfound powers had allowed me to simultaneously occupy a thousand different faerie rings and choose the one I wanted to step out of all in the blink of an eye, I now saw another series of possibilities and a way to choose among them, to make chance work for me.

The current arrangement of particles in my body was only one of a number of such patterns available to me. The vast majority of routes to rearrange them would result only in my tearing myself to pieces, a sudden explosive death. But there were other options, and I reached for one of those now.

It hurt! Chaos and Discord, but it hurt! I was trying to rip every single atom of my being away from every other atom and put them all back together again. And I was trying to do it in the femtosecond before the universe caught on to the trick and pointed out that it should have been fatal.

Shara slipped from my grasp as I ceased to have fingers, but before she could fall into the water I caught her again with one clawed foot. I didn't want to take her with me, but it was that or let her fall. Bunching my shoulders, I threw myself skyward and spread my great black wings. I was truly the Raven now, in form and function, and I gloried in the moment. The feeling of wind sliding through feathers. The deeply rewarding effort of fighting up and away from the bonds of earth and soil. The sheer sensuality of experiencing everything with a new skin.

In that instant, I understood that Raven the power was not some alien creature completely outside the domain of the old hacker Ravirn, but merely an extension of what I had always been. Quantum mechanics tells us that many things that really shouldn't be possible are, though so unlikely that entire universes could live and die without their ever happening. The atoms of my body rearranging themselves was one such occurrence. Incredibly, almost mind-bogglingly improbable, but not utterly impossible—a tiny loophole in the programming of reality, and finding and exploiting loopholes is what I do. Becoming the Raven merely gave me a shortcut around a lot of the coding Ravirn would have had to do to achieve the same effect.

Simple, elegant, and incredibly dangerous. I had no doubt of that last. One of the nice things about precoding a bit of magic, then running it through a spell-checker is that it gives you the chance to see whether you've made a mistake beforehand. If anything had gone wrong with the Raven transformation, I would still have been floating above the Styx, but I'd have been doing it in Charon's ferry instead of on wings of magic. Whether I'd experienced beginner's luck on this one or whether I'd touched on something deeper and more basic—the Raven form going with the name—I didn't know. I did know that I would have to be more careful about shape changing in the future.

"He's escaping!" The voice seemed to come from a great distance, traveling through a slurry of time and space to reach my consciousness. "Get him."

I shook my head, trying to break loose of such petty concerns.

"Uh, Raven?" This time it was Shara.

I pulled myself back into the moment. "Yes." My voice came out harsh and gravelly, half word, half caw. "What?"

"The Furies can fly, too."

I looked down. The fight on the banks of the Styx had ceased, the three heads of Cerberus bent in close conference with the three bodies that made up the entity known collectively as the Furies. How I could tell it was the two governing intelligences consulting and not a conference of the constituent personalities I didn't know, but I had no doubts. When six heads bobbed in mutual agreement I knew things were about to get ugly again.

Cerberus turned away from the Furies and leaped into the water, swimming powerfully to get beneath me. A moment later, and with a single coordinated motion, the sisters of vengeance launched themselves skyward. I was above them, and I thought I might be able to keep my height advantage if I worked at it, but that was only going to work for a very little while. The Styx and both its banks lay in a cavern under Olympus. Up was a finite resource, and I didn't want to get out anyway. I needed a plan. Well, actually I had one. It was just a bad plan. I'd come to the underworld to speak with Persephone, and I knew that if I wanted to do that, I had to enter Hades once again.

Before the arrival of the Furies, I hadn't fully decided whether I was willing to take that risk, especially after Cerberus had pretty much confirmed that I hadn't "escaped" last time. I'd been let go. I still wasn't thrilled by the idea, but it did have the added advantage of putting me in one of the few places the Furies, and Cerberus, for that matter, wouldn't follow. I turned in the air, lining up on the gate.

"Shara, I have to get to Persephone. I'll drop you outside the gate before I go through."

"No. You're going to need a webgoblin inside."

"I can't take you back in there."

"You have to. I need to see this thing through, and I don't think you can solve the problem without a goblin. Without me. Besides, I've got to get my soul back in one piece before I crack. I'm coming."

"You're staying."

"I'm coming."

"I'm not taking you, and that's final."

Shara didn't answer, and I took that as agreement. It might have been defiance, but I just didn't have time to argue. I was almost to the roof, and the Furies were coming up fast.

"If I don't make it out, tell Cerice I love her."

"Tell her yourself," said Shara. "'Cause I'm not breaking that news for you."

I felt the feathers of one wing brush against a stalactite. I had just run out of leeway. Folding my wings, I dropped like a stone. The Furies rolled toward me one after another, arrowing along an interception course, with Megaera flying point. It was going to be a close-run thing. We got closer and closer together as I headed for the floor, until finally we met in the air. Or almost met. I felt a stabbing pain in my tail and caught a puff of black feathers out of the corner of my eye as Megaera swiped at me and just missed.

I breathed a mental sigh of relief that turned into a curse as I realized how close I'd come to the ground. Cerberus himself served up the reminder, leaping for me like a lesser dog going for a Frisbee.

"Yarghh!" screamed Shara as she yanked her feet up to avoid Mort's reaching jaws.

Then I was at the gate. "Good-bye, Shara." I opened my claws.

"And hello," she answered me back, catching a grip round my ankle and hanging on as I flew through the opening.

We had both returned to Hades.

Considering the commotion kicked up by our arrival, I decided not to hang around the gate, flying on toward the heart of Hades. But I knew that no matter how hard I flapped, I wasn't going to get us where we needed to go fast enough, not if Hades started looking for us. So after I'd put some distance between us and the entrance, I spoke with Shara. I hadn't wanted to bring her with me, but I'd have been a fool not to make use of her now that she was here.

"When we came to break you out, Melchior was able to get root access to Hades' intranet so we pretty much owned the place." My voice came out harsh and croaking, and I found myself wanting to "caw" at every full stop. "I'm sure he's beefed up his security since, but if we can't LTP this trip, we're going to be in serious trouble."

"I told you, you needed me," said Shara. "Hang on a second. Melchior gave me the details on the system while you and Cerice were playing slot-in-the-RAM. I'll see what I can do."

She went silent, and I felt her body relax as her mind went elsewhere. She was gone much longer than Melchior had been. I began to worry that we were shit out of luck. But then I felt a slight tremor, and she returned to me.

"I can't do root. Hades shut that down solid, but I managed to crack the IM daemon and go from there to Hades' personal user setup, which gives me most admin privileges. Gating us around will be easy, likewise anything else the system is already set up for; but I won't be able to cover my tracks very well, and I can't guarantee I won't set off any alarms."

"After the mess at the gate, I doubt alarms are going to matter much in the long run. In fact, I doubt that we've got a long run. Can you find Persephone and take us to her?"

"On it." A couple of more precious seconds ticked past. "Got her. You'll have to land so I can set up the gate."

I bobbed my head and started a downward glide. We landed on a bluff overlooking a dell where the ghosts of trees played at being a forest. But they had no vitality, and

I could feel the weight of death pressing down upon me like a great stone on my chest.

"You planning on staying a giant Raven forever?" asked Shara as she began the LTP process.

I cocked my head to one side and croaked, "Nevermore." I couldn't resist. If I got killed in the next few hours, I might not get the chance again.

Shara rolled her eyes and turned back to the business at hand. "I'll take that as a no."

I took a few hopping steps away and thought about turning myself back. I'd never done this before, so I didn't really know how to go about it. I tried reaching inward to the place I'd touched earlier, my own personal interface with the Primal Chaos. It was like sticking my tongue in a light socket, or maybe inserting a cattle prod directly into my frontal lobes. Energy poured into me.

I no longer *had* a link to chaos. I *was* a link. It was wild. It was seductive. It was terrifying. Once upon a time I'd used a direct chaos tap to turn my cousin Moric into charcoal, and I'd almost gotten fried in the process myself. This was like that, only more so. I had infinitely more power available to me than I could possibly manage to control. If I wasn't exquisitely careful, I'd end up a briquette. If I'd still been in my old shape, I'd have been pouring sweat. As it was, I could feel every barb of every feather on my entire body standing on end.

The temptation to skip the whole thing and live out whatever time I had left as a raven was strong. I thought about it. I really did. But in the end I decided I had to master this thing. Besides, I'd miss my opposable thumbs. To say nothing of my lips. So I dipped a mental toe into that incredible flow of power and tried to picture the outcome I wanted. Again I was presented with a million, a billion possibilities.

A myriad of paths led from raven shape to a spreading smear of plasma, even more to a loose cloud of carbon compounds, and one or two to an application of $E = mc^2$

that would completely eclipse the Hiroshima bomb. I steered my way between these options to the tiny subset that ended with me alive and in one piece, finally selecting the one that matched my internal image of myself—Ravirn, late of House Lachesis, child of Chaos and the Fates. Once I had that firmly fixed in my mind, I constructed a set of commands that would take me through the intervening steps, a reprogramming of my own internal reality.

It was harder than the transformation into a raven, much harder. Then, I hadn't had time to really internalize all the ways the process could go wrong. I'd needed to act, and I had. But now, making the same decisions in cold blood and doing it with the unlife of Hades surrounding me—the ultimate reminder of the true and fatal meaning of a mistake—I shuddered. If I wanted to make Ravirn the master of the Raven, I had to master this. I knew that. But I didn't know if I could.

"Ravirn," said Shara, tapping her little purple foot. "The gate's open."

"All right." *Now! Just do it.*

I did. With a little mental twist, I set the transformation to running. Soul-searing pain filled every iota of my awareness. For an instant I existed only as agony, while my body ripped itself apart and reassembled in a new shape. Or rather, an old one. I was Ravirn once again.

"What's with the court rig?" asked Shara.

"Huh?" I asked. Then I looked down at myself and swore.

I was no longer wearing the racing leathers I'd had on earlier. Instead, I'd reverted to the formal wear of my youth. Apparently, no matter how much I might claim to have completely given up any allegiance to my grandmother, some deep part of me still longed for the days when I'd been part of her House. Either that, or the Raven had a wicked sense of humor.

My motorcycle boots had stretched themselves thigh high and grown cavalier's cuffs. Leather pants had vanished in favor of emerald tights. T-shirt had become tunic, likewise green. Instead of a jacket I had a black leather doublet. My pistol was gone, replaced by my much-loved but frankly obsolete rapier and dagger.

I swore again. I was really going to miss the built-in armor of my leathers and my pistol, but I didn't have the time, and I wasn't willing to take the risks necessary to get them back.

"Well?" Shara raised an eyebrow.

"Don't ask. Let's just go."

"Step into the light," said the goblin, bowing me before her. I did so, and she followed. "Gating."

The column changed from green to blue, and the world from outside to in. We stood on a narrow landing at the top of a long, curving flight of stone stairs. A thick door with a narrow window blocked our way forward. The bars were verdigrised bronze, as was the heavy lock. I leaned forward and looked through the window. Beyond lay an opulently furnished chamber with a huge bed and an elaborate table spread with a banquet in the traditional Greek style. For all that, it was still a prison. I needed only a glance at its sole occupant to know that.

Persephone.

CHAPTER EIGHTEEN

Persephone sat on the floor in the corner, her back firmly to the tower room and its appointments. Her face was pressed tight against her knees, her arms wrapped around her shins, and she was shaking. Though I couldn't see her face, I knew that it would be covered with tears and that the pain I had seen there before would be even worse.

I glanced again at the table. On a gold plate in the very center sat a pomegranate, its rind half-peeled away, and a gap showing where a few—no, three—seeds had been pulled loose. Other details that I hadn't seen, or hadn't wanted to see, leaped into clarity. The rumpling of the bed-covers, the fact of Persephone's nakedness.

"Oh gods," whispered Shara, who was peering through the keyhole. "This is the place where . . ."

"Where Hades imprisoned her the first time, preserved like some sort of twisted shrine."

I felt rage pouring though me. I wanted to reach into the chaos again, to unleash the fury that had scared me so much earlier, to render this place down to its constituent particles. But that wouldn't do either her or us any good.

"Persephone," I called, as quietly as I could. She didn't move. "Persephone."

She didn't turn. "Go away." The words were soft and dead, like a bird shot out of the sky. The pain in them made my joints sag like a rag doll's, but somehow I stayed on my feet.

"Persephone, please. I've come to . . ." I trailed off. How could I ask anything of this woman, this goddess of suffering? What had I done that would give her any reason to help me? But I had to try. "The virus, or whatever it is, that you released into Necessity's network. What was it supposed to do?"

"Why should I tell you?" Again, the pain.

She turned then, and I cast my gaze down toward the floor. I didn't want to meet the anguish in her eyes again, or witness her nudity, her vulnerability.

"Aren't you going to try to bargain with me?" she asked, rising and walking toward the door. "Won't you offer to free me from this place in exchange for my help in whatever it is that you want?" There were razors in her words, and I felt them bite deeply.

"I don't know," I said, forcing myself to look at her, to meet those eyes. It was like seeing the tearing agony of my transformations set in stone, an agony that never ended. "I might have tried that if I hadn't seen you like this. I did come here to bargain with you, to ask for your help in stopping the destruction. But I don't know what to ask you now. If you want, I'll try to get this door open."

"This cell is only the symbol of my imprisonment. Even if I walked out now, I would still be in Hades and my jailer could put me back here anytime he wanted it. It's not the cell I want to escape."

"But that's all I can promise," I said. I was learning to live with the dreadful weight of her words. "Shara?"

She whistled a burst of binary. It was a spell of unlocking, similar but not identical to the one I'd programmed with Melchior. The latch clicked, and the door opened. Nothing stood between me and Persephone. Before I could say anything Shara whistled another spell, clothing Persephone in one of Cerice's outfits.

"Thank you, little one." Persephone knelt in front of Shara. Reached out. Touched her brow. Winced. "I'm sorry. I didn't know it would tear your soul like that. I used you."

"It's all right," said Shara. "You were driven to it."

"No," said Persephone. "It's not all right. No thinking being should ever use another. Of all the people in all the worlds, I should know that better than any. I forgot it for a while. I was wrong. I apologize. If I could make it right, I would."

"What were you trying to do?" asked Shara.

This time Persephone answered the question. "Win my freedom. What else?"

"How does wiping out mweb connections address that?" I asked. It was as much a hacker shop-talk question as it was one about the vital issue. Her tactics baffled me.

"Necessity's networks govern more than the proper relationships between the worlds. They also dictate the fate and placement of the gods."

Shara whistled. And well she might. That was two bombshells in one sentence, and I should have figured out the thing about the gods in advance. I'd had all the clues.

"I'd always thought of the mweb as just a way of linking different levels of reality," I said. "Are you saying it controls their positions as well?"

"Yes and no," said Persephone. "The part of the mweb run by Fate may control how you get from world A to world B, but it's Necessity that says where those worlds should be, and even whether they should exist. Not every decision leads to a split in reality, only those that Necessity approves."

"If she's that powerful, how could you hope that just erasing the record of where you're supposed to be would cut you loose?" I asked. "Wouldn't she just fix it all later?"

"Is she fixing the problems my little virus has already created?"

"No. But now I'm not sure why that is." I was getting

more confused by the second. "If Necessity's really the final arbiter of everything, why can't she—I don't know—just wave her hands and say 'poof, all better now'?"

"Because she doesn't have hands anymore," said Persephone. "The gods are finite, the universe infinite. Surely you've heard that before."

I had. It was practically an axiom in the Houses of Fate. The mweb and the Fate Core had both been created to manage a multilayered reality that had outgrown the control of the children of the Titans, and I said as much.

Persephone nodded. "Good, you're halfway there. So, if that's true, how is it possible for even Necessity to handle it all? If only the ever-expanding capacity of a massive computer network is capable of keeping an eye on everything, what does necessity make of Necessity?"

Then I saw it. Necessity wasn't the Deus Ex Machina of Greek tradition. Not the God-in-the-Machine, but the Machina-Deus, the Machine-God.

"Necessity *is* the network!"

"She is indeed," said Persephone. "And if you can once strike something free of her memory, it's gone forever."

I suddenly found myself sitting on the floor. I hadn't just helped Persephone set a virus loose in Necessity's network. I'd helped her set one free in Necessity's mind. The Shara clone was messing around with the fundamental management structure of the whole shebang.

"You knew this when you recoded Shara?" I whispered.

Persephone nodded. "What did I have to lose?"

So she'd deliberately set out to hack the source code of *everything*. That took moxie. If the full truth of this ever came out, Eris was going to lose her place as the patron of hackers. Well, she would if Persephone's hack didn't destroy the universe.

"What's happening with the world resource locator forks?" I asked.

"I don't know," said Persephone. "It's not what I intended. Just as tearing this little one's soul in twain was not what I intended. Something's gone wrong with the plan."

I'll say it had! Big-time. But what to do about it now?

"You mentioned something about making it right," said Shara. "About my soul, that is. Did you really mean it?"

"I did. It's the least I can do. But I don't know how to go about it."

"Help us get into Necessity's system," said Shara. "Into Necessity herself, I guess. If anyone can fix things there, it's Ravirn."

Persephone looked at me, her eyes cold and hurting. "Why should the Raven want to do that? What's the benefit to chaos?"

"None that I know of, but I'm more of an accidental chaos power than an active advocate for disorder."

"Yeah," said Shara, "he can do more damage by mistake than most people can manage with careful planning. Still, his heart's in the right place."

"All right," agreed Persephone. "If you ask it of me, I'll try." She let out a sigh. "Though, it would be a harder choice if the thing had gone as planned. What do you need me to do?"

As Shara set up an LTP transfer, I filled Persephone in on what we knew about the seals guarding the gateway to Necessity.

"Fair enough," she said when I was done. Together we stepped into the light of the gate. "But I don't know that I'll be able to help. I can't actually touch Hades' computer. If I even try, all hell is going to break loose. You know that, right?"

"Let's call that part my problem," I said, as we arrived. I crossed out of the gate on my way to the desk where the machine in question sat. "Shara, get your little purple butt over here and run a hard connection."

She grinned and wiggled her hips. "I thought you'd never ask. My ass and I are at your service . . . for anything."

"Right," I answered, "and Cerice would kill us both. Let's see . . ."

Again, Hades had improved his security but not much. Hades123 didn't do it, but my third guess, "Cerberus," did.

People should never use the names of their pets as passwords.

"You ready?" I asked Shara, lifting her onto the desk
and arranging the cable running from her nose to Hades'
machine.

She looked scared but nodded anyway.

"Then, Shara, Laptop. Please."

Her flesh flowed and shifted, remaking her from a curvy
webgoblin into a curvy laptop. Cerice had taken the idea of
clamshell computer design much more seriously than I had
when I built Melchior, and it showed in the elegant scallop-
ing and subtle iridescence of Shara's machine form. I
turned my attention to Persephone next, beckoning her
over as I inserted an athame cable into one of Shara's networking ports.

"Come here. Shara's plugged into the desktop machine, and . . . let me see." I typed madly on her keyboard
for a few seconds, testing my interface with Hades' system. "I'd normally just plug you and me both directly into
Shara, but that's really just a hard link to the desktop at
one remove. I can't imagine that Hades didn't take precautions against it."

"So, what are you going to do?"

"Assuming Cerice was right about the seal barring the
way to Necessity, it needs both your signature and Shara's
to unlock it. If you're willing, I'm going to provide the
bridge between the two."

"How? It's not possible to fake a magical signature."

"No, but I've been thinking about this since Cerice told
me about the lock. I can't fake your signature, but if I'm
right, I can temporarily tie it to mine using blood as a
bridge."

"I don't—oh wait. I think I see. You're going to put the
athame through both of our hands."

"Yes." I pulled it out of my pouch and connected it to
the cable. "Through mine first, then yours. The blood link
should bind your magical signature to mine as I go into the
machine. Putting my flesh physically between you and the

interface cable should block your soul from actually entering the system and triggering whatever it is that Hades uses
to prevent your access."

"Interesting. That might work. But if it does, I'm going
to be sitting here with a dagger stuck through my hand."

"Yeah, I was going to mention that part in a second. It's
going to hurt like all get-out, but I don't see any way around
it."

Persephone laughed a small hard laugh, barely more
than a cough. "I think I can handle the pain. The question
is, can you?"

It was my turn to say, "Huh?"

"The link you're talking about is going to temporarily
tie our souls together. What I feel, you'll feel. The pain of
the blade is going to be the least of it. Can *you* handle it?"

I hadn't thought about that, but she was probably right.
Normally, you lose track of your body when you enter the
world of the mweb, but I was going to have a doubled link
back to the world of the physical, plus all of Persephone's
other issues.

"I don't have much choice. I want to fix the mweb. We
both want to fix Shara. Neither of those things is going to
happen unless I can get into Necessity's mind."

"All right," said Persephone. "Consider yourself warned."
Then she smiled. It was a bitter thing that chilled my soul.
"I'll try to think happy thoughts."

I swallowed. "Let's do this before I wise up and run for
the hills. Or worse, Hades arrives to shut down the party.
OK?"

She didn't say a word, just reached over and covered my
left hand with her own. I lifted the blade into the air above
the palm of my hand, then stabbed hard and fast. The pain
was blinding, and it didn't end when I left my body as it
usually did. If anything, it got worse.

Instead of the sharp sure bite of iron in flesh, it felt like
I'd driven a thorn branch through my hand, then lit it on
fire. A suicidally depressed thorn branch. I could feel all of
Persephone's pain embedded there in my flesh like a spike

of pure emotional poison, and I felt darkness growing around the edges of my vision. I suddenly understood how a wolf caught in a trap could gnaw its own leg off. Yet somehow I found I could bear it. The darkness remained around the edges, but it didn't take me under.

Whether it was because I'd already learned how to live with the pain of being ripped apart at the atomic level, or because Persephone was thinking her "happy thoughts," or just the sheer luck that the pain was confined to one finite part of my body, I don't know. Whatever the reason, I was able to force myself to look around and take in the world beyond my agony.

Shara's anteroom to the mweb appeared as a simple windowless room, its walls lined with bookshelves packed with paperback romances. I was tempted to look through the titles, but what little time we had was fast trickling away so, moving like a man underwater, I passed through the room's sole door.

It led into Hades' portal to the mweb, a perfect mirror of his real-world office, with its leather chair and thick carpeting. Apparently the Lord of the Dead didn't have much more imagination than his younger brother, Zeus. Shara was waiting, an electronic projection of her goblin self on Hades' desk.

"About time," she said. "I felt your arrival more than five minutes ago. That's like a week in mweb time. What took you so . . ." She met my eyes and trailed off rather abruptly. "Don't take this the wrong way, but you look like shit. I can see Persephone's pain looking out of your eyes. How can you bear it?"

"I don't know. I think she's shielding me from most of it somehow. It's only my hand."

I tried to raise my left arm, but it wouldn't move. The thorn branch apparently weighed about five hundred pounds, and thinking about it brought the pain back to the forefront of my mind. I felt my knees sag.

"Can you get us moving?" I asked. "I don't think I should drive right now."

"Done," said Shara.

An instant later she expanded, growing so that she stood about nine feet tall. She stepped closer then and scooped me up as a mother might her child. I wanted to argue about that, but I just didn't have the energy. Too much of my attention was devoted to the pain. The branch seemed to be growing into a tree and tearing my hand apart in the process. Things blurred out for a while. The next thing I knew Shara had set me down.

Looking around, I found myself in the translucent cityscape of the server where we had originally lost Shara's e-mailed self. But where the gigantic black cube had stood then, there was only a flat space, like a blacktop parking lot. In its center was a small indentation with three purple pips at its core. I stared blankly at the spot for long seconds.

I knew it was important, but I was having trouble remembering why, remembering anything besides Hades standing over me, his hot eyes staring down as he slowly removed his clothes. I wanted to die, but even then I knew that it would be no escape. I—

A sharp smack drew my attention. I blinked and saw Shara looking into my eyes. I knew that she'd slapped me by the sound, but only by the sound. I was numb to everything but the pain in my hand and the daggers it had driven up my arm toward my heart.

"Ravirn!" she said. "Snap out of it. I need your help in the here and now."

"Right." I forced myself to focus, but it was hard. The pain tugged at me, pulling me toward a whirling maelstrom centered in my left hand. "The seal."

I knelt and tried to press my wounded hand to the mark of the three pips. I couldn't make my arm respond to my orders. But I had to do something. Turning my whole body, I lowered the torn flesh until it met the purple stain. The thorn tree turned into a terrible tower of chain lightning, and I thought I would die. But I couldn't. If I died, HE would have me forever. Somehow I forced myself to live even there in the heart of pain. Vaguely, like something through fog or tears, I saw Shara's hand come down beside my own. The black slab underneath changed then, softening so that we began to sink into it.

As my head dropped beneath the surface, I felt a pressure in my ears and heard a voice, like something coming from a great distance.

"There." It was Persephone. "You're in. And I'm gone."

The thorn tree vanished as if it had never been. The relief was something physical like crashing through a wall of ice water into a world of peace. I almost passed out from the sheer pleasure of not hurting. I felt as though I was falling, then realized I was. Before I could do anything about it, something caught me. Shara, grown even more, from loving mother to colossus, her gorgon locks twisting and writhing, each snake wearing its very own miniature set of mirror shades, echoing the ones on Shara's huge face. I rolled over and pushed myself to my feet and Shara, returned now to her normal size, did the same beside me. Only then did I realize where I was, and on whose hand I stood.

"I could crush you both," said gorgon-Shara. "I should crush you both. The system would back me. I own the system."

I was in no shape to argue, so I was glad when Shara fielded that one.

"You can't crush me," she said. "I'm you, and we both know it."

"I can still crush you," said the gorgon. "Crush you and roll you into a ball and eat you. That way you'll be a part of me, and the world will make sense again. I can achieve my purpose." The giant's fingers lifted, curling above us like a wave about to crash. I prepared to jump over the side.

"Wait!" Shara held up a hand. "It won't work." Her voice was gentle, but the gorgon paused. "You'll destroy yourself, and me with you. You don't want that, do you?"

"I want . . . I want to be whole, to achieve my purpose, to stop Her pain. But I can't find it."

"I can help you," said Shara. "We can help you, but only if you'll let us. Only if you'll tell us what you need."

"I need to find the door."

"What door?" I asked, cautiously joining the conversation. I would help, but this was Shara's play, her soul we were dancing with. "I'm good at finding things."

"The back door into summer. It's not here."

The gorgon gestured with her free hand, waving it out over the strobing lightning of the mweb map with its infinitude of fractal connections. We were back on the island with the data ocean surrounding it, only now I viewed it differently. Instead of frost on windowpanes I saw interconnected neurons, the mind of Necessity. It was a scary picture. There were more dark places, gaps where worlds had been cut out of the system, neurons fried, the mind of the goddess fractured.

"You can do that, can't you, Ravirn?" Shara's voice sounded breathy, a little bit desperate.

I looked at the patterns, searching for anomalies other than the dead spots, and not finding them. "I don't know. I can try. If I do find it, what happens next?"

"I'll open the door," said the gorgon. "Let summer into winter, make it spring forever." She sounded more than a little bit crazed. "Two have to become one." She looked up and away then, staring into space.

"And there she's right on the money," said Shara after a long pause. Then she frowned. "Or I am. This split-personality business makes for funny sentence structure. We have to get back together."

"Are you sure about that?" I asked. The gorgon didn't seem to be listening at the moment, and I wanted to take advantage of that. "She's a little out there."

"She's me. Or I'm her." Shara cocked her head to one side. "Think of her as *my* Raven."

I smiled a wry smile and nodded to acknowledge the hit. "Better you do the assuming then. Let me see what I can do."

Again, I stared at the sea of lightning. There had to be some clue there, some trapdoor I could exploit. Then I saw it, and I laughed. I'd been a fool.

"Gorgon," I called, and slowly the giant turned her head back toward me. "I've a deal for you."

"What is it?"

I glanced a question at Shara. She nodded.

"I'll show you the way into summer if you'll agree to become one under Shara's guidance."

"I am Shara," said the gorgon, and she, too, nodded. "How can I refuse? Swear to do what you have promised, and I will surrender the point."

"How indeed?" I pulled an athame from my belt and cut my virtual finger, letting binary blood flow. "On my blood and honor, I so swear."

The blood might be nothing more than magically charged ones and zeros, but the oath was as real as if I'd made it in the flesh. I felt the weight of geas settling on my shoulders. Such is the way of the mweb, which we enter in the soul. I handed the athame to Shara.

"Over to you."

Pulling a cable from within her belly pouch, she plugged one end into the athame and the other into her nose. Inelegant, but oh well. Then she knelt and jabbed the blade deep into the hand on which we stood. The effect reminded me of e-mailing Shara out of Hades, a cartoonlike moment when the gorgon's whole body collapsed in on the point where the athame went into her hand, like a giant balloon punctured by, and sucked up through, a straw. As she shrank, we were swiftly lowered to the ground until we stood alone on the island of rock.

"Well," I said to Shara, "did it work?"

"Why don't you come over here and find out, big boy?" Shara said in her best Mae West and winked at me. She was back!

"All right, but don't tell Cerice." I stepped up close and lifted her for a big old kiss, then set her back on her feet.

"How do you feel?" I asked.

"Very, very strange. My other self spent a lot of time literally living within the mind of Necessity, and that's going to take some getting used to. Huh." An odd look crossed her face. "She did something very strange with Ahllan, something to keep her safe . . . I don't understand it. But there's a lot here I don't understand. There's also a good bit of Persephone's programming still in here. Between the two I see why the other me was a bit crazed. The way Persephone's code is pulling at me would be enough to send anyone around the bend all on its own. It keeps trying to force me to find a way for her to escape, even if it means destroying the universe. It's like an itch I can't scratch, and it's getting worse fast."

"Well then, let's redeem my oath."

"How?" she asked.

"By opening the trapdoor. The island, that is."

"Of course," said Shara. "It's so obvious it's hard to see."

She resized herself, becoming the gorgon in stature if not in feature. Lifting me up, she stepped onto the surface of the frozen sea, then turned and caught one edge of the island with her fingertips. Beneath was a smaller data set. More orderly and less chaotic, something like a traditional circuit board only graven in light. At various junctures were little hologramatic emblems. A cloud with a lightning bolt. A three-headed dog. The planet Earth. A Raven.

It took only a matter of seconds to locate the fire-eyed skull that denoted Hades. A line of chain connected it to a recess in the board. In the recess sat three seeds from a pomegranate. The rest of the fruit lay next to the globe of the Earth. Squatting, I reached for the seeds, lifted one.

Pain! Blinding, mind-numbing, soul-searing pain! The thorn tree was back, and it had brought a forest along for company. My hand jerked, and the seed dropped next to the recess. The pain went on, built even. As I groped for the seed, my fingertip touched the recess. The pain vanished, and I fell back on my heels. I looked down. Now the recess held two seeds and a tiny black feather. The third seed had returned to the pomegranate.

"Chaos and Discord," I whispered.

"What?" asked Shara.

"Apparently the recess has to be filled. If we free Persephone, someone has to take her place."

"Shit," said Shara.

"Yeah, and—" My head twisted involuntarily to one side, and I felt a burning in my cheek. My body had just taken one hell of a slap. "Something's happening back in Hades! I've got to get back there, and quickly."

I glanced at the board. There had to be some way to free her that didn't involve getting stuck in Hades for three months of every year. I just needed time to figure it out— my head rocked the other way—time I simply didn't have.

"Go!" said Shara.

"But—"

"Go! And take this." Leaning forward and shrinking back to her normal size, she plugged one claw tip into the recess, freeing the feather. She handed it to me. "I think I've got an answer."

"Cerice will—"

"Go!"

She pursed her lips and blew at me. In that place and time she must still have had some of the power of Necessity's security system, because her breath hit me like a hurricane. Before I could argue further, I flew up into the air and through a patch of blackness above, popping out into the world of the mweb server. I wanted to turn back, but a third slap changed my mind. In the ever-mutable world of the mweb, changing shape was as easy as changing your mind, so I took on the form of the Raven once again and flew like the wind back to the place I had left my body.

Persephone was drawing back her arm to hit me again when I slid into my body and then, with it, out of my chair. Shaking my head, I met her eyes. Her pain had redoubled, but there was something else there as well.

"What did you do?" she asked, sounding breathless. "He's coming, now. I can feel it in the pulse of the underworld. But I can also feel that his grip on me is looser. What's going on?"

Before I could answer, the door of the office ceased to be, the dead wood decaying into dust in an instant. On the other side stood Hades, and the fire in his eyes was every bit as strong as the pain in Persephone's.

CHAPTER NINETEEN

Hades the place is not Hell, and Hades the god is not Lucifer, but he holds the black fire that withers souls in his keeping. It burned hot in his eyes as he crossed the threshold.

"You're mine," he said, letting the flame of his gaze fall on Persephone so that she flinched. A sob escaped her lips.

The heat touched me next as hot agony burned along the line that connected our eyes. I saw hate there, and fury, and a terrible, devouring sort of lust.

"She's mine. And you will be. Forever. Death I will bring you, and as Death I will collect you, and though heat will bake you and flames burn you, never will Lethe's sweet waters pass your parched lips. You will envy Prometheus."

As he spoke I could feel the fire of his will eating away at my soul, pushing me already toward death, and fear filled me. Persephone stood then and stepped between us, breaking the link, and I sagged against the desk, my chin coming to rest inches from Shara's laptop shape. I noticed words on the screen.

Type: "Escapee. Execute."

There was a cursor prompt right after a big chunk of the programming language that Cerice had written for her dissertation.

Why? I typed. Neither Cerice nor I ever used the "Execute" command anymore, preferring "Please," which allowed the webgoblin freedom of choice in the question of a program run.

Trust me.

I did. *Escapee. Execute.* Then I hit return.

Data flashed across Shara's screen too fast for me to follow. It looked like a complete read-off of her memory, but I couldn't tell for sure. Out of the corner of my eye, I caught a flickering and realized that whatever was happening within Shara was being mirrored on Hades' monitor. But I didn't have time to think about that, not with Hades himself on the spot.

Catching the edge of the desk, I pulled myself to my feet. Hades had crossed deeper into the room, coming to stand only a few feet from Persephone. The weight of his gaze had bowed her down, pushing her own eyes floorward. It was the first chance I had to really look at him.

He was dark, with black flame in his eyes, and thick black hair like billowing smoke. His frame was long and lean, and he looked hungry, with his bones too visible under his skin, a skeleton playing at being a man. If Zeus is thunder and lightning, bluster and brawn, Hades, his older brother, is smoke and shadow, a fire burning underground. He smiled as he took another step, then backhanded Persephone with a crack that suggested a broken cheekbone.

Without so much as a whimper, she crumpled to the ground. Now only a desk stood between me and the Lord of the Dead. Hades raised his hand. Dark flames streamed from his fingertips, reaching for that last shield. Where they touched, decay ate into the rich mahogany, points of dry rot racing outward like ants escaping a shattered hill. It was mesmerizing, and I watched as one long line of rot slid under the now blank monitor, making it sink and tilt. Only then did I think of Shara, reaching to catch her up. Halfway there, my hand stopped as suddenly as if I'd run it into a wall.

Her screen was black and empty, off and more than off. Her case had lost its shine, fading from true purple to mauve as it had when she'd been killed. I didn't know what "Escapee" was *supposed* to do, but it was clear that Shara was no longer at home. Whether that meant I'd finally finished the task I'd set out to perform on my first trip here was something only time would tell. While I was still trying to decide what to do next, her mortal shell fell into the collapsing desk and vanished from sight. Dust puffed outward as the last bits of wood lost their structural integrity. Hades stepped forward, smiling still, his eyes level with my own.

The darkness within leaped between us, driving me to my knees. I might be a power now, but the Raven was no match for Death. I could feel my inner strength fading. I wouldn't last long, and I knew it. But I refused to look away from his gaze. I would meet my own personal death eye to eye despite the terror in my heart, even if it hastened the outcome. Shadows closed in around the edge of my vision again, narrowing my view till all I could see was the dark fire. Soon, even that began to fade. I was dying. Blackness and . . .

Discontinuity.

The world rolled under me like the deck of a ship in strong winds. I realized I was lying facedown. Something had changed, though I had only the haziest idea of what. There had been a sound, a wild, wonderful, totally unexpected sound, and Hades had released me. What had it been?

Laughter?

That was it. The light ringing tones of pure living joy, a sound utterly alien to this land of dust and ashes. I didn't understand. But I was alive still, and that meant I had to go on trying. My arms felt as heavy and dead as old logs, but I forced them to move, dragging my hands up beside my chest and pushing myself onto my knees again. What had become of Hades?

There he was, standing over Persephone, and the fires engulfed him now, a continuous sheet of black flame that wrapped around him like a shroud. But Persephone didn't seem afraid. Didn't even seem to notice him, looking through Hades rather than at him, and her eyes held . . . joy? That couldn't be right, but it was. The pain was still there, would always be there, but it had been pushed down into the depths and Persephone was laughing. Laughing in a bright clear voice like a stream foaming over polished rocks on a sunny morning high in the mountains.

Hades tried to strike her again. But his hand passed through her face without touching it, and I realized that she was fading. Or perhaps *clarifying* would be a better word. I could see through her, but she didn't look one iota less bright. Rather it was as though she were being transformed from flesh into light in a process that was accelerating steadily.

She turned to look at me then and paused in her laughter. "Thank you," she said. And, "freedom," though I could not hear that last word, only see the movement of her lips.

Then the light filled her, and she was the most beautiful thing in the world, perhaps in all the worlds. This is how she must have looked in the beginning, before her long imprisonment, and I cried for the joy of seeing her so. But the vision lasted only for an instant. Then she was gone, leaving me alone with Hades, who now turned his wrathful gaze full upon me.

But I was no longer afraid. Somehow, with Shara's help and against the longest of odds, I had righted one of the oldest and harshest of wrongs in a universe full of them. Persephone was free. What better epitaph could anyone ask for? Now I could, and would, face Death with a smile. After all, I had triumphed over him once, and in a way that would echo down the long years into eternity. Even if I was doomed to fail, Hades would know he'd been in a fight.

The black fires shot from his fingertips. My clothes rotted around me, my blades rusted, and I actually felt my hair going gray. But this time I did more than stand and take it. I reached deep into the chaos at my core and re-shaped myself, changing my hair back and clothing myself once again. Not with the court garb my grandmother de-manded, but in the leathers of my own choosing. I had bro-ken the chains that bound Persephone. I was the Raven and master of my own House, a child of Fate no longer.

But the fires fell on me again. This time the gray hair burned completely away and took some of my suddenly wrinkled skin with it. Arthritis blossomed in my joints, and my bones creaked as microscopic fractures raced through them like threads of lightning. I reached inward to tap chaos again, but the response was weaker now in my premature dotage. I knew, even as I started to renew myself, that the next round would kill me. This was not a battle I could win. Not this way, and probably not at all.

Then, as the old do more often than the young, I thought of those who had passed into Hades before me, and espe-cially of those I had sent here. Laric, the cousin that I had loved as a brother. Moric, the cousin I had hated but would not have killed had I any choice at all. I wondered if Moric were here still, and whether I might meet him again and apologize. His death in the fires of chaos haunted me yet. Suddenly, on the edge of death, it also gave me an idea. It was a bad idea, and one that probably wouldn't work, but as Melchior would have pointed out were he there to re-mind me, that wasn't a big surprise.

The Primal Chaos, $X\alpha os$, is the source of all things and the matrix in which reality is embedded. The Titans formed themselves from the stuff using nothing more than an act of will, and it flows in the blood of their children and their children's children unto the last generation. For any child of the Titans the Primal Chaos is no farther away than a moment's thought, or a heartbeat, or a razor's edge. For the Raven it lay even closer. With a flick of thought I opened a door in my soul and let the stuff of creation roar through it.

I felt it fill me to the brim and beyond. It was hotter than the plasma that fuels the sun and colder than the liquid helium that rains out of an outer planet's skies. It was pain and pleasure and sheer condensed sensation. I was baked and boiled and frozen and fractured, all from within. Then it overflowed. Mad, swirling, impossible colors shot from my eyes and mouth, from the pores in my hands and follicles on my scalp. A great tumbling ball of the stuff built around me and rolled outward, an ever-expanding sphere of destruction. It burst over Hades like a wave, knocking him down and tumbling him as easily as a twig in a tidal bore.

He tried to get to his feet, but the flow never stopped or slowed, just kept building and building. Where it touched, things melted, the walls, the floor, the very substance of reality. I was no exception. This was not a process I could control or—realistically—survive. The chaos that ate away the building housing Hades' office and even the bedrock on which it stood would also devour me. I had become the Raven, a creature of chaos, and more resistant to its extremes because of that. But resistant is not immune. Even as I watched the stuff of creation destroy the heart of Hades' domain and burn and bite the god himself, I could feel the thread of my own existence unraveling away into nothingness.

I was hurting Hades terribly, but I would not, could not win. Just as I was thinking that thought, the chaos ate through a final wall, the one between the universe and the sea that surrounds it. In the blink of an eye, here became there, the stuff of Hades poured into the Primal Chaos and vice versa. There, in the heart of creation and destruction, I felt my flesh fail and my soul fray, then nothing at all.

Nevermore.

EPILOGUE

■ ■ ■

"Ravirn," said Cerice, her voice barely a whisper.

Ravirn.

"Oh my dark bird, where have you gone?" Cerice sounded drunk.

"Shall I bring you another daiquiri, Madame?" The voice belonged to Haemun, and it held a note of chiding.

"Two, and keep them coming." Drunk and bitter beyond the power of speech to express.

Came a ripping then, a tearing in the air. Another voice.

"Nothing," it said. "Nothing at all. He's really gone." It was Tisiphone, and she sounded nearly as broken as Cerice.

"But he didn't show up in Hades?"

"No. But I'm not sure that means anything. The Primal Chaos is the exception to a lot of rules. Alecto thinks it destroyed him completely, that there was nothing left to make that final journey across the Styx. Not that he'd have wanted to go anyway. Hades is a miserable place under normal circumstances, and right now it looks like it was hit by a combination tidal wave and giant tornado followed by a force-ten earthquake."

"Good," said Cerice, her voice bitter. "I hope the god is in as bad a shape as the place."

"Worse," answered Tisiphone. "Burned and bitter, but returned from his jaunt into chaos."

Cerice gave a small sob. "What about Shara?"

"It's complex, though she's not in Hades either."

"Tell me."

"She's inside Necessity's system, merged with it somehow. She seems to be occupying the memory space that used to hold Persephone's tie to Hades, freeing the goddess to return to her mother, where she is now."

"I don't understand," said Cerice.

"Neither do I. Nor my sisters for that matter, though Megaera has a theory."

"And?"

"She thinks that Shara's soul will stay in the system, tied to the bits holding the bond, until the first day of spring, when she'll be released to do as she pleases."

"And when winter comes?"

"Back into the machine."

"I guess that's better than Persephone's lot. I'll have to build her a new case. The old one went with Ravirn."

Ravirn.

I heard another sob.

"I'd be careful when I put the new one together," said Tisiphone. "Shara's time with Necessity may have changed her."

"I'll remember that," said Cerice. "Oh, Tisiphone, thanks. For looking for him, and for telling me what you found out. You didn't have to do that, and I appreciate it."

"You're welcome, though I didn't do it for you. I still don't like you, but I owed it to his memory. Good-bye, forever."

The ripping noise came again.

"And good riddance." Very drunk.

I felt bad about that.

"Oh, Ravirn, how could you?"

Ravirn. I liked the sound of that. I? I. I!

"Haemun!" yelled Cerice. "Where's that damn drink!"

"Here, Madame."

"Thanks." There was a long pause. "I'm sorry for yelling at you. You don't need that."

"It's all right, I understand."

"Let me offer my apologies properly." Cerice started to whistle, something in binary, a spell of creation.

She was out of tune. Badly. And the spell went wrong, as such things do under the circumstances.

"What the—" Cerice whispered.

Another rip, this one felt rather than heard. A small hole between here and there. Pure chaos poured through into the world beyond. I went with it.

By will alone the Titans formed themselves from the stuff of creation. By will alone I duplicated the feat. Ravirn could never have managed the trick. But the Raven is a thing of chaos. And I am the Raven. From chaos was I born, to chaos returned, and from chaos born once again.

I stood on the balcony of Raven House. It looked much as it had the last time I'd seen it. Black and green and perfect. It was home, and Cerice was there, sitting in a chair with a drink in each hand.

"Ravirn?" said Cerice. Her voice held both tears and pleading. "It can't be you."

I smiled. It felt wonderful to smile. To feel the muscles sliding under my skin. To have skin. To have identity even.

"You're probably right," I said. "I'm likely a hallucination. Where's Melchior?"

"It is you. Nobody else could be so difficult in the very instant he's returned from the dead. Melchior's inside somewhere, drunker than I am. You scared us both nine-tenths of the way to death." She dropped her drinks, and the glasses shattered on the floor. "You bastard!"

Then she threw herself out of her chair and into my arms. "I hate you!"

"I love you," I said, and realized it was still true. Hers was the voice that had called me back from the sea of Primal

Chaos. My name on her lips with love behind it. "I really do love you."

"I love you, too," she said, squeezing me so hard that my ribs creaked. "But if you ever do anything like that again, I'll kill you myself."

"Wouldn't it be a bit late for that?" I asked.

She leaned away from me and opened her mouth to speak, then stopped, looking more than a little shocked.

"What?" I asked.

"Nothing important," she answered, but I could see that whatever it was, it frightened her. "I love you, and it'll wait. For now, I just want you to hug me a little longer. Then we'd better find Melchior. He's missed you as much as I have. Did I mention that I love you?"

"You did, but I wouldn't mind hearing it again."

"I love you."

"Your deal," said Dave, with a doggy grin.

I passed the cards from one hand to another in a fancy cascade. As they went, I adjusted probabilities and stacked the deck. Then I passed them back the other way and unstacked it.

I looked past Cerberus to the Styx and beyond. Hades the place is not Hell, and Hades the god is not Lucifer; but I would never cross that river willingly again, not with Hades back on his throne, with its empty place beside it. I had hurt Hades, probably more than anyone since Cronus the Titan, who had fathered and devoured Hades, but nothing can make an end of Death. I knew he would be there waiting for me for as long as it took, because though I am a power, I am not immortal. I shivered.

Things had changed since I'd sat in that very spot all those weeks ago contemplating a reprise of the journey of Orpheus. I had changed. And all my relationships had changed.

The most visible manifestation of that was the thing that

had so startled and disturbed Cerice, and one that made my skin crawl when I first saw it in the mirror. My eyes no longer match my colors, emerald and ebony, iris and pupils. Now chaos dances in the slits of my eyes, and in the dark, they give their own light.

The internal changes are bigger. Orpheus made his passage to the underworld on the strength of his music, his special divinity. I had hoped to make mine a copy of his. Foolish, really, to think that I could get in and out of that final gate without playing my strongest card. Little surprise that my first trip turned out to be nothing more than the first leg of the real journey. My special divinity is exploiting loopholes, first in programming, then reality, and now chaos itself.

"Are you going to deal those cards or marry them?" growled Bob.

"Deal," I said, flipping him a card from the bottom of the deck. I did it the old-fashioned way, with sleight of hand. Anything else would have been cheating.

KELLY McCULLOUGH has sold short fiction to publications including *Weird Tales*, *Absolute Magnitude*, and *Cosmic SF*. An illustrated collection of Kelly's short science fiction, called *The Chronicles of the Wandering Star*, is part of InterActions in Physical Science, an NSF-funded middle school science curriculum. He lives in western Wisconsin. Visit his website at www.kellymccullough.com.